How To Wrangle a Woman

SUSAN X MEAGHER

How To Wrangle a Woman

© 2012 BY SUSAN X MEAGHER

ISBN (10) 09832758-3-1
ISBN (13) 978-0-9832758-3-1

THIS TRADE PAPERBACK ORIGINAL IS PUBLISHED BY BRISK PRESS, BRIELLE, NJ 08730

EDITED BY: LINDA LORENZO
COVER DESIGN AND LAYOUT BY: CAROLYN NORMAN

FIRST PRINTING: JANUARY 2012

THIS IS A WORK OF FICTION. NAMES, CHARACTERS, PLACES, AND INCIDENTS ARE THE PRODUCT OF THE AUTHOR'S IMAGINATION OR ARE USED FICTITIOUSLY. ANY RESEMBLANCE TO ACTUAL PERSONS, LIVING OR DEAD, BUSINESS ESTABLISHMENTS, EVENTS, OR LOCALES IS ENTIRELY COINCIDENTAL.

THIS BOOK, OR PARTS THEREOF, MAY NOT BE REPRODUCED IN ANY FORM WITHOUT PERMISSION.

By Susan X Meagher

Novels

Arbor Vitae

All That Matters

Cherry Grove

Girl Meets Girl

The Lies That Bind

The Legacy

Doublecrossed

Smooth Sailing

How To Wrangle a Woman

Serial Novel

I Found My Heart In San Francisco

Awakenings: Book One

Beginnings: Book Two

Coalescence: Book Three

Disclosures: Book Four

Entwined: Book Five

Fidelity: Book Six

Getaway: Book Seven

Honesty: Book Eight

Intentions: Book Nine

Journeys: Book Ten

Karma: Book Eleven

Lifeline: Book Twelve

Anthologies

Undercover Tales

Outsiders

Dedication

To Carrie, my fiancé

CHAPTER ONE

FEW SIGHTS CAN TURN a person's guts to water quicker than a set of flashing blue lights in the rearview mirror. Brooklyn closed her eyes for just a second. *Maybe he's after someone else.* But no, the lights drew closer and the siren started to blare. This was gonna be bad. *Please, God, let the cop be a fan.*

She slowed, put on her blinker, and pulled over to the curb as safely and responsibly as was humanly possible. It was late for that, but nothing else came to her. A warm breeze wafting in through the passenger window carried the sounds of the officer's boots crunching on the pavement.

Lowering her own window, Brooklyn tried to appear sober and respectful. "Yes?" She'd learned that the less said in these situations, the better.

"License and registration," the brawny, leathery-faced man said, his eyes locked on hers.

He was older than any patrol officer she'd ever seen. He must have made some enemies among the top brass to still be on patrol, or he liked the thrill of watching people pee their pants in fear. She shivered, feeling like her life was about to take a very bad turn. "Here's my license." She fumbled for it, cursing her nerves. "It's a rental." She moved her passenger's knee to reach into the glove box and extract the rental agreement. When she handed it over the officer's attention shifted entirely to her passenger.

"It's a crime to litter in Georgia, Miss...York," he added, taking a glance at her license.

"Litter?" *What the hell?*

"Yes, litter. Your passenger threw these out the window a couple of blocks back." He pulled a plastic bag, the type used to handle evidence, from his back pocket. Brooklyn strained to see what it held. It was very late, or very early, depending on your perspective, and the streetlights were so dim she couldn't make out what he dangled in front of her. Removing the massive flashlight from his belt, he shined the light on the contents. When a pair of bright pink panties shone luridly through the baggie, Brooklyn nearly vomited on the officer's shoes. A few minutes earlier the woman beside her had asked if she wanted to see something hot, but Brooklyn hadn't realized she'd taken off her panties to show the goods. His light passed into the car and landed on the passenger's face. "Is that your…daughter?"

Brooklyn gazed at the young woman, seeing her as a stranger might. She'd appeared much older and much more sober at the club. Hell, she'd seemed bright and interesting, not like the drooling mess she was now. Slumped against the door, one arm dangling out the open window, she could have passed for fifteen.

"No. I don't know her. I'm just giving her a ride home." *And it's none of your business what we were gonna do when we got there!*

"A ride home?" He let the question hang there, not saying another word.

"Yes. I was at a gig and I stayed to have a"—*Don't say drink!* —"conversation with some friends, and I was heading in her direction so I offered to give her a ride."

"Right." He could not have been less convinced. He went back to his cruiser, taking his sweet time. Finally, he returned. "Please exit the car for me, Miss York."

Putting on that fake politeness made the command worse than it was. They must train them on how to make people feel insignificant. She opened the door, knees shaking so badly she was afraid her legs wouldn't hold her up. Then she noticed he had something under his arm. He opened a black bag and extracted a device she'd seen more than once. "I'm not drunk," she insisted.

He held the machine up to her face, and instructed, "Blow into the mouthpiece, please."

She took a breath, now both frightened and frustrated. You try to be nice and give a pretty girl a ride home, and you wind up huffing into a breathalyzer. There's no justice in the world.

After she blew into the machine he checked it, but didn't comment. "Will you wake your passenger, please? I need to see her identification."

"Why? She wasn't driving."

He was close enough to aim the flashlight into the car again. "The age of consent in Georgia is sixteen, Miss York."

"Consent? Consent to get a ride home?"

"I need to see your passenger's identification," he repeated slowly. "Now."

I must have passed the breathalyzer. Thank fuck! I know she's over sixteen, so I'm out of here if she isn't the police chief's daughter. It took a few minutes to get the woman moving, but Brooklyn got her to her feet and found her purse on the floor. The woman, whose license indicated her name was Cassidy, plastered herself against the car like it was a warm blanket. *Thank the good Lord she's nineteen!* Brooklyn handed the license to the cop, who took it back to his cruiser, leaving her to keep Cassidy from collapsing onto the ground. The drink the girl had chugged right before they left the club must have hit her like a freight train.

By the time the cop returned, Cassidy was semi-lucid and standing mostly on her own. He flashed the light quickly past her face, making her pretty features scrunch up like a baby eating a dill pickle. "Stop it," she whined while her hands fought to find her eyes to shield them.

"Are you with Miss York voluntarily, Miss Adams?"

"What?" she said, her Southern drawl combining with her drunkenness to render the word almost unintelligible.

"Are you with this woman because you want to be?"

3

"What are you implying?" Now Brooklyn was angry. This guy had no reason to infer anything other than what she'd told him.

"We might have had to overturn our sodomy law, but it's still a crime to force a girl into an aberrant act." His mean little eyes glared at her, and she realized this was personal. He did know who she was…and he hated her. Her skin prickled with sweat and fear. He could do whatever he wanted at this point, and she cursed herself for driving, for drinking, for offering cute young women rides home, and for having to go on the road to make a living.

Once more his light flickered over Cassidy's face. Instead of answering him, she fell forward and vomited, spraying Brooklyn's slacks and shoes. "Please help your…guest to my patrol car. We're going to go to the precinct until she can communicate."

"You have no right to do this." Brooklyn knew she was moments from exploding. Her voice was clipped and tense and her hands were curled into fists. "You're harassing me because I'm a lesbian."

His light landed right between her eyes and she was certain she heard him chuckle. "Into the car."

—⁓—

"You've done a kick-ass job of putting my nuts in a vice, funny lady." Arnie Glen sprawled in his massive chair in front of his cavernous desk and carefully removed his new camouflage baseball cap. He flicked his fingers across the *Reveille* insignia embroidered on the front, even though it couldn't have had a fleck of dirt on it. Then he ran his hands through his thinning hair, the gray at its roots joining with the craggy lines on his face to betray his age. It was clear he was wasting time, trying to make her squirm, and damned if he wasn't doing a good job of it.

Brooklyn swallowed, and tried not to show her fear. Fear always made him go in for the kill. She'd seen him eviscerate members of congress in moments, leaving them blithering fools, and they had much more experience in being tortured for sport than she did.

Arnie drummed his tanned, freckled fingers on his desk. A huge regulator clock behind him ticked off the seconds, the sound very loud in the carpeted room. "I'm sure you think it doesn't much matter if you're here or not, and frankly, I agree with you."

"That's not what I think at all. I explained—"

He squinted, his dull, gray eyes almost lost in the wrinkles. "You didn't have to explain shit. The tabloids did that for you."

"I wasn't charged because I did nothing wrong. I was only giving a woman a ride. I wasn't drunk, and I hadn't touched her!" *Much. Yet.*

"That's not how it looks."

"I can't help that. It's the truth."

"You were absent yesterday. That's the truth. You missed a whole day of work."

He made it sound like she'd forgotten to show up, not that she'd been in a holding cell for no good reason.

"Do you know how many days I've missed?"

"I'm sure not many—"

"Is zero many? You're damn sure it isn't. Twenty-nine and one half years, and I haven't missed one day. You've been here, what? Three months?"

"Actually, it's been six months."

Impossibly, his squint grew more pronounced leaving only the tips of his lashes visible. "Six months. And you've been late at least five times."

"I think it's only been four…" she trailed off when it looked as though he might reach across the desk and throttle her.

"Well, I've got good news for you, kid. One more time…one minute late…one second late…and you won't have to get up at the ass crack of dawn anymore."

Lectures were one thing, but threatening her job was another. "Arnie, I've got a guaranteed contract. You can't fire me for being a second late."

"I can fire you if I don't like the way you wear your hair. And I don't, as a matter of fact. Since you're the only woman here, I'd like a few men to enjoy looking at you first thing in the morning. Given you don't say a fucking thing that makes sense, the least you can do is be eye candy."

Now she was angry. "I'm not here to be eye candy. I have a point of view that I don't get to exercise much, but that point of view is why I was hired."

"Point of view," he muttered. "Socialist bullshit's more like it."

"Let's be honest. Everybody in radio knows you didn't want to hire me, but I've got a guaranteed contract."

"So you do. How many lawyers you got?"

"I have a lawyer."

"Good for you. But I've got dozens of 'em. They're all sitting around waiting for something to do. They'd love to spend their time getting rid of you. And by the time they're done, you'll have spent most of your criminally high salary fighting me." When he grinned, his eyes popped open and focused on her like a snake's. "Have fun, bitch."

An hour later, Brooklyn stood outside the door to her loft. Music was seeping from around the door and she leaned her head against the time-battered steel, trying to rein in her disappointment. She wanted to go to sleep immediately, not socialize. Grumpily, she opened the door, finding her friend and manager, Kat, sitting on her sectional.

"Hey, gurrrl," Kat called out.

"Hi." She put her bulging messenger bag on the dining table and walked over to Kat. "What are you doing over here at this time of day?"

"Nuthin' much. I thought we could watch some movies." She pointed at the television with the remote. "I've watched about ten minutes of four different movies on pay per view, and they all suck."

"No movies for me."

Even on a day when she'd come into Manhattan only to lie on Brooklyn's couch and watch bits of movies, Kat was dressed better than Brooklyn was. And Brooklyn's image had been broadcast to thousands of people. But it had always been like that.

They'd been friends since high school, and Kat had been her manager since Brooklyn earned enough money and had enough gigs to need one. Brooklyn knew they'd never have become friends at all if they hadn't both been fairly open about their sexual orientation when they were kids, but they'd somehow managed to stick together for all of these years. They were like sisters who wouldn't have chosen each other as friends, but they were family, for good or ill.

Brooklyn collapsed onto the cushy leather sectional right next to Kat. It felt so good to be horizontal, she considered staying right there until the next morning. "That bastard rode me like a plow horse today. I am worn out." She didn't need to use Arnie's name. He was the source of all of her animosity.

"He's a dick," Kat said absently. Her attention was now focused on another movie that would join many others to make Brooklyn's cable bill shoot for the sky. "He can't hurt you."

Whose show does she think it is? "He thinks he can, and I have no reason to doubt him. He said he'd fire me if I'm even one second late in the future."

"He can't do that! Can he?"

"I don't know. I mean, he can try, but I don't know who'd win if I sued him. I'd rather not find out."

"Boy." Kat shook her head, while staring balefully at the distressed wood floor. "He's such an asshole. He should feel sorry for you, having to sit in a holding cell for twelve hours because some jack-off cop hates lesbians."

"He's not the type to feel sorry for me." She headed for her bedroom, hoping Kat kept the noise down for a change. "Once you're famous, nobody does."

—⁓—

Two weeks later, during the broadcast, she received a note on her computer instructing her to go to Arnie's office as soon as the show was over. Fuck it, fuck it, fuck it. She'd been on time since the day she'd missed, but even she had to admit she'd been off her game since the incident. Trips to Seattle one weekend and Denver the next had screwed her up more than usual, and she'd been groggy and out of sorts both at home and on the air.

The after-work meeting preoccupied her, but she wasn't caught daydreaming. One of Arnie's favorite senators was in the studio, and he took up so much time gas-bagging that she was off the hook. One of the good things about being hated was that Arnie had rearranged the studio when she was hired to make sure he had to turn his head to see her. The angle of her placement meant the TV director had to go to a camera right over her workspace to capture her. Luckily, the two-shot that picked up the guest and Arnie stayed locked in place, and she didn't say a word that would cause that to change.

As soon as the "On Air" sign went dark, she grabbed her bag and headed to Arnie's office. The door was open and she walked in, stopping short when she saw a man sitting at the conference table. He looked up and her stomach sank. It was never good to have to meet with the guy who'd signed your contract when someone wanted to tear it up. "Mr. Manuel," she said, extending her hand to shake.

"Hello, Brooklyn. Have a seat."

She looked pointedly towards Arnie's empty chair.

"He won't be joining us." Tomas Manuel took a sheaf of papers and rapped them against the table. "We're concerned about you, Brooklyn."

"Concerned?" That was bullshit-speak for angry or worried about their investment.

"Yes. Arnie believes that you've been abusing drugs and—"

"I don't use drugs! Get someone in here right now and I'll take a test."

He ignored her offer and continued. "You might recall that there's a clause in your contract allowing us to force you to get help if we deem you need it."

"A totally ridiculous clause that you wouldn't have muscled in there if Arnie hadn't been on the air for years while he was on cocaine."

"That's not relevant to your situation. We reach thousands of people on the TV broadcast and hundreds of thousands on the radio simulcast. Every one of those people is important to us. What is relevant is that we at Spectrum and Arnie agree that your performance has been weak for the past month. That might be because of drugs. So we have the right to compel you be monitored."

"Fine. Monitor me." She leaned back in her chair, relieved that the issue was such a minor one.

"Even if you're not using drugs, you need to improve your performance. You'll also recall that we can force you to curtail or eliminate outside work if it's deleterious to our interests."

Now he'd hit a nerve. Losing stand-up would kill her. But you couldn't let management know they'd scared you. "Why would you want to screw things up? Ratings are great! Isn't that what matters?"

"Yes, of course. But we want to make sure you can help keep those ratings up. Being caught with that young woman wasn't wise. We could easily lose sponsors because of that type of behavior."

She jumped to her feet. "I was giving a stranger a ride!"

"Sit down," he said quietly. "Let's get this over with."

"So you're firing me?"

"Of course not. Who said anything about firing you?"

"Arnie threatened me after the incident in Atlanta. He said he'd fire me if I'm as much as a minute late."

The smile that flitted across his lips was hard to read. "Everyone at Spectrum loves Arnie, but he can be a little bellicose."

Was this guy a lawyer, or a vocabulary teacher? "So, if you're not going to fire me, why are we here?"

"We're here because I have an offer to make. We're going to hire someone to supervise you for a while. She's going to make sure you're not taking drugs or doing anything else that's hurting your performance."

"That's your offer? You can take your offer—"

"Brooklyn," he said soothingly. "We can make this hard or easy. Why not just play along?"

"Because I don't want someone in my business!"

"It will only be for a few weeks. Maybe a month. We'll play it by ear. And, to be honest, you don't get a vote in the matter. If you won't cooperate, we'll sue you for breach of contract."

Brooklyn jumped to her feet once again, blood pounding in her ears. "The ratings are good!"

"I know they are. And I assume your reputation in the industry is good too. When we sue you it's going to take a hit. Maybe not with the viewers, but with other employers. I'd think this through carefully if I were you."

"How does it help you to hurt my professional reputation?" Her tone sounded perilously close to a plea.

"Any time any one of our staff is in the news, ratings go up. It's a win win situation for us. I doubt the same is true for you."

—⁂—

There was a little more negotiation between her lawyer and the lawyers at Spectrum, but she was forced to give in. She'd be supervised for as long as Spectrum wished, and their spy would submit a detailed report about her and her outside activities.

Once the agreement was reached, she'd forgotten about the details until the next Sunday morning. The always-annoying, overly-loud doorbell rang, waking her from a sound sleep. She tried to lie there and ignore it, assuming it was some jerk buzzing only to get into the building. But after it was silent for a few seconds it started up again. Moments later her cell phone started to ring, showing an unfamiliar number. Then it hit her—the babysitter was coming. Hooray! There was no way to get out of this, so it was best to get it over with. Then she could show her the door and sleep for another few hours.

A cranky lower back and aching hip reminded her that travel took more out of her than it used to, and that reminder only served to darken her mood. Not bothering to double-check to see who it was, she hit the buzzer, almost wishing her visitor was a homicidal maniac who would blow her away and end it all.

She threw the door open and waited. The building had an elevator, but it was ancient and slow, meant for loading machinery and materials rather than people, so it took a good long while for guests to reach the fifth floor. Spectrum had said next to nothing about the babysitter, but she had a mental image of a person who would agree to watch a relatively healthy, relatively intelligent adult for a month. Someone kinda like Mrs. Doubtfire, but less attractive. That image was smashed, shredded, and immolated when a young, pretty, happy-looking woman appeared in front of her. It took Brooklyn a few seconds to make her mouth follow her brain's directions to speak. "Uh, hi," she said sounding about as witty as she felt. "Are you the babysitter?"

The woman laughed, sounding like the angels must when someone in heaven tickles them. "I don't think I've ever been called that, to my face at least." She stuck her hand out and took Brooklyn's limp one. "Most people call me a personal assistant, but I'm also known as a talent wrangler."

Brooklyn backed up. "Come on in." Standing there stupidly, she tried to make herself move. But she was so shocked by the babysitter's appearance, she wasn't thinking straight. It wasn't just that she was young and cute. What was odd was how much she looked more like one of the healthy, active women who moved around New York at breakneck speed, going to the gym or racing along the streets, desperate to get somewhere important. There was nothing about this woman that looked like she spent her days watching other adults do God knows what.

Finally, Brooklyn had to say or do something. She took a quick look around the loft and cringed. It looked horrible. Worse than horrible. It looked like someone had come in and ransacked the place while she'd been out of town. "I just got back from Tucson." She consciously tried to stand up straight, figuring she could at least control her posture, but she was too stiff to even pull that meager goal off. "We took the redeye, and I was supposed to be in business class, but something got screwed up. I don't think I've ever been on a trip where something didn't go wrong."

That was way too many words. Be cool! She started to lead the way over to the main seating area, still babbling. "I don't usually leave the place this messy, but I was running late on Friday and had to get packed. Obviously I changed my mind about what to take quite a few times." Clothes, shoes, newspapers, magazines, paperback books, and hundreds of 3 x 5 cards littered most of the open space. Brooklyn started to dash around, picking up armfuls of stuff.

"Don't worry about it. It doesn't look bad at all."

The babysitter was a liar, but she was polite. "Did you say your name? If you did, I missed it."

"I don't think I said it. It's Kerri. Kerri Klein. And I assume you're Brooklyn."

"I assume I am, but you could convince me otherwise."

"Do you want me to call you Brooklyn?"

"Versus…?" She stood there, her arms full, knowing she looked like a dope.

"I assumed Brooklyn York was a stage name. Isn't it?"

"No, no, it's my real name. My mom's from Brooklyn."

Where could she throw all of this junk? She chose the sliding glass door to her bedroom and hurled everything inside. But what kind of idiot would think that throwing mounds of trash into another room made the place clean? It was akin to turning your underwear inside out and wearing them for another day. Things moved around, but they didn't improve.

While having this blabby discussion with herself, she was standing close to the dining area, so she headed for that, figuring that was a better place to talk business. Kerri took a chair right next to her and leaned close, making Brooklyn lean back in her own chair, trying to keep a comfortable space between them.

"I'm going to be really honest with you," Kerri said. It was like she was going to reveal the secrets of the universe.

The sun was coming in from the massive windows behind her creating what Brooklyn assumed was a visual trick, but certainly seemed like a halo.

"I'd never heard of you until Spectrum contacted me."

Even though Brooklyn had tried to have a little space, she could smell Kerri, and her scent was amazingly alluring. It was impossible not to lean forward just enough to keep her nose twitching with pleasure.

"I wasn't crazy about coming to New York right now, but I did some research before I accepted and decided I couldn't turn down my first opportunity to work with an out lesbian."

Brooklyn's brain wasn't keeping up word for word. Kerri was beautiful in the "fresh out of the package, never been used" sense, and that kind of woman was among Brooklyn's favorites. She looked like she'd always smell like daisies and snowflakes and cinnamon buns.

"You what?" she asked, knowing she sounded like a dullard.

"You're out, right? The clips I saw on You Tube—"

It hit her like a slap to the face. "Did you say you were a lesbian?" That tinkling laugh that made Brooklyn squirm in her chair graced her ears one more time.

"I didn't say I was, but I am. Why? Do I look super straight?"

"Kinda." Amazed at the witticisms that were veritably flying from her tongue, Brooklyn could only smile stupidly.

"Well, I'm super gay, so looks must be deceiving. Now tell me about this job."

"This job?" She pointed at herself. "Or my job?" God, she could sound like a moron given the right circumstances. No one would believe she made her living with her wit.

Kerri smiled, showing one perfect dimple. "Why don't you start with yours. I've got to be honest again and tell you I haven't heard your radio show, but I watched a ton of clips from your stand-up shows."

"How much do you know about me? Did they give you a dossier or something?"

"No. I actually try to avoid reading too much about a new client. I'd rather make up my own mind about a person, and that's hard to do when you read information that's been heavily edited."

"You won't find much about me on the internet. I don't even have a web page."

"Hmm." Kerri smiled inscrutably. Did she think it was cool to swim against the tide or stupid to ignore a huge marketing opportunity?

"I hear that my entire act is on the web if you want to take the time to piece it together. I can't figure out why anyone comes to hear me in person."

Kerri grinned so attractively that it was impossible not to mimic her.

"Watching someone in person is so much better. Especially for your women fans. I'm sure you know how popular you are with lesbians."

"There's not a lot of competition," she said, trying to sound modest. "I bet there aren't many clips of *Reveille* on You Tube, since no one under eighty listens."

"What about the televised feed? I was going to take a peek, but I couldn't find a listing for it."

"The TV simulcast is on a station only about ten percent of the country gets. It's on the News and Entertainment Network, a new name for the Farm Report channel. If you don't see hay when you look out your window, you won't get it."

"Hmm. That's not great. Still, your demographics aren't that bad. Your show just tilts a little old." She smiled winningly. "Okay, very, very old."

"So you'll do demographic but not personal research?"

"Sure. Those are facts. It's opinion I'm not interested in."

"Got it. Well, you've heard of Arnie Glenn, right?"

Making a vague gesture with her hand, Kerri said, "I'd heard his name, but I didn't pay any attention to him until he called the secretary of state the "C" word. That gave him a lot more publicity than he deserved."

Brooklyn laughed, even though she hadn't found the situation funny in the least. "Arnie's had a charmed life. You'd think that doing something that stupid would have been enough to ruin him. But when he said he'd been misquoted and meant to call her a stupid dyke rather than a stupid C-word, I think he gave the country a pretty accurate view of who he really is." It was impossible to keep the disgust from her voice, then she realized she didn't have to. The babysitter wasn't there to make sure she liked Arnie, just that she showed up for work. "The only good thing about the whole situation is that his being a moron got me the job."

"What's the inside story on your being hired? They told me next to nothing about that."

"Spectrum was getting harassed from more groups than they knew existed. They didn't want to fire him, since so many big politicians and media types come on, so they offered to hire a woman to at least throw feminist groups a bone."

"From what I read he was really against hiring anybody new, much less a woman."

"Not to mention a lesbian. They tell me he used to be liberal on social issues, but that's changed. I guess he saw more money in it if he went over to the religious wrong."

"Why did they pick you?" She put her silky skinned hand upon Brooklyn's.

That was a strangely intimate move. Not entirely unwelcome, but most people didn't touch you for no reason. Maybe she was trying to flirt so Brooklyn would lower her guard.

"Not that I'm sure you didn't deserve it, but it seems like they were asking for trouble by hiring you."

"I think that's why he agreed. He wanted somebody that most of the audience wouldn't like and that he could pick on." She felt a smile come to her lips and she sat up a little straighter. "I think I've held my own."

"If the ratings are any indication, and I assume they're hugely important, you've done more than hold your own."

Brooklyn could feel her chest puff up. "We had thirty percent of the audience in the eighteen to thirty-five demographic in the first ratings book after I started. That's softened a little, but overall ratings are better than they've been in ten years."

"How long has his show been on?"

"Almost thirty years, and he's never missed a day," she recited in a singsong manner. "But he's not out every weekend doing the college lecture circuit like I am."

Kerri's hand moved gently, sending shivers up Brooklyn's spine. Who touched people this much? Was she a masseuse?

"Oh, you were sleeping, weren't you. That's why it took so long for you to answer the bell. I'm sorry I didn't come later in the day."

"Don't worry about it. I sleep all day most Sundays."

"Because you want to?"

That was an odd question, but what the hell. "I was on stage until after eleven last night, then caught the one a.m. flight to JFK. I tried for hours to get to sleep on the plane, which was impossible, since I was in a seat meant for someone five inches shorter and fifty pounds lighter. I had a couple of drinks, but even that didn't help relax me. When I finally got in this morning at six or whatever time it was, I took something to relax and I'm still groggy from it." She ran her hand through her hair, realizing what a mess it was. "My schedule is so screwed up it's not funny."

"We'll get to work on that soon. I guarantee we'll make progress."

Brooklyn laughed at her naiveté as well as her pluck. Just because she was supposed to write a report didn't mean she got to tell her when to go to bed. "Good luck. I have to be in Fort Lee, New Jersey at six a.m. four days a week, and on some college campus every Friday and Saturday night that I can get a booking."

"Aren't most radio shows on five days a week?"

"Yeah, but Arnie's got a huge place out in The Hamptons where he spends his weekends, and he doesn't want to travel on Friday. He must have some secret power over management, because he gets everything he wants." She shrugged. "It's fine with me, since I get paid the same if we work five days or four."

"Do you really have to work every weekend? That sounds like it would be a real grind."

Kerri gave her such a concerned, empathetic look that Brooklyn almost felt sorry for herself. And she completely lost track of the fact that Kerri was there to spy on her. "It's my choice. I've gotta make hay while the sun shines, and the radio show makes it sunny."

"Hmm."

Now that Brooklyn was sure the halo was an illusion, she spent a moment gazing at Kerri's fair hair. It draped across her forehead, skimmed her brow, and grew significantly shorter as it went towards the sides and back of her head. They might have called it a pixie cut…or something like that. A few actresses had recently started cutting their hair just this way, and Brooklyn thought it looked adorable on the right face. Kerri had the right face.

"We'll look at ways to do things differently. There have to be ways to make your life easier."

"Right." Now was the time to talk about Kat. "About that. I've got a full-time road manager. She travels with me and handles all of my arrangements. She doesn't really need help…"

Kerri moved that soft hand on hers again. Just enough to make goosebumps rise. Damn, that was soft skin, and it'd been weeks since she'd felt a woman's touch, making it all the more delightful.

"I'm here to make things better, not worse. If I'm doing anything that your manager doesn't like, just tell me and I'll back off."

She smiled such a confident, reassuring smile that Brooklyn felt the stiff muscles in her hips and back begin to relax. Having someone act like she was really there to help made the whole stupid schedule seem like it was manageable.

"My schedule is completely out of control. I've tried a couple of things, but they're not working." She felt herself let out a deep breath. "You know, I wasn't happy about having you here. I had an image of a drill sergeant kind of person." She tried to show her most charming smile. "I'm glad that's not what I got."

"Up to this point, you are the most compliant client I've ever had, so I'm very pleased too. Tell me what you've tried so far in getting your schedule set up properly."

"Last week I experimented with staying up all night. I think it went okay, but I didn't look very good and the make-up artist ratted me out the first morning."

"There's always one rat in every office, isn't there?"

"We're loaded with them. When you have to fill four hours of air-time a day you spend an inordinate percentage of your day looking for weak spots in your co-workers' armor. It's really a ridiculous way to earn a living."

"Did you stay on that schedule all week? I've got to switch my schedule around a lot, and I know how hard it is. It can take some people the better part of a week to feel right after a change."

"I tried to stay on it all week, but I kept waking up earlier in the evening, and by the weekend I was completely screwed up. I feel awful now. Really awful."

"You look terribly tired. Why don't you lie down and sleep until you wake up naturally. Then we can talk."

"You'll…what? Call me later?"

"I'll stay right here if that's okay. I've got lots of things to entertain myself."

Brooklyn looked at the big backpack that sat on the floor. "Really? I'd love to head back to bed, but I don't want to ruin your day." She looked at her watch. "Damn, it's just noon and I didn't get to sleep until nine. Three hours of sleep isn't going to cut it."

"Don't worry about it. Helping you figure this out is my job. So go. Go right now." She made a shooing motion with her hands. "I'll be here and we can have dinner and talk things over."

It shouldn't have been possible to feel better already, but Brooklyn did. "Okay. Want me to show you how to use the TV?"

"No, I'm fine. Can I take these keys if I need to go out for anything?"

"Yeah. Those are mine." She got up and headed for her bedroom, feeling very odd going to sleep with a perfect stranger sitting at her dining room table. "Is this really okay?"

"It's great. Get some sleep. If you're out until tomorrow morning I'll get you up. What time?"

"Four thirty."

"Do you drink coffee?"

"Hell, yes."

"What kind of coffee do you like?"

"I get a giant mocha latte with an extra shot."

"Great. If you sleep all night I'll have coffee ready for you at 4:30." She took out a phone and started making a note, her fingers flying across the screen.

"Is this all you have to do? Just look after me?"

"No, after I agreed to take this job, I grabbed another that I'd previously refused. My other client should be super easy. I just have to get him ready for court in the morning. That job should only last a couple of weeks."

Brooklyn's brow shot up. "Court?"

"Yeah. He has to be in court at nine."

Chuckling softly, Brooklyn said, "Another one who can't get up?"

"No, they say he's always up from the night before. I have to make sure he has on fresh clothes and doesn't smell like...whatever he was doing earlier."

"Smell?" Now she was interested.

Coloring just a little, Kerri said, "He likes to party, and that usually means strip clubs. Strippers wear a lot of perfume. They've taken to wearing body glitter too." Her brows knit together and her head tilted a bit. "Why women do that is beyond me. Most guys don't want to advertise that they've just been to a strip club. Strange."

"Is it Little Thug? He's on trial for criminal assault."

"No, no, not him. I wouldn't have said as much as I did if my client was well-known. Discretion is part of the service."

"So you won't tell people you're waking me up?"

"I signed a confidentiality agreement that will cost me megabucks if word gets out." She attempted to form a stern expression, but she couldn't carry it off. "Don't blab."

"I'm not proud of this, so I'm not gonna blab."

Brooklyn went to the counter and ran her hand through a big bowl of change, keys, receipts and loose cigarettes. "I've got an extra set of keys here...somewhere." She pulled out a keychain and held it up. "Success. You can keep this set."

Kerri took them and put them in her backpack. "I'll see you when you wake up. Would you mind if I brought my bike up?"

Brooklyn finally noticed that Kerri had a helmet hanging from her pack. "Sure. You can't hurt these floors."

"Your place is delightful," Kerri said, her voice so low it sounded like she was telling a secret.

"Thanks. I'm awfully far from my job, but I like TriBeCa. At night it can be almost deserted. It's like a ghost town that's all mine."

"I like that too. It's much easier to get around neighborhoods that aren't jammed with people." She held her hand up and jiggled her fingers. "See you later."

Brooklyn smiled weakly. "From your lips to God's ear."

—⁓—

Now alone, Kerri idly wandered around the open space, trying to get a feel for her new client. She wasn't a neat-nick, that was for sure. But someone had taken a lot of time to remodel the place, and it looked like that remodel was recent. The loft still bore the aroma of paint, and the grout in the bathrooms was perfectly white.

Brooklyn had gone with an industrial look that fit the old building perfectly. It was cold and not traditionally homey, but it had a very appealing New York edge. She must have spent a fortune, but she wasn't taking great care of it. It hadn't been cleaned, really cleaned, in a while. Once the clutter was gone it looked fine to an untrained eye, but it was dusty and that fine New York grit was on the tables and floors. So, either she didn't have a cleaning service or she had a really bad one. That was an interesting choice. What kind of person didn't clean her place and didn't hire anyone to do it for her—when she was rich?

Having done a little research when she'd gotten the address, Kerri found that the building was once a warehouse for goods imported from Germany. It'd been built in the late 1800s, and when she stood on the balcony and looked at the old warehouses that surrounded her, she had an image of men loading shelves full of foodstuffs from their homeland. What would they think of their hot, dim, noisy workplace now filled with multi-million dollar lofts? They wouldn't even have the language to express the concept.

The space was a long "I" with gigantic double-hung windows on the south and west sides. The original walls were brick, but the bathroom and portions of the living room and kitchen were plastered. Probably to cover up old doors or unrepairable brick. Brooklyn had placed a bedroom and bath on either end of the space, enclosing them in tall frosted glass with sliding doors. They added to the chill of the room, but it was nice to have light from the big windows reach all the way across the very tall space. Closets and drawers were built into the walls of the bedrooms and baths, removing the need for almost any furniture and adding another ice cube to the chilliness.

The huge TV hung on the wall of the main living space, and she'd created an entertainment center around it, with a massive leather seating area, a couple of tables and expensive-looking, modern lamps. Behind the sectional was another seating area, that looked like it was never used. A mauve fainting couch and two deep-blue, upholstered chairs sat there looking lonely.

Further across the room, the dining table was eye catching and unique. It was a huge piece of metal with a big hole in the middle. It must have been some sort of gear or machine part, and someone, probably not Brooklyn, had used some kind of tool to make interesting swirls on the surface. It was also so cold and hard that it wouldn't have appealed to most, but Brooklyn must have liked it, since it occupied such a prized spot. Brooklyn had taken pity on her guests and had furnished the table with very comfortable swivel chairs in a leather that matched the sectional. That was the mark of someone who wanted herself and her guests to enjoy themselves while they dined. Strangely, Kerri had seen many dining areas furnished with chairs that looked like torture devices. It was nice to know that Brooklyn, or her designer, considered the comfort of the people who would visit.

The kitchen was one of those ridiculously expensive, nearly all white, European-designed spaces. It was beyond clean and was so streamlined that it almost faded into the white walls. When she opened the oven, Kerri found the instructions on how to operate it still lying on the top rack. So much for cooking.

The guest bath looked like it could have been in a high-end spa. That room alone must have cost more than most people earned in a year, yet it had no personality.

The loft didn't give any real clues to who Brooklyn was, but years of working closely with people had attuned Kerri to a few things. Brooklyn watched TV and read, she didn't cook, she didn't spend much time tending to her own needs, and she seemed pretty easy going. That was always a plus.

Brooklyn was going to be out for a while, so Kerri took a small cushion from her backpack and placed it on the floor. The sun was coming in through the huge windows, adding both real and emotional warmth to the chilly loft. She sat cross-legged on the cushion and tried to quiet her mind, but it took a while. Meeting a new client was always slightly unnerving, and it took time to center herself afterwards. But she whisked away every intrusive thought one by one and finally reached a deep, peaceful state. She sat there, almost immobile for over an hour, and when she came out of the zone, she was remarkably refreshed and ready to launch herself into her new adventure.

—⁓—

It was very dark and unnaturally quiet in the loft. Brooklyn had no idea what time it was, but given how her bladder felt, she'd been asleep for a very long time. Her body still ached, but she felt better than she had when…what was her name? Kerri. Kerri something-or-other. She got out of bed, used the bathroom, then her empty stomach decided it was time for dinner, or breakfast. Whatever it was, it was time to eat. She walked out into the living area, stark naked. By the time she passed the sectional she heard a groggy voice say, "Are you up for good?"

"Shit!" She grabbed for the first thing that seemed big enough, and stood there trying to cover herself with a throw pillow. "I thought you'd gone home."

Kerri sat up and stretched. "I told you I'd be here when you woke up. Are you awake?"

"Well, I am now. There's something about showing a stranger your ass that really gets the blood moving!"

"If you like your privacy, I'll go hangout somewhere while you get dressed. But if it doesn't bother you, it certainly doesn't bother me."

Playfully, Brooklyn lowered the pillow for just a second and then covered herself again. Kerri laughed, her pretty eyes almost hidden when she did. She was so cute it hurt just to look at her. Her hair was a little mussed, and there was a pink line down her cheek from the welt on the sofa cushion. There was no doubt that she had all of the important attributes: beauty, intelligence and playfulness. But there was no sense in wasting time on a futile effort. Might as well let her see the dreadful reality now in case she only liked women as perfect as she was. Brooklyn dropped the pillow for another half second. "Did I burn your retinas?"

"Not a bit. I've seen just about everybody I've worked for naked, so it seems quite normal for me."

"I'm not very shy, but this body is nothing to be proud of."

"You look just fine. I'm a big believer in loving the body you have."

That was damned good news. Perfection had been left at the curb not long after high school graduation. "I'm in favor of feeding the body I have. Are you hungry?"

"I am. I decided not to eat while you were asleep, so I'm famished. Would you like me to cook?"

"I'm sure I don't have any food, and I'm not sure I have pots or pans, so we can order in."

"There are lots of places still open, why don't we go out?"

The call of a nice pizza and a few hours of watching the cable news networks was strong, but poor Kerri had been waiting for twelve hours. She should get to do what she wanted. "Should I take a shower and get ready for work now?"

"I wouldn't. If you shower right before you leave for work you might feel more like it's just a regular day at the office."

"I haven't had one of those yet."

―᠁―

It was after one a.m. when they left the loft. It had cooled off appreciably, and now felt more like fall. They'd each donned jackets, with Kerri pulling hers from that huge backpack. Brooklyn walked out into the middle of Desbrosses looking for a cab. The street was empty, as was Greenwich when she peeked around the corner. "The only place I know that's open is a deli on the Lower East Side. Is that okay?"

"I know someplace good, and they serve food until three. Best of all, we can walk there."

"Really? It's a little chilly, isn't it?"

"No, not at all. We'll warm up while we walk."

Who wanted to walk around TriBeCa in the middle of the night? But admitting that walking wasn't on her favorite-things list was embarrassing, so Brooklyn lit a cigarette and tagged along, thankful that she could at least use the walk to smoke. It didn't take long to get to a yuppie hangout that served a strange mix of Asian/Mexican food, but none of the Mexican food looked even vaguely familiar.

"I see a suspicious frown," Kerri teased. "Let me order for you. I promise the food here really is good."

Brooklyn slapped the menu closed. "Okay. I guess I should expand my diet past pizza and hamburgers."

"You don't have to. But I think you might like the food here, and it'll give you a spot to spend a couple of hours if you're looking to kill time at two a. m."

"That's a good idea. I tried going to a bar last week, but being in a bar when you're not drinking just highlights how much alcohol screws with your perspective. After enough drinks everybody at a bar seems funny and good looking, and God knows that's not true."

When their server approached, Kerri asked some questions, pronouncing a few words with a good-sounding Japanese accent. When he left, Brooklyn said, "Do you speak Japanese?"

"Oh, gosh, no. But I've been to Japan quite a few times. When I'm in a country for a while, I try to learn the cadence of the language. If you can get that and learn the phonics, you can pronounce anything—even if you're not sure what it means."

"Were you in Japan for work?"

Kerri took a sip of water. "Uh-huh. I was there for almost six months once. I spent some time learning the basics—just things like ordering food, giving directions, calling the paramedics." She showed a teasing grin. "I can describe the symptoms of alcohol poisoning in perfect Japanese."

"I've never been poisoned, so you don't need to know how to do that in English."

"That's good to know." Kerri looked at Brooklyn with a sunny smile and said, "What did Spectrum tell you about me?"

"Not a lot. Just that you were supposed to keep an eye on me and report me if I screwed up."

Grimacing, Kerri said, "I hate when a client does that. Besides not being the truth, it's counterproductive."

"So you won't rat me out if I'm on drugs?"

That sweet smile dimmed. "I'd have to. But I wouldn't get any satisfaction from it."

"No worries. I don't even smoke grass." *Often.* "But I got the clear impression you were supposed to make sure I was getting enough sleep to be able to be sharp for the show."

"I'm going to be completely honest with you. My job is to give Spectrum a report at the end of our time together. They want to know if you're devoting yourself to the show. Anything that's harming your performance is something for me to note. That could be anything from drugs to sleep to not giving a damn."

Brooklyn didn't say a word. She tried to merely look interested. Inside, she was fuming. There was no way in hell she was going to help this woman ruin her gig. She could act compliant, but she wasn't going to start behaving like she was in prison. Spectrum could kiss her ass.

"The good news is that I'm not out to catch you or trick you."

Kerri's eyes seemed so empathic that Brooklyn almost...almost believed her.

"I'll do everything I can to help you in any way. I'll cook for you, run errands for you, travel with you, read bedtime stories to you. Anything you need to be better at your job."

It was impossible not to ask the obvious question. "Why? Why not just watch me for a few weeks and tell them I'm a screw off?"

Laughing softly, Kerri shook her head. "I haven't worked for Spectrum before. If I can make you do a better job, they might hire me again. The better you do, the better I might do in the future."

Wow. That seemed strangely honest. But Kerri wasn't up to the job of pulling things out of Brooklyn she didn't want pulled. She was a pro at keeping her secrets secret.

"Believe me when I say I'm not going to call Spectrum every time you're out late. I'm truly not your babysitter, Brooklyn. I can help, but only if you let me."

"I know I need some help." *But letting you see how much could cost me my stand-up career. I'm not going to slit my own throat.* "I'll cooperate as much as I can."

"That's all I could possibly ask for."

—∿∿—

Brooklyn found herself yakking almost nonstop. It wasn't generally her style to talk so much to someone she didn't know well, but Kerri had the ability to draw her out, and she used that talent very effectively. But they didn't talk about anything important, and Brooklyn made sure to keep the conversation away from her personal life and her less-than-stellar habits.

The kitchen closed at 2:30 and they stayed until the manager locked the door behind them at three, with Brooklyn insisting on paying for both of them. They walked back to the loft at a leisurely pace, stopping at a newsstand to buy all of the morning papers that she didn't have delivered. "If I could do this every day, I think I'd be pretty happy," Brooklyn said.

"It's worth a try. Let's spend a while listening to your body. If it doesn't behave, we'll have to whip it into shape."

She winked, her whole face involved in the action. Brooklyn didn't think it was possible, but she got cuter by the minute. It was going to be very, very hard to keep this relationship on a business level. Of course, maybe they wouldn't have to.

———

It was clear Brooklyn had wanted to hail a cab, but she politely let Kerri take the lead—something Kerri loved to do. Clients, when left to their own devices, tended to make the wrong choices. Repeatedly.

They set out walking back to the loft. Now was the perfect time to ask about Brooklyn's recent troubles with the tabloids. She was relaxed, her belly was full, and walking generally allowed people to be reflective. Seeing how she responded would give a clue about her honesty.

"So…even though I tried not to learn much about you, I did read about the incident in Georgia. What was that all about?"

Brooklyn's eyes had been darting around while they walked, perhaps because she was the type to observe her surroundings or maybe she was hyper-vigilant. Now they landed and focused directly on Kerri.

"Everybody thinks they know what happened, but no one believes me when I tell them the truth."

"Give me a try. I like the truth." She tried to make her smile look very welcoming.

"Okay. I'd finished a gig and went to a local bar with the guy who opened for me. He called a couple of his friends and we hung out until closing time."

"That sounds pretty innocent."

"Yeah, it was. There were a couple of girls…women…there and they made it clear they'd like to hang out after the bar closed."

"And one of them picked you?"

Brooklyn looked almost embarrassed when she said, "Both of them seemed interested in me." She laughed, while shaking her head. "Times have changed. Every straight girl wants to have a fling with a lesbian now. It's like a badge of honor."

"Don't sell yourself short. You're awfully attractive."

"That's not what I see when I look in the mirror, but I'm not going to try to change your opinion."

She had the sweetest smile, and she looked so sincere that it wasn't possible to doubt her. "So how did the police get involved?"

"I said I was staying by the airport, and one of the women said she lived in that direction. So I gave her a ride home. But right before we left she took her drink and guzzled it. That must have put her over the edge, because she was a drunken mess twenty minutes later."

"Were you speeding?"

"Hell no! I was driving all over Atlanta with a drunken liar. Her apartment was so far from the airport it was probably in a different area code!"

Brooklyn was practically fuming. Was she angry about being lied to, or having to go out of her way for sex?

"Is it against the law to drive away from the airport?"

She stopped and quickly composed herself again. "No. But my passenger threw her panties out the window, right in front of a cop. He picked them up and clipped me for littering."

"Oh, my. I didn't read about that part."

Brooklyn scratched the back of her head in a mildly annoyed fashion. "I don't have a publicist, so there wasn't anyone to manipulate the press in my favor. Besides, I wouldn't have told anyone about that. The kid was nineteen. How would you like it if the things you did when you were nineteen got splashed all over the news?"

"So you really didn't do anything wrong?"

She stopped once again and stared boldly into Kerri's eyes. "I picked up a girl who could have been underage. She wasn't, but I didn't even bother to check. That's on me." Then she jammed her hands into the pockets of her jeans and started to walk again.

Kerri put a hand on her arm to slow her down, but Brooklyn gave her a mildly annoyed look so she removed it. "You really spent time in jail for littering?"

"No," she said slowly. "I spent the night in jail for being a lesbian with opinions the cop didn't like. He jacked me up because of who I am and what I represent. And that's the truth."

She said those last words so forcefully that Kerri almost stepped back. Whether that was in fact the truth, Brooklyn was really able to sell it.

"It sounds like you could make a stink or at least get some gay advocacy groups on your side if you wanted to make a point of it."

Brooklyn looked like she'd stepped in something nasty. "No, thanks. No one is going to make closed-minded people open their minds because of a protest. Besides, I don't want to drag the girl's name through any more mud. I'm sure her parents are still fuming." She let out a bitter laugh. "Probably at me, even though she's the one who tricked me into taking her home."

They didn't speak of the incident any more, but Kerri had a strong feeling that Brooklyn had told her the truth. Nothing about the story made her look very good, save for keeping her passenger out of the press. And if that was the truth, there was a good chance she wasn't a self-involved jerk. Wouldn't that be a nice change of pace?

—⁂—

Once they were back inside the loft, Brooklyn said, "I guess I'd better get in the shower."

"How can I help?"

After just a moment's pause, Brooklyn started to take her clothes off. Excellent. She'd gotten over her brief embarrassment about being naked. There would undoubtedly be some situation where Brooklyn would have to show at least some part of her body, so getting her over any skittishness was good progress for the first day.

"I can't think of anything. I'd love to have some coffee, but the local place doesn't open until five."

"Do you have a coffee maker?"

"No. I've gotten addicted to espresso and now coffee tastes like dirty water."

"If you get an espresso machine, I could have the drink you want ready for you the minute you wake up."

Brooklyn's eyes lit up. She was awfully cute when she showed her unguarded side.

"You can do that?"

"Yeah. A good machine costs a lot of money, but you'll pay for it in a few months with what you'll save not going to a coffee shop."

"I'll tell my...I'll get one. Tell me what kind to buy."

"Okay. I'll shop around today and leave you a note."

Now she was completely naked, although she held a T-shirt over her private parts. "Okay then," she said, giggling softly. She turned and headed for the bathroom, saying quietly, "This is so weird."

When the water stopped running, Kerri knocked and opened the door just a crack. "Would you like me to get some clothes out for you?"

"Sure. It'll be obvious which ones are for work."

Kerri opened the closet and tried to guess what kind of clothes Brooklyn would choose. She was a little hard to figure out. From the way she walked, she looked like she'd been an athlete. She had a smooth, rolling gait that suggested a woman who was confident with her physicality. But looking at her naked made Kerri wonder if she'd been wrong. Brooklyn was, at best, doughy. Her shoulders were broad, but her arms lacked any definition and there was a significant roll of fat encircling her midsection. Perhaps she'd once been in good shape, but had stopped exercising at some point. Stopped entirely. Or maybe she'd always been a couch potato and simply had an athletic gait.

Luckily for her career, Brooklyn's face was striking; lovely, actually, and it didn't reveal her excess weight. A woman didn't have to be pretty

30

or in shape to be a comedian, but it certainly didn't hurt. The same wasn't true for TV. To appear frequently on politically themed TV shows, a woman had to be better than average looking. Kerri didn't know a lot about Brooklyn's segment of the entertainment world, but she knew a terrific amount about movies and television in general, and good looks were the coin of the realm. Anyone who had tried to be a success on looks alone, however, had been in for a rude awakening. A pretty face didn't make up for an empty head, and Brooklyn's head seemed quite full.

Her head, or more specifically, her hair was the thing that got the most attention. Kerri had seen it referred to as "heavenly hair," and she had to admit it was pretty close to an accurate description. Brooklyn had the kind of hair that most women lost when they were in their teens. It was the color of dark chocolate, quite long, very shiny, and straight enough to glide across her back and shoulders when she turned her head. She could have sold it for large coin if she was in the market, but it was part of her image and most people didn't fool with something elemental to their being recognized.

Most surprising was how very gay Brooklyn looked, despite her overtly feminine hair. There was something about her that screamed lesbian. It wasn't easy to say what tagged her, but Kerri was sure other lesbians would have picked up on it. Straight men probably picked up on it too, and that was the part that was both surprising and pleasing about Brooklyn's success. When a woman could look like a lesbian and live her life in the open while still being on television almost every day—things were getting better. Of course, having the opportunity after a man called a high government official the c-word cut against that argument.

Kerri went through the closet carefully, picking out an emerald knit shell and a pair of slacks still in the dry cleaner's plastic. Then she rummaged through the very messy drawers and found a bra and panties. Another clue hiding in plain sight. Either Brooklyn wasn't seeing anyone, or the women she was with didn't mind her wearing really old dingy bras and undies. All of the shoes looked vaguely alike, so Kerri decided that

Brooklyn could choose them for herself. When Brooklyn came out everything was lying on the bed. "Is this okay?" Kerri asked.

"Sure. The station sends over new stuff and I just put it on. It all sucks, but it all matches."

"It's hard not to match several pair of black slacks. I could shop for something you'd like better."

"Nah. You don't have to do that."

It was too impolite to say that Brooklyn needed "a look," but she did. The clothes she wore on the clips Kerri had watched on the Internet were lifeless and said nothing about her style. But it was too early to push. "It's all part of the job. Let me know if you want me to shop or do anything else."

"I think I'm set. You can take off now if you want."

"If you don't mind, I'd like to hang out for a while. I don't go to my next client until seven thirty and he's just in SoHo."

"No, I don't mind." She headed back into the bathroom, but stopped abruptly. Looking a little sheepish, she said, "My manager might show up. She's not normally in the city in the morning, but you never know. If she comes…" Her lips pressed together, and it was clear she was thinking hard.

Who the heck was this road manager? Was she a girlfriend? "I'll introduce myself and take off. I'm good at disappearing."

"Really? I don't want you to think I…"

"I don't think a thing. It'll take a few days until you're used to me and how I work. I'm probably the only person in your life who doesn't want anything from you, and I'm sure I'm the only person in your life you don't have to worry about offending. Now go! Get ready!"

Giving her an almost shy grin, Brooklyn went back into the bathroom.

Kerri quickly made Brooklyn's bed, considering what she'd learned so far. Brooklyn was much more civilized and polite than she would have guessed. Her schedule was definitely screwed up, but it didn't seem like she was on drugs, and she showed no indication of being violent or mentally ill. So far this job was a slice of pie.

—⁓—

Brooklyn was fully dressed, her hair was dry, and her eyes were wide open when her driver buzzed at the door. She looked remarkably good for five a.m. Her eyes were a lovely shade of brown, and her strong features made her look as bright and confident as she was. She smiled at Kerri and said, "I've never felt so good about being up at this time of day."

"You look good." She touched her chin, tilting her head back so she could see her eyes. "No dark circles. Maybe we're on the way to figuring this schedule out."

The smile Brooklyn gave was rakishly charming. "We reached the moon today, let's not head for the stars just yet." She grabbed a jacket from what looked like a cage near the door and was off.

—⁓—

Now that Brooklyn was gone Kerri could dig a little more. Nothing too personal, but knowing the traps that lay everywhere was a must. The time she'd learned a big star was gay by denying his boyfriend access to the beach house was a lesson she didn't need to learn again. Snooping wasn't to learn gossip, it was simply job protection.

First, she attacked the armfuls of stuff Brooklyn had thrown into her bedroom the previous afternoon. Not being a reader herself, the ridiculous number of things on the floor was sobering. Brooklyn obviously read enough for two or three people, and it wasn't just the quantity that was amazing, it was the quality. She read things with no pictures and almost no color on the covers. There were journals about politics and the economy and international relations that looked as dry as hay. But she also had all of the gossip tabloids in the bathroom. Maybe that was a comment on their quality, since the boring-looking journals were neatly stacked by the bed.

She obviously made notes on 3 x 5 cards, since her angular writing was on cards of various colors stuck into magazines and books. Kerri didn't disturb any of them, but she took all of the loose cards from the floor and put them into neat, color-coded piles, hoping the color meant something.

Then she put the books and magazines and newspapers into stacks in the TV area. That looked like where Brooklyn hung out. Oddly, there wasn't much else to see. Her cursory search produced one bottle of vodka, a few beers in the fridge, some Chinese takeout, a bottle of Xanax that looked like it had been legally prescribed, and no pill bottles hiding behind couch cushions or taped to the lid of the toilet tank. There was not a syringe in the place, and no discolored coke spoons stashed anywhere. When she finished her scan and locked the huge steel door behind her, she was humming a happy tune. If things stayed this placid, she was going to have a great time.

—⁂—

Brooklyn opened the door at eleven and smiled when she saw Kerri sitting at the dining table. "I don't need help going to sleep, but you're welcome to watch."

"I'm just checking in. I would have watched the show, but I couldn't figure out how to turn on your mega-TV. So I listened instead. You sounded really sharp, but the other people are tough to take."

"Thanks. I thought I did all right today."

"You don't even look too tired."

"No, I'm not. I guess I'll stay up until I'm sleepy, huh?"

"Yeah, that's what I'd do. Just listen to the signals your body is sending. I'll come by late tonight in case you wake up early."

"You don't really have to…"

Kerri walked over so they were face to face. There wasn't two inches of air between their noses. The small distance violated her personal space, but Brooklyn found she didn't mind. Having the space-violator be adorable must be the key. "Did you enjoy having someone to talk with last night?"

"Yeah. It was really good. It helped a lot."

She patted Brooklyn on the shoulder and said, "It's my job to do anything you need. The goal is to get you into a good groove. Once your schedule's set you'll be great." She walked out, waving as she closed the door.

It was probably outside the job description, but maybe Kerri would be interested in putting her to sleep after a nice long bout of steaming hot sex.

At around two a.m., Brooklyn quietly slid the glass door of her bedroom open. She was wearing a T-shirt and panties this time, partly because it was chilly, and partly because she fully expected to find Kerri sleeping on the sectional. But Kerri was lying on a thin, rubber mat, doing some sort of difficult yoga pose. So that's where that body came from.

Too bad you couldn't look like Kerri while sitting on your ass eating potato chips. Given how taut and toned Kerri's body was, she'd never come within fifty feet of a potato chip. She had one of those lithe, supple, muscular bodies that top-tier swimmers had, and she was more flexible than anyone Brooklyn had ever seen. She was wound up like a pretzel, her head facing away from where Brooklyn stood, but she still caught her. Kerri let out a whoosh of air and said, "I see you over there."

Brooklyn approached, while trying not to look at her too intently. No one liked to be ogled. "Have you been up all night?"

"No. I woke up a little bit ago. I wanted to be alert when you got up."

Flopping down on the edge of the sofa, Brooklyn said, "I'd give half of my salary to have your pep."

"I like that word." Kerri stuck her legs out in front of herself and stretched for a few moments. "It sounds old, but kinda young."

"That's me. How long have you been doing yoga?"

"Years and years. I like to go to classes for the camaraderie, but I've been doing it long enough that I don't technically need supervision."

"I should do something like that."

"You can't walk ten feet in this neighborhood without seeing a yoga class going on. Try one out."

That didn't sound fun at all. Having Kerri try to put her into one of those poses was a lot more appealing. "Maybe I will."

"I'm ready to go get some dinner if you are."

"Sure. I'm starving."

"When did you go to bed?"

Scratching her head while trying to give some order to her hair, Brooklyn said, "I wasn't tired until about three, but I had a hard time falling asleep. So…maybe four?"

"You'll probably need ten hours until you make up some of your deficit." She jumped to her feet, the muscles in her thighs rendering the need for an assist superfluous. "I've got some tricks to help make your body believe it's time to get up, but we shouldn't do that until you're sure what you want your schedule to be."

"I want to go to bed at three and start my day at ten am. That's my sweet spot."

"You're not going to get that, so let's make the best of four thirty." Once again, her sunny, infectious grin precluded Brooklyn from smothering her for being so damned happy.

―⁓―

They were settled in a booth at another remarkably healthy-cuisined restaurant. Brooklyn was going to have to get her daily grease quotient from other sources if Kerri kept choosing their early morning dining locations. Brooklyn stirred three packets of sugar into her iced tea while giving Kerri a long look. "So tell me how a woman who seems normal got into the adult babysitting business."

"Who says I'm normal?"

"I just said you seemed normal. You could be as wacky as a far-right closet case."

"I'm not a closet case, that's for sure. As for my job, it's something I kinda fell into. I didn't want to go to college, and my mom knew a guy who knew a guy who knew a manager for a pretty big rock band."

"And the name of the band was...?"

"I never babysit and tell. Anyway, some of the members of the band had pre-teen kids. I traveled with them for two years and kept the kids out of the way. I liked it, it paid well, and I got to see the world. So I kept at it, and gradually switched to adults. The pay is even better, but they're actually more challenging than kids."

"They can buy drugs and drive." Brooklyn chuckled.

"That's part of many problems. But it's not a bad job. I like being organized and I like helping people. This pays a lot better than nursing, and I got to skip years of school—which I hated."

"It sounds like a good fit." *You're a freak! No one in her right mind would want to babysit adults. If you like doing that you should have been a prison guard. At least they get to carry a gun and wear a spiffy uniform.*

CHAPTER TWO

THE NEXT NIGHT BROOKLYN crept out of her room to find Kerri dead to the world. Checking her watch, she saw that it was only 9:30, much earlier than she'd woken the previous two nights. Might as well go get a little work in. She went back to her room, put on a pair of jeans that had been lying on the floor, then added a T-shirt and a button-down shirt. A navy blazer spiced her look up enough to go on stage. The hair needed a wash, but she didn't have time, so it went back into a ponytail. All things considered, she didn't look half bad. After leaving a brief note for Kerri, she was ready to go.

Finding a cab was easy at that time of night in TriBeCa, and she made it over to the Comedy Cabin by ten. The place was ancient, dirty, grimy, and smelled worse than it looked. But just going down the greasy stairs into the basement made her smile. This was where they made the sausage.

Scanning the back of the club, she saw some of the regulars and headed over. Being with her gang was akin to once again sitting in the back row of class with the delinquents. "Yorkie!" a slick looking older man called out.

"Hi, Manny," she said, going over to hug him.

"Where've you been?" a young guy with an expensive haircut and a suit asked, scanning his eyes up and down her body.

"Hello, Charles." She kissed him on the top of the head and sat next to a grizzled-looking, overweight guy whose body strained the seams of his dress shirt. "And, of course, Mike."

Mike put his beefy arm around her hips and left it there until she scooted out from under it. "Aww, come on," he said. "It doesn't hurt you to at least look like you like me. Other girls'll see and I'll do better with 'em."

"Other girls could see you getting blown and it wouldn't help," Charles snickered. "Besides, York's a dyke and that doesn't give you the same points a normal girl would give."

Flicking a finger hard on Charles' cheek was moderately satisfying, and they all sat quietly while a comic jumped onto the stage and started his act. He was very young and not very funny, and everyone around the table lost interest only two jokes in.

"Are you looking to work tonight?" Manny asked.

"Yeah. I've got a couple of things I'm trying out. Nothing very solid, but I'd like to see if they have any life to 'em."

"You better go talk to Sal. He said he's tight tonight. He might not have room for you."

Brooklyn stood and reached for the wallet in her back pocket. "His schedule opens up when it's caressed by a twenty."

The room wasn't very crowded, and she was able to slither through the haphazardly placed tables and chairs to find the owner of the club.

"Sal," she said, smiling her best smile. "Got five minutes to spare?" She held up the bill and he snatched it from her before he checked the notepad he tended to look at obsessively.

"After Manny. Just don't stretch it out too long."

"I will not." She lightly punched him on the shoulder, then started to make her way back to the table. A pretty young woman standing behind Manny winked at Brooklyn when she got near.

"*Dobryj vyechyer*, Anya," she said, smiling at the comely woman. "How are things in Mother Russia?"

Anya flipped her blonde hair while sticking her nose in the air. "We're not speaking at this moment. I want to go to visit my grandmother, but the flights are too expensive. The winter is coming and everyone wants to go before it's too cold. Mother Russia does not love me enough to make herself affordable."

"Who wouldn't love you? We all do, don't we?" Looking at her friends for support, every head nodded. "See?"

"You're sweet. But sweet is not money, which I need. What will you want to drink?"

"Just a Coke."

"No vodka?"

"Maybe just a small one. I have to go to work at six."

"One vodka," Anya said, chuckling wryly before taking off to fetch the drink.

"You've gotta get off that radio show," Charles said. "It's not helping your career."

She'd had this discussion with several dozen comics and they all felt the same way. But everyone knew comics didn't know crap, so she'd ignored them. Anya returned and Brooklyn handed her forty dollars. "For your trip fund," she said, smiling broadly when Anya placed a soft kiss on her cheek. It wasn't possible to tell what Anya's sexual orientation was, but spending the night with her would undoubtedly be fun. However, the day after might be a different matter. Anya could be as cold as the Volga in February.

"Do you think I have a chance with her?" Charles asked, when all of them openly watched her walk away.

In unison, three voices said, "No," but he continued to watch her move around the room. "She's the first pretty waitress they've had here in years. I think I should make a serious play for her."

"Go ahead," Manny said, chuckling. "But you're not gonna get anywhere. She's out of your league."

They switched their focus back to the guy dying up on stage. "That bit sounds a lot like one Louis CK does," Brooklyn said.

"Yeah," Charles agreed. "It's not too far from one Garry Shandling did twenty years ago either. Some of these idiots just watch You Tube and try to tweak good material." He let out a bitter laugh. "They might fool the audience, but they won't fool a comic."

That was the absolute truth. Once you had a reputation as a thief, it was damned hard to kick. The guy finished his set on a weak closing and Manny got up and said, "Wish me luck, ladies."

The group at the table listened to him with rapt attention. Manny was a real pro, a guy other comics respected. Brooklyn had heard some of the jokes he was working out, and they sounded better, sharper than they had before. His new stuff had promise too. He didn't kill, but he'd put in a really good five minutes of work—much of it new. That was a good night.

When Manny wound down, Brooklyn started tapping her foot and fidgeting. Nerves were always good when you were going on stage. When you weren't a little nervous, you bombed. Hubris was lethal.

There were only about twenty people in the house, mostly young guys. That group tended not to like political or current event humor, so she didn't have high hopes for her stuff going over well. But trying out new material was a must. She hadn't been putting in the time since she'd been on *Revielle,* and it would start showing in her performances if she didn't crank it up. She'd often wished she could pop in a new joke while headlining, but she didn't have the guts for that. Trying out each story and each joke, time and again in tiny clubs, was the only way to hone material. It was painstaking, and it was hard to find time when you had to be up at the crack of dawn, but it was still required.

Manny jumped off the stage, and after waiting a beat, she jumped on. Looking out through the bright lights, she caught a glimpse of her buddies and felt a smile settle on her lips. It was like punching in at the office after being away on vacation for a while. She was among friends.

―――

One vodka turned into three, but it was impossible to refuse a drink from a friend. Besides, it was only midnight. She'd be perfectly sober by six.

When the club closed, the four of them walked a couple of blocks to a dreadful pizza joint that was open all night. Rumor had it that it stayed open because the door not only didn't have a lock, it was so severely out of square that it didn't close. That was probably apocryphal, but she liked the image, so she chose to believe.

Charles produced a joint and Brooklyn took a hit. His weed was so powerful one hit was more than enough. They were all slightly high and pitchers of beer further lubricated the foursome until they were laughing loudly at each other's jokes. Eventually, the manager came over and told them to shut up. "This ain't the Four Seasons," Charles dryly observed. "No one there has ever called me an asshole."

"Give 'em time," Manny predicted. "Go often enough and any place would throw you out."

Mike checked his watch. "I've gotta go home. I've got to take my boy to school in the morning."

As a wave of fatigue hit her, Brooklyn knew she had to go. "I'm right behind you." She took some money from her wallet and laid it on the table. "Thanks for keeping me company tonight guys. And thanks for the feedback on my bits."

"Don't be such a stranger," Manny said. "Tell that prick on the radio that you've got to work on your craft."

"I'm sure he'll be very sympathetic," she said, then placed a kiss on his head. "G'night all."

It was two-thirty when she rolled into the loft; happy, optimistic and a little toasted. Kerri was once again doing some remarkably sensual yoga moves. "Hi," Brooklyn called out. "Did you see my note?"

"Yes. Thanks for doing that. Did you get something to eat?"

"Yeah." She stood by her bedroom door, and another wave of fatigue rolled over her. "I'm gonna lie down for a little while."

Kerri snapped out of the trance she seemed to be in and looked at Brooklyn sharply. "Are you sure that's a good idea?"

"Yeah, yeah. I do fine with naps. Besides, you said to listen to my body, right?"

"Unless your body's telling you to do something unwise."

"We won't know 'til we try. I'm gonna crash." Not bothering to undress, she dropped onto the bed, and was asleep before she could have counted to ten.

Three vodkas, one hit off a joint, and a few mugs of beer was not an excessive night for her, but it was just enough to make waking up all but impossible. She knew Kerri was shaking her, but she convinced herself it was a bad, bad dream. But once she was pulled into a sitting position by the lapels of her jacket, her confidence in that belief was dashed. "Leave me alone," she groused.

"I can't do that. You have to get up now. Right now." Kerri pulled again, almost dragging her onto the floor. Brooklyn caught herself right before she would have fallen.

"Hey!"

"It's time to get up," Kerri said clearly. "There's no time to play around."

Brooklyn got to her feet, then stumbled into the bath. Acid roiled up from her gut and burned her esophagus. While the shower warmed, she let out a few belches that reverberated against the tile and made her head hurt. Kerri opened the door and stared at her. Her smile was absent, blue eyes devoid of playfulness. "How much did you have to drink?"

"Not much."

"Why were you drinking at all a few hours before work?"

"You can't go to a comedy club and act like a little girl."

"You smell awful."

"Thanks."

"This reflects on me, Brooklyn. I don't like having my client show up for work half drunk and smelling like a brewery." She leaned in and sniffed. "Even though you're running late, you have to wash your hair. Unless you want everyone to know you were smoking weed."

"I had one hit!"

"Wash…your…hair. I won't allow you to go to work smelling like grass."

"I get it, I get it. It's all about you." Now that she thought about it, Kerri wasn't all that cute when you looked at her in a certain light. She was actually kind of a bitch. Brooklyn got into the shower and let the water hit her right in the face. It helped to wake her up somewhat, but she was definitely not looking forward to seeing Arnie's ugly mug for four freaking hours.

———

When Brooklyn got out of the bathroom, her work clothes were lying neatly on her bed. She heard the front door close and saw Kerri scamper by, heading for the kitchen. Brooklyn had her slacks on when Kerri appeared in the bedroom with a giant mocha latte, a pack of green apple gum and some freshly rinsed sprigs of parsley. "Did you brush your tongue?"

"I brushed and flossed my teeth. Not that it's any of your business." *Is she supposed to help me get up or be my dental hygienist?*

"It *is* my business. Making you productive is my business. Making your employer think you're serious about the show is my business."

She was speaking in a clipped, precise manner, and Brooklyn would have guessed she was angry, if she cared to consider anything other than her own throbbing head.

"Stick out your tongue."

Brooklyn reached for the coffee, but Kerri pulled it away from her.

"Let me see it."

Feeling like an idiot, but desperate for the coffee, Brooklyn extended her tongue.

"It's coated. Go brush it. Then you can have your coffee."

Cursing to herself, Brooklyn did as directed. She almost gagged, but kept at it, mainly because Kerri was watching. Funny how dangling the promise of a cup of coffee could feel like getting a dose of methadone.

The coffee, then the parsley was doled out. "Put this in your pocket. It might help your breath if you eat it after your coffee."

"Parsley?"

"I'm not sure it'll work, but it might. Sour gum helps sometimes." She handed it over. "Just keep chewing it. The sour flavor makes you produce more saliva. That can help."

She dashed from the room and returned with a tiny atomizer, then sprayed cologne around Brooklyn's head and torso, not stopping even when Brooklyn coughed and sputtered. "Whatever you do, don't exhale when anyone's close to you."

"I'll be too busy eating parsley and chewing gum."

"Not in front of people!"

"I understand," Brooklyn grumbled. "I'm a multi-celled organism. I can figure a few things out for myself."

"You couldn't figure out not to drink and eat something disgusting just a few hours before work. I can smell the beer coming out of your pores."

Another belch was coming on fast. Brooklyn was very proud of herself for turning her head before letting it explode. A lesser woman would have done it right in Kerri's pushy little face. Angel indeed. She looked more like the spawn of Satan, and her dimple was probably a richly deserved scar.

"Stand still," Kerri commanded. She grabbed a towel and briskly rubbed Brooklyn's back. "Did you dry off?"

"Of course!" That sounded testier than she'd intended, but this was ridiculous.

"Well, your back looks like it hasn't been touched. Who puts her pants on before she dries off?"

It wouldn't be too hard to grab that towel and snake it around her neck, would it? Anyone who'd been under her domain would understand —and probably approve.

Kerri was waiting for Brooklyn when she arrived home. She'd spent some time thinking about what she wanted to cover, and was now ready for the first of what she assumed would be a few confrontations. They were inevitable.

When Brooklyn entered the loft, it was clear she felt guilty about her behavior of the night before. Maybe she had a lot of practice, but whatever it was, she had perfected the hangdog look. She dropped her messenger bag on the dining table, shrugged out of her jacket, and walked right over to Kerri. "I really screwed up last night, and I'm sorry. Lying down for that nap was stupid. You knew it, and I would've been better off if I'd listen to you."

From her position on the sectional, Kerri looked up, seeing Brooklyn's heartfelt expression. Regrettably, it didn't matter whether or not she was sincere. Her instincts were bad and she needed to learn new habits.

"It wasn't the nap. It was needing a nap because you had too much to drink that was the problem."

Brooklyn flopped down onto the sectional. "I don't think you know much about comedians and the clubs we work in. I have to keep current. That means going out and putting in hours. And the only hours I can put in are after ten o'clock. The later the better."

"I can understand that. And staying up late once in a while wouldn't hurt you. But I don't believe you only had one or two drinks. I have too much experience to fall for that."

Brooklyn put her hands in her hair and shook it briefly. It looked like she wanted to tear a hank out, but she merely sighed and spoke quietly. "I had a couple at the club, then we went out for some food and people kept filling up my glass with beer. I can't afford to look like a girl. I have to keep up with the guys."

How many times had she heard this doggerel? It must have been printed on the sides of beer cans. "There are a lot of people in every form of entertainment who've gotten sober. You need to find people to hang out with who can support your need to drink less."

"If I wasn't drinking at all, I think it'd be easier for me. But when the guys know I'm a drinker, they torture me when I try to stop early."

Kerri looked at her for a moment while she collected her thoughts. "Here's the truth. You wouldn't put too much ketchup on your hamburger just because your friends told you to or teased you about never having enough ketchup. That would be silly to give in to their teasing, right? Well, you drink too much because you want to drink too much, and blaming it on other people is usually a pretty good sign that you have a problem."

Brooklyn got up and headed for the kitchen. She didn't seem to need to be there, she probably just needed some distance. She leaned heavily against the refrigerator, glaring across the loft at Kerri. "I don't have a problem," she said, enunciating crisply. "I can stop any time. But I don't want to, and I don't need to. A drink or two helps me sleep, and I desperately need that."

Kerri got up and followed her. Brooklyn clearly didn't like having people stand too close, so she stood nearer than was polite even in Egypt, where people nearly touched noses when they talked. "Alcohol is a central nervous system depressant. It's not going to help you be more alert or clever in the mornings, and that's what you've got to be."

"I said I heard you." Her eyes were sparking with a fire Kerri had yet to see from her. That was good. Anger was better than disregard.

"You'd feel better if you stopped drinking, but at this point that still is your choice."

Brooklyn's eyebrows shot up. "At this point? At which point will I lose my right to choose my own behavior?"

"I don't want to tell Spectrum that you need to go to rehab, but I will." She made sure her face showed how serious she was. "In a heartbeat. I'd much rather have you hate me than know I failed to stop you from harming yourself."

"Harming myself." She said it with such disdain that Kerri would have been offended if they'd been friends. "That's imbecilic. I had a few

47

drinks with friends. People at Betty Ford drink that much before breakfast."

"That's not true. People who can't control their intake need help—even if the amount isn't huge. If you can't resist a drink when you don't want it…" She trailed off, allowing Brooklyn to finish the thought.

"Bullshit." Brooklyn slid away and started to stalk towards her bedroom, but Kerri called after her.

"Would you mind coming over here please?"

She turned and glared. "Do I need to ask permission to go to my room?"

"No, but I'd like to show you something. It's about your career, so you might be interested."

Dragging her feet, Brooklyn made her way back and stood over Kerri. "What?"

"Sit down next to me. I want to show you some fan sites of yours."

As Brooklyn sat, her expression changed from annoyed to puzzled. "How do you know about them?"

"They're very easy to find. There's one from Germany that only has pictures of you. No words." She chuckled for a second. "I think most of them are put up by lesbians, but there's one that a guy has showing your hair."

"My hair?"

"Yeah. Every picture you've ever had taken that shows your hair clearly. I assume it's a fetish."

"That's whack. I've never looked at these sites, but I've heard they exist."

Kerri caught her gaze to make sure she was listening. "These are your biggest fans. These are the people who tell other people about you. They can help you a lot. They can also hurt you a lot." She handed the computer to Brooklyn. "Read the thread I have up there now."

"The thread is all of these things that keep getting indented?"

"Yeah. You page down with this key." Kerri watched her face carefully as Brooklyn read the increasingly angry posts from her fans. Kerri hadn't chosen the worst of them, but she'd made sure to choose ones that would sting.

Brooklyn sat there for a moment, then pushed the computer back onto Kerri's lap. "What a bunch of assholes."

"They might be. Or they might be real fans who can give you feedback before your declining bookings show you're not clicking. These people are telling you that you're not as sharp as you were. They're telling you that they feel that you're their voice and that voice isn't being heard."

Grabbing the computer again, Brooklyn said, "I want to read more. I want to read all of it."

Gently, Kerri took the machine back. "That's not a good idea. The Internet is a cruel, cruel place and you should have somebody give you a synopsis of what's being said."

Brooklyn's eyes widened. "Who in the hell can I get to do that?"

"Your manager should be doing it. You're giving her fifteen percent of everything you earn, right? Make her work for it."

"No, Kat wouldn't be interested in doing that. Besides, I only give her ten percent."

"Then how about your agent? It's not too far outside the job description to have an agent do that."

"No, no," she said thoughtfully. "He's stretched to his limit."

"Then I'll keep an eye on things as long as I'm with you. Later on you can decide how you want to handle it in the future."

"I want you to keep doing it," Brooklyn said, showing her first sweet smile of the day.

———

After having some lunch, Brooklyn sat down on the sectional and said, "I'm really screwing up, huh?"

"I wouldn't go that far, but your fans aren't happy. That's something to take very seriously."

"But what do I do?" She leaned all the way back, then gathered her hair into a bundle and tossed it back over the cushions. That was a delaying tactic. Dozens of times already, Kerri had seen her playing with her hair to take her mind off topics that troubled her in some way.

"Get on and stay on a good schedule. I know you have to work on material, but put it off for as long as you can. Being sharp in the morning is very important. If you want to make the most out of the opportunity, you've got to give it the best you can."

"I think I have been. The truth is that the show isn't a good fit for me. I'm not at my best when I have to jump in once in a while. But Arnie hates me and never sets me up right." She bent over and held her head in her hands for a few seconds. "The money's irreplaceable, but I hate the damn job."

She looked worn out. And her face had lines in it that Kerri hadn't noticed before. Maybe it was the harsh light from the windows, but Brooklyn could have passed for ten years older than she was. Kerri kept that tidbit to herself. Reminding Brooklyn that her fans liked her for her looks at least as much as her brain wouldn't help motivate her in the least.

When Brooklyn came home from work the next Monday morning, she carried a huge nylon bag from the cleaners, a dozen things on hangers, also from the cleaners, and a canvas bag, big enough for Santa to carry a large family's Christmas toys.

"What in the heck is this?" Kerri got up and ran to her, grabbing the canvas bag and almost stumbling under its weight.

"My laundry and my mail. I didn't pick it up last week."

"Your mail?" It was hard to keep her voice in its normal register. Who was this manager? Or the agent, for that matter? People at Brooklyn's level of fame didn't lug their own mail around in a bag.

"Yeah. Kat and I have a pretty good way of dealing with it."

Kerri dragged it over to hide it under the dining table. "What's that?"

"Well, first the station opens any boxes in a secure area. To check for explosives I guess. They give me everything that doesn't look dangerous."

"So this is only from the radio station?"

"Yeah. Every week or two Melvin, my manager, sends me a box of things that go to his office. Most of the letters that go through him are nice. Not so much at the radio station."

"Tell me about this system."

"I go through it, and put a post-it note on each piece that needs a reply. We came up with ten form letters that cover most situations. So I can just say number seven and she sends it out."

Had Brooklyn never met another celebrity? Most of them didn't even know their own home address. Answering this amount of mail was madness. "You open it yourself?"

"Uh-huh."

She was so cute! Her dark hair moved across her shoulders when she nodded her head, and her big brown eyes were earnest enough to melt the hardest heart. But how did she stay so innocent? There must be a legion of handlers hidden somewhere to keep her pure. Now try to sound casual, she doesn't like to be pushed. "Have you ever considered hiring a mail service?"

"Uhm, no. What's a mail service?"

Kerri wanted to throw the bag out the window, but she satisfied herself by discretely kicking it while considering how badly Brooklyn's handlers were treating her. "It's a way to get all of your mail handled quickly and properly. Do you want me to set you up for one?"

Those curious eyes clouded over in thought. "If it's quick and easy, why didn't Kat do that?"

"I don't know, but I have the time to get it set up. You just decide which things you want to see and that will be all you ever have to look at again."

"What do you mean 'which things I want to see'?"

"Say you're interested in hearing from kids, or young lesbians struggling with their identity, or the elderly. They can sort those all out. They can also throw away anything that's cruel or vicious, or give it to you if you like that kind of thing. It would save you hours and hours of work."

"But I'd still have to sign everything."

51

Oh, she was as pure as an infant! "No, you don't have to do that. They sign the responses automatically off a sample of your signature. It looks like the real thing if you want to spend enough to have it done right."

"I do," she said, now decisive and even cuter, in an adult kind of way. "But some of the stuff has to go to the police."

"Threats from cranks?"

"I hope so." She stuck her hand in the bag and pulled out a fistful of letters. "If the threats are from sincere lunatics, I'd better count my days."

"Is it that bad?"

She shrugged and didn't look too concerned. "I get a lot of cranky mail. I bet there's one in this bunch." She opened them one at a time and scanned them quickly. "I win. There's three. This one's good." She cleared her throat. "'You dirty commie whore,' Nice salutation. 'You Jew-loving, God hating bitch! I'll be waiting for you one night and show you what women were made for.'" She crumpled the letter and tossed it onto the table. "I don't send this type to the police. They'd have to have a whole squad to follow up on the ones who want to rape me to show me what I'm missing out on by being a lesbian." She deliberated for a moment. "I can usually tell if they hate me because I'm a woman, a lesbian, a liberal, or a New Yorker. Some seem to hate each part equally. It gets really bad if I say anything even mildly positive about Jews or Muslims."

"I'll have it all taken care of. You shouldn't even see things like that. And I'll handle your laundry from now on. Do you send everything out?"

"Everything. I'm not even sure if there's a laundry room in the building." She grinned, now half-way between the attractive adult and her innocent child personas.

—⁓—

On Thursday morning, Brooklyn didn't wake up until four, just a half hour before Kerri was going to have to wake her. They didn't have time for breakfast, but Brooklyn waved it off, saying they always had a ton of food at the station.

"I couldn't get to sleep until ten o'clock," she grumbled. "I'm back to six hours a night. It's like my body wants to stay up when it's light, then it starts winding down."

"That's pretty natural. I don't think this schedule is working very well. Why don't we try going to bed at nine? Most people do better if they're early to bed, early to rise."

"Ugh. That's so not my style. But I'm willing to try. By the way, I'm leaving town right after the show, and I'll be back on Sunday afternoon."

"Do you need me to travel with you? I'm more than happy to."

She really did look happy. Kerri could probably make things run pretty damned smooth. But no one asks the fox into the henhouse. "No, I think I'm good. My manager travels with me."

"No problem. Do you want me to come over on Sunday evening?"

How would that work? Logistics weren't her strong suit, but it seemed like a huge waste of Kerri's time. She was probably dying to have a few days to herself but was too polite and professional to say that. "No, don't bother. I've got to go to a party in Jersey as soon as I get in. I've got it all planned out. I'll be dead tired, so I'll come home and crash right after the party. That should have me ready for you at 4:30 on Monday morning."

"Are you sure? I'm happy to sleep on the sofa. It's really comfortable."

"No, need. Sleep in your own bed for a change."

⁓⁓⁓

On Monday morning, Kerri carefully rolled her bike into Brooklyn's loft. When she switched on the light, she stepped back in shock. What in God's name had happened? Once again, papers of all kinds and color dappled the floor from the front door to the sectional. But they hadn't been there when they'd left on Thursday morning. Bad sign.

Running into Brooklyn's room, she found the bed neatly made. Dashing back into the main living area, she jerked to a halt when she saw Brooklyn lying on the sectional. A pair of headphones was haphazardly on her head, and gruesome footage from World War II flashed on the television. A pizza box collapsed under her foot when Kerri approached.

53

The blue light from the TV reflected on a half empty bottle of vodka that lay on its side on the table.

It was going to be nearly impossible to get her out of the house in thirty minutes, but that's what they were going to do. It had been so stupid to trust her to handle the transition from a gig to Monday morning. No one hired a talent wrangler if the talent didn't have a big problem, and now it was clear Brooklyn's problem wasn't that her alarm clock wasn't loud enough.

Eschewing the gentle approach, Kerri started pulling her into a sitting position. The nauseating aroma of cigarettes, vodka and pepperoni that oozed from Brooklyn's pores almost buckled her knees, but Kerri closed her mind to it. Once she got her upright, she crouched down and nestled herself into her armpit. Holding Brooklyn's hand around her neck, she tucked her other arm around her waist and stood.

"We're getting in the shower now."

There was no indication that Brooklyn had heard her, but her feet moved along, making the job immeasurably easier.

When they got into the bathroom, Kerri turned the water on, then tried to undress Brooklyn without letting her fall. If she hadn't done the same thing fifty times in her life, she would've had an impossible time, but she'd figured out how to brace her leg against a client's knees while pressing her shoulder right into their solar plexus. That move had kept a 350-pound NFL lineman upright, albeit not for long. But Brooklyn was a manageable size, and Kerri had her naked in three minutes flat. Kerri kicked off her own shoes and got into the shower too. It wasn't fun for either of them, but she kept reducing the amount of hot water until it was running almost all cold. That did the trick, and Brooklyn finally stood on her own and started to wash herself, mumbling something incomprehensible.

Once Kerri was sure she was going to finish the job she got out of the enclosure and toweled off quickly, then went back into the bedroom to pick out clothes. As soon as the water stopped, she went back in and started to blot Brooklyn's body with a towel, commanding, "Start drying your hair."

Brooklyn didn't move fast enough, so Kerri grabbed a towel and ran it over her head roughly then started to blow it dry. Brooklyn's hair was such a lynchpin to her image that it had to be perfect. When a client was drunk it was vital that they look normal. Haphazard hair styles had led to more than one star dropping out of a movie because of "exhaustion."

Brooklyn's limo driver buzzed, and Kerri cursed quietly. She didn't have many options, so she grabbed a robe and put it on Brooklyn, then snagged the clothes, shoes and bag she'd assembled, as well as her own backpack and headed for the door. "Just don't fall down," she commanded, marching her charge to the elevator.

They got to the car a few minutes after five, and the driver was waiting with the door of the car open. "Oh, my lord, what have we here?"

"I'm not sure. All I know is that she's gonna be on the air in one hour. Pray that this isn't her last day."

—∿—

The driver closed the smoked glass window between the front and back seats and Kerri fought with the drunken woman for fifteen minutes, finally getting her bra and blouse on. Brooklyn was helping, but not very effectively. Getting the panties and slacks on were another level of hell, but Brooklyn was dressed by the time they hit the George Washington Bridge. It was 5:45 when Kerri held her own thermos, full of green tea, up to Brooklyn's mouth and watched her as she took a long swallow.

"My fucking head," she groaned.

"Drink this, and don't spill it." Kerri tried not to be too gruff, but she was very clear and concise, as years of experience had taught her to be. She held the robe under Brooklyn's chin just in case of spillage. "You've got to look like you're sober. Practice on me."

Brooklyn gave her a vague scowl.

"Now!" She spoke so loudly the driver rolled down the privacy glass. "Are you okay?"

"We're fine," Kerri said. "I'm just trying to wake her up."

"I'm up, I'm up."

Kerri faced her again. "Convince me you're sober."

"I am. I'm just tired. Groggy…I took a sleeping pill."

"How many?"

"One." Her brows knit together. "And maybe another."

"How many drinks?"

"A couple."

Kerri leaned into her and sniffed her breath. "Thank God you drink vodka. Drink a cup of coffee as soon as you get to your studio."

Giving her a scowl, Brooklyn said, "Really? Never would have thought of that."

"Can you give me a hand?" Kerri asked, getting the driver's attention.

"Yes, ma'am?"

"I'm Kerri, by the way. I'm working with Brooklyn."

"I can see that, ma'am. I'm Terry."

"Good to meet you. Have you heard any earth-shattering news this morning?"

"No, nothing too bad." He fiddled with the radio, tuning it to the local all-news channel. "The only thing I heard was that Senator Hartline died in a helicopter crash."

That woke Brooklyn up. "What? Hartline?"

"Yeah. He was flying over the damage from that big earthquake in Mexico and he crashed."

"Shit." Brooklyn settled back into her seat, her arms dangling listlessly between spread legs. "I should know more about that. Arnie hates him, so I'll have to talk about his accomplishments."

They arrived at the building, and the big car slid noiselessly down into the garage. As Brooklyn started to get out Kerri thrust her phone at her. "I pulled up the latest news from NPR. You can read it on the way to the studio."

"You're going with me?"

"I have to." Kerri wasn't dripping wet, but it was clear she'd been in a serious downpour or a shower, though the day was dry and clear. Adding to her allure, her hair was plastered to her head, her long bangs hanging down to her eyes. And she was barefoot. She slid out and said to Terry, "Do you have time to take me back to New York?"

"No, ma'am, but I can call for another car. Is that all right?"

"Of course. I'll be back down here at 6:01."

Brooklyn stood there, holding the device in her hand. "How do you…?"

"You put your finger on the screen and flick it." Kerri demonstrated, then took Brooklyn's arm and led her to the front door. Brooklyn had to show her ID, and Kerri managed to sign in as her guest, getting no help from Brooklyn, who was raptly reading. They went up on the elevator together, not speaking. As soon as they reached the proper floor, Kerri snatched the phone back. Brooklyn started to say something but Kerri jumped in, "Don't acknowledge me. Someone from the station might be near the elevator. Later."

The doors opened and a man blinked when he saw Kerri. Brooklyn got out and casually flipped him off when he said, "Hey, York, you left your trash on the elevator."

Kerri was sitting at the dining room table when Brooklyn got home. She slowly walked over to the sectional and fell onto it face first. She lay there for a moment, then rolled onto her side and said, "Let me die here in peace."

Regarding her for a few seconds, Kerri decided that she might actually not be long for this world. Her eyes looked like they'd sunken into her skull, dark circles lingered below each bloodshot orb and her skin was the pasty white of an invalid.

"I know it's hard to get up when you're hung over…"

"I wasn't hung over," Brooklyn snapped. She sat up and took a moment to straighten her sweater and brush her hair back into place. "I just didn't get much sleep."

Because you were drinking until the wee hours. "We need to reassess. We can't repeat what happened this morning, so I'll need to be here much earlier. Every working day," she added.

Brooklyn stood and stumbled slightly getting her feet under her. She grasped the arm of the sectional, while obviously trying to look casual. But it just made her look like a hungover woman who didn't want to be called out.

"This isn't normal for me. I had a weekend from hell."

Every client had far more difficulties than normal people, so she waited patiently for Brooklyn to recite the list of horrors that had befallen her.

"The problem, well, part of the problem is that people take advantage of me."

"Uh-huh." *Look up air fares for India as soon as you have a minute. As soon as this gig is up, there's an ashram with your name on it, and not one person there will complain about having to get up early to make suitcases full of money.*

"I try to be a good person. I really do. But I try to help and I wind up getting screwed."

Brooklyn stared at her with such intensity that Kerri found herself nodding agreement, even though she'd heard this exact spiel from every celebrity she'd ever worked for. Each of them was a chronic victim. She'd actually been hoping for more from Brooklyn, but she was obviously just like the rest of the pampered, privileged class. Sad.

"I was supposed to take the last flight out of Minneapolis on Saturday night. I would've gotten home at two or three in the morning, but I planned on sleeping until noon and getting over to my party. But some really nice young woman came up to me after the show and told me this tearjerker story about her uncle who was burned really badly while he was fighting a fire."

"What did she want you to do about it?"

"The usual. Someone had organized a bunch of local comics to do a benefit for him. I didn't want to do it, but she looked so sad I couldn't say no."

She probably slept with the niece, twice, then did the benefit. "So you missed the plane."

Brooklyn looked mildly annoyed. "No, that's not the point. The benefit was Sunday, so I had to stay another night. That wouldn't have been too bad, I didn't have to go to the party, even though I wanted to."

"So you skipped a party and stayed an extra night just to help a stranger?" Maybe she hadn't heard this story before. Was that too much to hope for?

Brooklyn waved that off. "I got to the benefit, which was in the afternoon, like the kid said, but I was, by far, the biggest name there. Of course they want the biggest name to go last, so I didn't get out of there until almost eight o'clock." Her expression blended puzzlement and outrage. "I don't know where the hell the plane stopped between here and Minneapolis, but we stopped twice and changed planes once. I got in the door at two a.m. and I was starving, and furious, and I couldn't get to sleep."

The question would probably set her off, but it was important to know who or what was the source of Brooklyn's ire. Once you knew that, you could make sure never to be on that person's side. "Who were you mad at?"

She stood there for a moment, looking like she might snap off a biting response. Then her body settled into itself, making her look smaller and more fragile. "I don't even know. Myself? All of the friggin' airlines? All I know is this kind of thing happens all of the time, and I've got to put a stop to it. I've *got* to."

That was strangely introspective. And wanting to change something that wasn't working was a very good sign. Maybe she wasn't as spoiled as most people in her category. At least she didn't blame the entire world for being stacked against her, which was super rare. Now if she could be led to realize how she'd gotten herself into a bad spot, they might make some progress. "So you had a drink…"

"That was on the plane. Then Kat gave me a sleeping pill. She said it was all natural. I guess I thought it would…" She shook her head. "I don't know what I thought. I just needed to sleep."

"I'm sure you don't want to hear this, but there aren't any sleeping pills you should take with alcohol."

"I know." Her head hung down, and she actually looked disgusted with herself. "And I must have had more when I got home. I don't remember doing that, but I must have. I wouldn't get a headache this bad from one drink."

"Do you remember taking a Xanax?"

"No." She shook her head briskly. "I didn't do that."

"The bottle was right there, stuffed in between the cushions. I think you took one or more and chased it with vodka."

"That's really not my style. I don't even carry those when I travel."

She actually did look disconcerted. Was it possible she was telling the truth? Doubtful. No one told the truth about substances. "Then how did they get here?"

"I honestly don't remember getting them out," she said, looking uncomfortable and embarrassed. That was probably the lie. Of course, the rest of it could be a lie too.

"In LA they call that the Clark Morgan Cocktail."

Clearly incensed, Brooklyn snapped, "I wasn't trying to kill myself."

"Neither was Clark. He had chronic sleep trouble and he took one too many of his lawfully prescribed drugs and now he's taking a permanent dirt nap. Twenty-eight years old and enough talent to run rings around most of his peers, but still dead."

Brooklyn got up and went to the refrigerator, noisily rummaging around. Kerri'd gone too far. Brooklyn wasn't the kind of woman who'd listen to a lecture. She was probably the type who'd take four sleeping pills just to show that it wouldn't hurt her. Time to grovel. You couldn't help people if they didn't believe you were on their side. She got up and went over to Brooklyn who was drinking out of an orange juice carton.

"I'm sorry I said that. But I met him when I was working with another actor, and he impressed me. He was a bright, sensitive guy, and his wife and son are never going to see his face again. It's gonna take me a while until I stop seeing every prescription sedative as a loaded gun."

Brooklyn wiped her mouth with the back of her hand and replaced the orange juice. "Don't worry about it. And you don't have to worry about me tomorrow. I'm going to bed right now and staying there."

Given that it was one in the afternoon, Kerri didn't think that was the best idea she'd ever heard, but she had to pick her battles. "Wasn't Kat able to make things go a little easier?"

"What's Kat got to do with anything? I'm the one who agreed to stay." That quick flash of irritation said something. It just wasn't yet clear what that was. Maybe it was time to probe.

"If I were your manager, and I knew you had a tough time saying 'no' I wouldn't let you get into a situation like that."

Brooklyn gave her a wry smile. "And just how would you stop me?"

That was the smile that made lesbians swoon. Other lesbians. Lesbians who weren't employed to keep an eye on her.

"I'd be by your side. You don't let your client wander around alone before or after an appearance. Every third person there wants something from you and you look like a jerk if you say 'no' to them. That's your manager's job—she's the meanie and you're helpless."

"That's not how we do things. I don't need anyone to protect me."

Kerri didn't reply for a moment, hoping Brooklyn recalled that she currently had a babysitter.

"Sure, I know that. But every celebrity needs help in keeping the wrong people away. There are a million things that can go wrong. Your manager has to anticipate them and prevent them, if she can."

"Kat does a fine job. I wish everybody would get off her back."

"I've never met her, so I'm not sure she could carry me. I wasn't criticizing her, just telling you what I'd do. But uninvited opinions are like feet. Everybody has two and most of them stink."

Laughing, Brooklyn said, "I'd always heard that about assholes."

"That's odd, I thought most people only had one." Kerri stood, put the papers she'd been working on into her backpack and headed for the door. "See you tomorrow at four. If you wake up before then and want company, just call."

"Not four, four thirty."

"Sorry, Brooklyn. four thirty isn't working. We've gotta have a little more wiggle-room."

———〰———

Brooklyn went into her room and flopped onto the bed. It was impossible to tell if Kerri believed her. She probably didn't, but the story was fairly solid. It sucked to have to blame Kat for the sleeping pills, Kat wasn't the lab rat under observation. So long as Kerri didn't ever get into the station and check Brooklyn's office, she'd never see where the real stash was. And if she believed that legit bottle of Xanax was the full extent of her drug inventory, the report to Spectrum would make Brooklyn sound like a Mormon.

———〰———

Kat stopped by the loft at around nine o'clock that night. She used her key to enter, and the fact that she didn't bother to knock first set Brooklyn's teeth on edge. Dressed in her usual clubbing attire, Kat walked over to the sectional where Brooklyn was watching a pseudo-documentary about people fighting addiction. Brooklyn held out a chilled bottle of vodka, and Kat took a quick slug right from the bottle.

"Whatcha watching?"

"Have a seat. It's funny." She poured herself half a shot and downed it. "These people are so screwed up, but they keep insisting they're fine."

They watched for a few minutes, laughing while a woman who was lying on the ground in front of her apartment insisted she was completely sober. Then Kat got up and stood right in front of the television. "Let's go!"

"Where?"

"Out."

"Ahh...I don't think so. I'm on thin ice. Really thin."

"Come on. You slept all day. At least I assume you did since you never picked up your phone."

"I slept a little. Now I'm vaguely awake and I should be going to bed. So I'm screwed again."

"Oh, for Christ's sake. Don't act like such an old woman. You don't need exactly eight hours of sleep at exactly nine thirty at night to be able to work."

"I slept for five stinking hours today. It just took me nine hours to get it done." She turned her head and malevolently stared out the kitchen window. "There was a fire somewhere with a million fire trucks blowing their sirens. I'm gonna try to get back to sleep by midnight so I can use my brain in the morning."

"Come on," Kat whined. "Angie's having a huge poker game and she's got an extra seat. Remember how much you took them for last time?"

The thought of that epic game brought a smile to her lips, but that was before Kerri arrived, which made it the distant past. "Oh, yeah. Back in the day I could have lived for a week on the money I made that night."

"It's still fun even if you don't need the dough as bad as you used to. Go straight to the station after the game."

"I don't think so. I promised I'd go to sleep."

Pouting, Kat plunked herself down next to a slumped Brooklyn. "You don't want to do anything anymore. Get up and go with me." She jumped to her feet and took Brooklyn's limp hands, trying to pull her up. "We don't go to comedy clubs any more, we don't go to movie premieres. Nothing. Being a recluse doesn't help your image."

"I put up with four hours of crap today because of the way I looked. My image sucks."

Kat tugged on a lock of Brooklyn's hair. Her voice was softer and carried more emotion than it had. "Ever since you got the radio show you aren't the same person."

Tiredly, Brooklyn said, "I am the same person, but I can't afford to get fired. I need the money, but even if I didn't, this gig is a huge chunk of Melvin's income. I can't screw this up for him."

"Melvin would make more if he was a better agent. It's not your job to provide for him. He's not your kid."

"I know that. But he was there for me when I was only getting open mic nights. He's my guy."

"So Melvin's your guy and the babysitter's your girl. What am I?"

"Don't be nuts. Kerri isn't my girl. She's my supervisor."

"Yeah? Well you stayed up late with her last week. Why can you do it with her and not me?"

"All I did was get up when I was rested and have breakfast. How exciting is that?"

"Not very. But you could play poker tonight, which is exciting. Then you could have breakfast and go to work. You'll be nice and tired tomorrow night."

"I can't afford to drink two nights in a row."

"Then just play. You don't have to drink."

Playing cards was one of her favorite hobbies, and the women Angie invited were terrible players. But winning was fun no matter what. She could feel her resolve slip away. "Well, I guess I could play a few hands." Just saying that gave her a burst of energy. This could work.

"That's my girl. Put on your TV clothes and let's get going."

"I've gotta leave a note for Kerri."

"I'll do it for you." Kat took a notepad and wrote, "We don't need you today," tossed it onto the dining table and went to turn off the TV.

CHAPTER THREE

KAT WASN'T A GOOD drinker. The more she had, the feistier she got. If she stayed there, everything was fine. But feisty sometimes led to pugnacious. They were in a cab, heading for a diner after the poker game broke up and she started in on an old refrain. "How much are you paying the babysitter?"

"I'm not paying her anything. Spectrum is footing the bill."

"So how much are they paying her?"

"I have no idea. Given that she's not doing much, I hope she's getting about fifty bucks a week." She laughed evilly. "Maybe she'll quit if they pay her little enough."

"I bet she makes more than I do." Kat was leaning against the door, putting on her most aggrieved pout.

"Can we not have this argument again? It never gets us anywhere."

"That's because you won't budge!" She said this so loudly that the cabbie turned and scowled at her. But that didn't stop her. When she drank, she got louder, as well as more convinced of her position. "If I'm your manager, I should get fifteen percent of everything you earn. Everything!" The last word was shouted and the cabbie yanked the car to the curb.

"Get out!" He stared at Kat, who merely opened the door and hopped out, leaving Brooklyn to pay, as usual. Now they were in Hell's Kitchen at four a.m., with no cabs in sight.

Kat didn't seem to notice they were stranded on Ninth Avenue. She was still grousing, although a little quieter. "Why do you screw me over? I'm your friend!"

It only took a few seconds. Just a few seconds to decide to finally tell the truth. "You're not acting like a manager. You're acting like my friend. I'm glad to have you with me, but it's not the same as having a real, experienced road manager."

"I've been with you for fifteen years, and I'm not experienced?"

"Kat, I give you ten percent of every dime I make doing comedy. That's fair."

"Then give me ten percent of *everything*. That'd be fairer."

"I'm not going to give you a cut for the radio show. You don't do a damned thing for it! Nothing!" She was upset now, and words she'd never had the nerve to say started to spill out. "Part of the reason I don't get to sleep on time is because I'm worried about being late and getting fired. And I wouldn't be in this position if our travel plans weren't continually screwed up."

"You were the one dragging that teenager around Atlanta, buddy. Not me! You missed work because your ass was in a holding cell!"

"That one was mine. All mine. I learned a good lesson that night. But every other time I've been late is because of you. That can't continue."

"You're the douche who can't say 'no' to anyone. I would have told the girl in Minneapolis to beat it, and we would have been home on Saturday —as planned—by me!"

"If I could trust you to handle things with sensitivity, I'd have you speak for me. But I can't. You don't know how to let people down gently, and that's a must when you're representing me. I can't have people badmouthing me because of the way you treat them."

"When has that happened?" Kat's breathing was heavy now, and beads of sweat formed on her forehead.

"Are you serious? I can name three clubs that have banned me— because of you. You told my cousin to her face that I didn't want to see her after the show in Ft. Lauderdale. I had to make up a lie about that and send her a gift—because of you. The truth is"—she still had time to turn back, but she didn't hesitate—"I'm *over*paying you."

"Every manager gets fifteen percent!"

"You're my friend who hangs out with me when I travel. You make our reservations online, and that's it. For God's sake, you order so much room service and so many goddamned movies that I'm probably paying you twenty percent when I take that into consideration." The list of small things that she'd been keeping inside started to pour out. She was powerless to stop them. "You're never around when I need you. I can't count the times I've needed a wingman for something and you're not even at the venue! I'm giving you ten percent of my gross pay so you can chase girls and have fun all over the country, and that's gotta stop."

"Fuck you!" Kat shouted. "I could make more tending bar in a dive!"

"Shut the fuck up!" A man yelled down from his apartment.

Brooklyn took it down a notch. "It's not my problem that you could make more elsewhere. If you were a real manager, you'd handle my whole career. To start, you should be working with Melvin to make sure I'm getting the right gigs."

"He doesn't need my help. You're plenty busy."

Brooklyn's head hurt, but she kept going. "It's not about being busy, for Christ's sake. There's a difference between getting ten K for a job and twenty-five, you know. You could make sure I got more of the big jobs and fewer of the little ones."

"How in the hell am I supposed to do that? That's Melvin's job."

That wasn't true, but it was a waste of time to dwell on it. "Fine. Then how about my main job? Why is some stranger at my house waking me up? Why don't you help me instead of luring me out at night?"

"Why do I care when you go to bed? I don't get a cent from the radio show. It'd be better for me if you got fired."

The sidewalk swayed beneath her feet. She was finally hearing the truth, and her stomach turned violently. "I can't believe you'd hurt me like that just for money. I honestly can't believe it." She thought she was going to be sick, but she had too much pride to vomit on the sidewalk. Holding on out of nothing but self-respect, she managed to say, "So you convinced me to go out tonight *hoping* I'd get fired? You really don't give a damn about me?"

"Nobody's breaking your arm. Don't be such a cunt." Kat was so close Brooklyn could smell the cigarette smoke on her breath. "The radio job is making you old before your time. If you had half a brain you'd quit."

"It's none of your business what jobs I take. None!"

Kat grabbed her jacket and scrunched a fistful of fabric into a ball. She shook her hard, just once, then leaned in so they were eye to eye. "That's finally the damn truth. You don't want advice. You don't want a fucking manager. You set it all up this way, buddy. But I'm through with being screwed. I want my fifteen percent."

"I won't pay you a dime more. Not one dime!"

"She told you to fire me, didn't she." Her eyes were filled with tears, but her voice bore nothing but rage.

"No one has told me to fire you." *Besides my parents and Melvin and everybody who has had to work with you.* "I'm not firing you. But I'm not going to pay you any more."

"You can take your measly ten percent and see who you can hire. Good luck!" She stormed away, heading up Ninth Avenue, away from the Port Authority Bus Station, where she would have to catch a bus to get home.

Brooklyn watched her march up the street, then turned and headed East. Strangely, she felt remarkably light, as though a burden had been taken from her. Saying what was in her heart had freed a part of her that had almost rusted in place. That lightness lasted for several seconds. Then images from their years of friendship hit her, one after the other. Fifteen years of mostly good times. Hanging out, traveling together, chasing girls together, heading down the shore for a week with all of their friends. She hailed the lone cab gliding down Ninth, got in and brooded all the way home.

—⁓—

Once again Brooklyn was lying on her sectional when Kerri arrived an hour later. But this time her eyes were mostly open and she waved weakly when Kerri stood over her. "Are you okay?"

Brooklyn shrugged, then slowly stood. "I had a bad night. But at least I'm up, huh?" Her smile was strangely sad.

"Need any help?"

"No. Well, you could pull out some clothes for me. That saves a few minutes."

"Okay." She watched Brooklyn walk into her room, then spent a little time folding up the papers and pillows and magazines that were strewn on the furniture. She was pleased to note the absence of liquor bottles. At least Brooklyn would smell better than she had the day before.

Kerri pulled an outfit from the closet, then placed it and some underwear on the bed she'd just made. Brooklyn came out and started to get dressed, obviously unconcerned with her nakedness. "Could I talk to you about something?"

"Sure. Anything." Kerri stood there, waiting. Her nose got to work, and she sniffed the faint smell of alcohol, probably Scotch or whiskey. Given there was no Scotch in the house, she'd been out again. But it was best to leave it alone, since she wasn't showing any other signs of being impaired. No one at the station would notice unless they got very close, and it didn't seem like they were a close knit group.

"After work. I don't have time now."

"Okay. I'll come back around eleven?"

"I can come to your…apartment? Hotel? Damn. I don't even know where you live."

"Santa Monica." Kerri smiled, pleased that Brooklyn was grounded enough to know that other people had lives. That was an unquestioned strong point.

"Long commute."

The half-smile that the girls loved made a quick appearance. Brooklyn really was attractive. Kerri tried to look at her as a stranger would. She wasn't a woman you'd ogle on the street, but she had strong, symmetrical features, kind eyes, and a very pretty mouth. Not to mention the perfect hair. She wasn't a showy woman you'd take to a club to make a statement about your own attractiveness. But she was the kind of woman you'd like to wake up to. There was no doubt about it. If Brooklyn wasn't a client, and wasn't a screw-up, she'd be just the kind of woman Kerri would go for. Sadly, even though she didn't have a thousand-dollar-a-day heroin habit, she was definitely a screw-up. "I'm staying on the Lower East Side. I never know when my roommate is going to be around though, so it's best to meet here."

Brooklyn looked around the room and Kerri followed her lead. She wasn't sure why they were looking around, but Brooklyn finally said, "How about lunch? Could I take you out to lunch?"

"Sure. I'm free all afternoon. Where would you like to meet?"

"Do you know where Daniel Laurant is?"

"Yeah, I think so. It's on Spring, right?"

"Yeah. Meet me there at noon."

"I'll call for a reservation," Kerri said, giving her a wink.

"Damned good idea. I never would have thought of it."

⁓

Brooklyn was sitting in the makeup room, with Toni working away, chatting nonstop as usual. This wasn't the morning to enjoy hearing about Toni's current boyfriend, and Brooklyn was paying almost no attention to her. She almost leapt from the chair when Tomas Manuel strolled in, leaned over, and said, "How are things going?"

"Fine," Brooklyn managed. *Go away! Go away!*

"The…service we talked about is working out?"

"Sure. Yep. Everything's great." She tried to slide out of the chair, but Toni picked up a pair of eyelash curlers and used them to effectively pin her to her seat.

"I hope so." He stood up, nodded to Toni, and continued on his way.

"Why's the big boss talking to you?" Toni asked.

Brooklyn tried to sound casual, but it was tough. She was shaking from the surprise of seeing Manuel at the studio, coupled with trying to think of a way to deter Toni from prying. "I work here."

She reached up and forcibly removed the curler from Toni's hand, tossed it onto the table and got up. Wrenching the smock from around her neck, she deposited it on the chair as she scampered away, moving faster than she ever did. Toni's eyes almost left a mark on her back, and Brooklyn knew the rumor mill would be grinding away in seconds.

———

They'd been on the air for a half hour when Arnie surprised Brooklyn by saying, "The big kahuna was at the station today."

"That sounds Hawaiian," the Wild Man offered. "He should have a Mexican name."

"He's from Brazil," Brooklyn said. "That's not in Mexico, in case you don't have a map in front of you."

"Still," the Wild Man persisted, "he needs a Spanish nickname. How about El Bosso?"

"He speaks Portuguese, not Spanish." Brooklyn rued her need to correct people who were blatantly wrong, but she couldn't help it.

"How do you know what he speaks?" Arnie asked. "How do you even know he's from Brazil? Are you two buddies? Is that how you got this sweet deal?"

"Yes," she said, trying to think of an answer that would shut him up. "It's time to confess. I'm Tomas Manuel's long-lost sister. You may call me...Esmerelda."

"That's easier to believe than him having a thing for you, Madam Resident."

"He's not blind!" Chick piped in.

The camera was on her. She could see the red light out of the corner of her eye. Putting on every bit of charm, charisma, and poise she possessed, she looked right into it, smiled sweetly and shrugged her shoulders. She'd never aped for the camera before, but this seemed like the perfect time. Brooklyn slipped a hand under her hair and gently let it trail away, glossy strands cascading onto her shoulder. She lowered her voice to its sexiest register. "I know women are only good for one thing, so if Mr. Manuel isn't my lover, you'll just have to think of why he might take an interest in me." She blew a kiss at the camera, knowing that Arnie would drop the subject when he saw he hadn't rattled her. As soon as the red light cut out, she grasped her sweater and pulled it away from her body, trying to dry the flop sweat she was covered in.

―――――

Kerri spent a while deciding on the appropriate attire for lunch at the very upscale French restaurant. One could get away with just about anything if you had the right attitude, so she went for bohemian, wearing skinny jeans, an ironic T-shirt advertising a 1950s French bicycle, and a thin black cardigan. A grey felt, narrow-brimmed fedora and a snug, grey leather jacket made her indistinguishable from the androgynous TriBeCa-style mavens.

Brooklyn was still in her TV clothes, another jade green shell and those omnipresent black slacks. Her shoes were black, and they were clunky—almost matronly. Not a good look. The dresser at the station must have been a straight guy who didn't like or understand lesbians. A black leather jacket looked like it was actually hers, but it didn't go well with the rest of her clothes. Kerri would have to do something about that.

"Hi," Brooklyn said, getting up from the bar. She made a clumsy move that looked like the start of a hug, then backed away and stood there awkwardly. "You look cute. Not a bit of Santa Monica to be seen."

"Thanks. I wear the same size as my roommate so I've increased my wardrobe a hundred percent."

Brooklyn signaled the hostess, a lovely young woman, who led them to a table. She stood there for a moment, then leaned down and said, "I love seeing you on The Daily Report. You're always funny."

Kerri watched Brooklyn project a persona she'd not seen before. She gave off a vibe that said both, "Please approach," and "I've got all day to talk to you." Her speech slowed down and she leaned back in her chair like she was relaxing with close friends. "Thanks. It's a fun show to do."

"Is James as smart as he seems?"

"Oh, yeah. He's a great guy too. He's not a psycho, like most comedians I know."

"Well, you're always great." She turned to Kerri and gave her a smile, showing scads of perfect, white teeth. "Isn't she great in that kind of situation?"

"She's great in every situation." Kerri smirked at Brooklyn who was grinning happily. "She's naturally clever."

"That's exactly it. She's clever. You can't fake that." She placed her hand very gently onto Brooklyn's shoulder, then leaned over and said, "Have a great meal."

Brooklyn gazed at the young woman as she walked away. "Think I could have gotten her number?"

"I think so, although it's hard to tell with a hostess. She's paid to be friendly, and she might just be a fan. Do you want it? I'll ask her for you."

"Nah." An amused smirk settled on her face. "Do you have to do that a lot? Hook people up with women?"

"And men." By breaking eye contact, Kerri tried to signal that she'd said all she would on the topic.

Brooklyn was pretty good at receiving subtle hints. She picked up her drink and took a sip. "Do you want one? Sorry I didn't ask when we were at the bar."

"No, thanks." Kerri picked up the water a bus boy set in front of her. "I'm happy with this."

They spent the next few minutes perusing the menu, listening to the specials and finally choosing their meals. "Are you a vegetarian?" Brooklyn asked.

"Mostly."

"Just mostly?"

She seemed genuinely interested. That was odd. "You could call me a flexatarian. I eat meat when I'm at a party or a dinner where it's being served. I just don't order it if I have a choice."

"Ethical grounds?"

She shrugged. "Partly. I'm very much against feed-lots and factory farming, but I honestly feel better when I get my protein from other sources."

"Get my protein." Brooklyn laughed. "That's a California thing to say. We just eat here."

"Oh, yeah. That's New York. Nothing pretentious around here."

"Oh, we're pompous pricks. But most people I know don't spend a lot of time deciding where to get each of their required nutrients."

Kerri took another drink of her water, then took a bite of a whole-grain roll. She batted her eyes, trying to get back to business while still seeming playful. "I bet you didn't ask me to lunch to talk about my diet."

"No. No, I didn't. Here's the thing. I have to manage my travel better. Kat quit," she said, looking down at her drink for a second. When she lifted her head, her eyes were dark and sad. "I'd rather not replace her, since there's a chance she's just mad and will come back when she's cooled off. Can you help me figure out how to do whatever I have to do?"

"Sure. I'm very good at making arrangements."

"I feel kinda funny asking you to do things like this…"

"Brooklyn." That made her lift her head and look directly into Kerri's eyes. "I don't think you understand why I'm here. I've been charged with making you more productive and more alert. That includes doing whatever it takes. Anything at all."

"I don't think I've been using you very well. Stuff has been sliding more than usual. I just missed a nephew's birthday."

"I can easily set up reminders for all of your important dates."

"On what?"

"On your computer. As soon as we're finished with lunch we'll get busy."

"I don't have a computer."

"I saw one in the second bedroom."

"That's an old one of Kat's. She'll probably be by to pick it up soon."

"Then that's another reason why we have to get busy."

———

There wasn't a lot for Kerri to choose from, but she managed to enjoy two tiny salads and two vegetable side dishes. She was still eating after

Brooklyn had demolished her steak *frites*. "Would you like for me to travel with you for a while?"

"Are you able to? I know you've got your other client."

"He never has court on Friday, so I could easily go with you so long as I'm back by Sunday night."

"That would work perfectly. Wanna try it out?"

"Definitely. You shouldn't be on the road alone."

A flash of something…maybe anger showed in her eyes. "I don't plan on giving rides to any more teenagers."

"You shouldn't be on the road alone because there are too many things to handle. All performers need help when they travel. All of them," she emphasized. "I wasn't singling you out."

"Sorry I snapped at you. I'm touchy about what happened."

She looked so sincere when she apologized. It might have been a well-rehearsed fake, but it sure looked real.

"No offense taken. Now I can't be your long-term solution, but I can help you figure out what you need, and maybe I can even do some pre-screening for a new manager, if you want one."

"That would be a huge help. I can't imagine having to interview people."

"Let's do this one step at a time. Do you have a gig this coming weekend?"

"Yeah, in LA. Are you up for it?"

"Absolutely. I can check in at home while we're there. Give me the details on the venue and I'll get busy."

"I'm not sure which day or which place I'm appearing. Melvin knows. Could you call him?"

"Sure. I can figure out the details. Don't worry about it."

Smiling contentedly, she looked like a Labrador getting its belly scratched. "'Don't worry'—that's a lovely phrase. I'd give a lot to hear it more often."

Going against Brooklyn's desires, after lunch they walked to the SoHo Apple store.

"I've never been in a computer store," Brooklyn whispered as an enthusiastic young man in a blue T-shirt approached them.

"We need a phone and a laptop," Kerri said, ignoring Brooklyn's squawk of protest.

They shopped for over an hour, with Kerri patiently explaining how a laptop would make Brooklyn's life on the road easier. But Brooklyn's attention wandered and she drifted away after a few moments. She walked back to the salesman and Kerri saying, "I like that iPad. Isn't that the same as a laptop?"

"It can be a substitute," the salesman said, "depending on how you use it."

"Do you want to write while you travel?" Kerri asked.

"Yeah. I do a lot of writing when I'm on the road."

"Then you might prefer the laptop. I'd have trouble typing on the virtual keyboard."

The salesman jumped in. "The iPad is more of a media device. It's great for watching TV and movies and listening to music and looking at photos and playing games. But it's not ideal for lots of typing, and its memory isn't very large."

Kerri added, "And the iPad doesn't let you see Flash websites. The laptop will."

Brooklyn shrugged. "It's only a thousand bucks. Add it to the pile."

The salesman asked if they had an American Express card, since using that would extend Brooklyn's warranty. She looked through all the nooks of her wallet and produced a sparkling card that she hadn't bothered to sign yet. "I didn't even know I had this one."

He ran the card through the reader but didn't get automatic approval. "I'm gonna have to call on this. Maybe it's because you haven't used it." He walked to a door near the main counter and disappeared for a long time. When he came back he looked very apologetic. "They refused the card. Actually, they think it's stolen."

"It's not stolen," Brooklyn grumbled. She whipped out the card she usually used. "Screw the warranty. Your stuff's supposed to be perfect anyway, right?"

The sales clerk gave her a winning smile. "You'll be a fan girl in no time."

———

It was four o'clock when they exited the building into the hordes of people who seemed to move down the narrow sidewalks of SoHo en masse. Brooklyn stepped out into the street, and started to hail a cab, but Kerri put a hand on her arm and said, "It's only a few blocks. Let's walk."

"And carry all this stuff?"

"You think this is a lot of stuff? I carried a forty-pound pack for over a week when I went camping in the Sierras. Hand it over, weakling."

"I can do it," Brooklyn said defensively. "I just don't want to."

Kerri snatched the bag from her quickly. "Come on. It's a nice day, and we can walk off some of that lunch."

"It's gonna be hard for you to walk off all of those vegetables—steamed, no butter. We might have to go all the way to Philadelphia." Brooklyn's grin was one Kerri had learned went along with her sarcastic comments.

"I guarantee you'll feel better tomorrow if you keep your blood moving today. Walking a little will make you sleep better."

"I knew this was a trick! Nobody in New York walks."

"Everybody in New York walks. If you want to see people who don't walk, come to my hometown. If people could get cars inside their houses, they'd drive from room to room."

"I thought everyone had a huge house in LA."

"Not everyone," Kerri said. "Come to my apartment and you'll see how the little people live."

———

They'd only gone a couple of blocks before Brooklyn had enough. "Come on, let's get a cab. I can barely put one foot in front of the other."

To Kerri's experienced eye, Brooklyn looked a little better than she had earlier in the day. There was a bit of color in her cheeks and her eyes didn't have the dull sheen they'd had that morning. She wasn't sure it would work, but Brooklyn seemed like a competitive person who would react poorly to being bested. Even though she personally eschewed competition, she guessed she could push Brooklyn's buttons with little effort. "I'm sorry. It was rude of me to try to make you walk. You go ahead and get a cab."

Brooklyn already had her hand up in the air, but she pulled it halfway down. "What are you going to do?"

"I'm going to walk."

"To my place?"

"Yeah. My bike's there."

Brooklyn placed her hands on her hips, looking like a stern, puzzled teacher. "So I'm going to take a cab, and you're going to walk."

With a teasing smile, Kerri said, "I only have control over the last part, and I like to walk."

"Ridiculous," Brooklyn growled, but they continued to walk together.

"I don't want to pry, but you seem a little down. Are you feeling bad about Kat?"

"Yeah, I guess. I'm kinda sad."

"If you want her back, why not send an apology gift and write her a nice note. Tell me what she likes and I'll shop for something."

Brooklyn lit up. "That's a great idea. I'll think about it." Her phone rang and she pulled it from her pocket. "My mom," she said as she pressed the talk button. "Hey, Mom. What's up?" They spoke for a few minutes, with Kerri focusing on the people they passed and her schedule for the next day. She was a little surprised when Brooklyn hung up and said, "Did you catch that?"

"Hmm? No, I wasn't listening."

"I found out why my credit card didn't work. The company called my mom to verify a big purchase and when they told her it was for computer stuff she said the card had to have been stolen." She laughed hard, looking unguardedly happy. "Isn't that fantastic?"

Kerri was stuck on one point. "Why would they call your mom?"

"Oh." Brooklyn sobered up immediately. It took her a few seconds to reply. "I use my parents' address for a lot of things. They're always home."

"Got it." That made no sense at all. Brooklyn was gone a lot, but only for two or three days at a time. Maybe she had a gambling problem and her family had to keep an eye on her money. Maybe her parents had to apply for the card because her credit was ruined. God only knew the permutations of trouble talent could get into.

Before Brooklyn had time to complain about the walk again they were back at her loft. Once inside, Brooklyn headed immediately for the sectional, which was obviously her favorite place. Her cell phone rang and she answered after glancing at the screen. "Hey, Melvin. What's up?"

She listened quietly for a moment, then started to bite on the tip of a finger. A line formed between her brows and her lips were set in a horizontal line. "No, I didn't know that." She nodded. "I definitely can't go to the funeral." Another brief nod. "Yeah, I'm sure they don't have much money. Jimmy was a great guy, but most of his money went into a vein." She met Kerri's eyes and shook her head mournfully. "Yeah, of course I'll do it. I wish you'd told me about it earlier, but I guess it wouldn't have mattered much anyway. How do I get there?" She collapsed into the soft leather, looking like she'd heard very bad news. "Okay. I can use my GPS." Her eyes showed a little fire when she said, "But I'm not showing up until the last minute. I've gotta get some sleep." She nodded once more, then mumbled, "Bye," and hung up.

"You don't look very happy."

Brooklyn stretched out to her full length and yawned. "I'm not. I have to go way out on Long Island to do a benefit for Jimmy Martin."

"I don't think I've heard of him."

Brooklyn shrugged. "He's a local comic. Melvin was his manager. Jimmy overdosed a couple of months ago and has been in a coma. A bunch of people put together this benefit for him, and now it's a memorial. He died yesterday."

"Was he a friend?"

"No. I knew him, but we never hung out. Anyway, people must have dropped out, because Melvin wants me to do an hour. That's ridiculous for a benefit. They usually cut your mike off if you go longer than ten."

"When is it?"

"Tonight," Brooklyn grumbled.

"Tonight? He wants you to do an hour of your set tonight?"

"Yeah."

Why wasn't she angry at being summoned at the last minute? And why had she agreed? The guy wasn't even a friend. Kerri had never known talent who let herself be treated so shabbily.

"Maybe I should hire a car service. I'm not sure I'll be awake enough to drive home."

"I'll go with you."

"Aww, you don't want to do that." Given her expression, she might as well have said, "Please!"

"I'd like to see you work. It'll be fun."

A grin desperately tried to peek out, but Brooklyn must have ordered it back in. "You don't know how to have fun if you think this is it." She looked longingly towards the TV. "I'd love to listen to the news. Will it bother you?"

"No, why would it?"

"Because I'll be asleep in a few minutes and I'm not sure if I snore."

"You're really not sure?"

"I didn't use to, but my throat has been sore and dry in the morning for a while. That might be a clue."

"That's not a problem. Do you mind if I use the other bedroom? I can try to convince myself to take a power nap."

"No, go ahead. Just wake me up at eight…if you're up."

"Oh, I will be. Don't worry about a thing."

—◆—

It wasn't easy to order herself to nap when she was wide awake, but that wouldn't stop her. Kerri was justly proud of the years of work she'd put into convincing her body to be a help, not a hindrance in life. If a nap would help, a nap would be had. She moved about the space, trying to get comfortable enough to sleep. The loft was so large that the bedroom didn't look very spacious. In fact, it was probably bigger than the whole apartment she was staying in. Thankfully, she didn't feel even a flicker of envy or jealously for the multi-million dollar property Brooklyn owned. Material goods were nice, but they could never, ever replace anything important. It was truly sad that so few people seemed to get that, but it was a fact. How many people had expressed envy of the celebrities she worked for? Most. But Kerri wouldn't have traded places with any of them. Not one person she'd worked with liked who they were, and no amount of money or fame could buy that.

It took a while to clear her mind because Brooklyn kept popping up. She was harder than most celebs to figure out, mostly because she didn't have the big, outsized personality that most actors had. She also didn't seem to need a lot of fawning by her fans, much less by her manager or agent. That alone was odd. The strangest thing was that she didn't seem particularly…funny. Kerri assumed she'd be like a jazz musician riffing on topics all of the time, always looking for a way to turn a phrase or make something click. But Brooklyn was quiet, introspective, and strangely flat for a performer. That didn't sync with the clips Kerri'd seen on the internet, so seeing her perform in person might be fun…or tedious.

—⁓—

Kerri had no idea how much the car Brooklyn had stowed in a garage just down the block had cost, but it was probably a whole lot. It was black, undoubtedly foreign, plush, and terrifyingly fast. The car growled as it leapt over potholes, and Kerri had to place a hand on the dash to secure herself more firmly to her seat. "Do you drive very often?"

"No. Just to go see my parents. I've only got"—she looked at the glowing orange lights on the dash—"nine hundred ninety-five miles on her."

"How long have you had it?"

"About a year. Maybe a little more."

"It's really nice." She didn't add that she'd once worked for a movie star who had a Porsche custom built with his name cast into the engine block. Celebs were a competitive bunch, and Brooklyn might be on the phone with Germany in the morning.

⎯⎯

They drove over an hour to get to the club, and there was nowhere to park anywhere near the place. Brooklyn scowled as she drove slowly around the vaguely seedy neighborhood. "I guess I'm gonna have to just leave my car out here, but I don't feel good about it."

"Do you think someone will steal it?"

"Maybe not the car, but the wheels. They're pretty rare, and every kid around here will want them." She sat there, the car in park, with the engine still running. "I just hate to have to go through the whole insurance process. And getting home without a car will really suck." She chewed on the tip of her index finger for a second, then brightened up. "Will you wait here for a sec? I've got an idea." Then she jumped out and jogged, slowly, for the club.

Fifteen minutes later she was back, accompanied by a skinny guy in an ill-fitting suit. Brooklyn opened the door and said, "Come on, Kerri. Mike's gonna sit in the car and watch it."

"Okay." She got out as Mike slid in. He was holding one bottle of beer, and another was in his suit pocket.

"Don't spill," Brooklyn warned as she closed the door.

They started to walk. "Sorry that took so long, but it took a while to find someone who didn't smoke. Even when a guy says he won't smoke in the car, he'll stand right outside and do it, then get back in and stink the thing up." She grinned, with the strong lights of the lot glinting off her very straight teeth. "Experience."

Did Brooklyn not realize the car already stank of smoke? How could it not, when she and her clothes smelled of it? People didn't seem to realize smoke was oily and pervaded fabrics of every kind. It must be very easy to be oblivious if you wanted to be.

The club was crowded and loud with people jammed in every corner of the relatively small place. They threaded their way across the rear, sliding past tables, Brooklyn shaking a few hands on the way. She scooted out a side door, where a gaggle of comics was standing and smoking. Brooklyn gave one guy a rough, guy-like hug and snatched a cigarette from a pack he had in the pocket of his Hawaiian shirt. "Bruno, it's been years!"

"It sure has," he said, looking very happy to see her. "That's 'cause we're heading in different directions, York. You're going up, and I'm going…" He pointed to the ground. "But I'm happy for you. Really, I am."

"Really?" She asked, giving him an utterly charming smile. "Come on, tell the truth."

"I've never been happy for anybody in my life. I hope you get shit-canned from that radio show so they'll give it to me."

"That's more like it. Hey, meet my…friend." She looked nonplussed. "This is Kerri Klein. Kerri, this is Bruno Macaluso. He and I go way back."

"Girlfriend?" Bruno asked.

"No," Kerri said, "just friends."

"We work together," Brooklyn amended. "Kerri's my temporary road manager."

"Where's the other chick? The cute one?" His eyes grew wide and he turned to say, "Shit! I didn't mean you weren't cute, honey. You're lots cuter than her friend. That's just how all of us talk about the other girl. What's her damn name, York?" he demanded.

"Kat. She's mad at me right now and I'm not sure if she's coming back. So Kerri's filling in."

"If I ever get a road manager, and I'm sure I won't, I'm gonna let you do the interviewing for me, York. You're a good judge of"—he gave Kerri a lascivious look—"talent."

"Yeah, I'd love to do that for you, Bruno. Right after I need a warm jacket in hell. How's the benefit going? Are you done?"

"Long ago. I was third. You're probably up next. But don't worry, Melvin will find you. I've gotta go take a piss." He winced visibly and looked to Kerri alone. "I'm sorry for my mouth. I forgot I'm around a lady."

"I'm not offended," Kerri said. "Not in the least."

When he walked away Kerri said, "Aren't you a lady?"

"Hardly." She laughed. "There are probably women comics who other comics treat with some level of politeness, but I'm not one of them."

"Why's that?"

"Honestly? I don't know. I used to think it's because I'm a dyke, but I don't think that's it. There's just something about me that makes them think of me as a guy."

That was odd. Brooklyn didn't seem like a guy at all when she was at home. But here, around her fellow comics, she did come off like one of the guys. Back slapping, grabbing cigarettes, shaking hands instead of kissing cheeks like the other women did. Was that natural for her, or had she worked on that persona to fit in?

Brooklyn rocked on the balls of her feet, looking nervous and uncomfortable. She snuck a few glances at the other people standing outside. "I don't know anyone else."

"Jimmy must have been popular. This place is packed."

"He probably played this place seventy-five times. Same for every other club on Long Island." She smiled, showing a hint of sadness. "That's not true, but he didn't go further—or higher—than the New York circuit."

"Is there really a circuit for New York?"

"Sure. You can play small clubs within a day's drive and stay busy. Then you don't have to pay for a hotel room. A lot of guys do that."

A balding, bespeckled, middle-aged man in a beige shirt and brown and gold tie walked through the door and shook Brooklyn's hand. "Hi. We're dragging on a little bit. Just sit tight and I'll find you when you're next up." He turned and smiled when he met Kerri's gaze. "Are you Kerri?"

"Yes. Melvin, I presume."

They shook and he stood there, looking like he couldn't think of a single word to say. "Well, I'll see you later." Then he quickly went back into the club.

"He doesn't seem like a very talkative guy," Kerri said.

"No. He never is. But he's worse around women. He's a decent guy, though. I trust him."

"That's important in a manager."

"For me, that's important in everything."

The way she said that made Kerri take notice. When Brooklyn spoke with such gravity, she meant it.

After standing out in the chilled air while Brooklyn bummed three more cigarettes, they went into the club. She grabbed a chair and took it into a corner, insisting Kerri sit. "I've got a lot of nervous energy, so I'm going to walk around. I'm going to do my old act, and it's really rusty."

"Why do your old act?"

"Because these people want to laugh. People only chuckle at my current stuff. This isn't my crowd…anymore."

Another comic approached, and he and Brooklyn chatted quietly. Kerri didn't try to become part of the conversation. Being as unobtrusive as possible was always the best choice. Instead, she listened to the comic onstage and wondered where the woman fit on the food chain. She was young, and fairly attractive, but her act consisted of her making fun of herself for being a slut who drank too much. The women's liberation movement had really given women a lot of freedom—to make the same dumb jokes that men used to make. But they had more sting when a woman delivered them. *God, please don't let Brooklyn do that kind of thing.*

Kerri was still musing when the next comic came on, and the next. Brooklyn was wandering around the club, talking to a dozen people, acting more vital than Kerri'd ever seen her. Finally, Melvin walked over to her and gave her the high sign. She caught Kerri's eye, mouthed "wish me luck," and headed over to a curtained area behind the stage.

An older comedian, the master of ceremonies, introduced her. "You know her from *Reveille*, where she keeps you entertained for hours every morning, from *The Daily Report*, from *Strictly Speaking*, from *Late Night*, and from *Still Later*. She's so successful she makes me sick! Ladies and gentlemen, I'd like you to welcome Brooklyn New York!"

She bounded onto the stage, where a buoyant wave and matching grin made a good portion of the audience sit up straighter and lean forward. "Thanks for coming out tonight, everyone. As Buddy said, I'm Brooklyn York. Yes, that's my real name, but the New part was a fabrication." She turned towards the man who introduced her. "That means you made it up," she said slowly. The crowd laughed much harder for that small joke than they had for the previous comic's entire set. It was fascinating watching a crowd fall under the sway of someone with charisma, and Brooklyn definitely had it. Just the way she occupied the stage as though it were her home made her stand out. When you added in her brilliant smile, sparkling eyes and robust intellect, there was no competition.

Besides her advantage in charisma, Brooklyn's jokes were undoubtedly sharper than the other comics'. It seemed as though she observed things that the other guys weren't able to. She let the audience in on her way of seeing things, and they seemed to have many "ah-ha!" moments when they shared her view. But there was something missing. Brooklyn didn't seem engaged, at least not in the way she'd been on the internet clips. Maybe she was just going through the motions for this unpaid appearance, or maybe she was too tired to give it her all—but it was slightly disappointing. Kerri had definitely expected more.

—⁓—

Brooklyn stood by the deceased comic's family, having her picture taken by fans and a few photographers who looked like they might be from local newspapers. Kerri saw Melvin standing off to the side and she sauntered up to him. "Hi, again," she said.

"Uh, hi." He looked like he wanted to escape, but she blocked his exit.

"Brooklyn was telling me about her upcoming dates, and I was wondering why she was playing such a small house in Los Angeles. Since she sold out the smallest venue at UCLA and has to do a late show, why not try to move her to the Wadsworth or even Royce Hall?"

"Oh, do you know Los Angeles?"

"Yes. That's where I'm from."

"Ooo, I could use someone like you. I don't have many contacts out there. I scramble to get her in anywhere. And they tell me it's hard to fill a big theater. I've heard that people there like to be outside most of the time."

Oh, my. Sometimes it sucked to have your suspicions turn out to be true. Melvin didn't have the goods. "I think it's harder to get people to buy tickets for things in LA, but it's a cultural center. I can't imagine many people in LA listen to *Reveille*, so she's got to make a name for herself via her comedy."

"I haven't seen any numbers on how *Reveille* does." He looked troubled. "Maybe I should do that."

"It couldn't hurt."

Brooklyn was on her way over, so Kerri stood aside and let Melvin escape. Then she turned and smiled at Brooklyn. "Great job!"

―⁂―

After having a drink in the bar with a dozen comics, none of whom Kerri had heard of, they went back to the car to wake Mike up. Brooklyn paid him for his time and they headed back to the expressway. "What should we do?" Brooklyn asked. "It's one thirty."

"I can't imagine a couple of hours sleep will help much. If I were you I'd power through. What do you think?"

"I think I can. Besides, I need to eat and that'll take up even more time. I can't sleep on an empty stomach."

Odd. That was the best way to sleep. "I'm happy to go anywhere you like."

"Then I hope you like pizza."

—⁂—

They went to a grimy, seedy looking place on the Lower East Side. There were no parking spots nearby, but Brooklyn stuck the car in a part of the bus stop and got out.

"Is this okay?" Kerri asked. "I'd hate to see you get towed."

"Nah." She stretched and yawned noisily. "This bus doesn't run all night. The cops don't care."

The inside of the restaurant wasn't as nice as the outside, which wasn't nice at all. The lights made Brooklyn look a sickly shade of yellowish green, a color no one looked good in. "I like pepperoni," Brooklyn said. "Do you want veggies on your half?"

How to refuse politely? This was always tricky. "I don't think I'm going to have any."

"No pizza?" She looked as if Kerri had refused to breathe air.

"No, cheese doesn't always agree with me." That was a lie, but one that shouldn't trip her up in the future. "I'll have a salad."

"Don't you like something that sticks to your ribs?"

Her concern was actually touching, but it probably had a thread of "why don't you do what I do?" in it. "I had a big breakfast, and a couple of snacks."

Raising her eyebrows, Brooklyn got up and went to the counter to order. When she came back, she tilted her head and looked at Kerri for a few moments. "Tell me about your diet."

"Really? It's not very interesting."

"Yeah." She nodded.

Brooklyn's gaze was intent and she really did look interested, but why? "Okay. I usually have fruit and yoghurt and oatmeal for breakfast. If I'm really hungry, I'll add a couple of eggs and a bagel."

"That is a big breakfast. And it's at four a.m."

"First thing in the morning is when I'm hungriest. Plus, that's one part of my day I'm in control of. Sometimes I'm running around like a maniac. Then I have fruit or vegetables for a mid-morning snack, then a little pasta or a bean salad for lunch. I try to eat around nineteen hundred calories a day, so I don't want to spend them all at once."

"Hmm. I have no idea how many calories are in things. Heck, I don't know if I eat a thousand or ten thousand."

"Really? I don't know many women who haven't spent a lot of time thinking about food and calories."

"You can add me to your short list."

"I will."

Brooklyn sat there for a few moments. For reasons that befuddled Kerri, it was clear this was of interest to her, but for some reason she looked sad. "Do you ever get to eat pizza?"

Kerri almost burst into a laugh. But the look on Brooklyn's face was so sweet, it was like she was asking if Santa ever went to Kerri's house. "Sure. I love pizza. But only if it's really excellent. Then it's worth blowing a thousand calories on."

"That sounds like a lot of work. It's easier to just eat when you're hungry, and order what you know you like."

"You probably have a point." It was impossible to tell if Brooklyn was teasing, or if she honestly didn't know that eating whatever and whenever you liked almost always led to dragging a lot of extra weight around.

Their food was delivered and Brooklyn dug into her pizza. She ate so fast and so determinedly it was more like an attack than an enjoyable meal. She'd obliterated the first piece before Kerri had time to touch her salad of iceberg lettuce with two slices of cucumber and four slices of pink tomato. She wouldn't think of eating a flavorless tomato, but she ate all of the rest to make sure Brooklyn didn't feel sorry for her.

"Don't you like tomato?"

"Yeah, I love tomatoes, but only when they're ripe. I try to eat things that are in season, so that leaves tomatoes off my plate for nine months out of the year."

"Huh." She stared at her, as though she were trying to divine what made Kerri tick. "Tomatoes are in everything."

"I don't eat out when I don't have to. I like to have control over what I eat."

Laughing, Brooklyn leaned back in her chair and regarded Kerri for a long time. "We couldn't be more different."

"Oh, I don't know about that. We both like women."

"Very much." Brooklyn showed that saucy smile that was impossible not to return.

They didn't talk too much after that, and Kerri got the feeling it wasn't only because of Brooklyn's furious eating. "Do you want to talk more about what happened with Kat? You still seem a little off."

"I feel pretty shaky, to be honest. I pushed her little bit, just a little, and she got her back up." That half smile peeked out. "Cats get their backs up. Kind of funny."

"Not bad for someone who hasn't slept. So how did you push her?"

"Do you really want to know? Because you're involved."

Kerri reached across and put her hand on Brooklyn's. She flinched, and Kerri reminded herself once again to stop being so physical with her. It was clear that Brooklyn wasn't a woman who liked a lot of contact. "Tell me."

"You were telling me about things she should have done or could have done and I called her on some of them. It really pissed her off, and that's what made her quit."

Kerri wasn't sure, but it certainly seemed as though Brooklyn was angry with her. She would've tried to reason this out with a friend, but never with a client. Apologize and retreat were the bywords of her job.

"Damn, Brooklyn, I'm really sorry. I shouldn't have offered my opinion. Can I help fix this? I could call Kat and explain that I put some ideas in your head…"

Brooklyn shook her head briefly. The sigh she let out was poignantly sad. "No, you were right. She's not doing what I need her to do." She gave Kerri a speculative look. "Could I convince you to take a permanent job? Fifteen percent of my annual income is a pretty good chunk of change."

Kerri would've immediately said no, but you had to let talent down very easily. They were like thin-shelled eggs. "I wish I could, but I really need to be located on the West coast. My grandfather's ninety-five and he has Alzheimer's."

"That sounds tough. Really tough."

"Yeah, it is. My mom's caring for him now, but when he needs round-the-clock care, I'm going to move in with them."

"Wow." Brooklyn didn't say another word. She just met Kerri's gaze and held it, showing what looked like true empathy. That got uncomfortable quickly, and Kerri jumped to change the mood.

"It won't be too bad, but Alzheimer's has no clear path, so I'm only taking short-term jobs."

"Right. But that really sounds like it'll be hard on you."

She waved her hand in the air. "It won't be that big a deal to move. No pets, no kids."

"Still…"

"So what do you want to do about Kat?" She could've talked about her grandfather all day, but it wasn't wise. A client couldn't throw anything at you if they had no ammunition.

"I'll just send her something and apologize. I actually hope she doesn't come back, but that's her choice."

Her choice? How was it her choice? Did Brooklyn not understand that she, not Kat was the boss?

—⁓—

When they got into the car, Brooklyn said, "Let's go for a drive. I like to drive around when there isn't a lot of traffic."

"Why not. We've got hours to kill."

The car rumbled to life and they set out. After cutting over to the middle of town, they headed north. It was cool but not cold. The moment Brooklyn opened the sunroof, she took in a deep breath that seemed to calm her. "So. What did you really think of my set tonight?"

Oh, damn. This was like walking into a field of land mines. But Brooklyn had a funny look in her eyes that was sort of cagey. *Tell the truth.* "I was a little surprised, to be honest."

"Why?"

"I watched a lot of internet clips, and I didn't see you do any of those kinds of jokes. They seemed more...I'm not sure what word to use, but your set tonight was hugely different from what I've seen."

"Yeah, it was. I told you I had to do my old act. Did you like it?"

That look was back, and her dark eyes seemed like they'd cut through any lies.

"I like your current act a lot better. It's sharper and more...brainy? Is that the right word?"

"I like having a brain, so that might be it."

"And you seem more engaged when you're doing your newer material."

Now a lovely smile brightened her face. Thank god.

"Yeah, I am. Tonight was a ninety minute set that I had to cut down —on the fly. I was always thinking about how to work the next joke in. That's tough."

"I can't imagine doing that! It sounds terrifying."

Brooklyn's gaze was strangely modest. "It's not hard when you're used to it. But my timing was really off. I sucked, but the crowd didn't seem to care."

"No, not at all. They loved you."

Shrugging, she said, "Maybe. It helps to be famous. People want you to succeed when they've heard of you." She chuckled, the sound almost like a purr. "It's really unfair. When you're starting out you don't get a break from anyone. You have to fight tooth and nail to get a smile out of 'em."

"That does seem unfair. I'd assume that people root for the underdog."

"Not in comedy," she said, her tone brooking no disagreement. "Standing on stage and claiming you can make someone laugh is almost like daring the audience not to like you. You start off in the hole."

"Fascinating. So…why did you want to be a comedian? It looks like a tough way to make a living."

"It's not, really. If you've got the nerve and are relatively good, you can make a decent living, so long as you don't mind working crummy clubs and traveling. It's a great career for people who can't handle a real job."

"You didn't answer my question," Kerri reminded her. "Why did *you* choose it?"

They'd made it up to the fifties, and Brooklyn turned towards Broadway. In the distance there was nothing but light. Times Square throbbed with colored lights and giant monitors showing commercials and movie trailers. Once on Broadway, Brooklyn slowed down even more than the traffic, almost idling down the street. She gazed up through the open moonroof and her voice had a bit of childlike wonder in it when she said, "Isn't this magical?"

Kerri leaned back in her seat, looking up at the blitzkrieg of light, sound, and motion. "It is. I've never seen it like this."

"I do this every once in a while. I really love it." She snuck a glance at Kerri. "I've always wanted to be where something big is happening. I absolutely love being on stage. I guess it's my drug." She took a deep breath, as if to inhale the excitement of the street. "I can't sing well, and I didn't have much talent for playing music. And I didn't want to be another person, so acting was out. Luckily, I was funny. As soon as I realized I could be funny for a living"—she grinned like the world's happiest woman—"my choice was made."

Just talking about her calling made her personality come alive. Her eyes sparkled in the bright lights, and her smile looked even more content. She looked like a woman who'd just been given a very impressive award and was luxuriating in the glow.

They drove on, the excitement of the street diminishing quickly as they started to pass nothing but stores selling cheap junk to tourists. Then even that connection to the hub of the city faded, replaced by workaday office buildings, all deserted. But even though the surroundings were now bland, Brooklyn wasn't. She still had a vibe that was remarkably alluring. There it was. The thing that successful people had. Kerri had never, ever met a celebrity that didn't have it, and now that she'd finally seen it, Brooklyn fit in with all of the rest of her celebrity peers.

"How old were you when you decided?"

It took a few minutes of thought for Brooklyn to reply. "I met a funny kid when I was in fifth grade. He changed my life."

She looked so serious, Kerri was unsure what to say. "Uhm…how?"

"Knowing that there was someone else who only wanted to make people laugh was validating. Really validating. I'd gotten a lot of praise for my grades, but I wanted praise for being funny. Jaden gave me that. We spent every minute we could spare together, doing some of the dumbest things imaginable. His mother and my mother were ready to send both of us to reform school." She laughed for just a moment, then turned somber. "But by eighth grade he wanted to be my boyfriend and I thought that was decidedly unfunny."

"You weren't attracted to him?"

"Have I mentioned I'm gay?" she asked, one eyebrow raised.

"Oh! Yes, of course. I just assumed…I'm not sure what I assumed, but that seems young to know your sexuality."

"I knew long before that. I just didn't have a name for it. But Jaden wasn't interested in me for jokes once he wanted me for a girlfriend. That was hard to get over."

Kerri found her hand on Brooklyn's arm, squeezing it in sympathy. "I'm sorry you were hurt."

"It was the first, but not the last time I had to stop hanging out with a guy because he couldn't believe I didn't want more than friendship. It still happens today."

Kerri was fairly sure most straight men would have been attracted to Brooklyn, especially if she showed them any reciprocal interest. Even a guy who liked women to wear sexy dresses could undress a hot androgynous woman with his mind. Why didn't Brooklyn know that? "Tell me more about starting out. What was your first time like?"

"Are we talking about comedy or lesbianism? I recall my first attempts at both."

Her eyes took on a very sexy look when she made even a moderately racy comment. Why was she single? "Comedy, please."

"Ahh, comedy. I was eighteen, and I'd only been out of high school for a couple of months. I was ready to break my cherry, as it were, and I found a club that had an open-mike night. I was so nervous I thought I'd have a heart attack. I swear, Kerri, my socks were wet when I got off stage." She laughed quietly for a few seconds. "I don't know if I was good or bad, but I assume I was bad. I still can't recall if I got laughs. But once I was on that stage, I knew I didn't have to go to school or look for a career. I was done." She looked completely happy with herself, even now, after all these years.

"But if you didn't know whether you'd done well, how did you have the courage to go do it again?"

"It didn't matter. I knew I could get up there and be myself. All that was going to stop me was me, and I knew I'd work my butt off to be good." She leveled an intent gaze at Kerri. "I have."

—◊—

It was four a.m., and they'd long since run out of things to do. They'd gotten coffee, watched the news, and read the paper, but the clock wasn't moving very fast.

"I've been thinking," Brooklyn said, breaking the long silence. "I keep thinking I should force myself to continue to stay up all night. Things like this benefit come up all the time, and I hate to say no to everything."

"I've thought about it too. On paper, it seems like the right thing, but it's not ideal."

"But I could be on the same schedule all week. If I slept from noon to eight I'd be able to be up for the radio show and my comedy gigs."

"That's true, but you'd miss something important."

"Besides bad headaches and getting yelled at for being late?"

"Yep. You'd miss the sun. You get to the studio before the sun's up, and you'd probably go to bed as soon as you got home." Or more likely sit on the sectional and watch TV for a few hours, which was almost the same. "By the time you got up again, it'd be dark, even in the summer. It's possible that wouldn't bother you, but it would drive me mad."

Brooklyn sat on her sofa, her head resting in her hand. "I really like the sun." She sighed heavily. "When I was younger, I loved getting up in the morning and going for a run before breakfast. Then I'd go to school, and as soon as the bell rang, we'd play tennis until it was too dark to see."

She looked so sad, Kerri could have easily shed a tear.

"Now I'm considering seeing the sun for a half hour a day. What kind of mess have I set up for myself?"

"Let's try to stay on an early-to-bed early-to-rise schedule for a while. If it's too awful we'll switch. But you deserve to get outside, Brooklyn. Don't give that up unless you absolutely have to."

Brooklyn looked at her watch and sighed. "Time to get in the shower." She started for her bedroom, then stopped and looked at Kerri curiously. "How do you think it's going? Is this a decent job for you?"

Odd. Most people didn't ask something like that unless they'd bit you and were afraid you'd file assault charges. She got up and walked over to stand next to Brooklyn. Not as close as she usually stood to people, but close for Brooklyn. "It's going great for me. You're delightful to work for."

"No way."

She really looked like she wanted to be reassured. But about what? "I'm being perfectly serious." Without thinking, she put her hand on Brooklyn's shoulder and stroked her arm. There was still a brief flinch, but it wasn't as noticeable as usual. Maybe they were getting used to each other. "Most people hire me when they're in a lot of trouble, either with the law or a movie studio or something like that. You're just tired. I'm really enjoying myself. I just wish you didn't have to be so exhausted that you needed help."

Brooklyn's smile was so sweet that the hair on the back of Kerri's neck stood up.

"I think you're just really polite. But I appreciate it. I hate to be a jerk."

"You haven't shown one bit of jerkiness, if that's a word."

"Thanks," she said, and Kerri stood there watching her cross the room.

Brooklyn was very hard to categorize. But she was absolutely, positively not a jerk.

CHAPTER FOUR

KERRI WAS IN THE apartment when Brooklyn returned home from work. Given Brooklyn's instincts, she'd be asleep on the sectional within minutes. They had to get on a regular schedule, but keeping her awake today wasn't going to be easy.

Brooklyn was almost stumbling when she dropped her messenger bag and coat on the dining table. "My whole body hurts," she groaned while flopping onto the sectional.

"I have a good lunch for you. You can eat, then relax for the afternoon so you're nice and tired tonight."

"Yeah. Tonight." She laughed quietly at the joke she alone heard.

They ate, then Brooklyn retired to her favorite spot, where she slowly got more and more horizontal. Kerri knew she had to be more creative to keep her up, but she wasn't sure what would work. Maybe the new computer would be of interest. "Hey, can I look at your phone? I want to put your contacts on your laptop."

"Sure." She took the phone from her pocket and handed it over. Kerri played with it until she could figure it out. There were only about ten contacts listed, and Brooklyn had to have hundreds of them. "I'll check the PC. That's probably where Kat put things."

"Feel free. I've gotta warn you that I'm gonna fall asleep in about two minutes though. If you need anything, ask now."

Rather than checking the old PC, Kerri went back to the table and took the iPad out of the box. She had to ask Brooklyn a few questions to get her registered with the on-line music store, then she started downloading applications that she knew Brooklyn would be unable to resist. "Oh, this is cool!" She started playing a game that was just like a pinball machine.

"Can I see?" Brooklyn sounded like a five-year-old. A very cute five-year-old.

"Sure. We can play together." No competitive person could resist a well-designed game.

They played the game for hours, only stopping when Brooklyn complained of being hungry. "I'm gonna call for Chinese. What do you like?"

"You keep playing. There's a really good place just a couple blocks from here. I'll go get us something. Do you like spicy food?"

Brooklyn was already lost in her game, but she nodded. Kerri took off, returning a half hour later with a variety of vegetarian Indian food. Brooklyn got up and started poking through the containers. "How can you tell what any of this is? It's just brown stuff and green stuff."

"I promise you'll like it. Go sit down and I'll make up a plate for you."

Looking suspicious, Brooklyn did as she was asked, and a few minutes later she was happily shoveling the food into her mouth. "This stuff is really spicy! It's good too."

"I thought you'd like it. I'll take their menu and check off all of the things I've had. Then you won't make any mistakes if you get it delivered."

"It's a deal." She pointed her fork at something and said, "This is chicken right?"

"I'm not sure what half of it is," Kerri lied. She normally liked to tell the truth, but lying for her clients' best interests was an exception she happily, and routinely, made. If a client thought tofu was chicken, it was fine for the client…and the chicken.

―――

At seven o'clock, Kerri stood up. "I'd better get going. Four a.m. comes pretty early."

"You're gonna take a cab right? It's too cold to ride your bike."

With a sincere smile, Kerri said, "I appreciate that you're concerned. Now give me that tablet or you'll be up all night playing." Brooklyn reluctantly handed it over and Kerri pressed a simple switch to turn the machine off. She knew Brooklyn wouldn't be able to figure how to turn it back on without investing a few minutes, and she could tell by her drooping eyelids that she'd be asleep before her curiosity got the best of her.

—⁂—

The next morning Brooklyn didn't exactly jump out of bed, but she got up fairly willingly. By the time she got out of the shower her eyes were wide open, and she was speaking in complete sentences.

"You look good today," Kerri observed. "Did you sleep well?"

Brooklyn paused a moment, then looked at her with true curiosity. "You know, I did. I wonder why?"

"Just good luck, I guess." *And nine hours of sleep, no afternoon nap, no greasy food, and no vodka. Other than that, just luck.*

—⁂—

Surprisingly, it turned out that Brooklyn had not only an aptitude, but a real interest in learning how to use her computer. They spent a long time the next afternoon going over various things, with Brooklyn sopping up the information like a sponge. Sitting there, her head bent close to the screen, she looked like the best kind of student—the kind who desperately wanted to learn.

Kerri found herself saying fondly, "For a Luddite, you're surprisingly into this."

The smile Brooklyn gave her was so charmingly sweet that it almost took her breath away. "Luddite. People say that all of the time, but I don't know the origin of the word. Tell me about it."

Slightly embarrassed, Kerri shook her head. "I can't. I thought it meant someone who didn't want to use technology."

Brooklyn petted the computer like a cat. "I bet the answer's in here. Show me the best way to find it."

Kerri sat next to her and they performed her first Google search. Brooklyn then spent a while reading about the Luddites, finally saying, "It's apt, but not really precise. There should be a better term differentiating people who fear technology from those who reject it."

"You should do a bit about that."

Brooklyn leaned back against the sectional and regarded Kerri with the smirk that indicated she was about to taunt her. "A bit, huh? Tell me more about how this bit should go."

She just sat there, looking smug. That was bad news. The worst news, actually. Kerri was the model of virtue when it came to most vices and temptations, but she could not resist a cocky woman who had something to be cocky about. It was a dangerous fault, since most smug people were pains in the butt or insufferable in other ways. But this was the first time Kerri'd seen this cocky side of Brooklyn. Maybe it was a fluke. Please let it be a fluke!

"Uhm, well, I can't help you much on that one. It just sounds like the kind of thing you could make funny."

Brooklyn patted her on the shoulder, all traces of conceit vanishing. Now she seemed kind and friendly, her usual manner. "The idea's the hard part. I'll see if I can come up with something.

Brooklyn settled more deeply into the sectional and started going through her various newspapers and magazines, sticking notecards into the articles she wanted to make sure to read. Kerri mentioned almost casually, "Almost everything you're saving is on the internet."

"That's what they tell me," Brooklyn said, giving her a half smile. "I like it this way."

"No problem. But for when you're traveling you might want to use that app I put on your phone. It lets you save articles on your computer and read them later on your phone. You also might be able to download some podcasts from sources you wouldn't otherwise see."

"What is this…podcast?" she asked, in the comically bad Russian accent she often used when she was unaware of something. "I hear people talk about it, but it's over my head."

Kerri sat down at the computer and showed her the remarkably long list of news and current events from which to choose. It was obvious that Brooklyn would lose herself in the abundance of choices, but Kerri couldn't stand to sit still one moment longer. She'd been stuck in the loft for two hours, doing basically nothing, and that was too much. So she got up and started searching. It took some time, but she found all of the cleaning supplies Brooklyn owned. There wasn't much—just enough to dust the whole place thoroughly. Then she got the vacuum from a well-designed hiding place in the spacious kitchen and started to clean all of the wood floors. Brooklyn didn't move. It honestly didn't look like she'd done more than breathe, much less notice that Kerri was making a very loud racket.

Brooklyn spent a solid hour choosing podcasts she might like, and by the time she was done downloading just the most recent episodes of each, she had thirty hours of listening to get through.

"You might want to edit that a little bit," Kerri teased, having put the vacuum and the cleaning supplies away without comment. "You'll find some of them aren't worth your time. But some definitely are."

"If I'd had something like this when I was younger, I would have been a very happy kid. I was always curious, but I didn't really have a way to satisfy my curiosity. I just daydreamed."

"Did you do well in school?"

Brooklyn made a face. "Yeah, after I got off to a bad start. First grade was the worst."

"How do you get off to a bad start in first grade?"

"I missed so many days they made me repeat. The other kids teased me for being stupid."

"Oh, wow. Were you sickly?"

She looked truly puzzled. "I don't remember being sick, but I was always tired. It was hell on my parents getting me up in the morning. Maybe I was a bad sleeper even then." A sunny smile appeared. "I've done pretty well for myself after flunking first grade. I hope the little jerks who made fun of me recognize me when I'm pontificating about something or other on TV."

"Pontificating?"

Brooklyn blanched. "Bad choice of words. I meant being dogmatic."

"Dogmatic? I have a vague idea of what that means—"

Now Brooklyn looked like she wanted to swallow her words. "Pompous!"

Kerri couldn't help it. She reached over and gently squeezed Brooklyn's leg. "Don't feel bad when you use words I don't know. I ask about them because I like to learn things."

"But...most people get offended when I use uncommon words."

"I'm not one of them. You don't use them to make other people feel stupid, do you?"

"No!" Her eyes nearly popped from her head. "I read a lot and words just creep into my head..."

Kerri squeezed her leg again. "I was kidding. I don't have a fantastic vocabulary, but I like words. Now, what does pontificating mean?"

"It's when someone talks as though they were the pope. He's the pontiff."

Kerri nodded slowly. "I like that. Pontificating." She took her iPhone and made a note. "I'll try to use it."

Smiling, Brooklyn said, "It's not usually a compliment."

"Got it. I'll use it when I want to insult someone. Especially if I think they won't know what it means."

CHAPTER FIVE

KAT COULD WELL HAVE kept her notes on napkins, carry-out menus or receipts from the deli, but she didn't make them on the computer she'd abandoned in the spare bedroom. Given that Brooklyn knew absolutely nothing about her own schedule, Kerri either had to call Kat and beg for information or re-create it. Without wasting a moment pondering the best course of action, she called Melvin and spent almost an hour with both him and his secretary, logging every date he'd booked. When they were finished, the calendar was filled in for the next four months, and Kerri was beaming with pride from a job well done.

Next she called the radio station and eventually got connected to the VP in charge of programming. His secretary confirmed all of the dark days for *Reveille*, including vacations. Now all she had to add were Brooklyn's personal notes, and those would be tougher to find, since Brooklyn was the last person who knew her own commitments.

On Thursday morning, Kerri was waiting for Brooklyn right outside the front door of the radio station. Oddly, she had her bicycle with her. Brooklyn walked out of the building, shaking her head and laughing. "Don't tell me you rode that bike all this way."

"I didn't have time to get any exercise this morning, and I hate to take a long flight if I haven't at least gotten my heart rate up for a while."

"That's where fear of flying can help." She clutched her heart dramatically. "I used to be petrified. My heart rate was up for two days before a flight."

"Okay, how about this? Riding my bike saved me from having to take the subway, then a PATH train, then a New Jersey Transit bus."

"Much better. Are you planning on taking it to Los Angeles?"

Chuckling, Kerri said, "I'm too cheap to pay to check it. I thought I'd just leave it here. I can chain it up in the parking garage."

"This is one thing I can take care of." They walked down the ramp to the garage, where Terry greeted them.

"Your trunk is big enough for this bike, isn't it?" Brooklyn asked.

"I've got room for the bike and both of you."

"I'd really appreciate if you could swing by my apartment at some point this weekend and drop the bike off. I'll give you my key."

"I'm happy to do it. You just have to promise to bring me some of that Los Angeles sun."

"I'll do my best, but the weather might be out of my control."

—⁓—

They'd been in the car just a few minutes when Brooklyn's phone rang. "My mom," she said before answering. She was on the phone until they reached the airport, and when she hung up she said, "My daily review."

"Huh?"

"My mom calls after the show to tell me how great I did."

"Every day?"

"Yep. She listens at work. Given how closely she listens, I'm surprised they haven't fired her." She chuckled, then checked her phone for any other messages.

Kerri sat there thinking about how it would feel to have her mother call her every day to talk about her job performance. The mere thought made her skin crawl. Being close to your mom was nice, but there was close…and there was too close.

—⁓—

They'd gotten lucky and were upgraded to first class from business, giving Brooklyn a seat that reclined horizontally. They'd been in the air about an hour when she looked at Kerri gravely and said, "I know I'm going to have to screw up my sleep schedule this weekend, but I hate to think of losing the little progress we've made. What should I do?"

She looked so sincere and genuinely troubled that it took Kerri back. She'd never, ever worked with a celebrity who seemed to believe that her own actions played a part in the results she got. Her heart clenched in sympathy for Brooklyn's dilemma. Being tired much of the week was no fun, and when your job required mental sharpness, being tired was made worse by the stress of worrying about your performance. Still, in reality they'd made very little progress. "How late do you think you'll be up tonight?"

"I'm going to swing by the Comedy Crib to work on a few things. The manager told me to come by around nine."

Teaching Brooklyn about schedules was going to take some time. "When you need to do something like that you need to tell your road manager. We can't keep things in control if we don't know about them." She reached over and squeezed Brooklyn's arm. Despite being skittish about close contact, she seemed to accept mild criticism better when it was mixed with a gentle touch.

"You're right. Even though he said to come at nine, I'll never get on that early. I'll be lucky to be finished by eleven."

"Do you think you'll go right home afterward?"

Brooklyn revealed a little of her dashing grin. "That depends on how good I want to be."

Kerri was powerless not to return that smile. It was almost intoxicating. Brooklyn could have women dangling from each limb if she wanted it, but if she wanted it frequently she was hiding it well. Unless, of course, she'd been having sex with Kat. Kerri would have to probe a bit to find out what that relationship entailed. "Well, let's come up with some different scenarios. The earliest you can get to bed is midnight, which is four hours later than optimal. To counteract that you could take a long nap now. Remember, your first radio interview is at seven."

The smile was gone. "I forgot about those damned radio interviews. I hate them with a passion."

"The publicist for the venue is going to pick us up at five thirty a.m." The tension that immediately settled on Brooklyn's face made it hard not to feel sympathy for her. Because she required more sleep than the average person, she had a bad constitution for an early morning show And not getting enough sleep made her slow-witted and less than funny. But this was the hand she'd dealt herself and they'd have to make do. "Is it common for just the publicist from the venue to shepherd you around? No one on your side to make sure things go your way?"

"What's my way?"

Brooklyn looked deadly serious, and a little perplexed. How had she gotten as famous as she was without feeling the world revolved around her? Most people were led around by their manager, their own publicist, their own hair and makeup person...the list could easily go on. The manager should have had several conversations with the radio station producer to make sure the DJ asked questions that portrayed her in the best light. But Brooklyn acted like a consultant who was scheduled to show up at a new office in the morning. No big deal.

"I'll come by at five to help you wake up. Just sleep when you're tired this weekend. That's all you can do."

"That's right now."

"I'll wake you a half hour before we land, okay?"

"Done deal."

Brooklyn closed the shade and reclined her seat. In fewer than five minutes she was sound asleep, her face, in repose, touchingly innocent. Kerri gently covered her with a blanket, then asked the flight attendant not to disturb them, even for meals. Although she was hungry, she didn't want the smell of her lunch to rouse Brooklyn. But she was prepared. She'd brought a number of high energy snacks with her, and they satisfied her hunger in a fashion only a few rungs below a first class airline meal.

—⁓—

Brooklyn slept for four hours. When she started to shift and move around in her seat, Kerri softly called her name. From the way her eyes darted around it was clear she was disoriented.

"What... Oh. Hi. Are we there?"

"Not quite. I hated to wake you up, but you looked like you were at the end of a sleep cycle. I find it much easier to wake up and feel alert if I can time it right."

Brooklyn raised her seat, and shifted her shoulders around. Surprisingly, her smile was remarkably sunny, very much in contrast to her usual waking demeanor. "I feel pretty good. Now all I need is someone to wake me up at a certain time, and someone else to watch me while I sleep to make sure I'm at the end of a cycle. I don't know how poor people afford this."

She showed the self-mocking smile that Kerri had grown fond of. It was nice, though rare, when a wealthy person reminded herself of how good her worst days were.

―⁂―

By the time they got a rental car and Brooklyn checked into her hotel, it was five p.m. "It's awfully early for dinner," Brooklyn said. "Maybe I should take you over to your apartment."

"Oh, don't worry about me. It's easy to get to my place on a bus from Westwood. I think I'll go home and check on the old homestead, then I can meet you back at the Comedy Crib at nine. It's on Sunset, right?"

That was a pretty clear sign that she didn't want to hang out. Maybe she wanted to simply do the work things and keep her distance. But being in a strange city for the whole weekend sucked. Hanging out with Kerri would sure beat sitting in a hotel room, hoping for something wonderful on TV. It couldn't hurt to drop a hint or two. "I thought I might go over to the ocean and walk around. Can I drop you off if I'm going to Santa Monica anyway?"

"Sure. I don't have an unnatural fixation for public transportation, it's just easier for me than owning a car."

"You don't own a car? At all?"

"Not at all. I've actually never owned one."

"You live in Los Angeles, and you don't own a car."

"I'm a third-generation Angeleno, so I should know better. But my parents make up for it. Together, they have three."

That was more than quirky. Maybe she had epilepsy or something. There had to be a compelling reason to never drive when you lived in LA. Unless you had a limo, which didn't seem likely.

—◇—

Traffic leaving LAX was horrid as usual. Brooklyn propped her left knee up and rested her elbow on it as they crept along. "Tell me about being a third generation Angeleno. Was it weird growing up in LA?"

"No, why would it be weird? It's just a city."

"Not really. It's…I'm not sure what it is, but it seems more like a big movie set than a hometown."

Kerri laughed. "Maybe it's not typical, but it seemed normal to me. My parents both worked in the business, but I grew up in the Valley in a very middle-class neighborhood."

"There are middle-class neighborhoods? I've only seen wealthy and poor."

"Go to the Valley. There were definitely no movie stars or billionaires in our orbit, but we weren't poor. Having my parents work for a studio was like being in any industry town. Aerospace, mining, whatever. It seems normal if that's what you grow up with."

"Does it seem normal now?"

"Yes," she said, looking thoughtful. "But people act like it's very odd, so it must be, at least a little."

Maybe growing up that way made her a little quirky. No matter what she said, having your world revolve around movies had to be strange.

"What do your parents do?"

"They're both artists."

"Really? That's cool."

"Yeah, that part really is. It's nice to live in a town where you can make a living as a commercial artist. My mom drew cartoons for Warner

109

Brothers, and now my dad does special effects for films. He's working on a blockbuster for Pixar right now. He said he's been putting in sixty-hour workweeks."

"Wow, that's tough. How old are they?"

Kerri gave her a puzzled look.

"I just asked because you said your grandfather is in his nineties. I figured…"

She reached over and stroked Brooklyn's arm. The way she touched people unconsciously was very LA. It wasn't unpleasant, but it was really taking some time to get used to it. She hoped Kerri hadn't noticed.

"I'm not offended. My mom's sixty-two and my dad's seventy."

"And he's still working?"

"Yeah," she said looking proud. "He's a technical wizard and he'll work until he can't do it any more. I like that he does something that really gets his creative side engaged."

"My dad hangs wallpaper," Brooklyn said. "He's such a perfectionist, it's a good job for him. I wonder if he feels creative when he works?"

"Probably. At least a little. Anything you do well can stoke your creativity."

"I guess that's true. I wish I could feel more creative on *Reveille*. Right now it's just punching the clock."

They went up Wilshire Boulevard, and when they were near the ocean, Kerri said, "Turn right at the next block."

The turn brought them onto a street of smallish bungalows, notable for not having been mansionized the way so many homes on the West side of LA had been. This actually looked like a neighborhood a normal person could afford.

"Do you own a house?"

"Oh, no." She laughed as though that were a ridiculous concept. "You can stop right here." She put her hand on the door opener and started to get out, but her politeness must have prevailed because she said, "Do you have anything to do?"

Brooklyn knew it was a low blow, but she threw it anyway. Kerri didn't seem like the kind of person who could be guilt-tripped into doing something she didn't want to do, so it didn't seem too underhanded. "No. I thought I'd just wander around for a while and then stop and get a couple of hamburgers or some tacos on my way to the club. There's every kind of junk food in existence right on Santa Monica Boulevard. Maybe I'll stop and have a drink or two also."

Kerri's expression was troubled and Brooklyn almost felt bad for manipulating her.

"Why don't you park and come in with me? I just need to spend a few minutes here. Then we can go for a walk and have a nice dinner. I know a good place not far from the Comedy Crib."

Trying to look innocent, Brooklyn said, "Are you sure? If you want to spend some time alone, I totally understand."

Kerri smiled at her. "I get a lot of alone time. It'll be nice to have some company."

Sweet!

They both got out of the car and walked down a narrow sidewalk between two bungalows. Hidden behind the one on the right was a small two-story apartment building sitting on what was probably once the back yard. As they climbed the stairs, Brooklyn saw that there were two apartments on both the first and second floors. Kerri took out her key and jiggled it into a cheap-looking lock in a veneered door that Brooklyn could have kicked in without much effort. When Kerri opened it, they entered a room that looked to Brooklyn like a brightly-colored monk's cell. Everything, including the kitchen cabinets, was painted either bright blue or a bright shade of green. The living room contained a futon with a tropical print cover, and a wooden rocking chair. Some photos, probably taken from Kerri's travels, were simply framed and hung on the walls. A wooden table, painted blue, sat between the chair and the futon and was the only other thing in the room. There was no TV, no stereo, no books, no cabinets or anything that might hold the stuff most people accumulated. The room wasn't particularly large, but it was so sparsely furnished it seemed spacious.

The place smelled dusty and stale, like damp old plywood. Kerri went to a sliding glass door at the front of the building and tried her best to get it to open. "These two dollar aluminum doors were not meant for buildings only fifteen blocks from the ocean." She gave it a real good yank, and it started to open slowly and noisily.

Brooklyn wasn't sure what to say. She had no idea if Kerri just couldn't afford the things most people surrounded themselves with, or if she didn't want them. So she went with, "I like the minimalist look."

Kerri grinned at her. "I can tell that from your apartment. You don't have a lot of things sitting around."

"Is this a one bedroom?"

"Yeah. The bedroom's right there." She pointed. "Take a look around. I'm going to go see if my neighbor's home. She takes my mail in for me." Kerri left and Brooklyn walked into the bedroom, which was almost as barren as the main room. The only difference was a wooden dresser with the drawers painted alternating stripes of blue and green, and a few extra-colorful pillows on the bed. But there was a good-sized double window over the bed, which, even though it faced the alley and the back of the buildings across from it, gave the room a nice warm glow. The bathroom was tiny, and the fixtures were original, probably early sixties. Brooklyn indulged her natural nosiness by opening the closet door in the hallway. Kerri was clearly a woman who didn't like to have a lot of possessions. The only thing in the closet was an extra set of sheets and a couple of bath towels. When Brooklyn heard the front screen door creak, she walked briskly back into the living room.

Kerri dumped two shopping bags full of mail onto the futon and started going through it. "If you just give me a few minutes, I promise this won't take long."

"Is that all just from a couple of weeks?"

"No," Kerri said absently, flipping through the envelopes and flyers. "I was in the Balkans for almost four months before I went to New York. I got to stop in LA for two days, but I went straight to see my grandfather and stayed in the Valley rather than waste time coming over here."

"Tough schedule. Is that common for you?"

She grinned, teasingly. "That was my first time in the Balkans, so it was pretty unusual. I was working with an actor who was shooting on location. As soon as that wrapped, I was going to come home. But your job came up...and that leads to this kind of junk piling up." She finished going through the pile remarkably quickly, saving only two items. "What a waste of money." She started shoving all of the trash back into the bags. "I'll put this in my neighbor's recycling bin on the way out. Then I won't have to leave mine out against Santa Monica regulations," she added in official-sounding voice.

"How do you pay your bills?" Brooklyn asked, still perplexed.

"I do everything on-line. It's much easier than writing checks."

Brooklyn stood up, feeling uneasy. Maybe she had pushed herself too strongly into Kerri's personal time. "Is that really all you're going to do here?" Being gone for months at a time seemed to demand a longer visit.

"Yeah." Kerri stood up and put the two pieces of mail she was saving into her backpack and slung it over her shoulder. "I just wanted to get this done today in case I don't sleep here tonight and I can't get back here tomorrow."

"Where do you plan on sleeping?" Brooklyn asked, giving her an intentionally naughty look.

"One never knows. I'm ready for anything."

—∾∾—

They sat at a Japanese restaurant just a few blocks from the club where Brooklyn was going to work out some new material. Kerri had ordered for them, choosing things that would fill Brooklyn up but wouldn't sit heavily in her stomach while she worked.

"So," Brooklyn said, pointing her chopsticks at Kerri. "I used my sharp powers of observation to see that you don't have a girlfriend."

Kerri took a bite of food, not replying for a few moments. "Not true. You just know I don't have a girlfriend I live with...in that apartment."

"Huh. I guess that's true." After a moment's pause, she said, "Do I have to ask you outright? Are you single?"

"Yeah, I'm single. Are you?"

"If I'm not, I'm hiding my girlfriend pretty darned well."

"You might not live with her. I know a lot of people who don't live together. It's getting to be a trend."

Brooklyn shook her head. "That wouldn't be my kind of trend. I like to live with a girlfriend. You don't?"

"Not any more. I had a very serious girlfriend for a few years. Actually, she had the apartment I live in, and I was able to get on the lease when we became domestic partners. That's why I've got such a nice place for such a sweet price."

"How sweet?"

"Less than the payment on a nice car. Not bad for walking distance to the beach."

"That's not bad at all. What happened to the girlfriend?"

Kerri waved her hand dismissively. "She would say it was because she wanted to move to New York to be an actress and that I didn't want to move. In reality, there were a lot of things we struggled with. I think that's true for most relationships."

"No one since?"

"What exactly are you asking?" She raised an eyebrow, hoping Brooklyn could tell she was teasing.

"Anything you're willing to tell me. It's like pulling teeth to get anything out of you."

Kerri decided she'd better loosen up. Clients didn't like to feel they were being excluded. "I've never lived with another lover. I travel too much to be able to make that kind of thing work." That should be enough to satisfy her. And it wasn't very far from the whole truth.

"Really? It's been two years since I've had a girlfriend, and I'd jump back in the first chance I get."

It was time to find out about the incident Brooklyn would probably rather forget. Acting as her road manager meant Kerri had to be prepared for anything. There would be no DUIs on her watch. "You weren't looking for a girlfriend down in Atlanta, were you?"

Blanching, Brooklyn shook her head, looking disgusted. "Hardly." She waved her chopsticks in the air, then jabbed them as if she was dotting an *I*. "I will never do anything that stupid again."

Kerri loved seeing her like this. Self aware and willing to accept responsibility for her actions.

"I swear to God the girl seemed smart and pretty mature when we were talking. But she was only nineteen and that's stupid young."

"So you're looking for a girlfriend, but willing to pick up a bedwarmer?"

"Mmm, not often." Her gaze shifted to her plate and it looked like she might not continue. A few moments later her gaze met Kerri's. "I get lonely. I miss having a lover and once in a while I take what I can get."

"Aww. That makes me sad. I hate to think of you hooking up with some stranger just because you're lonely."

A trace of her cocky self appeared. "That's not the *only* reason..."

"I thought as much. You probably have women throwing themselves at you."

"Once in a while. But, like I said, I'd rather have a girlfriend. Not you, huh?"

"No, not me. It's nice not having to consider anyone else's needs when I decide whether to take a job or not. And most women aren't fond of you spending twenty-four hours a day with a glamourous actress— even if she is a drug addict you can hardly bear to be around."

Looking slightly sad, Brooklyn said, "I hope you don't feel that way about me."

Once again, Brooklyn's soulful eyes made Kerri's breath catch in her throat. "No!" She found her hand covering Brooklyn's, which felt surprisingly good in hers. Her skin was amazingly soft. "Not at all. You're head and shoulders above almost all of my clients."

Brooklyn let out an audible breath. "That's a relief. My parents would be ashamed of me if I acted so badly that people didn't want to be around me."

"Then you should thank them sincerely. I can't tell you how badly some people behave."

"I've met a lot of them. Unfortunately."

It was clear she wasn't a diva, and she was pretty and bright. Having a load of money didn't hurt her prospects either. What kept her alone? "How did you wind up single?"

"We had our share of problems, but the big one turned out to be that Ashley couldn't get used to my schedule."

"You can't either," Kerri teased.

"I didn't have the radio show, so it was much easier then than it is now. But she worked on the weekends and couldn't travel with me. She didn't like that."

"Did she want to be with you more, or just not want you to be gone so much?"

Brooklyn shrugged her shoulders and gave the look that said she didn't want to explain any further. "Maybe she thought I was fooling around on the road. She wasn't very trusting."

Given the incident in Atlanta, Brooklyn's girlfriend was probably wise to want to keep an eye on her. "How long were you together?"

"Seven years. When we first got together, I was really struggling in my career, but our relationship was great. As things got better professionally, the relationship turned sour."

"You could always have been less successful."

Brooklyn's grin was sad, but still looked pretty charming. "That wasn't in the cards. I didn't work as hard as I did to play Hoboken for two hundred bucks a night."

"You'll get back in the game. From what I've seen, you're a really good catch." That was the truth. Brooklyn was the least neurotic, least demanding, least immature celebrity she'd ever worked with. That wasn't saying a *whole* lot, but still…she couldn't be looking hard if she'd been alone for two years. Something else was keeping her single, even if she didn't realize it.

—⁓—

The Comedy Crib was only half-full when Brooklyn took the stage that night. It seemed like the crowd knew her, but they didn't know her well. Early on a Thursday night the audience was made up of mostly couples, and they seemed quite well behaved and ready to laugh if the comedian was decent.

Kerri was sitting at a table close to the stage allowing her to watch Brooklyn very closely. She had a certain energy about her, but it wasn't substantially more than she displayed when she was at home. That seemed odd for an entertainer, but Brooklyn definitely had a relatively laconic style at home and she must have needed an excited crowd to amp it up.

She started off explaining that she was considered a cerebral comedian. Kerri hoped that the audience was equally cerebral, because they certainly weren't laughing. Maybe they were studiously considering the jokes for a later burst of laughter—or a test.

Brooklyn's delivery didn't get any more enthusiastic or engaging. She actually seemed as though she didn't care if the audience liked her or not. She told a fairly long, strangely involved story about the president of Russia. Carrie was quite sure she wouldn't know the president of Russia if he bit her, and the crowd seemed to be in the same boat. Nonetheless, Brooklyn got a pretty good laugh when she twisted the story around and started impersonating him. Her Russian accent was so awful that it was funny on its own, and by the time the laughter died down, she waved at the crowd and loped off the stage.

Kerri snuck away from her table and met Brooklyn at the bar at the back of the room. "How do you think it went?" Brooklyn asked.

"Well…" It was always uncomfortable when your client asked you for feedback. Entertainers had a massive need for reassurance. There was almost nothing you could say that would satisfy them even if you loved their performance. "I'm not a good judge of audiences, so I'm interested in what you thought."

The manager of the club walked over, and he and Brooklyn exchanged the type of hug that men gave each other—a half hug/ half back slap. "That went pretty good," the man said. He must have realized Kerri was with Brooklyn because he stuck his hand out and said, "David French."

"Forgive my bad manners," Brooklyn said. "This is my friend Kerri Klein. Kerri was just trying to not tell me what she thought of my set."

Laughing, David said, "You're a smart woman. Don't ever tell a comic what you thought about their act. Nobody has thinner skin."

"He has a point," Brooklyn said.

"I've got to get backstage." David caught the bartender's glance and said, "Buy these ladies a drink, Kevin." He hit Brooklyn hard on the back again and took off.

"Do you want a drink, or do you want to go home?"

"I can stay up if you'd like to, but I don't need a drink," Kerri said.

Brooklyn gave a quick wave to the bartender, catching his eye before she dropped a twenty. Then they headed for the street, where they'd left the car. "I think it went pretty well," Brooklyn said. "I've been trying to find a good tag for that bit about the Russians. I'm not there yet, but I'll get it."

It seemed like she was a long way from success, but Kerri wasn't going to point that out. "I told you I don't have any idea how you work through a joke. Is there a formula?"

They approached the car and Brooklyn popped the locks. It took her a minute to get in and get her seatbelt on, and Kerri could tell she was thinking of her answer.

"I can't talk for anybody else, but I tend to work on one or two jokes at a time. I try them out until I'm happy with them, and that can take forever if I'm not lucky. Sometimes I'll have the whole setup, but I can't get the tag right. Sometimes I'll know the tag but the setup's too balky. You just never know."

"That's fascinating. You really only work on a joke or two at once?"

"Sometimes more. It depends. But it always takes a long time to get a new hour together."

"A whole hour? Why so long?"

"Headliners have to do an hour. An hour and a half is better. Comedy has changed in the last few years. Heck, in the old days some people would do the same act for ten years. I don't know how they got away with it, but it wasn't uncommon."

"I can recall seeing some people on TV, and it seemed like they did the same jokes every time."

"Yeah, yeah. You can't do that anymore if you want to headline. I try to put a couple of new bits in every month, to keep it current. Still, I'll have to have a mostly new act by September. If I want people to come see me every year, I've gotta have a new frame to hang current events on."

"All new?"

"That'd be nice, but I can keep some of the old stuff if I need to. Just not a lot. People get mad." She laughed. "Of course, some people get mad if you don't do their favorite bit every time they see you. You can't please everyone."

"I'm sorry you can't see this from my perspective. It's fun for me," Kerri said. "It's really enjoyable to be around someone who does something a little different."

"Maybe that can be your new goal. Next you can babysit a plumber, then a chiropractor, then a Tibetan monk…"

CHAPTER SIX

THE EARLY FRIDAY MORNING radio interviews were thin slices of what hell must have been like. The hosts were unusually ill-mannered and their main purpose was to make people laugh at other people's expense. There was nothing about them that Kerri found interesting, but she forced herself to pay attention as she sat in the green room with the publicist from the theater Brooklyn was performing at the next night.

They were finished by nine, and were both exhausted. Tedium, even when broadcast to hundreds of thousands of people, had a way of wearing one out. Brooklyn only had an appearance on a local TV show the next morning, so they had all of Friday to kill.

"I could use another breakfast," Kerri said, feeling slightly grumpy. She'd only gotten a few hours of sleep since the time change had messed her up, and having to listen to Brooklyn waste her time and energy with the morons on the radio shows had irked her.

"I could use a first. I can't eat much first thing in the morning, so I usually just have my latte. Now I'm starving. Where would you like to go?"

"Well, it's awfully nice out. Let's go to a place by the beach."

They started off from Culver City, the location of the last of their radio interviews. "How do you feel about doing those interviews?" Kerri asked, hoping to sound neutral.

"If they weren't standard in my contract, you couldn't pay me enough. I don't think they draw one more customer. In fact, I think they repel people." Brooklyn was driving, but she slumped down in her seat as though she were about to nod off. "They suck hard."

"But you have to do them?"

"Oh, yeah. If there's one empty seat in the venue, I've gotta show up and try to sell it. I've had to talk to every bad boy DJ in the US, each one trying to be just a little more outrageous than the last. If only one of them tried to be different by knowing something about me or asking an insightful question, I'd wet my pants. But it's always snarky things about my being a lesbian or what it's like to work with Arnie. And half of the time they get my plug wrong."

"I've never been on a radio publicity tour, but I've tagged along on those horrible Q and A sessions for a big movie. The stars sit in a room in a hotel and movie reviewers come in every fifteen minutes. They last all day, and by the end of the day I actually feel sorry for the people making thirty-five million dollars. I mean, I know it's a lot of money, but it's grindingly tedious."

Brooklyn shot her a sly smile. "I might be able to tolerate it for thirty-five mil. Let's face it, people don't fight and claw to stay in show business because it's a bad way to make a living. I've got no right to bitch."

"No, you don't, but being treated badly sucks no matter how much you make. Just because you have money doesn't mean you have to tolerate everything thrown your way."

Brooklyn didn't say a word, but she gave Kerri such a warm, appreciative glance that it make her heart skip a beat. This woman had a big heart and a gentle soul. There was no way on earth she was voluntarily single. No way!

They went to a well-known café in Venice, just off the boardwalk. It had been a long time since Brooklyn had been to the boardwalk, and as they waited for their food she raptly watched the passersby. "I think I could get used to living in LA." Her lopsided grin was surprisingly sunny, given the time of day. "After the cold weather we've had recently, I might be able to get used to living in Somalia."

"It has been unseasonably cold this fall, but I don't expect a bad winter."

"So cute. So very cute and very naive. Keep your guard up." She looked out at the expanse of sand, thinking about how nice it would be when it was summer again in New York.

"I was thinking about some of the questions they asked you this morning," Kerri said, startling Brooklyn from her reverie. "And I noticed that they didn't seem to understand your current act."

Brooklyn took a sip of her latte and forced herself to ignore a man walking down the boardwalk with a huge green parrot on his shoulder. "They don't. They think all comedians are alike, but we run the gamut from old-school guys who set up a joke and a punchline without any real through-story to people who take on an entirely new identity."

"You certainly don't do that. You seem like a slightly bigger version of yourself on stage."

"That's about how I see myself. I started out just wanting to tell jokes, but that got old for me pretty fast. When that happened I started being more political, showing more of myself and my views on stage."

"I'm still amazed at how young you were when you started."

Laughing, Brooklyn nodded. "I was too young to know how hard it was going to be. I had to play open mic nights for over a year. Those were brutal, but I kept at it and eventually got to play some of the sleazy 'bring 'em in' clubs."

"I'm afraid to ask…"

"It's nothing shady. You get to be on stage the same number of minutes as the people you bring in. And, trust me, you can't convince many people to come more than once. I had just my mom and dad in the audience a few times, and doing the same two minutes for your parents isn't anyone's dream. I can't imagine how they must've hated it, but they were very supportive."

"From the start? I've heard most comics say their parents tried to talk them out of starting in the business."

"Yeah, they were great at the start. It was when it became clear I wasn't going to go back to college or get a real job that my dad got upset."

"I didn't know you went to college."

She grinned mischievously. "I went to college, but my first open mic was during orientation week. I quit after going to each class once."

"Once?"

"I wanted to give it a fair try."

"Your parents must have been thrilled with that!"

Giggling for a second, Brooklyn shook her head. "They weren't out any money, so my dad didn't take it too badly. He thought I was a dunce for quitting, but he thought I'd go back once I failed." She tried to hold back a little to not make it obvious how pleased she was with her success.

"So you lived at home and worked open mic nights?"

"Except for the lived at home part, that's correct. My mom would have let me live there forever, but my dad said his house was for students. I had to be good at comedy—or starve."

"Tough love."

"It was good for me. Very good. When I started making more money than he did, he thought it was a great idea to be in show business." It had been almost twenty years, and it was still sweet to think about. He'd almost swallowed his teeth when she'd shown him the 1099 form from a gig she'd done at a good-sized club in New York. Yep. It was still very sweet.

————

After breakfast it was still early, but Brooklyn could feel herself winding down. "I'd like to sleep all day, but I know that's not a good idea. Do you have any ideas on what I can do to stay awake for..." She looked at her oversized watch. "Twelve hours?"

"Well, I'm sure this isn't what you had in mind, but I was going to rent a car to go see my grandfather. I guarantee you won't be able to sleep over there, but that's all I can promise. I never know how his mood will be."

Kerri didn't seem her usual confident self. Actually, she seemed nervous. Maybe she needed some backup. Why not? Kerri was always doing the heavy lifting. "I'm up for it. If he doesn't want visitors, I'll go to a movie."

Kerri looked almost relieved to have company. "Great. He's almost always happy to see people. It's just hard when he doesn't recognize me. But I've learned how to suck it up and just be with him."

"Sometimes he doesn't recognize you?"

A pained look flitted across her features. "Not often, but yeah, that's happened. He still likes to have young women around, so don't be offended if he flirts with you."

"Does he ever flirt with you?"

Kerri blinked, then shook her head. "Not really. But he's gotten fresh with my mom a few times." She rubbed her eyes quickly. "It's only going to get worse, so I try to find something positive about the visit that I can hold onto and cherish."

"That sounds very mature, but I bet it's not as easy as it sounds."

"No, but a lot of things are hard. My grandfather is a wonderful man. That hasn't changed because his brain isn't working well. I just try to go with the flow and let him be who he is. I'm sure I was tough to deal with when I was a baby. Now it's his turn."

That was a darned nice sentiment, but who could actually do that?

⁓

Traffic was heavy on the 405, and they crawled along behind a huge eighteen-wheeler, breathing in his exhaust. Brooklyn fiddled with the unfamiliar dashboard dials, finally finding the one that shut out fresh air.

"I've been thinking about what you said earlier, about starting off as a comic," Kerri said. "When did you first think you wanted to be a pro?"

"I was young," Brooklyn said. "Really young. When someone I liked was going to be on TV, I'd tape them and then sit there and transcribe their act. Then I'd sit in my room and work on it until I could impersonate them. I wish I had footage of myself at ten or eleven years old trying to sound exactly like Chris Rock." She laughed, her eyes crinkling up in pleasure at the memory. "I had his CD *Born Suspect* memorized and could hit every beat."

"That's adorable! Did you do your act for your family?"

"No, not at all. I was more secretive about it than I was about liking girls. I told no one."

"I find this fascinating," Kerri said. "Most artists I know had a vision for their future that most of the rest of us don't have."

"I've never seriously considered doing anything else. If I couldn't get on a stage and grab an audience by the throat…well, I don't know how I'd manage."

"You make it sound kind of violent."

"It is," Brooklyn agreed. "We kill, we slaughter 'em, we murder the audience. Most of the terms we use are pretty harsh." She flashed that sexy grin. "I don't even want to know what's behind that."

Damn, that grin was lethal. Something about the way her confidence shot up when she talked about her work made her attractiveness shoot up. And it was awfully high to begin with. Sometimes almost too high to resist. It was getting harder for Kerri to keep saying "no" to her urges.

They were rolling along the 210 and Brooklyn opened the sunroof, taking in a deep breath. "I can see why they call this place Sunland. The sun seems brighter up here."

"It's bright everywhere in the Valley. That's why I like Santa Monica. I prefer the fog and the cool evenings. Oh! Get off at the next exit. I almost forgot something."

Brooklyn followed a series of directions and they eventually arrived in front of a small bakery. Kerri dashed inside, and returned a few minutes later with a big white box tied closed with string. "I got a few cookies for you. You and my grandfather should get along well since you share almost exactly the same appetites."

Brooklyn smiled at her. "Well, you said he still likes the ladies. God knows that's one of my weaknesses."

Kerri regarded her as they pulled out into the light traffic. That was all talk, very little action from what she had seen. Brooklyn was either hiding something important, or woefully unaware of a fatal flaw. Maybe both.

———

They reached a nice looking ranch-style house with a view across a canyon. When they got out, Kerri stood right next to the car and spent a little time breathing deeply. She had her eyes closed, and Brooklyn felt she was invading her space even to look at her, so she moved away from the car and looked across the dry, scrubby canyon. Seeing her grandfather must take a real chunk out of her. Poor thing. But how do you help someone get through something painful? Talk about it, or just be there?

She was so intent in her musings that, when Kerri came up behind her and touched her back, she jumped. "Whoa! I was just standing here trying to imagine what lives out there."

"Lots of things, but nothing very big or dangerous. Unless you're a house pet, that is. Lots of dogs and cats go out and don't return. Luckily, it's a state park, so my mom will always have a nice uncluttered view."

"It's hard to believe this and New Jersey are in the same country."

"I haven't spent much time in New Jersey. Actually, I don't think I've spent any time in New Jersey."

"We'll have to fix that. Are you ready?" She looked far from ready. Kerri was actually a little pale, and she didn't have a whiff of her usual confident, calm demeanor.

"Yeah. Let's go."

Brooklyn's stomach started to hurt on the short walk. She'd never been around a person with Alzheimer's and seeing Kerri so nervous was contagious. When they got to the door, there was a note that read, "Hi, honey. I hope you don't mind, but I ran out to get my haircut this morning. Rosalie is here, but her English isn't very good. I'll be back soon. Love, Mom." Next to the writing was a very cute drawing of a hedgehog with her hair so long it flopped down over her eyes.

Kerri pulled the note from the door, folded it neatly and stuck it into her pocket. "Whenever she knows anyone else can take over, she heads for the hills. Not that I blame her. She really needs more breaks than she gets."

Kerri put her hand on the door knob, and as she turned it, Brooklyn felt her stomach knot more tightly. She knew they were only going to see an old man with an addled brain, but she would have run back to the car if she wasn't determined to be there for Kerri. They walked inside with Kerri calling out, "Grandpa? Rosalie?"

A woman came out into the entryway and said, "Kerri?"

Looking much more confident, Kerri walked over to her and shook her hand. "Yes, that's me." She pointed at Brooklyn. "This is my friend."

Rosalie smiled and nodded and pointed towards the backyard. "Mr. Klein," she said and disappeared whence she had come. Kerri took in a visible breath, her shoulders rising and falling before she strode directly for the backyard. They walked through a large, sliding door, and approached a small, surprisingly dark-haired man who was lying on a chaise by the pool. His eyes were closed, but it wasn't clear if he was awake or sleeping. It was a warm day, over eighty degrees, but he was wearing a plaid flannel shirt with a cardigan sweater over it, a pair of khaki slacks, argyle socks and soft looking suede shoes. His hair didn't look dyed, which was rather stunning, given his age. Most striking was how amazingly well taken care of he was, as his smoothly shaved cheeks attested.

Kerri's expression so clearly showed her anxiety that Brooklyn's nerves got more jangled. She was about to suggest they dash back to the car, but Kerri sat down on the edge of the chair and put her hand on her grandfather's shin. "Are you awake Grandpa?"

His eyes opened immediately, but they were foggy and confused. It was clear he was trying desperately to figure out who this young woman was. Strangely, Kerri didn't identify herself. She just sat there, smiling at him.

It couldn't have been long, but it felt like an age before recognition dawned and he leaned forward and threw his arms around Kerri.

"Sandra! Where have you been? They won't let me go home. Can we leave? Please, honey, take me home."

Brooklyn had never seen a face move so quickly from a calm, sweet smile to heartbreak. Kerri didn't directly address his question, instead, she pulled on the string and opened the box from the bakery. "Look what I've brought." His watery eyes stared at the delights in the box, and he reached in and immediately took a eclair.

"I never get these anymore. Are they from that place in Pacoima? What's the name?"

"Yes," Kerri said, dabbing at the tears that rolled down her cheeks. "They're from the German Pastry Shop. Your favorite."

Their roller-coaster ride of a visit with Bernie Klein continued until the sun went behind a hill and he wanted to go inside. His mood was volatile, and besides not being consistent in whom he recognized, he had a wide streak of paranoia that popped up and disappeared with no notice. He seemed especially suspicious of Kerri's mom Joan, whom he spoke of bitterly, but even that faded in and out with no trigger.

What was remarkable through the day though was the way Kerri interacted with him. She was the soul of patience and kindness and, by the time they were ready to leave, she had climbed several rungs up the ladder of Brooklyn's respect. Big rungs. And being there had shown Brooklyn there was no reason to be afraid of people like Bernie Klein. He was just a guy who had trouble keeping it together. Kinda like some comics she'd known. Everybody needed to be connected to other people, especially when things were tough.

―――

When they were back in the car and heading for some dinner, Brooklyn considered a relationship she couldn't figure out. "Your grandpa kept talking about Sandra. Was that your grandmother?"

"No, that was my aunt. She died about a year after my grandmother did, and that made my grandfather go downhill a lot faster than anybody had predicted. Today was the first day he'd ever confused me with her, and it hit me like a kick to the gut."

"I can't imagine. But I can see why you like to visit him. Even when he's not really there, he's a pretty interesting guy."

Kerri grinned at her. "You just like him because he let you have an eclair."

"Not only that. He was going to let me have a cigar too."

"That's one area my mom and I don't agree on. She thinks we should be very careful about his health, and I think we should only be careful about his needs. I say whatever makes him happy we should give to him."

Brooklyn wasn't sure where Kerri's mom had been all day. Her note said she was going for a haircut, but if her stylist was within a hundred miles she'd made another stop or two. Still, Kerri hadn't mentioned it, so she thought she'd better not either. Maybe it wasn't obvious to her that her mom had blown her off. "He acted like a kid when we were outside and he smoked one of the cigars you brought him. That really seemed to perk him up."

"Today was a really good day. And I'm glad you were there with me. It made it a lot better." When Brooklyn glanced at her, Kerri was smiling warmly. "Thanks,"

It was just one simple word, but it meant a lot.

———

They grabbed a quick dinner at what Brooklyn considered a sketchy Thai place. But Kerri insisted it was good, and given that she didn't feel sick after an hour, Brooklyn guessed it had been. Now it was getting late, she was alone in her hotel room, and her mind was racing.

She had to get up at six to get showered and dressed and chug enough coffee to make her mind work for her TV appearance. And if she wasn't up for a good hour beforehand her eyes always looked puffy and red. That meant she had to get to sleep right then to look halfway decent.

She glared at her watch. Ten o'clock. It didn't matter that it was one a.m. in her body clock. Something in her screwed-up brain refused to acknowledge that it was a perfectly proper time for bed.

The thought of heading over to a club on Sunset was powerful. She knew all of the owners, and she could work on a bit or just hang out.

That's what years of habit had trained her for. Stay up really late, hang out in clubs, chat up other comics, have a few drinks, maybe get lucky, crash at four or five.

She paced around her room, which didn't seem like a suite. It felt more like a jail cell in a particularly cramped prison. Her whole body itched with anxiety and pent up agitation. This was all wrong for her! But she was stuck—stuck like a pig on a roasting spit.

Brooklyn stormed into the bathroom and started throwing toiletries around, scattering them until she found the bottle of aspirin where she hid her sleeping pills. She'd almost forgotten her stash at the radio station, and then she would have been entirely screwed. Popping two, she sulked back into the bedroom, got undressed and lay down after ripping the bedspread off. If the damned pills didn't take effect in ten minutes she was going to have to hit the mini bar, and even she knew that wasn't a good idea. But she had to sleep—no matter what.

Kerri paced in the green room the next morning, wondering how the lackluster host of the "Los Angeles Weekend" show had ever gotten a job. He was as exciting as dry toast, and even though she hated to admit it, Brooklyn wasn't much more dynamic. She looked flat and tired and a bit haggard. And the makeup guy hadn't done her any favors by making her fair skin look almost ghostly.

But the most damaging thing was how unengaged Brooklyn was. She clearly didn't want to be there, and when you coupled that with a boring interviewer, you got a big fat boring three minutes. There wasn't a person in LA who would have gone to UCLA to see her if they hadn't already bought tickets, and it was actually possible that people who had tickets would try to sell them on Craigslist.

Brooklyn had to shoulder more of the responsibility for making these interviews entertaining, or she had to find a way to stop doing them. This way was getting her nowhere.

They had breakfast after the TV appearance, and Brooklyn didn't seem to think it had gone poorly, which spoke volumes. But she seemed so listless that they went back to her suite in Westwood, and she immediately lay down for a nap that turned into what to Kerri was a full night's sleep.

Kerri sat at the desk in the living room and made phone calls, double-checking everything for the night's performance. Then she worked on some correspondence, keeping up with past clients and other personal assistants. She made it a habit to let everyone know where she was working and when she might be finished. The next job was never guaranteed.

When Brooklyn was finally awake, she immediately got on her laptop and started poking around.

"We've got to get going," Kerri said. "I want to stop by the venue to make sure everything's good to go."

"Do we have to go in person?" Brooklyn asked. "Can't you just call someone to check things out?"

"That's not a good idea. You need to do a sound check at the very least."

"A sound check? I never do those. Why should we?" She looked so puzzled that Kerri wished she could find Kat and give her a good tongue-lashing.

"You have to make sure everything's perfect before the audience gets here. They pay a lot of money to see you. They deserve a good show."

"Yeah, yeah, I get that," she said slowly, showing that she really didn't. "But how is this gonna help?"

"Two things. One, it makes the people at the venue know they have to treat you professionally and not make stupid mistakes. Two, if there are any problems with the set or the lighting or the sound, we can have them fixed now rather than later. People want the show to start on time."

"But it never does. Something is always screwed up."

"But it should," Kerri said firmly. She was the tour manager that weekend, so the tour would be managed—properly.

The theater was the smallest one on the UCLA campus. It was much smaller than Brooklyn should have been playing, but she didn't seem upset by the size. Kerri had done everything she could think of to get ready for the show, but a dozen things came up during the performance. She could hear the crowd roaring with laughter, but she was too distracted to be able to listen to many complete jokes, or stories, as Brooklyn called them.

At the end of her act, Brooklyn asked for questions and dozens of people headed for the microphones that Kerri had arranged to have students monitor. The crowd liked her a lot while she was performing, but they loved her when she interacted with them. There were a lot of lesbians in the audience, and every time Brooklyn made even a veiled reference to her sexual orientation, they hooted and hollered. Brooklyn didn't seem the least bit embarrassed by this, and nothing anyone said, no matter how ribald, even made her blush. Kerri was amazed at that, having learned that Brooklyn barely even cursed at home, and her sexual innuendo was always very mild. But she was clearly a pro, and she rolled with everything they could throw at her.

Brooklyn stayed onstage far longer than they had planned, but she and the crowd were having such a good time that Kerri didn't even try to signal her to quit. Kerri wasn't sure how Brooklyn knew it was time, but the second the energy in the room flagged, she called out "I'm out!" and took off, jogging across the stage. She came back for three curtain calls, but didn't do an encore.

Kerri had been in the back of the auditorium, reasoning that she had a better view of the entire venue from that perspective. By the time she got backstage, Brooklyn was drying her face and hair with a towel. Comedy didn't look like hard work from the audience, but she was drenched. Her mood was way up though, and she grinned happily at Kerri. "That was a little better than the Comedy Crib, huh?"

Finding herself amazed, Kerri could only nod. She wasn't sure where Brooklyn had pulled this font of energy from, but it was remarkably—no, stunningly—attractive.

It was going to be hard to ask the question artfully, but Kerri thought it was important. The difference between each of the times she'd seen Brooklyn on stage was so huge that she thought it was something she needed to understand. They were sitting backstage, watching students run around getting things ready for the second show when Kerri said, "Your energy seemed so high tonight. Is it different for you to play before a big audience?"

Brooklyn gave her a puzzled look. "Big audience? Oh, you mean between last night and tonight?"

"Yeah. There's a big difference in the way you come across."

"I hope so." Brooklyn let her head roll back and she laughed heartily. "When I'm working on a bit, I try to do it almost flat. If the bit's really good the audience will laugh at it no matter how you deliver it. But you can make a bad one seem funny if you sell it hard enough. I don't want to be fooled."

"Oh! So you're flat on purpose."

"Yeah. When I put a new bit in my act I sell it hard, but that's only after I know how good it really is."

"And you can really tell that by going to a small club?"

"Yep. The best audience for testing a joke is one that doesn't know you or like you. That's why it's vital that I go work out new stuff at different clubs on different nights. I don't want my fans to pick up a pattern and follow me. I want strangers."

"You know, one of the nicest things about working for you is that we can talk like this. I usually work with actors and none of the ones I've been with in the last few years are willing to talk about their craft. Maybe that's because they're in withdrawal, but still…"

"I'm not in withdrawal, and I love to talk about comedy." She sat there, looking strangely happy, even though they were at a very small

133

venue at a university and her dressing room was the size of a coat closet. It was great to be around someone who actually liked show business even when she wasn't being attended to like a queen.

—⁂—

Once again Kerri didn't get to fully appreciate Brooklyn's set. She had to handle a lot of small details, mostly in the front of the house. While she was running around, she kept returning to something she'd noticed. Brooklyn didn't have a drink before or after her first set. That was important. If she drank to prop herself up before performing it was more of a danger sign. It was looking more and more possible that she drank to excess only to relax. That certainly wasn't great, and it wouldn't be easy to fix, but it was better than knowing she was an out-of-control alcoholic.

They were both tired after the second show, but Kerri determinedly refused Brooklyn's offer of a ride home. After a minor squabble about taking a bus or a cab, Brooklyn deposited Kerri into a cab lingering near the buses; then, just as the car started to move, she opened the door and thrust forty dollars inside. Kerri was on her knees, glaring at her through the back window, while Brooklyn laughed her ass off. She was standing there, still chuckling, when a woman approached and said, "I hope I'm not annoying you, but could I take a picture with you?"

Brooklyn turned and saw a woman about her own age, standing there looking vaguely embarrassed.

"Sure. I don't mind at all."

The woman stood next to her, extended her phone, and snapped a photo. They both looked at it, and Brooklyn said, "One more. My eyes were half closed."

The woman hurriedly took another, and they pronounced it perfect. "That was really nice of you. I thought you'd be…distant."

"I'm actually pretty nice," she heard herself say. "That sounded stupid, but I really am."

The woman stuck her hand out. "Raffa Santiago. I was at your show."

"The second set?"

"I guess so. The one that was just over a while ago."

Raffa was attractive in that "I'm really smart" kind of way. There were probably a ton of thoughts going on behind the dark eyes framed by big brown glasses. Brooklyn looked around, seeing no one but a few students waiting in a circular drive for buses. "Do you live around here?"

"No, I live in West LA. I came over to wait for the bus, and saw you and…someone else."

"My manager. She lives in Santa Monica."

Raffa's eyes seemed to light up. "Are you going to your…hotel right now?"

"I was going to. But I'm not in a rush. What did you have in mind?"

"Well…" She didn't look a bit shy, but she fumbled for a few seconds. "Would you like to have a drink?"

"Sure. Do you know anywhere around here?"

Those big brown eyes blinked slowly. "Maybe your hotel has a bar."

Her hotel didn't, but she didn't think Raffa really wanted a bar. Still, it was best to be honest. "I have a nice room with a bar. How's that?"

"That's perfect."

They walked down the street together, with a spark of excitement welling in Brooklyn's belly. It had been weeks since she'd been with a woman, and Raffa looked like a very nice candidate to erase the dry spell.

—⁘—

Brooklyn was still wearing her bra and panties while she determinedly worked at bringing Raffa to another climax. Raffa was one of those women who was hard to please—at first. She wasn't very vocal, and Brooklyn had to guess at what she liked. But that was part of the fun. She imagined the clitoris like an intricate lock and herself as a deft safecracker. Raffa's clitoris was small and well hidden, and she needed a lot of pressure and patience to finally get off. But once she'd had an orgasm they flowed from her like water. Brooklyn enjoyed flicking her tongue across her now exposed clit, watching it jump, while Raffa caressed her hair, murmuring sweet nothings as her body spasmed. Brooklyn's tongue was heavy and tired and her jaw ached, but now that she'd found the combination she didn't want to lock the safe again.

Finally, Raffa grasped her by the shoulders and whimpered, "Enough. Please. I can't take any more."

Climbing up the bed, Brooklyn flopped down on her back and grinned. "Happy?"

"Very. Just let me catch my breath and I'll return the favor."

This was the touchy moment. The one that could easily ruin the night. Brooklyn cast a quick glance at the clock on the bedside. "That can't be right, is it?"

"Three thirty? Yeah, I think that's right. Why?"

"That's why I'm seeing double. That's six thirty in New York." She yawned, probably putting it on a little thick. "How about a rain check for the morning?"

Raffa put her hand on Brooklyn's belly and scratched it gently. "Why?" Her eyes searched Brooklyn's carefully.

Giving her a long kiss, Brooklyn lay back down. "I'm really exhausted. Honestly."

"Do you want me to leave?" Raffa started to sit up, but Brooklyn placed a restraining hand on her shoulder.

"No, I'd love to have you stay." Putting on her most charming smile, she gave her a quick kiss. "How can you pay me back if you don't stay?"

She looked suspicious, but Raffa nodded. "Okay. If you're sure you want me here."

"I definitely want you here. Let me go brush my teeth and I'll be right back." She slid out of bed and started to brush her teeth. Her clit ached with need and there was a tightness in her abdomen that she always got when she craved release. But there wasn't a one-night-stand in America who could identify Brooklyn York in a naked lineup, and Raffa wasn't going to be the first. If a woman ever said she'd given Brooklyn a good work-out, she was a bold faced liar. But if she wanted to sing her praises as a skilled orgasm-creator—that was perfectly fine with her.

She opened the door to find Raffa asleep. *Why not?* Placing a spare blanket over her lap just in case Raffa woke, she sat in a comfortable chair and proved her mettle as an orgasm-maker, this time in the independent category.

Raffa was dead to the world at five when Kerri texted Brooklyn. "R U up?"

She most definitely was. Knowing she'd never get up in time for her flight, she'd listened to podcasts on her phone while Raffa slept next to her. It was remarkably hard not to fall asleep as well, but it would have been harder to wake up. Still, it was a good night. She'd made love to a woman, which always gave her a charge, and she got the skin-on-skin contact that she craved like a drug after not having it for a while. Yes, a girlfriend would've been a heck of a lot nicer, but being with a woman like Raffa was much better than being alone.

She texted back and they decided that Brooklyn would swing by Kerri's apartment in an hour. Brooklyn showered, dressed and took the time to leave a nice note, then threw away the little liquor bottles they'd drained to get over their nervousness. Nothing was as depressing as waking up, alone, in a strange hotel room littered with dead soldiers. Then she snuck out of the room as quietly as a mouse.

―⁓―

They were on the plane two hours later, waiting for permission to take off. It was early, just seven, but Brooklyn didn't look as groggy as she had the day before. "I can't believe the difference it makes to have someone who knows how to get things done travel with me. Those were the best-run sets I think I've ever had."

"Thanks. I guess I can tell you now that this was the first time I've ever handled a live event."

"Shut up!" Brooklyn gasped, slapping at Kerri's shoulder.

"Yep. I've watched people manage everything under the sun, but I've never done an event myself. It was kinda cool."

"You were wonderful! You did a million things Kat never did."

She would never speak badly of Kat. It was never wise to say even an obvious truth about a client's friends or family. "Well, it was a great trip for me. I absolutely loved watching you last night, even if I didn't get to hear much of your show. And, just for the record, you could have fifty girlfriends if you wanted to. Those women were practically throwing their undies at you!"

"Those aren't the kinds of women I'm interested in—as girlfriends at least. A lot of them are the kinds of people who'd like anyone who's famous."

"But what about the women who like you and aren't star-chasers? Why exclude them?"

Brooklyn shrugged. "I dunno how to tell the difference. If they want to hook up, I assume they want me because I'm famous. Besides, how could I even strike up a conversation with your eagle eye. Do you always stand between the performer and the people asking for autographs?"

"Oh, yeah. You never know what someone's gonna throw at you. I don't want someone to hand you something embarrassing and have someone else get a video of it and post it on the internet. Things like that make you look bad."

Brooklyn looked at her approvingly. "You're really good at this."

"I just might be." Kerri sat there, ruminating on the weekend. Brooklyn had been the model of restraint. Not much liquor, a little less smoking, and her diet had even been relatively healthy. She was definitely taking better care of herself. Things were looking good.

—⁓—

A cab delivered them to Brooklyn's loft at four p.m. They started for the door, but Brooklyn stopped abruptly. "Hey, we should go for a walk or something."

Kerri stared at her for a moment. "Really? You want some exercise? It's pretty cold out."

Brooklyn smiled that charming grin. "Well, I don't really want it, but it would probably do me good. We could walk up to the Village, grab a pizza and some wine, then get to bed early."

"Is that my only option?"

"No, no, if you want to head home, it's totally cool."

"I'm not in a rush, and I do have to eat, but I'm not in the mood for pizza. How about this? We'll take a cab to a Thai place I love, then we can walk home."

"Do they have a bar?"

"They must. I've had a beer there."

"It's a deal." She reached for Kerri's bag and headed inside, saying, "I'll drop the bags off and be right back." She was gone before Kerri could utter a word of protest.

———

The cab kept going and going until Brooklyn scowled darkly. "I was tricked. We're almost in Hell's Kitchen. It's twenty miles back to TriBeCa."

"Probably three," Kerri said, snickering. "You're gonna get a great meal, so you'll be happy."

"Do you ever eat American food? It's good. You should try it."

"Yes, I eat American food, but I prefer Asian. I like a lot of spice."

"I do too, but I like it from pepperoni and barbecue sauce." The cab pulled up in front of a very nondescript storefront and Kerri reached over to hand the driver a twenty. "I can get this," Brooklyn said.

"You pay for me all of the time. This was my idea, so I've got it."

Brooklyn took her hand out of her pocket, a pleased smile brightening her face.

———

It took longer than Brooklyn would have thought to walk three miles, and she was beat when they got back. "Time for bed," she said firmly. "Why don't you just grab a cab so you can get home faster?"

"No, I'll come up and take my bike. I'll need it in the morning."

"You could take a cab back in the morning. I don't want you to carry your bag on the bike. You could easily fall over."

"Brooklyn, I had it on my back all the way to Ft. Lee." She continued moving towards the door, but Brooklyn jumped in front of her.

"Here's twenty bucks. Come on, take a cab." She waved the bill in front of her.

Kerri stopped and looked at her carefully. "Do you not want me to go into your place? Am I invading your privacy too much?"

Brooklyn dropped her hands and stood there, looking awkward. "No, you're not. I just read about people hit by cars and it worries me to have you riding late at night."

"It's not late at all. I promise I'll be extra careful."

When they entered, Kerri said, "The door to your patio's cracked open. You didn't leave it that way, did you?"

"Gosh, I must have." Brooklyn walked by the dining table, swiping a piece of paper off the surface and slipping it into her pocket. She went to the door and closed it, "I don't think I'll need to stand out there and have a cigarette before bed for a change."

"Maybe you had your fill while walking home. The power-walk/chain-smoking craze might take hold if you publicize it."

"Don't knock it if you haven't tried it."

"Mind if I get some water for my bottle?" Kerri went to the refrigerator and saw a big note attached with a magnet. It read:

"Hi, honey.

I hope your trip was good. Get to bed early and make sure you eat everything I left for you. And stay away from pizza!

Love, Mom"

"For you," she said, trying not to snicker as she handed the note over. "Your mom brings you food?"

"If she's in the neighborhood," Brooklyn said defensively. "She loves to cook."

Standing there for a few seconds, Kerri sniffed, moving her head around. "I smell cleaning products." She leaned close and smelled the stainless-steel refrigerator. "Windex." Then she ran her hand over the counter. "Not a crumb." Giving a guilty-looking Brooklyn a look, she said, "Does your mom clean your house?"

"If she's over here. She says she hates to head right home after dropping off some food. It's too much time in the car." She crossed her hands over her chest and looked vaguely defiant. "I don't ask her to do it.

As a matter of fact, I finally convinced her to just do the kitchen. She swears she likes to clean."

"Did I criticize you? I think it's sweet." She got her water, trying to prevent Brooklyn from seeing her smile. Then she walked over to her bike, loaded her pack on her back and secured her water bottle. "I'll see you bright and early." As she guided the bike out the door, she added, "I hope there's a mint on your pillow."

—·—

The next morning, while Brooklyn was in the shower, Kerri took a look at the food that had been delivered. Each dish was labeled with a note, explaining what it was. It was the food her grandparents had grown up on, things that seemed iconic in America. Ham and scalloped potatoes, spaghetti and meatballs with a huge loaf of garlic bread, meatloaf with mashed potatoes and gravy and lasagna with more garlic bread. Save for the spuds, there wasn't a vegetable in sight. Since Brooklyn clearly didn't shop or cook, she was living on only protein and simple carbohydrates. How did she not have scurvy?

CHAPTER SEVEN

ON THE WAY HOME from work on Monday, Brooklyn answered her cell phone. She felt herself brighten when a familiar voice said, "Hey, guurl."

"Hi, Kat. It's good to hear your voice."

"Really? I thought your babysitter would've replaced me by now."

"It's not like that. She's not a manager, and even if she was, she'd be managing somebody more important than me."

"So is the job still open? Do I have to interview if I want to come back?"

"The job is yours. And it will be as long as you want it." Wait. What? Why had she said that? Things were finally going well! Damn it, it was too late to pull back the offer. She was stuck…again.

"I'll come over tonight and we can talk things over."

"Make it this afternoon. I'm in bed by nine."

"Now I know why you've got a babysitter. I haven't gone to bed that early since I needed one."

—⁓—

Kerri arrived at four thirty the next morning to find Brooklyn glumly sitting at the dining room table. She had a paper cup of coffee in front of her and even from the the doorway Kerri was almost overwhelmed by the cigarette smell. "It looks like you and Kat got to meet up. Been home long?"

"Yeah." Brooklyn stuck her arms out and yawned noisily. "We didn't actually go out. Kat came over, saw all of my new computer stuff and started asking me questions about how I was going to use it. When I told her I was going to keep my own calendar, she got really angry and we had another blowout."

Kerri sat down and put her hand on Brooklyn's leg. A look made her remove it quickly. "What do you think made her mad about that?"

"I'm not sure. It seems like she's angry about having anybody else have an influence on me. That doesn't make much sense, since she's one of the least controlling people I know."

"Do you want me to go buy an iPad for her? You could send it to her with a note saying that technology can bring you closer or something like that."

Brooklyn got up and started to walk towards her bedroom. "That's what I've been sitting here thinking about. And I think I've decided to let her go." She walked into the bathroom and closed the door.

—⁂—

Brooklyn seemed particularly glum when she got home from work later that day, but she was polite as always. "It's really nice of you to come by to check on me, but you honestly don't have to."

If I could trust you to go to bed on time, I'd give you all the privacy you could handle. But you haven't come close to proving that. "I don't have anything else to do, and Spectrum is paying a lot for this job, so I want to be available. I thought we could talk today about the near future."

Brooklyn went to the refrigerator, took out one of the meals her mother had left for her, cast a quick glance at the instructions, then threw it into the microwave. Then she flopped down on the sectional, propped her feet up on the coffee table, and ostentatiously showed that she was giving her full attention. "Let's talk."

Kerri sat next to her and opened Brooklyn's laptop. "I'm on the payroll for two more weeks."

Brooklyn's eyes widened. "Two weeks? Why only two weeks?"

This was a nice turn of events. She'd never had a client who wanted to be monitored longer. "Someone from Spectrum called and said they only needed me for two more weeks."

"Hmm." She looked at Kerri sharply. "Have you given them any info on me so far?"

"Not a word. Whoever I talked to today didn't know much about either of us. She was someone's admin."

"Why would they make this such a short contract? Do you think they've decided to fire me and they're only using you for a smokescreen?"

Kerri spoke as soothingly as she was able. "I honestly think they're just trying to keep costs down. They had to pay a lot to get me at the last minute and for a relatively short time. They only guaranteed me a month, so I'm not surprised they want to stop."

"I am. It seemed very open ended to me."

She looked genuinely put out, but Kerri couldn't figure out why. Maybe losing Kat had hit her hard. She did say she got lonely on the road. "I can only physically travel with you until you play Salt Lake City. But I *can* do a lot of the legwork for the next month or even two. I can definitely make sure your travel arrangements are all in order. And I'm more than happy to help you interview managers."

"That's probably the last thing I'd ever like to do."

"That's why I'll do the first cut for you. I'll get it down to three people, check their references, hire a service to do a very thorough background check, then let you make your choice."

"I don't think you understand how much I hate letting strangers into my business."

Kerri was suddenly touched by the implication of what Brooklyn said. Everyone else in her life had been with her from the beginning of her career or from the beginning of her life, yet she'd let Kerri in almost immediately. "I think I do understand, but you need a manager."

Brooklyn sat there for a minute, then tilted her chin so she was gazing directly at Kerri. She held the look for a long time. "I'm really happy with the manager I had in Los Angeles. I just have to figure out how to keep her."

The microwave dinged and Brooklyn got to her feet. Kerri sat there, trying to figure out why goosebumps covered her body. It couldn't have been just from one look. But even thinking about that gaze made the goosebumps come back for another round. There was something going on between them, but whatever it was couldn't be realized. Just acknowledging that made her sad, but rules were not made to be broken.

A few days later, Kerri was busily laying out photos that she'd ripped from magazines on the dining room table. When Brooklyn arrived home just before lunch, she called out from the doorway, "So this is what you do while I'm gone. Is this the lesbian version of paper dolls?"

"Come on in and close the door. I don't want your neighbor to steal any of my ideas."

Brooklyn dropped her bag at the door and went to the table. "Are these women you want me to date? Because I will." She pointed at a pretty blonde woman. "Especially her."

"I don't know any of them personally. But I think you need a look."

"What is this thing…a look?" she asked in the cheesy Russian accent Kerri had come to enjoy.

"A style that people recognize as yours. I thought we could go shopping today and get you set up with some of the basics. So take a look at these and see if any of them reflect your sensibilities."

"I have no sensibilities."

"Everyone has sensibilities." She pointed to a woman wearing a tailored dress shirt. "Something like this would look good on you. You could wear it hanging out, which would look casual, and if we had them custom made, they'd fit you great and look tasteful."

Shrugging, Brooklyn said, "That's fine. Are we done?"

"No, we're not done. If we do this, you'll want to keep this look for quite a while, if not for the rest of your career. I want to make sure this is something you won't mind wearing."

"You see how I dress. I like to wear jeans and my basketball shoes. Other than that, I don't care."

"Fine. I think you should wear a brightly colored T-shirt and a dress shirt over it. That would look good over jeans and basketball shoes. But I think you should wear that to *Reveille* also. If you're going to have a look, you should keep it consistent."

"The wardrobe people will probably give me a hard time, but I guess I don't care. I think they were just trying to make me look a little less dykie with those dumb sweaters."

"You're not dykie. You're androgynous, and that's stylish. I got the names of a couple of tailors. I thought after lunch we could go pick out fabric."

"I don't have to go do that. You could do that for me."

"I…I suppose I could, but don't you care at all what fabric I pick out?"

Making a beeline to the sectional, Brooklyn flipped on the TV and sat there looking perfectly content. "You always look good, so you must have good taste. Therefore, you're better prepared to do this than I am." She grinned, an unrepentant delinquent's smile on her face.

"I can't get measured for you. You're going to have to meet me at the tailor's."

"No problem. I'll order some Chinese food and sit here like a bump on a log. I'll be waiting for your call when my measurements must be taken." She glowered playfully. "And not a moment before."

—∾∾—

When Kerri returned to the loft, a pair of big boxes were sitting on the dining table. "Cool. The espresso machine and grinder are here," she said, but Brooklyn didn't look up from what she was reading. Kerri walked over to her, making Brooklyn jump when she spoke. "Did you notice I didn't call you to come get measured?"

"Damn." She patted the area over her heart for a second. Then, as though the magazine she held had a spell over her, she zoned out again. Kerri went over to the table, noisily extracted the espresso machine and the coffee grinder from their boxes. The machine came with a DVD, which she watched while mimicking the steps shown. Getting them set up on the counter, filling the machine with water and doing a few test shots took an hour. She was getting ready to leave when Brooklyn slapped her magazine down on the table, stood up and stretched. "Wow! Did you…how did those get here? Did you bring them in?"

"No. They were on the table when I got back."

Brooklyn stood there for a moment, looking blank. "I kinda remember someone buzzing…"

Kerri laughed at her vacant expression. "You might want to pay a little more attention when you let strangers into your apartment."

"I was involved in…something. I don't recall what, but it seemed important."

Kerri stood close, close enough that she knew Brooklyn couldn't ignore her. "You didn't hear me come in. I could have ransacked the place."

Looking slightly embarrassed, she said, "I thought I had to go meet you someplace, so I wasn't expecting you. I was waiting for the call."

"The tailor didn't have time to measure you today, so I picked out fabrics. I have swatches if you want to see."

"I don't really care. You can surprise me. Hey, how about a nice latte?" She went to the chrome-fronted machine and lightly caressed it.

"Not tonight. The last thing you need is less sleep. I brought some things to make a good salad. Hungry?"

"For salad? Not really. But I guess I can gag down a vegetable or two." She jumped up onto the counter, and let her feet dangle while she sat there.

"There are about six vegetables here, so you can gag three times as much." She started washing the lettuce, having to dry it on kitchen towels, since Brooklyn didn't have a spinner or a colander. "What were you reading that had you so enthralled?"

"A really great article." She looked like she had a serious crush on the article in question, but she didn't add a word.

"Want to tell me about it?"

The look she gave was filled with regret. "It was about quantum computing."

Kerri stopped what she was doing and looked at Brooklyn carefully. "Quantum computing? I'm not sure what that is, but I'm surprised someone who didn't own a computer last week was enthralled by it."

"I'm clearly not a computer person, and I don't know much about physics either. But this is a very big thing. They think this type of computer will enable subatomic particles to be in two places at one time on the same piece of silicon."

She'd spoken only a few sentences, but each contained more of Brooklyn's obvious excitement. She was practically bubbling with interest, and was clearly happy to share it.

"How does any of that mean anything to you, given that you don't know much about the topic?"

Brooklyn sat there for a moment, her brow knit in thought. "I can't explain it very well. But I don't have to know a topic well to be interested in it. Actually, I'm more interested if I don't know anything about the it. I love having to force my mind to get around something difficult."

"Given what you've read, could you have an intelligent conversation with a physicist?"

Brooklyn laughed heartily. "No way! But if I keep reading articles about it, I'll eventually have a surface knowledge. Just enough to be able to have an intelligent conversation with someone who isn't an expert. My goal in life is to know a little bit about everything that interests me in any way."

Kerri smiled at the confident look on her face. "I bet you'll do it." She started to put the lettuce into a big bowl. "Do you like talking about the things you read about?" It was blatantly obvious that she did, but she'd never tried to share anything before.

Brooklyn sat there on the counter, her face contorted by deep thought. "I love to talk about stuff," she said quietly. "But I don't know anyone who's interested in the same things I am."

"Not your ex?"

"Oh, god, no. She and I had very different interests. Ashley liked to read, but she was very linear. She liked sci-fi and fantasy and mystery novels. I'm all over the place."

"Your parents?"

"No, not really. My mom would let me talk all day, but she…" She shut her mouth so quickly she made a snapping sound. "She's not into the same things."

Hmm. That sounds like a polite way to say that her mom doesn't understand the brainy stuff Brooklyn finds interesting. That makes two of us. "You probably would have found people who liked the same things in college. Do you ever regret not sticking with it?"

"No. Not even a little bit. There wasn't anything I wanted to do except make people laugh, and wasting four years before doing that wasn't for me. I'll just have to keep looking for people who understand nothing about quantum computing, but want to hear me blather on about it."

Kerri touched her leg, grimacing when Brooklyn twitched away. "You've got one here." What was that about? It had seemed like Brooklyn was getting more comfortable with casual touch, but here she was, jerking away from it again. But the luminous smile that made Brooklyn's entire face light up showed she was darned happy that Kerri was interested in hearing her talk. Talk about mixed signals!

―――

The next morning, Kerri stopped at a bodega close to the loft and bought a half gallon of skim milk. The espresso machine and grinder were waiting, and it took her quite a while to make the first drink just perfect, but she had everything ready to go by 4:15.

Being organized and thinking of different ways around problems might not have been the most difficult job in the world, but she got a lot of pleasure out of doing it well. There was an added bounce to her step when she sailed into Brooklyn's room and set the carefully-made mocha latte on the bedside table.

"Brooklyn, it's time to get up." Ugh. The gentle approach wasn't going to work today. She placed her hand on Brooklyn's back and rubbed it briskly. "Come on. Time to wake up."

Brooklyn was lying on her belly, with a pillow over her head. Her hands gripped the pillow tightly, as though she'd been holding on while someone tried to wrestle it away from her. Kerri felt bad for her, but her sympathy only went so far. She grasped the sheet and snapped it off Brooklyn's body, leaving her fully naked. Still, not a muscle moved.

"Brooklyn. Get up. Now." She grasped the pillow and yanked, encountering a surprising amount of resistance. "If you're fighting me, you're awake." It was getting late, and worse than that, that lovely latte was getting cold. There was no time to dance around this any longer. She whipped the pillow away, flipped her over, swept Brooklyn's feet off the side of the bed, slid her hands under the exposed armpits, and pulled her into a sitting position. "The next step is a lot less pleasant. Don't make me do it."

Brooklyn's eyes still weren't open, but she let out something between a whimper and a moan. "Ten minutes. Please. I"m so tired, I ache."

"Can't do it." She picked up the latte and held it to Brooklyn's lips. "Take a sip."

Brooklyn's nose wiggled while she took a tentative sniff, then she put her lips on the mug and slurped up a big gulp. Her bloodshot eyes finally opened. "That's good," she gurgled. "More?"

"Can you hold the mug yourself?" Kerri had been teasing, but Brooklyn shook her head. Patiently, Kerri let her take a few more sips, then said, "I'll go turn the shower on and then make you another cup. Do you like it this way?"

Brooklyn finally blinked and looked her in the eye, managing a wan but sincere smile. "It's perfect. Another sip, please."

⸺⁂⸺

It hadn't been easy, by any means, but Brooklyn managed to get up without too much trouble for an entire week. She thought she'd been a little sharper, and she knew she was talking more on the air, which was a big plus.

When she got home after her Thursday show, Kerri had good news. "I thought I'd let you know that people on your fan sites have been commenting on how much you've been contributing. You're getting a lot of good reviews."

It was embarrassing to let Kerri see how much that meant to her. Trying to be cool, she nodded. "That's good to hear. Everybody likes good feedback. I was looking at my calendar today, and tonight would be a very good night to go to the Comedy Crib. What do you think? Will I ruin my good work if I stay up until one?"

"You know that's not ideal. But I understand that you have to get your work in. Are you tired now?"

"No, strangely not."

"Then have some lunch and do whatever you normally do at this time of day. I'll come by at around four and teach you some of my nap tricks."

"Who knew there were nap tricks? I can't wait to hear them." She headed for the freezer and Kerri made for the door, unable to watch Brooklyn microwave another of those carb-loaded meals.

As promised, Kerri was back at four. She went into Brooklyn's bathroom and started running the tub. Always inquisitive, Brooklyn was right over her shoulder, looking into the empty porcelain. "I don't like to take baths."

"This isn't for getting clean. It's for relaxing." She pulled some things out of her bag and sprinkled something into the water. The room was almost immediately filled with herbal scents. "Lavender," Kerri said before Brooklyn could ask. "It's very soothing."

Like a dubious but compliant child, Brooklyn got into the bath when it was ready. "What's the most boring thing you generally read?" Kerri asked.

Immediately, Brooklyn replied, "*American Spectator.*" Kerri went into the living room and thumbed through the myriad of periodicals until she found one. When Brooklyn took it, Kerri reached down and twirled her hair into a twist, then grabbed a clip from the edge of the sink. "You don't want to get your hair wet, right?"

The smile Brooklyn gave her was knee-weakening. She looked so lovely, with her cheeks pink from the steamy bathroom, her eyes bright and alert, and an expression of true gratitude brightening her grin. My God, how could she avoid being snapped up?

Kerri found herself backing out of the room just to avoid those penetrating eyes. "I'll be back in an hour. You can add hot water if you need to, but don't make it too hot. That can make your heart rate speed up which isn't something we want."

As soon as she closed the door, Kerri went to her bag and took out her meditation cushion. She set it on the floor so that the afternoon sun warmed her, then slipped into the proper posture. Her back was straight, eyes vaguely focused on a spot a few feet in front of her. Normally, she could switch into a meditation mindset fairly easily, but today she had to work at it. No matter how many times she shooed them away, thoughts of Brooklyn's beautiful eyes looked up at her. That wasn't something she could allow. Even thinking about a client in that way wasn't a good idea, and when the client was available, it was even worse.

Kerri had gotten some subtle vibes from Brooklyn from the beginning, but she'd carefully ignored them. They were coming more frequently now, and that couldn't continue. Meditation helped her stay focused on goals, and one of her most prominent goals was to avoid getting entangled with people who could make her life more difficult. Brooklyn wasn't a train wreck, but she was at least a fender-bender. A fender-bender to be avoided.

An hour later, Kerri went back into the bathroom. Brooklyn was about halfway through her magazine, but she looked very pleased to be interrupted.

Kerri held up a big bath sheet and Brooklyn stepped into it then wrapped it around herself. "I feel a lot more relaxed, but still not very tired."

"We'll get that taken care of. Back to the bedroom we go." Kerri placed a sheet on top of the bed. "Lie down on the bed on your stomach, and I'll give you a massage."

"You can give a massage? And you haven't given me one until now? If you'd told me that the first day, you'd have a repetitive motion injury by now. I *love* to be massaged."

Smirking, Kerri said, "That doesn't surprise me." Brooklyn got into position and Kerri used some lavender scented massage oil to work on her neck and shoulders, which was where she carried a lot of tension. Breaking up the routine, she moved down Brooklyn's back, then down her legs before coming back up to knead her shoulder muscles. Brooklyn didn't say a word. Actually, she didn't make a sound, but when Kerri was finished she turned her head just enough to show a very satisfied smile. "We're gonna have to do that frequently."

"Just lie there for a few minutes. I'll be right back." It took almost ten minutes, but Brooklyn was still awake when Kerri walked into the bedroom with a mug of warm milk laced with a little honey. "This will help you relax even more."

Brooklyn turned over, sat up and drank it down, her compliance once again odd for an adult. Most people would complain about some part of this process, or at least ask questions. But Brooklyn clearly liked being told what to do by someone she trusted. When she was finished drinking the milk, Kerri handed her her iPhone. "I bought a bunch of classical lullabies. If you don't fall asleep to them, there's no hope." They exchanged warm smiles, then Kerri started to walk towards the door.

"Thanks a lot. Just having you go to that much trouble will help me sleep."

Kerri lingered in the doorway. "Why do you think that is?"

Brooklyn's voice was slow and soft, and it was clear she was very relaxed. "It's validating. I spend so much energy on worrying about when

I'll get to bed and if I'll be able to sleep. It's on my mind every day. Sometimes all day."

A pang of sympathy struck Kerri. There were worse situations, but being chronically tired was no party. "I didn't know it was that bad for you."

"The problem is that nobody understands how much of a problem it is. People ride me about it if I complain."

"Things that affect you are nothing to make fun of."

Brooklyn moved her head enough to meet Kerri's eyes. "That's one of the things I like the most about you. You take me seriously, and I know you won't make fun of me."

"I never would."

"If I thought you would, you'd be here to get me out the door at five thirty. Period."

"I'm glad I passed your test."

"Not half as glad as I am."

After closing the door, Kerri leaned on it for a moment, thinking. Brooklyn didn't often ask to be pampered, but she'd never refused an offer, no matter how small. She must have a boundless appetite for being catered to, an appetite Kerri had never developed. Nor wanted to. A client who needed pampering was a fatal combination. She just had to keep reminding herself of that when she looked into those kind, soulful eyes.

CHAPTER EIGHT

THEY WERE STAYING IN New York for a gig that weekend, and Brooklyn seemed almost giddy with the thought of not having to travel.

As Kerri was getting ready to leave on Thursday, Brooklyn asked, "Are you busy Saturday afternoon?"

"Not particularly. What time do you want to be at NYU?"

"The show's at eight, so you tell me."

"I'll make a few calls and see how things are. What do you have in mind for the afternoon?"

"Since this is the first weekend in I don't know how long that I'm at home, we're having a family barbecue. It's supposed to be in the fifties, and that should be warm enough to be outside. I thought you might like to go with me."

Kerri stood there for a moment, wondering about Brooklyn's motivation. She'd never accepted an invitation to do anything social with a client, but maybe this wasn't social. Maybe she needed help or protection from something. "Sure. What time should I come in the morning to get you up?"

"I'm setting my alarm for six. You can set yours for whenever you want to get up." She put on the self-mocking tone she sometimes adopted. "You get the *whole* morning off. If you can come by here at around noon, we'll head over to Joisey."

"You've got it. Good luck with getting up. Just remember, the alarm can be your friend." She closed the door and stood out in the stark, industrial-looking hallway. *Yeah, right. She needs protection at a family barbecue. It's one thing to agree to do something unwise, but don't try to lie to yourself about your motivations!*

———

The family home was in a relatively nondescript New Jersey suburban neighborhood. Most of the houses had been expanded, some of them to the lot line. Brooklyn's family hadn't put a second story on theirs, but it looked as nice as any on the block.

They followed the noise to the back yard, where a couple of dozen people tried to perch on what little land was left after the yard around the in-ground swimming pool.

A middle-aged woman rushed over to them, her smile very much like Brooklyn's, minus the sometimes sardonic edge. "You're so early! And you look so good." She pinched both of Brooklyn's cheeks, then hugged her tightly. "It makes me so happy when my baby looks healthy."

"You're embarrassing me, Mom." Brooklyn didn't look embarrassed in the least. When she was released from the hug, she said, "Mom, this is the woman who's helping me keep my job. Kerri, this is my mom, Donna."

Donna turned and gave Kerri a hug almost as enthusiastic as the one she lavished on Brooklyn. "I love you already."

"I love to be loved, so I'm happy."

"Mom, I'll take her to meet the men in the family while you make me something delicious," As they walked away, she whispered, "I promise no one else will hug you."

Donna ran over to supervise the barbecue and Brooklyn led Kerri to a tall man with salt-and-pepper hair and penetrating brown eyes. "Kerri, this is my dad, Richie."

As predicted, Richie didn't hug either of them, but he looked glad to see them. He shook Kerri's hand, surprising her with the hard calluses on his fingers. "Good to meet you," he said. "Do you know the boys?"

Up until that moment, Kerri didn't know there were boys, much less met them. "No, I don't."

He pointed at a pair of tall, broad-shouldered, nice-looking men, both of whom seemed to be older than Brooklyn. "Zack is on the left and Austin is on the right. Zack has Ethan and Henry"—he pointed to a pair of boys who were near the empty pool, throwing a football hard at one another—"and Austin has Cody. He's the one with the earphones, sitting over there wishing he was someplace else."

"A teenager?" Kerri asked.

"Yeah, he's…"—he looked at his daughter, clearly puzzled—"How old is he?"

"He just turned fifteen. I know because I forgot his birthday. To make it up to him cost me an arm and a leg."

"Oh," Richie said, "I forgot my daughters-in-law. That's Karla and that's Emily. They've been around so long I think of them as my own kids."

It looked as though everyone in the immediate family got along well, except for poor Cody, who probably wouldn't have been there if he'd had his driver's license.

Brooklyn said, "Everybody else is either a neighbor or a friend. You don't have to know their names." She chuckled, and her father gave her a gentle cuff to the cheek.

"Have some manners about you."

"I'm more practical than mannerly. I hate being introduced to people I don't need to know."

"Kerri might have something in common with some of these people. They might become lifelong friends. But you've screwed that all up."

"I can live with that," Brooklyn said. She looked happy and relaxed, and it was clear her father's teasing didn't bother her. "I'm hungry. It's time to forage."

As Brooklyn started to guide her away, Kerri turned toward Richie and said, "It was very nice to meet you."

"Same here."

There was a huge buffet set out on card tables by the house. Donna seemed to be everywhere, organizing every thing and every person. They got in line behind some neighbors and filled their plates. Kerri had decided to just go with the flow, so she took a hamburger and every kind of vegetarian side dish.

They sat on folding chairs that Brooklyn had placed just far enough away from the others to prevent them from being included in any of the conversations. That was strangely anti-social, but it was her family so they were undoubtedly used to her ways. Kerri had a bite of the burger, just to be polite. then methodically tore into each salad.

Brooklyn commented, "Don't take this wrong, but you eat a lot."

"It's late for me. I got up at three, the same as usual, so it's been ten hours since I've eaten."

Brooklyn reached over and relieved her of her hamburger. She waved it in front of her face saying, "If you leave this on your plate my mother will make you eat something else." She took a bite, smiling happily. "You can thank me later for being so considerate."

Donna, who seemed to see everything, walked over and asked, "Was there something wrong with the food?" Her dark eyes scanned Kerri so closely she felt a little uncomfortable.

"No, of course not. But the salads were so good—"

"She's a vegetarian," Brooklyn interrupted, grinning impishly. "Everybody in LA is."

"How about..." Donna looked like she was racking her brain. "How about a tuna sandwich?"

"Tuna's a fish, Mom."

"I don't need another thing," Kerri added. "I swear."

Donna seemed strangely agitated. "I hate to have someone come to my house for a meal and leave feeling hungry. Are you sure I can't get you something else? How about a cupcake?"

"I'm really full, but thanks. You're a great host."

"I'll take a cupcake," Brooklyn said, smiling sweetly at her mother.

"I'm bringing two," she said as she headed for the dessert table. "Maybe you can get Kerri to eat one."

As Donna walked away, Kerri pinched Brooklyn on the arm. "Making your poor mother get your food. You're shameless!"

"Yeah, I am," she agreed, drawling lazily. "She likes doing things for me. It upsets her when I don't let her."

Kerri nodded, but Brooklyn was full of it. It was unkind to let someone run around serving you if you could serve yourself. Just because someone was a willing victim didn't mean you should take advantage.

—⁓—

Donna wouldn't allow Kerri to lift a finger to help clean up the kitchen after the meal. She found it too frustrating to stand around not helping, so she let Brooklyn do that, obviously without guilt. Pulling up her coat collar against the chilling wind, she walked over to where Richie was closing up the grill. "Are you all going to be at Brooklyn's show tonight?"

"Just the adults. The kids aren't interested in anything she talks about." He laughed a little bit. "The boys aren't very interested either, but Donna makes them go. Same for me, I guess."

"Really? I'm not a big fan of politics, but I think she's very clever. I've only heard bits and pieces, but she hooked me."

"I know the kid's got talent, but she's way out there in liberal looney land. I guess that's where the money is, though. The liberal media has this country by the throat."

The only part of that entire statement Kerri agreed with was that Brooklyn had talent. But she'd learned long ago never to argue about religion or politics. Especially with your client's parent. "Maybe you could smuggle in some earphones and listen to music. Brooklyn would never know."

His smiling eyes reminded Kerri of Brooklyn's. "That's a damn good idea. Maybe I'll yank those things out of my grandson's ears and take 'em." After he finished his task, he guided Kerri over to the far side of the swimming pool. "Come back here and see the addition my neighbor's putting on. It's so big it's gonna block the sun."

They went to the back of the yard where Kerri looked at the addition. Though not finding it particularly big, she placidly agreed with Richie that it might cause the end of Western civilization.

"People are such idiots. You never get back what you put into a second floor. You do it so your kids each have a big room, then they leave home and you're stuck heating and cooling a whole floor you don't need. Who says a kid has to have his own room? My boys grew up fine and they shared until they moved out."

Kerri didn't have any insight into that philosophy, so she just nodded. He stood there for a moment, seemingly at a loss for words. Then, in a rush of them, he said, "Donna told me what you're doing for Brooklyn. No offense, but that's about the screwiest thing I've ever heard. Do you think there's something wrong with her? Do you think she's on drugs?"

That came out of nowhere. Brooklyn didn't show any indication of drug abuse. It was clear Richie didn't hang with the druggie set, but odd that he'd think that of his daughter. She'd never tell anyone anything specific about a client's life, but it couldn't hurt to reassure him. "I think the main thing that's wrong with her is that she can't get into a good routine for getting up early, but she's making progress."

"I don't mean for it to sound like I don't love her. I'm crazy about her. But the last thing she needs is another woman doing a bunch of things for her that she should do for herself. If Donna babied her any more, she'd be wearing diapers."

After having learned how intimately Donna was involved, Kerri tended to agree with him. "I've worked with a lot of celebrities, and Brooklyn is the most well-adjusted one I've ever been around. She's just not a morning person, and having to get up at four and then stay up until midnight on the weekends is really hard for her."

"Nobody wants to get up at four. But millions do it, and for a heck of a lot less than she gets. But she's had her head in the clouds since she was a baby."

"Since she was a baby? Really?"

"As soon as she could read. Her nose was always in a book, and by the time she was in junior high she was reading things I couldn't have understood if I had an encyclopedia."

"She's certainly bright. I don't think anyone will argue that."

"Yeah, she's smart, but a smart baby is dangerous."

That one didn't make much sense, but Kerri nodded again.

"I tell ya, it's been a struggle to force Donna to let her go." A strangely angry look settled on his face. "Do you know she kept the kid home so much when she started school that they failed her?"

"She told me she repeated first grade, but I didn't know..."

"Donna let the damn kid stay up so late that she couldn't wake up in the morning. So she let her stay home! I should have turned her in to the authorities. She wrecked her."

"Brooklyn didn't say anything about staying up late when she was young, but she does have some pretty severe sleep problems. Maybe they go back a long way."

"She might not remember staying up till all hours. Donna has to protect her, you know. Brooklyn can't hear about anything that might upset her." He looked like he wanted to spit. "It's amazing she ever got out of the house."

"But she's a very hard worker. If she wasn't, she would've turned down the radio show and never had to get up before eight o'clock at night. Then she wouldn't need me at all."

A gentle smile settled on his face, and Kerri could see a hint of Brooklyn in his expression. "She's a hard worker when it comes to her job, I'll give her that. Thank God, Donna didn't baby that out of her." His face took on a rough sweetness when he said, "She used to love to go on jobs with me, even when the other kids were out playing."

"What did she do to help?" It was hard to frame the question without showing she had no idea of what he did for a living.

"She could snap a great chalkline. And it was nice to have her get behind a toilet to cut the paper around the pipes."

Paper. Pipes. Wallpaper? That's the only thing that made sense. Oh, right. Brooklyn had mentioned that.

"I see all of these people taking advantage of her. That agent wants his ten percent, her best friend wanted her ten percent, and now…"

Unconsciously she reached out and grasped his arm. He looked down at her hand as though she were caressing him, so she withdrew it immediately. "I'm sure you worry about her, but you don't have to worry about me taking advantage of her. I'm ready to go back to California as soon as possible. When Brooklyn feels confident in her new schedule, I'm gone."

"I don't mean to insult you, but that's like giving a contractor an unlimited budget and telling him to let you know when he's finished."

Kerri laughed, having to concede the point. "I see where Brooklyn gets her sharp mind. You're right, but you're going to have to take me at my word. After I leave here, I'm going to go on a long-planned vacation, and I honestly can't wait. So I'm doing everything I can to help Brooklyn rely on herself, not other people."

"Then you'd better change the locks on her door so my wife's not over there every Sunday doing everything but clipping her nails." He stood there for a moment, his brow furrowed. "I shouldn't say that. She probably does that too."

It wasn't easy getting a minute alone with Donna, but Kerri managed by following her to the bathroom. When Donna emerged, Kerri was looking at the photos of the family that lined the hall. "You've got a great looking bunch of kids," she said.

"Oh, thanks. Ritchie's a good looking guy now, and you should have seen him forty years ago. He was a dream!"

"Brooklyn looks a lot like him, doesn't she?"

"Yes, a whole lot." They both looked at a photo of a young Brooklyn, sitting on her father's lap for a family portrait. "The spitting image."

"She's a lucky girl. Not many moms would make sure she got home-cooked meals."

Donna laughed, looking a little embarrassed. "You know about that?"

"I went up to her apartment one day right after you'd been there and saw a note you'd left her. Doing all of that work must take an awful lot of your time."

"It's not too bad. If I didn't do it, she'd just eat pizza. She's never cared about food at all, but she's worse now. She eats whatever is the easiest thing to grab. At least now I know she's getting a healthy meal."

Hmm, how to politely suggest the meals were way too high in carbs and fat? "I've been trying to get her to eat more Japanese and Thai and Indian food. She doesn't seem to notice it's got a lot more vegetables in it."

Making a face, Donna said, "I don't like that stuff. You never know what they're putting in it."

Unsure of who "they" were, Kerri tried another tack. "If she'd add a fresh vegetable to the food you bring her she'd be doing better."

"Better than what?" Donna asked with just a slight edge of sharpness.

"It'd be easier for her to get up if she had a little more energy."

"My girl needs nine hours of sleep. She's been that way since she was a little thing. If she gets her sleep, she's got enough energy for all of us." She nearly glared at Kerri, who reminded herself that no disagreement with the talent's parent ever worked out in the long run.

"She's very lucky to have you care for her so much, and I'll try to make sure she eats your meals rather than ordering pizza."

Donna gave her another quick hug. "I'm glad to know you're on my side."

"We're both on Brooklyn's side. Speaking of which, do you have an address book? I'd like to get all of her relatives addresses and birthdays written down for her."

Once again Donna gave her a squeeze. "Oh, my God, it would be so nice not to have to harass her a week before her nephews' birthdays. She wouldn't even remember Christmas if there weren't so many store windows decorated!"

Kerri stood backstage, watching Brooklyn chat easily with the stage manager, appearing happy, or maybe content. She had a lot of energy, more energy than Kerri had ever seen her display. Her energy added to her attractiveness, and Kerri thought that the blouse she'd given her as a present added even more to her allure.

She'd been around enough stage lights to know what looked good under their glare. Colors often looked too bright or too washed out. The shirts they'd ordered hadn't arrived yet, so she'd bought her an oversized, cocoa-colored, linen shirt. Wearing that over a darker brown T-shirt set off Brooklyn's dark hair and eyes. And the T-shirt would catch any sweat before it got to the lighter colored shirt. She would have chosen something other than the orange basketball shoes that Brooklyn had on, but it was the look Brooklyn had chosen, so it was here to stay.

Brooklyn walked over and stood right next to her as the announcer began the introduction. Her eyebrows popped up and down a couple of times when he went on and on about her accomplishments. Eyes dancing with happiness, she said, "I'm the shit!" Then she fist-bumped Kerri and literally ran onto the stage, holding her arms up over her head and dancing around like a boxer who'd just scored a knockout.

Kerri's body tingled all over. The excitement Brooklyn exuded was amazingly contagious. She started talking, and surprisingly, her cadence was a little slower than her normal speech. She didn't have much of a New Jersey accent, but what little she had was gone. Now she sounded like she could be from anywhere in the country, something Kerri hadn't noticed the previous times she'd seen her on stage.

As so many comedians did, Brooklyn started out with a long rant about flying. She incorporated some of the small indignities they'd experienced on their recent trip to Los Angeles, but she didn't stop at the easy joke. Instead, she added up all of those humiliations travelers were now subjected to and turned them into a surprisingly cogent indictment of how America holds itself hostage to the mere threat of terrorism. She worked on that thought for at least ten minutes, amazing Kerri at the way she would hit a line hard for a laugh and then quiet down to say something quite touching.

Brooklyn spent a few minutes blaming all of us for letting the government cave in to terrorists. That struck Kerri as decidedly different from most comedians' take. It seemed much easier to blame the government for the country's problems, but Brooklyn pointed out in several different ways that we were the government, and that blaming the authorities was like blaming your mom for your troubled adulthood. For a comedian, that was a mature way of looking at things. But how did that sync with lying in bed and letting your babysitter hand-feed you?

The act seemed significantly longer than it had in Los Angeles, and the crowd was with her the whole way. They got the inside New York jokes, they got the Jersey jokes, and it was clear to Kerri that this audience identified completely. At the end of her act, Brooklyn waved enthusiastically and bowed several times, then jogged over to Kerri. She took the towel that Kerri extended and dried her face and hands.

"It's hot out there," she said, grinning like she'd just stumbled from a wild roller coaster.

"You are the one who's hot, in every way."

The crowd demanded an encore, and Brooklyn strolled back out, nodding as though she expected the ovation. She told a cute, personal story about starting off as a standup comedian and slowly transforming herself into more of a political commentator. She said it was better for her family when she stuck to politics, even though most of them didn't agree with her politically. Then she told about the time she'd made her mother cry because of a joke about her cooking. She swore that her mom was a wonderful cook, and pointed her out in the crowd. Donna and the whole family stood up and took a bow, then Brooklyn said she realized that making up jokes about people she loved just to get a laugh wasn't something she could do in good conscience.

"Speaking of conscience," she said, the crowd listening raptly. "It's time for the legislatures of every state in this union to follow the lead of New York and vote to allow marriage to every man or woman who has the capacity to make that pledge to another adult." The crowd went wild, praising both the idea and their own representatives for their vote.

"It's a wonderful thing to know that I can one day find the woman of my dreams and make a public commitment to her. That reminds me of a joke. How many opponents of gay marriage does it take to change a lightbulb?" She paused, holding her hand up to her ear as people called out numbers. "The answer is none," she said, quietly. "They fear change and they'd rather stay in the dark than go towards the warmth of the light." She stood there grinning as the crowd hooted and clapped. "Go towards the light, people!" Then she held up a hand, shouted, "I'm out!" and ran off the stage, receiving claps on the back from everyone backstage.

Kerri walked with her to her small dressing room and closed the door, standing in front of it for a moment. "I don't think I've ever gotten into it like that backstage, and I've watched every kind of performer there is. You had that crowd eating out of your hand. That must feel amazing."

Brooklyn looked fantastic. Her eyes were bright, there was a flush of color in her cheeks and her body gave off an electric tension. "It's not better than great sex, but it's darned close."

Kerri wasn't sure what sex with Brooklyn would be like, but if she gave off the kind of energy she was giving off at right that moment, there was no doubt that it would be mind-blowing. It was almost painful to know she'd never be able to find out for herself.

Brooklyn started to doff her wet shirts, and Kerri handed her an oxford cloth shirt she'd brought from home. "You know, I don't get about half of your jokes."

"What?" Brooklyn had been wiping her damp body down with a towel, but she stopped abruptly.

"I think you heard me. I wanted you to know that your work is funny even for people who don't know what the heck you're talking about."

Brooklyn sat down on the chair in front of the small makeup table. "But...doesn't that make...how could that be?"

She looked adorably confused, with her big brown eyes wide and curious.

"I don't care about politics, or most world events. I don't read the newspapers, or watch much TV. So I don't know who the speaker of the house is, and I don't get the jokes you made about him. But they were still funny."

"Does that…" Brooklyn shook her head. "I can't imagine a joke isn't funny if you don't know the context."

"But it is." Kerri leaned over and took the edge of the towel, wiping a drop of perspiration from Brooklyn's brow. They were just inches from each other and, for the first time, she had a quick, strong desire to kiss her. Standing up so quickly she got a head rush, she managed to say, "The way you say things is almost as funny as what you say. I felt like a kid who laughs when the adults do. It's a group experience."

"And that's okay with you?"

"Sure. Why wouldn't it be? I'm not going to start being a news junkie, so why not enjoy myself?"

"That's a very good point." She still looked confused, but now she also appeared amused. "One that I really like."

Even though it was late, the Yorks wanted to go out for a drink. Kerri reluctantly joined them, figuring that Brooklyn might need to use her as an excuse to leave.

They went to a pub close to NYU that Brooklyn had obviously been to before. A couple of people recognized her the moment they walked in, and Kerri marveled at how a celebrity sighting worked. No one said a word, but people seemed to sense that the person behind them had stopped talking. So that person turned, then the one in front of him turned. In seconds the entire crowd was casting obvious or furtive glances, but it didn't seem to bother Brooklyn one bit. She smiled and nodded at anyone who made eye contact, then stood right inside the door and signed the slips of paper people thrust at her. By the time she'd posed for photos with several dozen people the rest of the family had ordered drinks, including one for her.

Brooklyn slumped down into a chair, nodded in pleasure when she noticed her drink, then took a big sip. "I'd love a glass of water," she said to Kerri. "I don't want to gulp this down."

Before Kerri could make a move Donna was up, slicing through the crowd and getting the attention of the bartender. Brooklyn caught Kerri's eye. "You've gotta be fast to beat my mom."

"I don't think I'll ever be that fast."

"You should all let her get her own water," Richie said, scowling at his daughter. "It's not like she's breaking rocks out there."

As usual, Brooklyn didn't give the slightest impression that she was offended or felt guilty. "Women like to wait on me." Her eyebrows popped up and down as she smiled at her father who eventually gave her a grin in return.

"Maybe I'm jealous."

"Maybe." Brooklyn sipped the water her mother set in front of her and tossed a few pieces of popcorn into her mouth. Donna had brought one small bowl of popcorn from the bar, and had placed it right in front of her daughter.

"Where's my popcorn?" Richie demanded.

"Right over there." Donna pointed at the bar. "Brookie, you were so fantastic," she gushed. "I couldn't believe how crazy the crowd was for you."

"Thanks," she said, after draining her glass.

Kerri got up this time, and she asked for two glasses of water—to avoid another trip. When she returned, a pair of young women were taking pictures, one of them standing behind Brooklyn while she pulled her tight shirt up, exposing her breasts. Kerri slapped the glasses onto the table and took off after the picture taker, but she couldn't get to her before she fled, giggling. She was quietly reprimanding herself when she returned to the table. "I'm sorry I didn't stop that girl from taking her picture behind you."

Brooklyn looked up and shrugged her shoulders. "No big deal. It happens all the time."

That might have been, but no one had done it while Kerri was on the job, and she was more than a little disappointed in her own performance.

After saying goodbye to the Yorks, they finally got into the car. Brooklyn started it up, then let it idle for a few moments. "I'm going to take you home. And by home I mean where you live. Don't bother arguing with me, because I'm not going to have you riding your bike at this time of night."

"I won't argue. After midnight on Saturday is pretty crazy in my neighborhood. It's really not a good time to be riding a bike. Besides, the roads look a little icy."

Brooklyn gave her a surprised look. "I think this is the first time I've ever won an argument with you."

Smiling sweetly, Kerri said, "That's because we weren't arguing."

<hr />

After going across town to the Lower East Side, Brooklyn crawled along Kerri's street, looking for a spot. "You don't mind showing me where you live, do you?"

"Of course not, but you'll never find a space." As she said that, a man got into a van and fired it up. Brooklyn sat there, feeling smug, then eased her car into the generously sized spot. She smirked, "Lesbian parking karma."

The neighborhood was a little on the sketchy side, but it was lively, with young people passing them as they walked in a hurry to get somewhere. They arrived in front of a modest red brick building and walked up the unimpressive staircase to the fourth floor. "Not having an elevator is good exercise," Kerri teased.

Brooklyn didn't reply, mostly because she was trying not to show how completely winded she was. She was trying to take deep breaths, but could only manage rapid, shallow ones. Kerri opened the door, and Brooklyn walked in. This apartment was even smaller than the one she kept in Santa Monica. It couldn't have been over three hundred and fifty square feet, but it had a nice sofa and a lounge chair and a tiny dining table. Brooklyn noted with approval that this apartment had a television.

The kitchen was more of a suggestion of a place to cook than a place where any work could get done, but there were bowls of fresh fruit sitting on the counter, and Brooklyn had to admit that was more than she ever had in her kitchen.

"Well, what do you think?" Kerri asked. "Does this look like some place I'd live?"

"It certainly doesn't look much like your place in Santa Monica. Do you own this or…"

She was interrupted by someone jiggling the front door knob then entering. An attractive blonde woman who could have been Kerri's sister walked in and threw her arms around her. "I got to go on!" She planted a lingering kiss on Kerri's lips, then pulled back and squealed, "I'm so excited!"

Brooklyn stood there, mouth agape, as Kerri squeezed her tight, then returned the kiss. She finally pulled away and said, "We have a guest."

The woman took one hand from Kerri's body and extended it to Brooklyn. "Dakota Chapman." Then she gasped. "Brooklyn York!"

"Yeah, that's me." *Who the hell are you?*

Dakota cuffed Kerri on the arm. "You're going out with Brooklyn York?"

"Uhm, Kerri and I are working together," Brooklyn said when Kerri didn't reply.

Dakota hugged Kerri possessively. "She tells me nothing. Nothing! I'm a big fan, by the way."

Uncharacteristically tongue-tied, Brooklyn affixed a smile to her face and managed to say, "Thanks."

Dakota finally let Kerri go and headed for the tiny refrigerator. "I've had a bottle of champagne in here for a year." She reached in and pulled it out and started to open it. "I was going to go out with some of the people in the cast, but I knew you'd appreciate me making my real Broadway debut more than any of them ever could." She looked at Kerri with what Brooklyn could only characterize as true love. "It's been a long time coming, baby, but I finally got to say a line on Broadway."

Brooklyn had never felt like more of an intruder, so she started backing up in the small space, blindly reaching for the door knob.

"Congratulations. I'll let you two celebrate."

Dakota let out a sad mew. "You're leaving so soon?"

"We can have dinner sometime. Kerri's just got me going to bed so early..." She was halfway out the door when she said, "Congratulations again. See you soon." Sweat prickled her neck, her stomach tightened and her vision swirled as she stood in the dim hallway. Who in the hell was Dakota? Did she just meet her in the last week, or was Kerri lying about not having a girlfriend? If Dakota wasn't a girlfriend, what did you call a woman you kissed enthusiastically and shared a sofa bed with? Brooklyn could hear the pop of the champagne cork and the sound of both women giggling. She took off, walking quickly, so she didn't have to hear another sound.

—⁓—

Brooklyn stood on her balcony, drinking vodka and smoking one cigarette after another. None of this made sense. Kerri was always available, and never seemed to have any plans. So who was Dakota and what were they to each other?

She hated to admit how certain she'd been that she'd be able to make a play for Kerri. Reluctantly, she had to acknowledge that was one of the detriments of being famous. Women were far too eager to fall for you, and you tended to forget it took a little effort once in a while. In the last two years she'd pretty much pointed at any woman who sparked a hint of interest and got her. But she hadn't wanted any of them for long. Kerri was different. She was a keeper. But it looked like Dakota already had her.

She stubbed out her cigarette, feeling an unpleasant rush in her head from smoking too many too quickly. Swallowing the last of the vodka, she went back inside. She hadn't been up this late recently, and it felt odd. Odd and bad. She walked over and plopped down in front of her television set, where she watched a gruesome story about a serial killer. The tone of the show matched her mood, and when it was over she still wasn't tired so she channel surfed, staying on each of her hundred plus channels just long enough to decide she didn't like what was on. Then she took her phone out and turned off her alarm. There was no way she was getting up at six. She'd just take her lumps on Monday.

——

When her phone rang the next day Brooklyn answered it before she realized what she was doing. "Hello?"

"It's Kerri." She sounded bright and chipper as always. Screw her and her jolly mood.

"Hi."

"I didn't wake you up, did I?"

"Yeah, you did, but I assume it's after six, so I should probably be up."

"It's after noon, Brooklyn. If you can manage it, you should probably get up and try to get some exercise so you can go to bed at your normal time."

"Yeah. That's the idea."

There was a short, uncomfortable silence, then Kerri said, "I just wanted to check to see if you needed anything today."

"No. Nothing."

"Okay," she said, sounding tentative. "If you want to sleep all day and stay up all night I'll gladly come over to be with you."

She wanted to be gracious, to thank her for her thoughtfulness, but she couldn't manage it. "No thanks. I'll try to get to bed early. I'll see you at the same ridiculous time tomorrow."

"Are you sure? Did your show take a lot out of you?"

"Yeah, it must have, but I'll be fine. See you tomorrow."

Now she was wide awake, giving her more time to stew about Kerri and the girlfriend she didn't have named Dakota.

——

Brooklyn spent the better part of the day trying to figure out an angle to get under Kerri's skin. There had definitely been a change in their interactions over the past week; something was starting to build between them. She was certain of that. Even though she didn't have to work hard at picking up women, she was darned good at telling when they were interested in her, and Kerri was at least partially interested.

But there was always the possibility that Kerri viewed her as damaged goods or at least in the bargain bin. Women didn't tend to want something that no one else wanted. In retrospect, it had been a mistake to tell Kerri how little she was interested in women who were only attracted to her because of her fame. Making that too clear cheapened the overtures Kerri had already witnessed women making. Damn it all.

CHAPTER NINE

"BROOKLYN. BROOKLYN. BROOKLYN!"

It couldn't be time to get up already. It just couldn't be. But there was no other reason for Kerri to be standing by her bed shaking her. And what was with this bed? How could such an expensive mattress feel so horrible?

"I'm up." Brooklyn started to sit up but her back bellowed so loudly that she stopped mid-movement and fell back onto the mattress. The light was wrong, all wrong. It was too intense and coming from the wrong direction. Finally, she was able to fully open her eyes and see that she was lying on her sectional, not her bed, and a halogen lamp was shining in her eyes. How in the heck did that happen?

"Are you able to take a shower? Alone?"

What kind of question was that? She started to get up, then dropped onto the seat again, a spike of pain hitting her right behind her eyeballs. It was all she could do to avoid vomiting. But she didn't want Kerri to have to witness that, so she steeled her nerves and tried one more time to stand, this time crushing a paper bag and some tin foil with her foot.

This was bad. She had no memory of ordering food, or draining the bottle of vodka that was lying empty on the table. All she could smell was cigarettes, alcohol, and the sweat of her own body, and that combo was enough to make anyone sick. Adding in the headache should have qualified her for a medal of some sort just to be alive. But they didn't give medals for having blackouts, and if they did, the other comics would have already earned all of them.

A blackout. That had to be what this was. She'd never had one before, and she wasn't about to admit to anyone that she'd just had one. This was one of those little "take it to the grave" moments, and if she could just manage to get in the shower and get to work, no one need be the wiser.

—⁓—

Kerri watched her stumble into the bathroom, keeping a close eye on her in case she tripped. As soon as Brooklyn got into the shower, Kerri set about compiling her wardrobe for the day. That only took a few minutes, and Brooklyn was taking forever, so she went into the living room and cleaned up from the previous night's bacchanalia. There was just one glass, so Brooklyn had apparently been alone again. Drinking alone was never a good sign, and one more such night was going to earn her a ticket to rehab. Spectrum probably had a family plan discount for all of their personalities who'd been on a twenty-eight-day vacation from alcohol.

—⁓—

As soon as Brooklyn left, Kerri began another search. This time, she didn't merely check obvious hiding places. She disassembled the loft just as she'd had to do to apartments, houses and hotel rooms the world over. While taking apart Brooklyn's dresser, removing each drawer, then turning the piece on its back so she could check every surface, she thought of the time she'd had to take apart a fifteen-room vacation home in the South of France. It had been a sweltering hot day, and the place hadn't been air conditioned. The film star she'd been monitoring had gone to Cannes that day, and her bodyguards were in charge of keeping others from harming her and her from harming herself.

Kerri had only had one full day to work, and it took every minute of it to find the heroin. It had been hidden in a hollowed out hardback book that had been stored in an airless attic in a box with dozens of other books. The completion bond company for the blockbuster movie set to begin shooting had been very grateful to her, but their thanks didn't help her exhaustion. Luckily, it was chilly in New York today, and opening the windows cooled her off enough to make the hours pass quickly.

Despite her suspicions, all she came up with was a bottle of pills that an internet search proved to be for a urinary tract infection. The last time she'd checked, an infection didn't give a woman a wicked hangover. Still, Brooklyn seemed more than hungover. She'd seemed drugged, and that was a suspicion Kerri couldn't afford to ignore.

Dropping onto a chair, Kerri sat for a few minutes, weighing her feelings. There was no doubt she was angry, but it was so unlike her to be angry with a client that she had to dig deeper.

No matter how she'd try to convince herself that Brooklyn was off limits, a tiny part of her couldn't stop wanting her. It was bad enough to desire a client. But a needy client who loved to be babied and might have a drug problem was "three-strikes-and-you're-out" territory. The embarrassing part was that she was disappointed. Profoundly disappointed.

It took a while for Toni to get her makeup on. "You look like the dog's breakfast," she whispered in her Cockney accent. "How late were you out?"

"I wasn't out." They weren't allowed to smoke in the building, but everyone in hair and makeup did. Grumbling to herself, Brooklyn took a deep drag from the cigarette she'd cadged from Toni's pack. When had cigarettes started tasting so awful? She needed them like she needed air or food, but they gave her less and less pleasure. Maybe that's why they called them a vice. Her head throbbed, the pain having settled behind her eyes. It was worse on the right side, and when she peered at herself in the mirror, she noticed that her eyelid was puffy, like she'd been crying.

"You're very chatty today," Toni observed. "That should serve you well on air."

Toni was the ideal person to get your day started off on the wrong foot. She did nothing but gossip, and she ran to Arnie with every tidbit she could pry out of her victims. Brooklyn usually humored her, or tried to sweet-talk her, but today she wasn't in the mood. "Thanks for the career advice." She took another cigarette, more to annoy Toni than anything, and lit it from the one in her mouth.

"Those cost me ten dollars," Toni snapped.

Ostentatiously, Brooklyn dug into her pocket and came up with seven dollars that she'd stuffed in there after buying another latte on the way to work. She tossed the money on the makeup table, not adding another word.

The TV director popped his head in and said, "Four minutes!" then ran down the hallway. It was always frantic on Monday, but this day seemed worse than most. People were running everywhere, clipping each other with things they were carrying, and snarling curse words as they passed.

Brooklyn started to get up, but she took a final look at herself before she did. Toni had obviously used the wrong color foundation on her, since she was at least three shades paler than normal. It was too late to fix now, and when she made eye contact with her in the mirror she could see a look a triumph on the younger woman's face.

This was the day she'd decided to try out her new "look." Not because she was ready to argue with the stylist, but because she wanted to wear something comfortable. Her jeans were her security blanket, and the pale green T-shirt and bright white dress shirt Kerri had laid out for her made her feel more like herself. Having some control over her image was important, and she was glad they'd taken the first step. Regretfully, the pale makeup and the green shirt just made her look sickly, something Toni probably got a lot of pleasure from contributing to.

When she entered the studio a PA dashed over to her and shoved a battery pack in her pocket, then hooked up her lapel mic. Being on both TV and the radio was a big pain, since they had to take direction from competing groups. The TV director had a very different goal than the radio producer and each department had their own sound guys. She put her headphones on and settled into her chair, hoping against hope that Arnie took it easy on her.

"Five! Four! Three!" The director held up two fingers silently, then one, and the "On Air" sign lit up. The normal bugle sounded, then their intro played. Arnie sauntered in and settled himself just as the final notes played. "Rise and shine, people. It's a beautiful day to be an American."

Brooklyn was scanning the newspaper, something she was usually allowed to do in peace. But the camera right over her head went on, alerting her by the red dot just above it. "You'd all better be careful," Arnie intoned. "It's cold and flu season. Look at our poor funny lady over there. Have you ever seen a Caucasian woman's skin that particular shade of green?"

"Is there a race on earth that's green, Arnie?" she asked, trying to sound snarky. Sometimes he backed off if he wasn't in the mood to fight.

"No, I suppose not. What do you think, Wild Man?" he asked his loyal lapdog, who'd been adding nothing to the show for twenty-two years.

"I don't know of any race that's green," he said. "Maybe Asians? Are they ever green?"

"Not that," Arnie snapped. "Doesn't Madam Resident look like she's got the flu?"

"She looks awful, that's for sure," Chick, the sports guy jumped in. "Did you know today was a work day, Brook?"

"I'm aware of that. Surprisingly, I wouldn't drive to Jersey to hang out with you guys at this time of the morning if it wasn't."

"Then why do you look like you just rolled out of a bar?" Arnie asked.

"If she just rolled out of a bar, she'd probably have a girl...I mean woman trailing after her," Chick added. "Right Brook?"

"I think she likes girls *and* women," Arnie said, his voice taking on a predatory purr.

Brooklyn tried not to shrink from the camera, but it was hard. When your head felt like it was in a vise, and three idiots were poking you with sticks, it was no fun having thousands of people trying to see how bad you actually looked. So she sat up straighter, tried to smile and tried even harder to keep her eyes open wide. "I feel fine, thanks for asking. How about you, Arnie? Were you avoiding the flu by hobnobbing with the beautiful people in the Hamptons this weekend?" He hated having the audience reminded that he made several million dollars a year from the show and spent his weekends with the ultra-rich.

"Speaking of beautiful people," he said, "a listener sent us a lovely picture of you posing with a fan." He held a photo up, and the camera zoomed in. They'd placed a censor bar across the woman's breasts, but that only made it look dirtier. It looked like Brooklyn had her head resting right between the woman's ample bare breasts, and the smile on her face indicated she was very happy to be there.

She was screwed. Going into an explanation was a waste of energy. Attack was the only option. "Don't be so jealous, fellas," she said, chuckling. "It's not my fault that women stopped hitting on you a few decades ago."

Arnie sniffed, "If this was the quality of woman that came after me, I'd be happy to have them stop."

"I didn't actually meet that fan, but she looks like a nice person. From what I can see of her, that is. There's something obscuring her face."

"A big pair of headlights," Wild Man offered. "Is that what you like, York?" The sound guy dropped a loud, old fashioned car horn in.

"I prefer to actually face a woman," she said. "When they come up behind me and flash their headlights for the camera the encounter loses something. But you guys would know more about that than I would. What's it like to completely objectify a woman into body parts?"

"It's a little early for your feminist crap." *Fantastic!* Arnie was really peeved. He hated to let the audience know he had a genuine feeling about anything, so he'd veer off. "I saw a photo of you at the Knicks game, Chick. Are they on a losing streak because you keep worming into those court-side seats?"

At last, Brooklyn took a deep breath and slumped down in her chair when the red light went off. A bullet dodged.

—⁓—

As always, Kerri was waiting for her when she arrived home. She enjoyed Kerri's company, and found herself perking up near the end of the show—just thinking about going home. But today she could only think of sleep—something Kerri wouldn't approve of.

Brooklyn hung up her coat and went to the kitchen, where Kerri was making something healthy looking. The sight of all of those vegetables was off-putting, and Brooklyn started to head for the freezer to pull out a home-cooked meal, but that didn't sound good either.

She stood there, trying to hide her annoyance at Kerri's mere presence. "I can't decide what I want for lunch."

The sweet smile that seemed to have a permanent residence on Kerri's face looked back at her. "Want a salad?"

"No, that doesn't sound good." She was an adult. She could have what she wanted. "I'm going to go out to lunch."

Kerri's eyebrows shot up in surprise. "Really?"

She looked so shocked that Brooklyn had to laugh. "Yeah, really. I'm in the mood for deli food. I think I'll head over to the Lower East Side."

Kerri stopped chopping vegetables and hurried over to her. "I'll go with you if you'd like."

Looking at that innocent face made her feel like a jerk to say no, but she put up with the discomfort. "No, I'm ready to go." She headed back to the door to get her coat, but Kerri was right behind her. Damn it. It was time to be a jerk. "I'd like to be alone, if you don't mind." There. Saying it softly made it a little less rude. "I had a bad day."

"It might help to talk about it."

"No, not today. I'm going to read something I've been avoiding." She went to the low bookcases that skirted the windowed wall. "I've got to read this crap." She held up the latest from a Republican former congressman who Arnie liked and had on often. "I might as well keep my crappy day going."

Kerri looked like she was about to insist on going, so Brooklyn went for the door as quickly as she could. "See you later."

When she got outside, the cold, moist air hit her like a slap in the face. It was too early in the year for this kind of weather, but it went along perfectly with the tone of the day.

—⁓—

A big, greasy Reuben was Brooklyn's favorite hangover cure. She wasn't sure what about the sandwich made her feel better, but it almost always did the trick. She'd gotten halfway through the boring book by the time she'd jammed the last bit of sandwich into her mouth, and was almost tempted to walk home. But she came to her senses and hailed a cab. When she entered the loft Kerri was cleaning the windows. "It's amazing how much you have to pay to have the help do windows these days," Brooklyn said.

"Only the insides. Your building can hire someone to do the outside." She put down the glass cleaner. "How was lunch?"

Brooklyn tossed her book on the table and took off her coat. "Good. Well, the food part was good. The book is horrible." She was as full as a tick, and knew that a long nap in front of the TV would make her as happy as anything on earth. So she broached the subject, hoping to catch Kerri off guard. "I'm gonna catch up on cable news. And I might catch a few winks while I'm at it."

As she'd feared, Kerri was next to her in a flash. "That's not a good idea. If you sleep this afternoon, you'll have trouble falling asleep tonight. It's really best to fight through your fatigue so you can get a full eight hours."

"I know, I know." She sat down, waiting for the lecture to continue.

"Let's go outside and stay busy. We can do anything you like." Kerri smiled, obviously trying to encourage her. "What are your favorite things to do?"

Something evil in her made the words come out. "Do you know what I really like?"

"No. What?" Her pretty face cocked just an inch, like a fascinated puppy.

"I like to go to a nice bar, have a couple of stiff drinks, pick up a willing woman and do what comes naturally. Oh, I like to read and watch TV too."

The pretty smile deflated like a ruined soufflé. "There has to be something you like to do that doesn't involve alcohol, sex, or sitting on a couch. Come on, think about it."

"Okay." She took in a breath. "I like going to museums, and to plays, and I like a good documentary. Plus lying on a beach," she added. "But I like to read on the beach, so that's redundant."

"Then let's go to a museum." The persistent good cheer was getting hard to take.

"They're closed on Mondays." She probably didn't know MOMA was open. "No plays are on either. You're supposed to sleep on Mondays."

"Then let's go for a walk. It's nice out."

Brooklyn got up and went to a window. They were the originals, and were so heavy they were almost impossible to open. But she wrenched one up and stood there, letting the wet breeze hit her like the salt spray on a beach. "Yeah, it's lovely. I'll put on my swimsuit."

"Oh, it's fine. I rode my bike here, and it was twenty degrees colder at four a.m."

"Just because you're nuts doesn't mean everyone is." She marched over to the sectional, her mind having been made up. "I'm going to watch TV. You can stomp around and make a lot of noise, but rest assured I can sleep through it." She sat down, kicked off her shoes and stretched out. There were few things that felt better than a long nap in front of the TV on a cold, drizzly day. When your head felt like it was in a vise and your stomach was still roiling from the morning, the thought of sleeping away the pain was that much more alluring.

Surprisingly, Kerri didn't argue. Instead, she packed up her things, walked over to the sectional and patted Brooklyn on the head. "I'll leave you in peace. Call me if you have trouble sleeping and I'll come back."

"Will do." She caught her eye and smiled. "Thanks."

It was after five when Brooklyn woke up later that afternoon, groggy, thirsty and grumpy. The Reuben had sucked every bit of moisture from her body, and she stumbled into the kitchen and downed two glasses of water.

The lure of the sofa called to her. She almost went right back to it, but she knew she should get up and try to get back on schedule. Thumbing through the movie listing in the Times, she found a documentary at the Angelika she'd heard about. Then she called a friend who liked movies as much as she did. Gerry was home, available, and willing, so they met at a bar across from the theater. You couldn't go to see a film about the genocide in Rwanda without a drink to soften the blow, so they had a couple.

You also couldn't watch a movie without popcorn, so they shared a giant tub. Gerry kept leaning over and whispering things like, "If I'd brought a gun, I'd shoot myself. This is the most depressing thing I've ever seen."

But Brooklyn knew that wasn't a complaint. Gerry liked depressing films as much as she did. Afterwards, they had one more drink, then took off in separate cabs. Once home, Brooklyn realized that she was wide awake and it was nine p.m., the witching hour. If she didn't get to sleep soon, she'd be groggy again on the show, and she couldn't allow that to happen. So she grabbed her jacket, went down the block to the garage where she kept her car, and found a spare bottle of sleeping pills in the glove box. Kerri probably wouldn't search the apartment, but just in case, she wasn't about to lose her last legally obtained supply. She took two for good measure, went back home and stretched out on the sectional once again, knowing that the pills and the drone of the news would knock her out within minutes.

The next morning was a freakish recreation of the day before. When Kerri shook her awake there were no liquor bottles to trip over, but she spied a takeout carton of something from her local Chinese delivery shop. She knew she hadn't ordered anything, but the noodles that lay on the coffee table like dried worms indicated that someone had. So either she was ordering food she didn't recall, or someone else was. Which was more frightening was hard to know.

Kerri kept pulling on her, and she got to her feet. "How late were you out?" Kerri screamed at the top of her lungs. Or maybe she spoke in her usual calm tone. Either was a possibility.

"I was home by nine. I just saw a movie." As she tried to locomote towards the bathroom, she could feel Kerri's eyes on the back of her head. Just that look was enough to make her head hurt even worse—if that was possible.

———

She wasn't going to admit that Kerri had been right about naps being her enemy; nonetheless, when Brooklyn returned home after the show, it was she who brought up the idea of going out. "I'm going to go up to the Met this afternoon to see what's been going on. I'm embarrassed to admit I haven't been there in a couple of years."

"I'm in the same boat. Can I tag along?" Kerri looked like she was about to burst from happiness. That look hit Brooklyn like a punch to the gut. Doing something positive for herself gave Kerri pleasure. Why not just give in and be a decent person?

———

They were wandering around the museum when Kerri said, "I wonder if anyone will see you and tag you on a social media site?"

"I assume I should know what that means, but I don't."

"When people mention you, and when they post a picture of you, other people can see it. Like last night when you were at Ryan's Bar and at the Angelika."

Brooklyn jerked to a halt and stared at her. "How did you know where I was?"

A smile that looked just a little devious showed. Kerri pulled out her phone, hit a few buttons, typed a few letters, and showed Brooklyn the result. There was a photo of the back of her head at the theater, and two, from different people, at the bar. Someone also snippily mentioned that she and the man she was with had been speaking too often during the movie.

Sputtering, she said, "It's like the KGB!"

Kerri nodded. "There's nowhere to hide."

As they continued to walk, Brooklyn mused that Kerri wasn't speaking in generalities. She was making it clear that she knew much more than she let on. Maybe it was time to get a safe deposit box for the sleeping pills.

———

Fairly early in the afternoon the following Sunday, the pair returned from a gig in North Carolina. Kerri's bike was at the loft, so they had their cab drop both of them off there. Once inside, Brooklyn poked through the small amount of mail she got. "I know I should stay up, but I don't think I can manage it."

"It's a nice day, let's go outside."

Brooklyn looked at her, marveling at her demeanor. "How do you do it?"

"Do what?"

"Stay so fucking peppy." She laughed at herself, realizing how silly that sounded. "I guess I just have to realize that once you hit my age, you're never gonna feel good again."

Kerri wore a sly grin. "I'm six years older than you are."

"Liar!"

Chuckling, Kerri took her wallet out of her backpack and handed Brooklyn her license.

Brooklyn spent a moment looking from the license to Kerri's sunny face. Handing it back, she added, "It's probably fake. You don't even drive."

"I know how to drive, I just don't have a car. And the secret to feeling good isn't really a secret. You just have to get the amount of sleep you need, eat well, and exercise. People have known that for thousands of years, but it still hasn't caught on." She gave Brooklyn that adorable smile that somehow never seemed judgmental.

"I'd like to be able to exercise, but the only thing I like to do is play tennis. And it's been so long since I've played, and I'm so out of shape, I'd probably have a heart attack."

"Do you have a bike?"

"Probably. But I think it's pink and has training wheels. I'm sure it's in a place of honor in my mom's garage."

"Let's spend the afternoon getting you set up with a nice bike. You can spend this winter getting in shape so that you'll be able to start playing tennis again. The key is doing things slowly, not pushing yourself so hard that you get injured."

Brooklyn took her wallet from her bag and stuck it in her back pocket. "Normally I wouldn't let you talk me into this, but I love buying stuff, and some of the bikes I see are ridiculously cool. I want one of those fixed gear ones the hipsters ride. All black...or maybe a strange green... or orange..."

―⁓―

They spent most of the afternoon at the bike shop, and by the time Brooklyn was properly outfitted with her new bright yellow single gear bike it was almost dusk. The bike shop Kerri had chosen was close to the West Side Highway, and they went over to the Hudson River bike path and rode just a couple of miles so Brooklyn's butt wouldn't hurt.

It certainly wasn't warm out, but they'd expended enough energy that they were able to sit comfortably on a bench while staving off the chill winds. After seeing several gay couples walk by, Brooklyn said, "After much prodding, you told me in California that you were single. Does Dakota know that?"

Her tone showed she was teasing, but Kerri could tell it was a serious question. "She should. She's the one who broke up with me." At Brooklyn's surprised look, she nodded, "Yes, Dakota was my first, and longest lasting girlfriend. We're still very close."

"So that's her apartment?"

"Yeah." *You want to know if we have sex, but I'm not going to tell you.* Big brown eyes continued to stare right at her, so Kerri offered a little more. "I visit her a couple of times a year, and she stays with me when she comes to LA."

"That's interesting. Ashley and I don't hate each other, but we're both happy to keep things at a Christmas-card level."

"Luckily for me, Dakota and I keep things at an 'I'd love to have you stay with me' level. It saves thousands." *That's all I'm giving up, Brooklyn. We've got to be real friends to share real details.*

Kerri led the way back to TriBeCa, and after they got the bikes upstairs, Brooklyn was famished. "I know it's time for bed, but I'll never be able to sleep when I'm this hungry. I'm going to order a pizza."

Kerri hadn't had to use trickery very often, but this was an ideal time for it. "I have one secret to getting myself adjusted to any time zone, but I haven't told you about it."

"You've got a secret that you haven't told me? Why are you holding out?"

"I'm not really holding out. It's just something I don't think you can do, and I didn't want to make you feel like a failure."

It was like waving a cape in front of a bull. Kerri could actually see Brooklyn's competitive nature engage. "Hit me," she said, standing tall and crossing her arms over her chest. She looked like she was waiting for Kerri to bull-rush her, and that she was completely confident she'd be able to stand her ground. Actually, when she behaved like this, she was almost irresistible, but that wasn't something Kerri allowed herself to linger on.

"I only mention it now because this is the ideal day to do it." Brooklyn was still glaring at her, her eyes sparking with determination. "In a way it's really simple, but it's very hard for most people to do."

"Are you going to tell me today?"

"Here it is. You need to wait about sixteen hours between meals. When you break the fast by eating, your body thinks that it's morning, no matter what time it really is."

"That's it? That's the whole secret?"

"Yep. If you go to bed now, without eating, your body will think four is a perfectly normal time to get up as long as you eat right away."

Brooklyn looked at her watch. "I could do that. Easily. But I always have a hard time relaxing on Sunday night. If I add my usual anxieties to an empty stomach, I'm afraid I'll be up for hours."

"How about this? You get ready for bed, and I'll teach you some relaxation exercises. I can't guarantee they'll work, but they sure do work for me."

Brooklyn stared at her for several moments. "It's a deal, but only if you stay here overnight. Now that I've been on a bike in the city, I'm going to be even more of a mother hen."

"I don't mind being mothered…a little."

———

Since they'd been traveling, Kerri had her yoga mat strapped to the outside of her backpack. Once she was in her pajamas, she took the mat and went to Brooklyn's room. They worked together for a little while, doing some very simple deep breathing relaxation exercises, then Kerri showed her some easy ways to relax her muscles. "Let me show you a pose that always makes my back feel better after a long flight." She had Brooklyn lie on the mat face down, and showed her how to do the cobra pose. Brooklyn almost got it right, but she was holding a lot of tension in her lower back and butt. Kerri got down on the floor with her and put her hand on her lower back, gently rubbing it. "Take in a deep breath, and on the exhale let these muscles release."

Their heads were almost touching and the thought hit Kerri that this was even closer than they'd been at NYU. Brooklyn's eyes were warm and welcoming and outrageously pretty. Just as she had that thought, Brooklyn leaned toward her and gently brought their lips together.

Years of experience sent messages to Kerri's brain, demanding, insisting that she pull away. But her body desperately wanted to ignore them. It felt so good, so right to kiss Brooklyn, but whenever there was a war between Kerri's brain and her body, the brain won. She started to pull back, then placed one very brief kiss on Brooklyn's cheek. She rolled into a sitting position and said, "If I were ever going to be inappropriate with a client, you'd be the one I'd start with."

It took Brooklyn a second, but she rather clumsily mirrored Kerri's pose. "I could get you fired."

That was so Brooklyn, and a big part of what made her attractive. She always had a quick reply, and an active mind was a huge turn on. "Yeah, you could, but then I'd have to go back to LA." This was the hard part. She'd had to get past this slightly embarrassing position more times than she could count, but it was so much harder this time. "Would you like me to tell Spectrum to find someone else right away?"

"No!" Brooklyn clambered to her feet, looking agitated. "I got lost in the moment. I really apologize. It won't happen again."

Kerri got up and put her hands on Brooklyn's shoulders, looking into those mesmerizing eyes. "You didn't do anything wrong. If we'd met under different circumstances…"

Her expression was sad and, as usual, self mocking. "Like if I were a completely different person…"

"That's not it at all. I never, ever, get involved with a client, no matter how ridiculously attractive"—she shook her a little to make her look into her eyes again—"or fantastic she is."

"You're even good at shooting people down."

"I'm not shooting you down. I'm just…"

"Not accepting my overtures."

"No, that's not how it is. I have a work ethic that I always follow, and for me, always doesn't mean most of the time."

"I appreciate that. This is just part of my laziness. I'm most attracted to women who are already inside my house."

Kerri was mightily tempted to kiss that adorable half grin. But no matter how attractive Brooklyn was, she was deeply flawed. Kerri's longstanding policy was not to date clients, and Brooklyn provided a textbook example for the sagacity of that rule. Brooklyn had people waking her up, cooking for her, cleaning for her, and doing a dozen other things that most adults could handle just fine. Her inability to care for herself, coupled with her bouts of binge drinking slammed the door on any possible romantic involvement. Her most adorable qualities, and there were plenty of them, couldn't overcome those problems.

———

It was remarkably easy to wake up the next morning. Somehow, even while smarting from Kerri's rejection, Brooklyn had gotten to sleep fairly easily. She gazed up at Kerri's happy-looking face and got out of bed without a whimper. "I hope you've factored in enough time for me to stop and have the biggest breakfast of all time," Brooklyn teased, trying to make it clear they wouldn't have to talk about the events of the previous evening.

"I can do better than that. I've got your favorite cereal, a nice muffin, and an orange. You can have the cereal here, then take the other things in the car."

Grinning before she closed the bathroom door, Brooklyn looked at her and said, "Thanks for taking care of me. I really do appreciate it."

———

Yeah, it was immature. It was impossible to argue that it wasn't. But the only way to get past rejection was to turn it around.

Kerri had a lot of good qualities, but she was a caregiver. Caregivers were awfully close to mothers, and mothers were a long way from sexy. It would suck hard to get involved and have the sizzle drain out of it because she was too maternal.

And why in the hell didn't she already have a girlfriend? If she'd shown an iota of interest, she would have been snapped up long ago. No, she didn't have one because she didn't want one. And you aren't going to change her mind about that.

Plus, and this was a big one, what in the hell was going on with Dakota? There was no way they were "ex" lovers. Something was going on there, and if seeing a woman a couple of times a year was enough for Kerri, she was totally screwed up. She hid it well, but she was damaged goods. And nobody ever got a real bargain when they bought from the damaged, dented, and dinged bin.

It was a sunny, cold afternoon, and the dusting of snow they'd woken to had melted from the streets; a perfect day for bike riding in Kerri's view. Brooklyn and Kerri started out from the long path along the Hudson River. It could be ridiculously crowded in the summer, but in early winter it was blessedly empty.

They'd made it up to the 79th Street boat basin and Kerri could tell Brooklyn was getting tired. The only way to make this pleasurable was to keep from making it too arduous—at least while Brooklyn was still out of shape. Kerri had brought some snacks, and they sat on a bench and ate while watching people stroll down the path pushing baby carriages.

After sitting there a few minutes, Brooklyn's phone rang. Kerri noticed she flinched when she saw the name. Brooklyn stood up and walked away to talk, just out of hearing range. She wasn't on the phone for long, and when she came back she said only, "Ashley. Tax questions."

Kerri didn't usually ask personal questions of her clients, but she thought it was clear to both of them that they were now somehow more than that. "Did you own a house together?"

"Yeah, we had a townhouse in Ridgewood. Do you know where that is?"

"No, I've never heard of it."

"It's in Jersey, not far from where I grew up. If we'd stayed together I'd have saved about a half hour of travel in the morning. For that reason alone, I should beg Ashley to take me back."

"Would she?"

"It's highly doubtful. She's getting married soon, and I don't think she's doing it just to make me mad."

"How does that make you feel?"

Brooklyn gave her a long look. "Haven't they retired that question to the psychotherapists' Hall of Fame?"

Embarrassed, Kerri slapped her hand over her mouth. "That was really lame, and I apologize. But I'm interested if you want to talk about it."

Brooklyn shrugged and sat there for a minute or two. Her sharp gaze scanned the Jersey palisades, which lay right across the river. "I think it's always sad when someone you've loved moves on with her life, but I think I'm better off without her. To be honest, I miss being in a relationship and having somebody to count on more than I miss *her* specifically."

"Make sure you put that in the card you send, I'm sure she'll appreciate it." Trying not to laugh, she lost the battle when Brooklyn gave her a sharp slap on the thigh.

"Ashley was great in some ways, but she had to be in charge. It got tiring to know you were going to lose every argument."

"You said you were together before your career took off, right?"

"Yeah, she was there for the lean years."

"How'd you meet?"

Brooklyn chewed on her inner cheek for a second, a habit she reverted to when she was seriously considering a question. "I knew a guy in high school who asked me out a few times. I never went, but he was pretty determined."

"I'm sure you were just as cool in high school as you are now. How can you blame him?"

Brooklyn gave her a smirk and continued. "I was working a club down the shore one summer, and Sam showed up with a bunch of people. One of them was Ashley." She grinned, looking a little smug. "His older sister."

"Ouch! You swiped the guy's sister?"

"I didn't take her hostage. We all sat in the club until they closed and when Ashley shook my hand when they were leaving, she slipped me her phone number. She could tell I was a lesbian in two seconds, unlike her brother who still isn't absolutely sure."

"That's a funny story. So she was a little older?"

"Yeah. Just a few years. We dated for a while, and eventually moved in together."

"And it was good, right?"

"Pretty good for the first few years. But things came up and we didn't work hard enough on resolving them."

"Do you have any examples?"

Smiling, Brooklyn said, "If you've been in a relationship for over five years you have a list as long as your arm."

"Just give me a finger."

Playfully, Brooklyn started to lift her middle finger, then let it collapse. "Okay. She didn't get along very well with my parents. My mother, specifically."

"Really?"

"She and my mom argued over the dumbest stuff, like which of my clothes should be dry cleaned, and what kinds of food I liked. Really dumb. Childish."

"What…what? How would they get into an argument about the kinds of food you liked?"

"Ashley would make something for me and when she'd mention it my mom would tell her I didn't like it. Then they'd start picking at each other. It was tiring to listen to."

"Did you get involved? Or was it just the two of them?"

She shrugged. "I stayed out of it and ate what was on my plate. I don't like to get involved in arguments I don't start."

I'm sure Ashley appreciated that. "Ashley cooked your meals?"

"Yes, Kerri," she said with exaggerated patience. "She also did the grocery shopping, the laundry, and most of the housework. I would have helped, but she wanted it done her way. And, just so you know the whole shameful truth, she did my bookkeeping."

"That's…interesting."

"Yeah, it was very interesting when we kept having less and less money, even though I earned more and more."

"She stole from you?" *What in the world!*

"I could never prove it, and to be honest, I didn't want to. But after we broke up, I had substantially more money than I did when she was paying the bills."

"Wow…that's…awful."

"Yeah, it cost me a lot of sleepless nights. I really should have broken up with her, but I couldn't be sure."

"Wait, wait." Kerri held a hand up. "You didn't talk about it? Confront her? Hire an accountant to do an audit?"

"Nah." She shrugged, as though this were a minor point. "It was only money. I trusted her in other ways."

"Like what?"

"She was loyal, and she never talked about me behind my back. That meant a lot."

"Brooklyn, you think she stole from you."

"Yeah, but living with me isn't any picnic. She probably deserved to stash some money away for putting up with me."

Kerri was stunned. What kind of sense did that make? "So what did you do?"

"Nothing. But when we broke up my mom took over everything Ashley was doing." She let out a sigh and rolled her eyes. "Yes, my mother is my accountant, and I don't want to hear a word about it. She does a great job."

Kerri moved her mouth a couple of times, but no sound came out.

Laughing, Brooklyn gave her a bump with her shoulder. "I like you like that. Keep it up. So, I know you can have someone close to you be very involved. It's just that Ashley wasn't the right person. Maybe she was just careless with our money. Like I said, I can't prove she stole it. But it was my fault for letting her handle it in the first place. She honestly didn't know more about bookkeeping than I did."

"She wasn't an accountant or a CPA?"

Snorting, Brooklyn said, "She was a bartender. But she said she could do it, and I let her. Hell, I should probably use a stranger now, since my mom gives me a hard time when I spend too much on things she doesn't think I should have."

"I hear you loud and clear on that. I left home at eighteen and that's the last time I allowed anyone to let their opinions overrule mine."

Brooklyn slapped Kerri on the leg one more time, then stood up and put her helmet back on. "That's also why you haven't been in another relationship." She stuck her hand out. "That'll be ten bucks for the psychoanalysis."

They got on their bikes and started towards home, with Kerri thinking about what Brooklyn had said. She seemed pretty perceptive when it came to Kerri's life, but couldn't she see how childish it was to rely on people who weren't experts for so much? Apparently not, since her mom was her accountant and Melvin was her agent.

They'd been back at the loft for a while, but Kerri hadn't been able to move on past the discussion about Ashley. It was weighing so heavily on her mind that she finally had to bring it up again. "Hey, do you mind my asking a little more about your relationship?"

In response, Brooklyn put the TV on mute and gave Kerri her full attention.

"You said you missed having someone to count on more than Ashley herself. Is that really true?"

Brooklyn's eyes scrunched up and she tilted her head back, as though the answer were on the ceiling. When she met Kerri's gaze again she said, "No, I missed her. But I had my doubts about her, and she thought I was cheating on her when I traveled."

"Were you?" *Please, say no.*

Brooklyn responded so quickly that it seemed like the truth. "I'm not like that. We had good sex. Why go looking for it somewhere else? Besides, I was never gone for more than three days. If you can't wait that long for sex—you need some help."

"Why do you think she wanted out?"

"I'm still not sure." Her face took on a sorrowful, dark quality, one Kerri hadn't seen before. "I think she stopped loving me, but I'm not sure why."

"That must have hurt."

"More than a little."

Kerri knew that her sad smile hid much more pain than Brooklyn admitted to.

"It was like being shot in the gut. I limped through life for a good six months before I could get any perspective at all."

"Did you see a counselor?"

Brooklyn gave one of her "you've got to be crazy" looks. "No. I'm not going to take drugs to get over a heartbreak. I simply went over what had happened between us and tried to figure things out."

"That's what therapists do too."

"For money." She grinned. "My way is free. Anyway, I realized that neither of us had been giving the relationship our best efforts. She wanted to start over with someone else, so I had to let her go. It sucked hard, but what I was left with was the realization that I desperately missed her companionship."

"That's really important."

"Definitely." Brooklyn nodded forcefully. "But that's not enough. So I decided that I needed more than physical attraction and companionship next time. So I'm waiting until I find someone who can be...more."

"More in what way?"

"I need someone who's my equal. I felt one level down from Ashley much of the time, and one level up the rest. That sucked. I want the kind of woman who'll challenge me, while still letting me be myself." She smiled, looking a little embarrassed. "I'll get there. Eventually."

"I know you will." Suddenly, Brooklyn didn't seem like a dependent woman who relied on her mommy or a minder for the simplest things. But that's who she really was. A childish woman who could also pull some perceptive thoughts out of thin air.

—⁂—

Kerri's last official day as Spectrum's eyes and ears was on Friday. She had compiled a lengthy report for the company, and she shared the gist of it with Brooklyn before she sent it off. "I can't show you the actual report, but I told them that I thought your problems could almost all be attributed to how early you had to get up."

"Really? Do you honestly think that's true?"

Kerri stood there for a second, then decided to be frank. "I think you have a drinking problem, but you seem able to control it when you're rested."

"Did you put that in there?" She looked like she was going to lunge for the report and destroy it.

"No, but I worry it could easily get worse. You don't seem to need to drink every day, but when you do you definitely overdo it."

"Yeah, I know. I don't even enjoy it. I just need to relax."

"I think you should work even harder on your schedule. You can make the changes you need if you'll dedicate yourself to it."

Brooklyn had been walking around the loft, looking agitated. "You didn't say that my schedule would be better if I didn't work at clubs on the weekend did you?"

"Of course not. The fact is, they hired a comedian to work hours that no comedian ever works. So in my view, your working on weekend nights was a given. If the radio show was at noon, you wouldn't have a problem in the world. So it seems unfair to point out what should be obvious to anyone."

On one of her loops through the loft, Brooklyn stopped to squeeze Kerri's shoulder. "Thanks for not making a big point about that. It's something everybody knows, but I'd still rather it wasn't emphasized."

"Now, remember, even though today is my last day, I'm still committed to helping you find a manager. I'm going to hang out in New York for a little longer, so it won't be a problem."

"How about this? Why don't you act as my manager until you need to go back to Los Angeles? I'll pay you whatever Spectrum was paying you."

"But that won't help you in the long run. You need a permanent manager."

"Fine. We'll keep our eyes open, and if any candidates pop up we'll snare them."

"You honestly don't have to pay as much as I'm making for a good manager, Brooklyn. I make a good salary because what I usually do is very demanding. But working for you is easy." She got up and walked over to her. There was something about Brooklyn that begged to be touched, even though she gave every indication that it was too intimate for her comfort. Kerri decided not to censor herself, so she put her hands on Brooklyn shoulders. "I don't want to take a pay cut, but I also don't want to take advantage of you."

For a change, Brooklyn didn't look like she minded the touch. She actually leaned into Kerri's hands. "You're not taking advantage of me. I know I could get by paying someone like Kat ten percent. But having you do this right has me really wanting your level of competence. I know you have to pay for that. But when you have to leave, I'll take some also-ran and try to be happy."

Kerri squeezed her shoulders and felt a thrill of excitement. She'd never wanted to be a manager, but maybe it would be fun for a while. Now that Brooklyn had made an overture that had been rebuffed there was much less sexual tension between them. And there was nothing wrong with having a nice long vacation from the usual train wrecks she normally had to corral. Before she could stop to give it a second thought, she heard herself say, "It's a deal, but only if you continue to try to normalize your schedule. I don't want you in worse shape when I leave than when I got here."

Her face broke into a massive smile. "It's a promise."

―※※―

They had been keeping a fairly brisk but moderate pace on every one of their bike rides. Brooklyn appreciated that Kerri was going slowly, and that it was clearly for her benefit, but she was starting to chafe against the reins. It was late afternoon and a very light rain started to fall, almost clearing the bike path of both walkers and bikers. Seeing all of that clear space in front of her brought out Brooklyn's competitive urges and she called out, "Race you to the end."

She stomped on it, going as quickly as she could, making up a few yards on Kerri who had been caught unawares. It felt great to make her body work full-out for a change, and the cool wind buffeting her face gave her a blast of energy.

When Kerri flew past her after about a mile, Brooklyn could hear her giddy laughter. Even though she hated to lose, she hated having someone allow her to win even more. Having Kerri play it straight up felt great, and she vowed that she would eventually kick her butt. She was gasping for air when she reached the end of the bike path, but partially soothed by the fact that Kerri was breathing heavily too. Dropping her bike onto the grass, Brooklyn shuffled over to the railing and leaned against it, searching desperately for oxygen. Her lungs felt like they were in a vise and after a second she started coughing, keeping it up until she spit something truly nasty into the river. "Oh, my fucking God. I have never, in my entire life, had something that vile come out of my lungs."

Kerri's sympathetic look was more annoying than a lecture would have been.

"No, really. Stuff shouldn't be coming out of my lungs. I don't smoke much at all."

Again, Kerri said nothing, but her expression showed her dismissal of the claim.

"I only smoke when I drink. And I don't drink that much." She hated to hear those words come out of her mouth. In her experience, the people who insisted they didn't drink much were the ones who practically had a spigot attached to their mouths. "It's not like I smoke three packs a day."

"You don't smoke that much compared to a lot of people," Kerri conceded, "but it doesn't take much to hurt your lungs. Although something has to kill you, right?"

Kerri looked so cute when she teased. That single dimple of hers took the sting out of almost anything she said. "It's not like you're trying to set any records. You can have fun riding your bike without going fast."

Instantly agitated, Brooklyn said, "Are you saying that the little bit of smoking I do is going to stop me from ever catching you?"

Kerri's laugh had just a hint of sympathy in it, which was irritating in the extreme."I can't say anything for certain, but I ride a lot, and I ride fast when I can. I'm gonna be tough to catch."

"I'm being totally serious. Do you really think the little bit I smoke will keep me from going fast?"

"It can't help, but I'm not sure how much it hurts. If you think about it logically that stuff you coughed up has to be taking up some space in your lungs, doesn't it?"

Brooklyn didn't reply. She stood there looking at the river, debating with herself, her toughest opponent.

———

They stopped on the way back and got a quick dinner, then Kerri took off from the restaurant to go to her apartment.

When Brooklyn returned to her loft, she went out onto the deck with a vodka and tonic and her cigarettes. She dropped onto a chair to watch the sun finally peek out as it began to set over New Jersey. It was cold, and her leather jacket barely stopped her from shivering. She didn't have a great view, but she could see up Desbrosses Street and catch the reflection of the sun from a building down the block. Even though she was chilled to the bone, she sat out there until it was time for bed. Her lungs ached, and she was foggy-headed from smoking nine cigarettes, but she was resolved. She took her lighter and set the pack on fire, dropping it into the bucket of sand that served as her ashtray. It was premature to make a permanent vow, but for now, she was done.

———

As she stood in the bathroom brushing her teeth, Brooklyn did something uncharacteristic; she assessed her body with a sharp eye. The fact that Kerri was older than she was while looking so much better was beginning to annoy her. Compared to her fellow comics, she was in great shape. But maybe people who spent every weekend on the road eating junk food and passing away hours in bars weren't the best benchmark to be judged against.

She grasped the roll of flesh that surrounded her midsection. Where had this come from? When she was in high school her jeans were always too big around her waist. Now, a roll of fat surged over her waistband, spilling out from every side. How had her body changed so much in just a few years? Okay, it was more than a few years, but it was odd to barely recognize herself.

Her face and neck still looked darn good. Luckily, her face was one of the last places she gained weight. Sliding her eyes down her body she saw the locus of every unhealthful thing she put in her mouth. The weight hadn't come on all at once. It was actually just a few pounds a year. But her size ten jeans gave way to twelves, then fourteens and now sixteens, the largest size many stores sold. It was time to make a decision. Going into plus sizes wouldn't be the end of the world, but as long as she was going to stop smoking, she might as well try to eat a little better too. If she took off two or three pounds a year by the time she died she'd be back to her high school weight. Fan-fucking-tastic.

CHAPTER TEN

THAT EVENING, KERRI WENT to bed at her usual time. She'd been in New York long enough to ignore the sounds of garbage being picked up, sirens blaring, and the wails of drunks going home from the bars that littered the neighborhood. Regrettably, she still woke up when Dakota came in at night, a habit she'd been unable to break.

Dakota's play was a hit, or at least enough of a hit that the producers expected it to run for another six months. If she came home directly after the performance, she got in around 11:30, but she rarely did that. There were a few bars near the theater district that a lot of actors went to, and it didn't take much prodding to get Dakota to tag along.

Kerri wasn't sure what time it was, but she was sure it was late when Dakota flipped the heavy deadbolt on the door. After a few minutes in the bathroom, Dakota crossed the small room and slid into bed. Even though she didn't like being woken, it was always soothing to have Dakota put her hand on her waist or shoulder and curl up behind her.

But tonight, the hand was a little adventurous. When a pair of fingers slipped into her panties, Kerri put her hand on top of Dakota's, holding it still. "Where do you think you're going?" she asked, sleepily.

"To paradise," Dakota whispered.

Kerri could tell from her laugh that she'd had a few drinks. "So you got bored with your friends and came home to me?"

Placing kiss after kiss across Kerri's shoulders, Dakota murmured, "I'd never do that. I've been thinking about this for days, but we're never awake at the same time."

"I'd love to, honey, but I've got to get up early."

Dakota put her hand on Kerri's shoulder and pressed down on it to roll her onto her back. Looking into her eyes, she smiled brightly. "No you don't. It's Saturday morning, and I came home so I'd be here right when you normally wake up."

Even if it had been a workday, it would have been impossible to resist Dakota. Even the dim glow of the streetlights showed her lovely eyes, so full of excitement. "Did you really plan this?"

"Yeah, I did. We haven't had sex in days." A very happy smile was affixed to her face, and Kerri felt the familiar tug on her heartstrings.

"How can I resist such a romantic invitation?"

They had sex whenever they could manage it, but the romance had been gone for a long, long time. Kerri wasn't sure when it had made its last appearance, but she didn't miss it. Being playful and staying entirely in the moment had taken all of the jealousy and risk out of their relationship. They could do what they wanted when they were apart; they had silently agreed to never speak of any outside activities. No fuss, no muss. She loved Dakota dearly, and knew she held a very special place in Dakota's heart. They were damned lucky to have each other, and damned lucky to have never crushed each other's dreams. It was practically the ideal relationship.

She took two fingers and ran them across Dakota's pretty features, giggling when they were sucked into her mouth.

Dakota slipped both arms around her and pulled Kerri atop her body. They grinned at each other for a second, then Kerri tilted her head and they started to kiss. Dakota was feisty, as always, and she flipped Kerri over onto her back. Now wide awake, Kerri returned the move and pinned Dakota, holding onto her shoulders. Dakota shifted her hips quickly, knocking Kerri off. Laughing, they grappled, wrestling for supremacy.

They were both exerting so much energy that they were panting, and Dakota leaned down and took a playful bite of Kerri's neck. "I'm going to get you down and fuck you like I've been dreaming about."

Kerri used all of her strength to topple Dakota once more. "Not this time." She scrambled to get her knees onto Dakota's shoulders, pinning her tightly. "I'm going to fuck *you*, and you're going to love it." Looking down at her, she saw the excitement building in her avid gaze. "I can never have my way at work, so when I get an urge at home, I have to satisfy it."

Dakota loved to dictate the action, but she'd let you be in charge if you earned it. In a lightning quick move, Kerri stretched out, now lying atop Dakota's entire body. "I'm going to take my time and do everything to you that comes to mind." She slid her hands under her shoulders and locked her into a tight hold. "And the last thing I'm going to do is fuck you until I have worn...you...out." She dipped her head and kissed her roughly. "You're mine until I'm done with you."

Dakota looked into her eyes and with just her gaze gave Kerri permission to do anything and everything she wanted.

—⁓—

The sun was coming up when they got out of the shower, still very connected emotionally and physically. Dakota went into the tiny space that served as a kitchen and started to make coffee. Lazy and uncharacteristically indulgent, Kerri went back into the living room and fell onto the unmade sofa bed. "I could do that all day," she said reflectively.

"I bet you could. For someone who likes sex as much as you do, I don't understand how you go for so long without it."

"I try to control my body, not have it control me."

Dakota walked over to sit next to her on the bed. "Then why do you have that big Magic Wand in your bedside table at your apartment?"

"Snoop!" She grabbed Dakota and wrestled her onto her back again. "I like to have orgasms. It's a way to nurture my body and keep my uterus in shape." She was snickering, but still tried to look serious.

"Bullshit. You love sex, and you'd have it every day if you could. I bet that wand gets a workout."

"It's new," Kerri admitted. "I burned the last one out."

"Ha!" She tossed Kerri to the side, and they played like a pair of puppies. Panting, they finally tired each other out. "I wish I could see you more often."

"I know, baby, but duty calls. I'm going to have a find a new gig back in LA soon. Let's hope I get one that doesn't drive me nutty."

"How about Brooklyn? Is she good to work for?"

"You know I won't tell you anything, right?"

"You never have, but I've never been interested in one of your clients. I have a crush on this one, even though she looks better on TV than in person."

"Everyone looks better on TV. Didn't they teach you that in one of your acting classes?"

"She still looks good, but she wasn't wearing makeup the night I met her. She looked pretty pasty."

"Mmm."

"She looks like she drinks a lot, to be honest."

Kerri shrugged.

"You know, they also say the camera adds ten pounds, but it takes it off Brooklyn. Where does she hide it?"

Kerri knew where those pounds were hidden, but she wasn't about to tell Dakota that Brooklyn's midsection was the place to look. "No comment, about that or anything else."

"When she came by here that night, she said we could have dinner. Was she just blowing me off?"

"I don't know, sweetie. If she brings it up, I'll let you know."

"But you won't ask for me? Better yet, you could say I'd like to call her and get her number for me."

"No way. I could never put her in that kind of position. I can't have a normal relationship with a client. You know that."

"You had her come up the other night." Her eyes opened wide and she gasped, "Oh, shit! Were you going to…"

"Of course not! I thought she was going to drop me off, but she wanted to come up. I would have had to be rude to stop her."

"Hey! That doesn't mean she wasn't trying to hit on you!"

"I wouldn't tell you if we went at it like rabbits. I also won't deny it. So stop asking, sweetie."

"It sucks to have you working for someone I think is cool, but I can't even meet her."

Kerri put her arm around Dakota and hugged her. "I know. I just don't like clients to know much about me. I like to keep my home life mine and mine alone."

Dakota leaned over and kissed her again, lengthening the kiss until it was a little more than friendly. "Do you have to work today? You'll notice I didn't specifically ask for who?"

Laughing, Kerri tumbled her over, showing her superior strength. "Yeah. I have to leave for the airport at noon."

"Then why don't we make good use of the rest of the morning? I might not have another morning with you for weeks."

"Have I told you that I love New York? And you?"

Kerri and Brooklyn stood outside the artists' entrance to the Hippodrome Theater in Baltimore that evening. In a foul mood, Brooklyn paced around in the alley looking very much like an addict waiting for a fix. Kerri had seen this behavior too many times to count, but she'd never seen it from Brooklyn. She knew that asking someone if she did drugs was a complete waste of energy, but she decided to see if there might be some other cause for Brooklyn's agitation, just to set her mind at ease.

"Have you played here before?"

"No, this is huge for me. It's over 2,000 seats."

"That *is* big."

"Melvin knows I hate to play venues this big, but they're willing to pay, so I've gotta do it."

"I don't know if you're like me, but when something's bothering me it helps to talk about it. Like if I was nervous or anxious…"

Brooklyn gave her a stern look. "I'm trying to figure out how to work that scandal about the congressman and his campaign aide into the beginning of the act. It's just not coming to me." She had her arms across her chest, her hands tucked into her armpits. She was so tightly bound it looked like she was in a voluntary straitjacket.

"Talk about it. What's interesting about the scandal?"

With a malevolent glare, Brooklyn snapped, "I quit smoking, okay?"

That was it! That's what looked so odd. Brooklyn didn't just smoke when she was drinking, as she claimed, she smoked when she was punching up her act. Kerri had seen her do it before each performance. She found some place outside the venue and paced around for half an hour, putting the latest local headlines into the beginning of the act to show the crowd she knew what city she was in. "Don't go anywhere. I'll be right back." She ran into the theater, asked around backstage, found what she was looking for, and ran back out. Handing it to Brooklyn with a flourish, Kerri presented her with a fresh cigarette.

"That's how you help? What if I wanted heroin?"

"Different problem. Not smoking has screwed up your routine, and not having your routine makes it harder for you to concentrate." She took the cigarette from Brooklyn's limp hand and popped it into her mouth. "I'm not going to light it for you. Just having it in your mouth and smelling it will help."

"Are you sure?"

It was clear she desperately wanted to be reassured, and Kerri was glad she could do so without lying. "One hundred percent positive. And within a few weeks you won't even need the prop. Now tell me about this scandal."

Brooklyn put her hand up, removed the cigarette and rolled it around between her fingers. As she walked, she stuck it back in her mouth, sucked some air in through it, pulled it out then started to gesture with that same hand. "Okay, this guy is a very conservative Catholic, married, four kids, and has a hot, young, busty campaign aide." She gave Kerri a dry look. "You'll never guess what happened."

When the show was over a comedian friend of Brooklyn's came backstage and invited her out for a drink. She gave Kerri a funny look, one that was hard to decipher. Taking a guess, Kerri said, "I don't think you have time. If we hurry we can get on the last flight back to New York."

"Don't I have time for a quick one?"

Now it was clear she wanted permission, but Kerri wasn't sure how she should respond.

"Come with us, and you can make sure I don't stay too long."

Ahh, she wanted supervision. It wasn't clear if she wanted Kerri to make sure she didn't drink too much, or didn't smoke, but she could do both.

As they walked out of the theater, Kerri once again marveled at how self-aware Brooklyn was about some things. Asking for help was something that was so rare in celebrity circles that she guessed this might be the first time anyone had asked for it before committing the bad act. Normally her clients asked for help when the squad cars were encircling the house and the news-copters were already buzzing overhead. Brooklyn would probably be miffed to hear it, but watching over her was like babysitting a ten-year-old. Bad things could happen, but generally you didn't have to do much more than keep an eye on things.

After spending a half hour in the bar, they went up to their floor in the hotel, arriving at Brooklyn's room first. She slipped her key in the lock and said, "Come in for a minute."

Kerri followed, assuming Brooklyn wanted a back rub or some other advice on how to get to sleep quickly. But she sat down at the desk chair and looked at Kerri with troubled eyes. "I didn't realize how addicted I am to smoking. It's on my mind every God-damned minute." She dropped her head, looking ashamed.

"Hey, don't be down on yourself." Kerri sat on the edge of the desk and put her hand on Brooklyn's head. "Nicotine is one of the hardest things in the world to quit. It's harder than heroin."

The dark head lifted. "That can't be true."

"It is. It really is. Get up and let me sit at the desk." Brooklyn relinquished the chair and Kerri opened the laptop. "I got this book for a guy I was working with a while ago. He wanted to know the science behind addiction. Knowing you, you'd really appreciate it too." She searched on Amazon for a minute, and found what she was looking for. "Here's the book. I'm going to have it sent to your iPad." She clicked a button and said, "It's on there now. It's pretty dry, but you'll get through it quickly."

Brooklyn picked up her iPad and checked it, smiling brightly when the book showed up. "That's awesome, isn't it? Much better than when I was a kid and had to badger my parents for a ride to the library."

"Much better. Now don't read the whole thing tonight." Kerri went over to her and put her hand on her shoulder, pleased when Brooklyn didn't flinch. "You need to sleep now. Our flight's early in the morning."

"Right." But those dark eyes were already scanning the book. She was probably going to be up for hours sucking up all of the info in those electronic pages. Giving it to her at night wasn't the smartest thing Kerri had ever done, but Brooklyn would have been up worrying about smoking and her addiction to it anyway. Sometimes you had to pick your poison.

After going to her room, Kerri spent a long time doing relaxation exercises. After seeing such an energetic set it was hard to calm down enough to sleep. It was no wonder Brooklyn had such a tough time, since she was the one who had to fill herself with adrenaline and then get rid of it without many healthy outlets.

Luckily, they didn't have to get up until eight, and after doing all of her exercises, Kerri was sure she'd be able to get a solid six hours of sleep. She was equally sure Brooklyn wouldn't be so lucky.

—⁓—

It sounded as though someone was doing construction, but nobody did that when it was pitch dark out. The pounding got louder, and Kerri got out of bed and went to the window, looking to see if there were emergency construction crews outside the hotel. All she saw was a deserted Baltimore street, but the noise was even louder by the window. It took a second to realize the sound was coming from next door. Moving quickly, she slid into a pair of jeans, grabbed her room key and went to Brooklyn's room. She knocked as loudly as was polite, but Brooklyn didn't answer. Her heart began to race and she dashed back into her own room to find the extra key to Brooklyn's. Many catastrophes had been averted over the years by having that extra key. She slid it into the lock and stood there for a second, frozen in fear.

Brooklyn was standing on an upholstered chair next to a waist-height window she'd managed to pry open. As Kerri stood there Brooklyn got one leg out, and was now sitting on the window track—fifteen stories from the ground.

Thoughts raced through her brain, trying to make sense of the scene. Suicide? That didn't make sense. There were far easier ways. Nothing else made sense either, and Kerri's instincts took over. Fighting every urge not to scream, she ran for Brooklyn and encircled her with her arms. Feeling that warm flesh pressed against her was unspeakably soothing, but her heart was still thrumming hard. She spoke as gently and confidently as she could. "Just relax, and I'll get you down."

"Need a cigarette," Brooklyn mumbled.

A fucking cigarette? She was going to hang out the window for a cigarette? Suicide made more sense than that!

"Come on now. You've got to come back inside."

Nothing. It was like Brooklyn had gone completely deaf.

Kerri tugged on her, then started to pull. But Brooklyn resisted, leaning further and further towards the abyss.

It was clear she wasn't in her right mind, but Kerri didn't have time to figure out why. She strengthened her hold and yanked hard, sending both of them tumbling backwards across the floor, falling into a heap.

She took the worst of it, but Brooklyn came out of her fog enough to be outraged. "Who are you?" she demanded. "Get out of my house!"

It was decision time. Call the police, or handle it herself. Something was seriously wrong, and the police would likely take her in for a psychiatric evaluation. That could be a career destroyer. Deciding that would have to be a last resort, Kerri tried to reason with her. "It's me, Kerri. I think you're having a bad dream."

Brooklyn rolled away from her, then sat up, staring at her through slitted eyes. "Kerri?"

She seemed suspicious, but also slightly worried. "Yeah, it's me. We're in Baltimore, remember? We just had a drink with your friend in the bar."

"I'm so tired," she said. A few tears escaped, trailing down her cheeks. "I'm always so tired." She leaned over and patted the floor, then lay down, sobbing softly.

What in God's name was wrong with her? It seemed like she was having a psychotic break, but she'd been perfectly fine an hour earlier. People didn't usually lose their grip on reality so quickly. She had to be on something. But what?

There were so many things to worry about, but Kerri had to make another decision. Leave her on the floor, or get her into bed? Bed was the better choice. Not so much for Brooklyn's comfort, but she'd probably wake up much sooner if she was uncomfortable, and keeping her asleep was a good idea—for both of them.

Kerri got to her knees and shuffled across the floor. Sliding one hand behind Brooklyn's neck and the other on her shoulder, she pulled her into a sitting position. "It's time for bed. Come on." This part of the job really stunk. It was very difficult getting a full grown woman to her feet when she wasn't willing to help. So Kerri used all of her tricks; pinching her, yanking hard on the waistband of her jeans, trying to lock her knees, anything that aided the task. Eventually, Brooklyn was upright, and Kerri could push her towards the bed. She landed with a thunk, then Kerri spent the next few minutes undressing her.

A cold wind was blowing in through the open window and it took quite a while to get it closed again. Brooklyn was obviously stronger than she looked, but she wasn't going to get another chance to prove it. That window was going to stay closed. Period. Kerri took the two upholstered chairs and the desk chair and moved them across the room to the entry door. Brooklyn couldn't have gotten the window open without the leverage she got from standing on the chair and if she tried to drag any of them back to the window Kerri would definitely hear her.

She was just about to lie down when Brooklyn started rambling nonsense again. It wasn't clear what she wanted, but it was very clear she didn't want to be in bed. This was the exciting world of talent wrangling. Wrestling with a crazed woman in the middle of the night while trying to decide whether to have her committed was super fun!

After a while Brooklyn calmed down and fell asleep. Actually, it didn't seem as though she fell asleep as much as she lost consciousness. Kerri was wired to the teeth, and couldn't even consider going back to sleep, even if she hadn't been on suicide watch. Seeing Brooklyn up on that window had filled her with an anxiety that she wasn't used to dealing with. She could argue all day that it wasn't wise, but she had feelings for Brooklyn. Deep feelings. And every time she let the image of her falling to her death creep back into her head, her stomach turned and her heart beat wildly. She'd keep her safe until they could figure out what was wrong. And they *would* figure it out. There was no way she was giving up on her.

She turned the light in the bathroom on, somehow feeling better not being in the dark. That little bit of light allowed her to see the desecration of the minibar. All of the tiny bottles of vodka were empty and lying on the floor, along with three candy bars, a package of cheese and crackers and one of mixed nuts. That was a good thousand calories–empty calories. It was amazing Brooklyn was only thirty or forty pounds over her ideal weight if this was a common occurrence. Actually, given what hotels charged for minibar items, it was amazing she came out ahead even after selling out a two thousand seat venue. Was this a common occurrence? Maybe Donna would let her see the hotel bills for the last month. Of course she'd want to know what Kerri was looking for, and upsetting her wasn't a good idea.

She kept busy cleaning up all the trash, then she picked up all of Brooklyn's clothes, which, for some reason, were strewn about the room. She sat on the edge of the bed and stared at her for a while. It was so difficult to know what was in a person's head, even someone you had known for years. Everyone had secrets, foibles, and elements of their personality that even they weren't comfortable dealing with. Was Brooklyn an alcoholic? Sometimes she seemed so, sometimes not. But if nothing else, she was a bad binge drinker. That could be very dangerous, but it was probably also going to be very hard to stop. Maybe that's why she had wanted her babysitter with her at the bar tonight. Maybe she knew she had a problem, and knew it was difficult to stop drinking once she started, but she wasn't ready to admit it in so many words.

It was silly to feel this way, but it was hard not to accept some responsibility for her getting into this shape. When you were responsible for the talent, you were paid to know what they needed, even when they weren't sure. Having her ask for help tonight should have been a bigger signal, and Kerri felt bad that she'd let her down. Brooklyn was going to have another hangover, and if Kerri had been on her toes she would have prevented it.

Why did this only happen after I wasn't working for Spectrum? She hated to be so suspicious, but she'd learned the hard way that addicts had more sneaky ways around things that anyone could properly foresee. Maybe Brooklyn had done things like this from the beginning but had some way of hiding it while Kerri worked for the enemy.

Brooklyn thrashed around on the bed, mumbling something. Trying to keep her asleep, Kerri gently stroked her leg. It seemed to work, and Brooklyn rolled over on her side and quieted down. But just a minute later her eyes fluttered open and she looked at Kerri for a few seconds. "Hi," she said, her voice raspy.

"Hi. How are you feeling?"

Brooklyn sat up, then pulled the sheet up over her breasts. She ran a hand through her disordered hair and shook her head a couple of times. "I'm not very clearheaded, but I must have fallen asleep on you, right?"

"At least once. You weren't asleep for long though."

Brooklyn scooted down the bed until she was just a few inches away from Kerri. Her voice was soft and strangely sensuous when she said, "I must've been out of my mind if I fell asleep with you in my bed."

What in the hell? Brooklyn never said things like that. But when she really thought about it her voice wasn't so much sensual as slurred. She was obviously very drunk and was holding it together by a thread.

"I'm not really in your bed, I'm on your bed." She got up and backed away. "You need to get to sleep now."

Slapping the bed with the flat of her hand Brooklyn said, "Come over here by me. You wouldn't have come to my room if you didn't want to play."

"I don't want to," Kerri said, trying to be as clear as possible without sounding angry. "I want you to get to sleep, and I want to get to the airport on time. If you go to sleep soon, you can get four and half hours of sleep and you'll feel much better."

Grinning sloppily, Brooklyn said, "I'll feel much better if you take that top off and let me get my hands on your titties."

Kerri took a quick glance down and saw that she had on a very thin pink cotton undershirt she sometimes slept in. The room was still cold, and her nipples were hard as rocks. When she looked back up Brooklyn's eyes met hers.

"They look good, don't they?" She twitched her finger. "Come over here," she said, more demanding now. "You won't regret it. Nobody ever needs to know."

"I'll know, and so will you. This is not what we do."

Brooklyn flipped the sheet away, looked down and saw that she was naked. "Did you undress me?"

"Yes, but only because you were too drunk to undress yourself." It was hard to keep the judgment and derision from her voice.

Shrugging her shoulders, Brooklyn continued to advance. "Whatever works." She got close enough to put her hands on Kerri's shoulders where they were quickly swatted away. "Come on now. Let's get busy."

It had passed the line from uncomfortable to unpleasant, and Kerri wasn't going to stand for another moment of it. "Listen to me," she said clearly. "We are not going to kiss. We are not going to touch each other. We are *definitely* not going to have sex. If you try to touch me again, you will regret it."

Laughing, Brooklyn stumbled backwards, landing on the bed, where she sat staring at Kerri with a strangely pleased look on her face. "I like a woman with a little fire, but you seem serious."

She glared at her, trying to look imposing. In fact, she was imposing. She knew she could put Brooklyn on the floor or in a headlock with very little effort. She didn't want to do it, but she could. "I'm deadly serious."

Her expression was no longer pleased. Brooklyn got up and went over to her suitcase and started pulling out clothes. "So you come up to my room, undress me, get me hot, then tell me not to touch you. What kind of bullish it is that?"

"You're not leaving the room." Kerri stood by the front door, blocking it. "You're too drunk to be out in public. At the very least you'd embarrass yourself."

"Who do you think you are? You can't tell me what to do."

"Watch me." She set her feet shoulder width apart and put on her most imposing glare. "You're not leaving this room. So get back into bed and behave."

Brooklyn completely ignored her. She struggled into a pair of panties and then into her jeans but Kerri moved to her, grabbed the back of them and pushed her towards the bed, where she fell in a heap. "You can take a shower, you can watch television, or you can lie there quietly. Those are your only options."

Now she looked more than puzzled. "What's going on? Who are you?"

"I'm the person who's going to stop you from hurting yourself. And right now I'm done playing with you. You've already drunk all the liquor and eaten all of the food. It's almost dawn and I'm out of patience. The bar is closed, so there's no one for you to bring up here, and I'm not going to keep an eye on you while you troll Baltimore for some poor soul who will accept your pathetic overtures." Once her temper started to rise it was hard to stop it, and it had definitely started to rise. "Now go to bed and shut up!"

"Fine. I don't know who the fuck you think you are, but I've changed my mind and I don't want to have sex with you anyway." She went back to the minibar and looked inside, obviously seeing no bottles of vodka. She slammed it hard, muttering, "assholes." Then she went into the bathroom and Kerri could hear her rummaging through her toiletries. Kerri got there just in time to see her slap her hand to her open mouth, obviously taking some form of pill.

Grabbing her, Kerri shook her hard, trying to get her to open her mouth. "What did you take?" she demanded.

Brooklyn swallowed hard, then let a mean smirk show. "None for you."

Kerri went through the few bottles on the vanity, finding an empty bottle of acetaminophen. There was a small chance it was really something so benign, but she knew that chance was infinitesimal.

Brooklyn had shucked her jeans and panties and gotten back into bed. "I'd really appreciate it if you'd leave. You seem like the type who'd steal my wallet."

Almost growling, Kerri snapped, "You seem like the type who'd let a complete stranger into your room when you were too drunk to know what she wanted from you. I could've come in here and cut your throat."

"Go ahead," Brooklyn mumbled before falling asleep so quickly it once again seemed like she'd passed out.

Kerri went into the bathroom again, and inspected the bottle of acetaminophen. The label indicated it had been filled with liquigels, but there were traces of powder at the bottom of the container. The bottle had not been there during her sweep of the loft, so Brooklyn had obviously added them for the trip. What else had she been able to hide, and where had she hidden it?

—⁓—

Kerri was sure things would be uncomfortable between them, but Brooklyn reacted as she did many normal mornings, pulling the pillow over her head and fighting to retain it.

"Come on," Kerri urged. "It's eight o'clock and we've got to be at the airport by nine fifteen."

"Why do we have to leave so early?"

For the first time since they'd been working together, Kerri felt her patience fray. "I don't care when we leave. You're the one who likes to go as early as we can."

Brooklyn opened one eye, and the look on her face reflected surprise mixed with concern. "Are you all right?" she asked gently.

Kerri let out a breath and tried to get into a good mental space. "Sure. I'm fine. Do you want me to see if I can switch us to a later plane?"

"God, yes. I'll do anything for a few hours sleep."

"Consider it done."Brooklyn seemed completely normal, so whatever she'd taken had left her system. They'd get into the details of the evening later. Now, it was time for some much needed sleep.

—⁓—

Since flights to New York left nearly every hour, they were easily able to get a six o'clock to JFK. Brooklyn still acted hung over and lethargic, but she also seemed to have absolutely no memory of what had transpired the night before. When to tell her what had happened was the next issue. It didn't do any good to bring things like that up if there wasn't a plan for how to deal with them in the future. If Brooklyn was merely a binge drinker and pill taker, Kerri was going to have to make her face that fact and take action. That wouldn't be much fun, but it was something she'd done many times. But the way Brooklyn had acted seemed much closer to psychosis than alcohol abuse, and a fix for that was much more complicated than a twenty-eight day stint in rehab.

What to tell and when to tell it consumed Kerri for the duration of their flight. She was able to reflect without interruption since Brooklyn was asleep for almost the entire time. She woke from a bit of turbulence as they started their initial descent and gasped when she saw her head had been on Kerri's shoulder. "I'm so sorry," she said, looking mortally embarrassed. "It's bad enough that you have to babysit an adult, but having her head draped over you is way beyond the call of duty."

How about having her try to force herself on me? But it was clear Brooklyn didn't remember doing that, and bringing it up now was just unkind. They would clear things up later.

—⁓—

Kerri was waiting for Brooklyn when she got home from work the next day. The radio show hadn't gone well and Arnie had probed Brooklyn's unguarded flanks for every weakness. After tossing her things down on the dining table, Brooklyn wandered over to the sectional and flung herself onto it. "That was four hours of suck fest. Were you unlucky enough to catch any of it?"

"Yeah, now that I know how to use the TV, I had it on from about nine until ten. I got the feeling the start of the show was pretty rough."

"It was hellish. He could tell I was running on fumes and he spent most of the first hour harassing me about caring more about my comedy than about the show. I think it's clear to almost everyone that that's true, so it's awfully hard to rebut. But I don't think he does his show any favors by making such a big deal about one of his performers not doing a good job. I find that befuddling."

"This might not be the best time to bring this up…"

Brooklyn's eyes popped open and she sat bolt upright. "That usually means that somebody wants to break up with me. Did you find a better job? Not that that would be hard…"

"Brooklyn, this is a really good job. I like working with you, and I like being in New York. But I'm worried about you."

She flopped back down, waving her hand in the air. "Don't worry about it. The worst he can do is fire me, and sometimes I think I'd be lucky if he did."

Kerri walked over and sat down on the sectional, put her hand out and grasped Brooklyn's arm. It made her smile to see Brooklyn look down at her hand just the way Richie had when she touched his arm. It must've been genetic. "I'm not worried about your job, I'm worried about your health, and your safety."

A quizzical expression settled onto Brooklyn's face, and she cocked her head slightly. "My safety?"

"Yes. You had too much to drink on Saturday night and you got your window open and tried to climb out."

"I did not!" She was up again, staring into Kerri's eyes like she'd been slapped.

"Yes, you did. I found you with one leg out of the window, sitting on that narrow ledge. You were moments from falling fifteen stories."

Brooklyn slapped both hands over her face and shivered roughly. "That can't be! I don't remember anything."

"Has anyone ever suggested you might have a problem with alcohol?"

Brooklyn stared at her, her eyes slightly narrowed. "No one normal."

"And that means?"

"The only people who've ever said that are people who don't drink at all. You know how people are. If they don't drink they think everybody else is a drunk."

"I don't drink much, but I don't think everyone else is a drunk. However, when someone has no recollection of trying to climb out of a fifteen story window…"

"God dammit, Kerri. I had two drinks at the bar. You were there. You saw me."

"And you drank all of the vodka in the minibar."

"I did not!"

"Then you had somebody else in your room who did. And if that's true, then you've got another problem."

"Shit." Her head dropped into her hands and she shook with fear.

"What kind of pills did you have in that pain reliever bottle?"

Her head snapped up and she stared for a few seconds. Kerri could see the lies flying by, just waiting for Brooklyn to choose one.

"Sleeping pills."

"What kind?"

"I'm not sure. I had them at work, and brought them with me."

"Where did you get them?"

Now she looked like she wanted to crawl into a hole and hide. "From a guy who opened for me in Seattle. He's got everything."

"So you have no idea exactly what you're taking?" She let that hang out there for a moment, hoping Brooklyn would hear how idiotic it was to trust a comedian/amateur pharmacist.

"No, I really don't know." She sat there quietly for a moment. "They always work, and they work fast. That's all I care about."

Kerri leaned closer, intentionally invading Brooklyn's personal space. "I know sleep is important to you, but is it more important than your life?"

"Of course not." She got up and started to pace in front of the TV. "Did you take the bottle? It wasn't there when I packed."

"Yes, I did, but it was empty."

"Shit," she muttered. "There were three pills left after I took one."

"So you took four and drank around six shots of vodka." She didn't add anything to this, figuring the facts didn't need another word.

"That's not good." Brooklyn sat down heavily. "And I don't remember anything. That's not good either." She looked at Kerri with raw need, silently begging for help. "What do we do?"

"First, we need to have your doctor do a complete workup on you. We should make sure you're healthy and tell him about your sleeping problems."

"She," Brooklyn said, "knows all about my sleeping problems. But I guess it wouldn't hurt to have a physical. I haven't had one in a long time."

"If you'll give me her number, I'll call and set it up. Until then I'm going to have to sleep here during the week and in your room this weekend in Eugene. I hate to invade your privacy, but I care about you."

Brooklyn looked like a deflated balloon. "This is bad. Really bad."

Kerri was so tempted to wrap her arms around Brooklyn and tell her everything would be fine. But she wasn't at all sure that was the truth.

—⁂—

Going to a relatively small town on the West Coast was the worst of all of Brooklyn's trips. There were no direct flights available, and a stopover always increased the risk of not getting back in time for work on Monday morning. When they went to bed a little after midnight after Brooklyn's Saturday show, she was already obsessing about having to get up in four hours.

"I know it's not something you've tried before, but I'd really be happy to teach you some simple meditation techniques," Kerri said. "They might help you relax enough to get to sleep."

Brooklyn paced around the small room, wearing a T-shirt and men's boxers. She was clearly agitated, and worrying about sleep was definitely not in her best interest. But she seemed unable to calm herself down, a very unfortunate trait in someone in her line of work. "Are you going to give me a hard time if I have a drink?"

Kerri got up out of her bed and went over to stand in front of Brooklyn. She looked into her dark, guarded eyes and said, "I won't give you a hard time about anything you do. I'm just here to help you feel better."

"No, you're here to help me do better. There's a very big difference."

"I don't see it that way. I know you'll do better if you feel better, so that's my goal. If you want to have a drink, go right ahead. Just remember that alcohol is a depressant and it probably won't help you wake up at four a.m."

"Then how in the hell am I supposed to relax?"

"We could go for a long, long walk, have breakfast someplace and then go right to the airport. You can sleep on the plane, and go to bed early tonight."

"I don't want to do that to you. You're a normal person, and you can get to sleep whenever you want."

"You're normal too, Brooklyn. Now let's put our clothes back on and go for a walk around this nice little town."

———

On the flight home, Brooklyn woke up enough to gaze at Kerri with sad eyes. "Given that I didn't have a drink and didn't take pills or try to climb out of the window does that mean I'm an alcoholic?"

Kerri couldn't help but pat her reassuringly. "You're going to see your doctor on Tuesday. After you talk to her, we'll talk about it together and see if it's a good idea to make some changes. No matter what happens, I have every confidence that you can handle it." *Maybe not every confidence, but most of them.*

———

Kerri waited at her apartment while Brooklyn spent the afternoon at her doctor's office. At least it seemed like an entire afternoon. It was strange to feel so connected to the outcome of a few tests, but Kerri couldn't get her mind to move on to other topics. Finally, her cell phone rang and she jumped like a frightened cat. "Hello?"

"Guess who seems to be in good shape?"

"God, I hope it's you." She blinked, wondering how that private thought had escaped. She sounded so relieved she was embarrassed.

"Yeah, it's me. Do you want to grab some dinner? I could come by your apartment."

"Uhm, sure. Actually, why don't we meet at a place I like on Second Avenue and Ninth? I'll leave now and we'll probably get there at the same time."

"Okay. I'll see you there."

Kerri hung up and clutched the phone to her heart for a second. She was as relieved as she would have been if Brooklyn was a relative. But she wasn't. She was a client; one that had problems the doctor clearly didn't know about if she believed Brooklyn was in good shape.

—⁓—

An hour later they were enjoying their entrees while Brooklyn revealed every detail of her medical odyssey.

"So you won't get the test results for a week, huh?" Kerri asked.

"Yeah. I'd normally hate to wait that long, but she made me feel so much better that I'm cool with it." Brooklyn took a bite of veal marsala. "Plus," she added, pointing the tines of her fork at Kerri, "the book you recommended has made me feel better. I'm confident I'm not an alcoholic."

"How did the book convince you of that?"

"I know you think I drink too much, and I probably do. But I don't have the drive, the compulsion they talk about. I drink so I can sleep, and that's not at all how the author describes alcoholism."

Kerri nodded. She'd heard every excuse and every justification ever created for why a person drank to excess. But one thing was certain. Brooklyn drank enough to have negative consequences, and that was a billboard-sized warning sign—no matter how she rationalized it.

—⁓—

The following Monday, the doctor faxed the test results to Brooklyn along with a note that said, "Everything looks surprisingly good. But work on taking off that excess weight!"

Smiling, and looking a little smug, Brooklyn handed them over to Kerri. "My cholesterol isn't even bad."

"And your liver function is really good." If Brooklyn had a long-term drinking problem that is where it would've shown up. But the mere fact that she hadn't been drinking heavily long enough to harm her liver didn't mean that she wasn't doing so now. She put her hand on Brooklyn's shoulder and gave it a gentle squeeze. "So, now we know that you either have a relatively recent serious drinking problem or there's something else

223

going on. Did you tell your doctor the whole story about trying to climb out the window?"

"I told her everything I knew. But since I didn't know I'd done it, I might not have made it sound as bad as it looked to you. But I think telling her that I found my manager in my room and she claimed I tried to jump out the window to have a cigarette was the most important point, right?"

"That would make the point for me."

"She did say that chronic sleep deprivation can cause sleepwalking. She can hook me up with a sleep lab if I want to be tested."

Thoughtfully, Kerri nodded. She looked at the results again, seeing nothing out of the ordinary, and she'd seen many, many blood panel results. This just didn't make sense. "Well, I guess we need to stay roommates until you can get to a sleep lab. That's my only suggestion."

"I don't mind a bit. You don't snore and you don't have any other bad habits that I could detect. You're the one who should get hazard pay."

CHAPTER ELEVEN

THAT WEEKEND FOUND THEM in Billings Montana. It was another brutal itinerary, and Kerri hated to acknowledge that the show hadn't been very good. She had a very big suspicion that Brooklyn's mind hadn't been completely on her set, and that her attention was diverted to thoughts about getting home. Brooklyn hadn't been exaggerating when she'd said she obsessed about sleep. It was on her mind throughout the day and got worse as the sun set.

They were in their room and after brushing their teeth and getting ready for bed Brooklyn looked at her watch and said, "At least I've got time to take a sleeping pill." She went into the bathroom and came out popping one into her mouth without water. "Taking a pill is the only thing between me and the loony bin."

"Are you serious? You're taking a pill after what happened in Baltimore?"

"Yeah," she said, looking truly innocent. "My doctor gave me a prescription."

"Did you tell her about the ones you got illegally?"

"Yep. She said they might have been anything." Smirking, she added, "Apparently not all comics are licensed physicians."

Kerri walked over to her and touched her chin, then lifted her head. "I wish you would have told me about getting more pills from your doctor. I'm not sure they're a good idea."

"She's got a license, Kerri. It's on the wall." She looked so earnest it was almost funny. Almost.

"I hear you. But you can't keep taking pills to sleep. It's still medicating yourself to do something that should be easy. You're far too good a person to cut your life short because of a dependency."

"Yeah, but this isn't the same as alcohol," she insisted. "The pills are from my *doctor*."

"Taking anything to sleep isn't good. You're risking your health no matter how you get them. Do you understand that?"

Brooklyn nodded, then almost scampered into the bathroom, obviously trying to get away from being lectured. It was clear she didn't understand, but also clear that she didn't want to. Brooklyn wanted to be able to sleep nine hours a night, get to work rested and refreshed at six a.m., and stay up late every weekend. That couldn't be done. Not by anyone over twenty-five. And even someone that young couldn't do it for long.

When something was bothering her or she was feeling tense, Kerri redoubled her efforts to meditate. It took longer to get into the right frame of mind, and it took longer to relax, but she always found it very worthwhile. Tonight she had a devil of a time, but she kept at it, never criticizing or chastising herself, just trying to get back into the now and focus on her breath. She completely lost track of time and focused only on her body, her posture if it got out of line and her breathing. When she finally felt peaceful she looked at the clock and saw that it was two a.m.

Even though her sleep was going to be curtailed, she felt fantastic. Her mind was clear and she felt light and peaceful when she slipped into bed. She was asleep in moments, but it seemed like less than another minute before she was woken by Brooklyn getting up. "Are you all right?" she asked.

Brooklyn didn't reply. She went into the bathroom and when she came out Kerri watched as she saw her slap her hand up to her mouth the way she had when she took her sleeping pill.

"Shit!" She scampered out of bed and shook her. "Brooklyn?" No response. Brooklyn got back into bed and pulled the covers up to her chin. In another few moments she was breathing like she was sound asleep. The only thing that made sense was that she was sleepwalking. They'd have to get to that sleep lab, pronto. Until she did, Kerri was going to be in charge of the sleeping pills. They were quickly tucked into a hidden pocket in her backpack. If Brooklyn started to look for them Kerri'd hear her banging around the room. She lay in bed for a few minutes, then got up and put the backpack into bed with her. Then she could finally relax.

—⁓—

She wasn't sure how long it took this time, but at some point she heard Brooklyn rifling through her clothes. "Brooklyn? What are you doing?"

She was trying to get into her pants, but didn't seem to know how. An arm went into a leg hole, then the other pant leg was draped around her neck. She took out another pair of slacks and tried to put them on in the same fashion. Now wearing two pairs of slacks around her arm and neck she headed for the door. Kerri leapt out of bed and stopped her just before she got there. Grasping her by the shoulders, she gave her a gentle shake. "Brooklyn, wake up."

"Offenders off the car. No way we can go now. Got a get back hurry up. No time to waste. I'm in a be late!"

Shaking her little harder, Kerri called her name again.

"Too late! If it's not now it'll be never and never too late. If the fenders are with this they have to be against us. I don't know how else to tell you."

This was bad. She had to be a very severe sleepwalker. Having never worked with one, Kerri was at a loss. She guided Brooklyn back to bed and pushed her to the mattress. Getting right into her face, she said, "You wait right here, and I'll take care of it."

She must've sounded confident, because Brooklyn nodded and stayed right where she was placed. Kerri grabbed her phone and frantically looked up info on sleepwalking. Most sites said to let it play out, so she did, watching her like a bird watches her fledglings during their first flights. After about twenty minutes, Brooklyn started to snore. At least it sounded like a snore. But maybe it was something else. Kerri was going to wake her up when it seemed as though Brooklyn was about to swallow her tongue, but she woke herself up—partially—then rolled over and fell asleep immediately. Sleep apnea? That was a definite possibility. But no matter what it was, they were going to get to the bottom of the problem —together.

———

Some determined research by Kerri led them to a physician who was both an internist and a specialist in sleep disorders. It took another week to get in to see him, and Kerri slept on the sectional the whole time. Brooklyn might have gotten up and wandered around but Kerri knew she would hear her if she tried to leave the loft.

When they went to see the doctor, Kerri got up and followed Brooklyn when the nurse called her name. "I think I can handle this," Brooklyn said not unkindly.

"I assume he'll want to talk about what happened in Baltimore. Your body was there, but your mind wasn't, so I'm the only witness." She grinned sweetly, and Brooklyn caved in.

The doctor came in after they waited for a few minutes and he took the usual medical history. Then he started to ask her about her sleep patterns. Brooklyn reported, "I had a lot of problems with sleep when I was young. I always wanted to stay up later than my bedtime, and if I pleaded enough I usually got to. But then, of course, I had a really hard time getting up in the morning."

"How'd you do in school?"

"Very well, but I was groggy most of the time. I was a great standardized-test taker, and that saved my butt."

"How has your sleep been since you've been an adult?"

"I haven't had much trouble because I rarely had to get up early. For the last fifteen years I just had to be awake at nine or ten o'clock at night, which isn't that hard to manage." She laughed a little bit. "But eight months ago I got a job where I have to leave my house at five fifteen… in the morning," she clarified. "Things have been a disaster since then. I need to go to bed by nine Sunday through Thursday, but I need to stay up until one or two in the morning on Friday and Saturday."

"I don't think there's any way to have that schedule and stay rested. Most people don't even attempt something like that without alcohol or drugs. How have you used substances to deal with this?"

He was very matter-of-fact, which seemed to make Brooklyn more forthcoming.

"I'm definitely drinking more than I should. Actually, I'm drinking more than I like, but I feel like I can't get my brain to slow down if I don't have a drink or two. I try not to take sleeping pills unless I really need them, but I need them more and more."

"So you've had sleeping pills along with alcohol?"

"Yes, I have."

"She's also taken more than one pill at a time. A few weeks ago we think she took four. And last weekend I saw her get up and take another one and I don't think she knew she was doing it. That's why we think she must be sleepwalking."

He thumbed through the pages of notes, then shook his head. "That's doubtful. Actually, my guess is that the answer is quite simple. I think you've been reacting to the sleeping pills. There are many, many people who react to them badly. Most people are fine if they only take one, but some people can't even handle that."

"Could they make her do things she doesn't remember? Like eating?"

"Yes, that's very common. People walk around, drive their cars, eat when they're not hungry. Almost any strange behavior can be attributed to them."

"I'm pretty strange anyway," Brooklyn said, "but I have had some blackouts in the last few months. Times when I woke up and found takeout food that I didn't remember ordering."

"Again, that's very common. I'm confident you'll find your symptoms disappear if you stop taking the sleeping pills."

"I think she should go to your sleep lab," Kerri said, hoping she wasn't overstepping her role too much. "Sometimes she snores and it seems like she stops breathing. Then she wakes up just enough to breathe, then falls asleep again."

He looked up at Brooklyn. "Do you recall waking up?"

"Not a bit."

"Are you refreshed in the morning?"

"No, but it's been a long time since I've felt really rested."

"That's not good. Let's set up an appointment in the sleep lab. If you have sleep apnea, we should be able to get you some relief on that issue."

"But what about sleeping in general? How do I get to sleep without pills?"

"I wish I had an easy solution. Most people can adapt to any schedule as long as it's consistent. Conversely, very few people can adapt to a schedule like you've described. The only thing I can suggest is to cut back on the alcohol, definitely stop taking the sleeping pills, and take naps when you need them."

"Is there a better sleeping pill that won't make me climb out of windows?"

"No, but I wish there were. I can give you a few long-acting anti-anxiety pills that will help you wean yourself off the sleeping aids. That's about all I have to offer."

Brooklyn stood up and shook the doctor's hand and she and Kerri walked out into the hallway. Kerri immediately started to berate herself. "I should have known. I'm so mad at myself for not recognizing that your problems could have been from sleeping pills."

"You didn't even know I was taking them until last week."

"I should have known," she insisted. "That's my job. I should have known you were hiding them."

"I'm the one who took pills that say all over the bottle that taking them with alcohol can lead to death. I guess I'm glad to know that I can fix the sleepwalking, but I'm not happy at all to give up the sleeping pills."

"Nobody is." She put a hand on Brooklyn's shoulder and squeezed it. "Maybe you'll figure out you have sleep apnea and when they fix that everything will be better."

"I'm not happy to be rooting for sleep apnea, but I guess it's something."

When they left the building, the clouds had disappeared, the sun was shining brightly, and it was definitely above freezing. People walking down the street all looked just a little happier than they had the day before. Kerri said, "Let's walk through the park. It's only five blocks from here."

"There's probably still snow on all the paths."

Kerri grasped the fabric of Brooklyn's jacket and tugged her along. "Don't assume the worst. Knowing New York, there will be people on the Great Lawn trying to get a tan."

No one was lying in the sun, but the paths were, by and large, clear. As they walked along, Kerri said, "I think it's obvious we need to change your schedule."

"Without sleeping pills, I can't get up early, so I have to change. I'd rather have my standup suffer than show up at *Reveille* every morning feeling like a pile of dog crap. I just can't take it anymore." She looked so tired, exhausted really, that Kerri's heartstrings were pulled.

"I've really let you down. We should have toyed with your schedule long before this. I'm so sorry."

She looked so penitent Brooklyn would have forgiven her even if she'd stolen from her. "Hey, you're doing everything you can. The doctor didn't have any great ideas, and he's a sleep specialist. We'll just try a new schedule and see what happens."

"When we first talked about this I said I was worried about you not getting enough sun. We'll have to make sure that doesn't happen. I think you'll want to sleep right after work, but I don't recommend that."

"But if I go to sleep by noon I'll be up by nine. Then I can go to a club to work."

"True, but that will guarantee you never see the sun. Trust me on this, you need some sun."

When Kerri was insistent, she had always been right. It was time to stop fighting and start trusting. "Okay. We'll try it your way."

Kerri took her arm and squeezed it, like she could make Brooklyn see things her way just by touch. Actually, it kind of worked. When those pretty hands were on her arm, Brooklyn felt calmer, or maybe she just felt cared for. Whatever it was, it was pretty nice.

"You're usually home by eleven, so let's try our best to soak up as much vitamin D as we can in the early afternoon. You can go to sleep at three or four and get up around midnight."

"Midnight might work. I'd have to get up a few hours earlier than that on Friday and Saturday, but that shouldn't kill me. With any luck I can make that up on Sunday night."

"Is midnight too late for you to go to comedy clubs to work on material?"

"It's definitely on the late side, but maybe I can work something out with a couple of clubs to let me come in right before they close. It might even help them out if they can promise the audience someone they've heard of will close out the night."

"I think this could work," Kerri said with confidence. "Let's go back to your loft, and I'll give you another dose of my nap-time magic. We can start on our new regimen today."

Brooklyn beamed at her. It was so remarkably wonderful to have someone this competent in charge of things. She turned and walked quickly towards Fifth Avenue where she stuck her hand out and hailed a cab. "I literally cannot wait."

―――

Brooklyn managed a long nap and woke at eleven p.m., hungry but still groggy.

Trying to be very quiet in the open kitchen was no easy feat. Kerri's scratchy voice called out, "Are you up?"

"Yeah, I think I am."

Brooklyn smiled as she caught sight of Kerri's tousled hair and squinty eyes. "You don't look like you are though. Go to the second bedroom and sleep some more." Kerri started to shake her head, but Brooklyn said, "Don't argue with me. You look wiped."

"But I want to keep you company." She yawned so wide Brooklyn could see her back teeth.

"I promise not to drink, smoke or gobble up a handful of sleeping pills. Nothing more exciting than vegetating in front of my beloved TV is on my agenda."

Surprisingly, Kerri got up and shuffled into the spare room without argument, leaving Brooklyn alone. The poor thing must have been exhausted to give up without a fight.

After flipping on the TV, Brooklyn lay on her side on the sectional, Sweet! The events of the day flashed in front of her, soothing her mind in a way she knew was counter to most people. Actually, this new schedule was going to suck for Kerri. If there was ever a morning person, she was it. But getting up early was never, ever going to work for Brooklyn. Even trying it had been stupid. She just hoped Kerri was more flexible in her habits than she was. Luckily, most people were.

—◆—

It wasn't easy staying up alone. Brooklyn used the TV as background noise while she read a great article about the economy. Finance and banking didn't normally interest her, but getting a well-written article about something difficult always got her brain going. When Kerri got up at three, Brooklyn felt a burst of energy. Having someone with you when you were trying something tough made the journey so much nicer.

"Are you up for resetting your stomach as well as your brain?" Kerri asked. "If so, you shouldn't eat anything after about nine a.m."

Brooklyn checked her watch. "I can do it, but we'd better go out for the biggest breakfast in history."

"I'm up for it. This is my normal breakfast time."

"It's my normal time to wake up and take more sleeping pills." She grinned. "But the old habits are being kicked to the curb."

———

"You know," Brooklyn said a while later, pointing with her toast, "I think I'm going to like this. It's much closer to how I lived before I got *Reveille*."

"I know it can work. The initial adjustment might take a while, but we'll do it."

"Nah," Brooklyn said with complete confidence. "There won't be any adjustment. This is natural for me."

———

She got home, as usual, around eleven. Kerri was waiting for her and before Brooklyn put her messenger bag down Kerri said, "How about ice skating in the park?"

Brooklyn felt as dull as a year-old razor blade. Her bag hit the table with a thunk and she shuffled towards the sectional. "That sounds nice. Let me know how it goes."

Kerri intercepted her before she made it across the room. "Oh, no you don't. You've got to get some sun."

Brooklyn pointed to the big windows. The day was as gray as slate, bitterly cold, and it looked like it would snow if it would only warm enough. "I don't have time to get to the Caribbean and back by morning."

"Well, it might not be very sunny, but you've got to reset your body clock. Falling asleep now won't work."

She dropped her head and took in a huge breath. "I'm beat, Kerri. Just let me relax for a while. I'll watch TV and chill."

"Nope." She put her hands on Brooklyn's back and steered her into her bedroom. "You hired me to make you feel better. To do that we've got to normalize your sleep cycles. That means you've got to get outside and do something active."

"I haven't ice skated in years," Brooklyn whined as Kerri forced her into her room.

"Then we'll do something else. But we're going to the park. Find your warmest clothes and put 'em on."

"I think I'd rather fire you."

"That won't help. You'll have to pay me for today, so I have to do my job—and that means getting your butt out of this loft. You'd sprout moss if I'd let you!"

———

It took a couple of weeks, but Brooklyn finally had a free night to spend in the sleep clinic. When the doctor called with the results, Brooklyn made notes, and when she hung up she read them to Kerri.

"Good news is that it's very unlikely that I'm a sleepwalker. Bad news is that I have mild sleep apnea. He's going to write a prescription for me to get either a mouthguard that might help, or a C-pap machine—which I don't think I want. I did a little research on them, and they're tough to travel with, besides the fact that no one likes using them."

"I know people who've used them, but they had to be in bad shape to be convinced."

"Luckily, I'm not there yet. Give me time," she said, grinning impishly. "I'll get the mouthguard and hope for the best."

———

After three weeks of being on her new late schedule, Brooklyn's mood was consistently upbeat. As usual, she'd put a lot of effort into doing things right. Amazingly, her diet had changed dramatically as well. Now she let Kerri have full reign over what, and when she ate. Vegetables, lean meats and whole grains replaced pizza and vodka, and a few of her excess pounds started to drop off. The best thing was that she had a surplus of energy that Kerri had never seen her demonstrate.

One morning when she was leaving for work she said, "I'm going to call Kat and see if I can patch things up with her. I clearly don't want to work together, but I hate to lose her as a friend."

"I think that's a great idea."

"If she's amenable, I'm going to ask her to come over tonight at midnight or so and go with me to a comedy club. She really loves to tag along and the other comics all love her."

"That's great. Call me if you need anything. If not I'll see you tomorrow morning."

The next morning, Kerri found Brooklyn already in the shower, singing, when she arrived. The loft smelled vaguely of smoke, and she followed her nose to the balcony. It was still dark out, but the balcony light was on. She couldn't help but laugh when she saw that every stitch of Brooklyn's attire was in a pile on top of a chair. She'd obviously been smoking, and had tried to keep the odor out of the loft. One thing she had to say for Brooklyn. She wasn't always successful at what she tried to do, but she always made a good effort.

Brooklyn was remarkably repentant about her slip, bringing it up repeatedly on their bike ride that afternoon. "I was so mad at myself for smoking yesterday, but once I had one I couldn't stop. But I think I'm back in Kat's good graces, and that made up for it."

"Don't be hard on yourself. Almost everybody relapses. If you want to try again, I guarantee it'll be easier."

"That book you got for me says that your brain changes when you're addicted to something. And when you use the substance again you're addicted immediately. That's why only abstinence works."

"Are you ready to go cold turkey again?"

"I've got to. I felt awful this morning. Come to think of it, I felt awful last night. Smoking might be the stupidest thing man has ever invented."

She got a pensive look on her face and pulled her bike over. Taking out her phone, she hit a button and started speaking, "Tobacco. How the first guy decided to inhale the aroma when it was dried and caught fire. Another guy suggested they get a lot closer, so the smoke would get into their lungs easier, and burn their eyes more. Who would do such a thing? It's like rubbing dog crap on your clothes so they stink, then have everybody say, "Wow, you smell like crap. I want to smell like crap too. Where do you get your crap? My crap is made for women. Well, mine has a sticker on the package that says dog crap will make you stink to high heaven."

She was smiling while she talked, and Kerri could almost see her mind working. It was cool watching Brooklyn get the spark of an idea. It would be even cooler to see if she ever put it into her act. Yes, that might be months, but no other jobs had come up—even though she hadn't asked her agent to pursue any—so maybe she'd still be around.

Brooklyn put her phone back into her pocket and they started to ride again. "I saw your clothes out on the balcony," Kerri said.

Brooklyn slapped herself with the flat of her hand. "I didn't know what else to do, and I didn't want those stinking clothes to screw up all my nice smelling ones."

"After you left this morning, I washed your underwear and took the things from the balcony to the cleaners. I added your sheets and comforter too."

"You washed my underwear?

"Yeah. It wasn't hard."

"Ugh. I'm not paying you nearly enough."

She knew it might be a touchy subject, but Kerri broached it anyway. "Would you like a little help in getting the smoke smell out of your loft? It might help your resolve."

Raising an eyebrow, Brooklyn said, "I've never smoked inside my loft."

"No, but you were wearing clothes when you were smoking outside. I thought I could do a sniff test on all of your stuff and send everything that fails to the dry cleaner."

Brooklyn looked so crestfallen it was almost funny. "You can really smell smoke in my place?"

"Sorry, but yeah. The first day I came in I figured you smoked infrequently or outside, but I could definitely smell it."

Slumping into what looked like defeat, Brooklyn shrugged her shoulders. "It's okay with me if you take everything out and burn it." She grumbled just loud enough to be heard, "Kat swore you couldn't smell it."

"Does Kat smoke?"

"Yeah, a lot more than I do."

"Smoking screws with your sense of smell, and taste too. She probably couldn't tell."

"Do whatever you want. I hate having a place that smells like smoke."

"You could easily hire someone to do a deep cleaning and then come once a week."

Brooklyn's head was shaking before Kerri finished her sentence. "No outsiders."

"Can I ask why you won't hire someone?"

"I don't want anyone messing with my stuff. Besides, it's always a driver or a housekeeper who sells you out to the tabloids. I don't want another thing to worry about."

"Uhm…I don't mean to be rude, but you don't do anything that the tabloids would be interested in." It was hard to keep a straight face, especially when Brooklyn looked so completely outraged.

"I might start!"

"Okay, fine." She patted her on the shoulder, waiting for the tiny flinch that followed. "Then we'll do it. But you'll have to hire someone to detail your car. I draw the line there."

"The car smells?" She was so shocked it was comical.

"Yep. Not as bad as the loft, but pretty bad."

"Fuck my life."

"Not until we're done cleaning," Kerri said cheerily.

—◦◦◦—

They had to stop at a grocery store to purchase the cleaning supplies that Brooklyn's loft was devoid of. They didn't buy much, just vinegar and bleach and ammonia. When they got home, Brooklyn went into her room and found a couple of pair of sweatpants that were now too large for her. They cut them into manageable-sized rags and Kerri outlined their responsibilities. "Why don't you start on the windows and I'll start on the kitchen cabinets."

"Okay." Brooklyn stood right where she was, peering at Kerri.

"What do you need?"

"How do I start?"

"Have you ever cleaned a house?"

Biting her lower lip, Brooklyn shook her head regretfully. "My mom did all that stuff when I lived at home, and Ashley did it when we lived together. I guess I'm not much of an adult."

"Sure you are. Everybody has to learn, and now you're ready to." She walked over to the sliding glass door and used the ammonia-scented sponge to go up as high as she could reach. "With windows, you start at the top and work your way down. Only use as much solution as you need, and assume you'll have to do each one twice. The smoke leaves a residue that's really hard to get off."

Kerri changed her plan and decided to clean all of the wood and metal furniture so she could keep an eye on Brooklyn. While she was working, she said, "Did Ashley really like cleaning?"

"I don't think so. She just wanted everything done in a certain way, and if she did it herself she didn't have to redo it if I screwed it up."

Kerri thought about that for a minute, wondering if part of the reason Ashley had been attracted to Brooklyn was because of Brooklyn's happiness in giving up control over almost anything.

It took a while for Brooklyn to finish the sliding glass doors, but when she was done they were sparkling. "Why don't you decide how you'd like to keep your reading material? You need a system."

Brooklyn shrugged, but walked over to the three tables that held most of her reading material. She took everything and piled it up on the coffee table, then started to sort through it. Kerri moved over to the kitchen and started to clean the cabinets. She enjoyed cleaning, and found herself lost in the work. She'd finished polishing everything before she looked back at Brooklyn, who was now nearly covered in magazines and newspapers. There was absolutely no order, and it actually looked worse than when she'd started. Deeply contemplative, Brooklyn was totally engrossed in what she was reading. Kerri chuckled to herself, seeing exactly how a controlling woman could quickly cut Brooklyn out of the process.

It took another hour for Brooklyn to finish organizing her reading material, but it was tidy when she was done. She stood up and said, "What now?"

Kerri was sitting on the fainting couch, playing a game on Brooklyn's iPad. She pointed at the remaining windows, all in need of cleaning. "They're waiting for you. By the time you're done I think you'll be an expert."

"Cool." Brooklyn got her supplies and went to work, humming to herself as she moved along. Kerri watched her, thinking that it wasn't so much that she was lazy. She just needed to know what was expected of her. Clearly, no one in her life up until now had expected anything at all when it came to housecleaning.

They arrived at their Dallas hotel on Friday at ten a.m. It was a cold, blustery day, just the kind of day made for sitting on a nice bed and watching TV. Brooklyn was going to a club to work on some material late that night, but they had nothing whatsoever to do until then.

After they'd checked into their rooms, Kerri knocked on Brooklyn's unlocked adjoining door. "Hey. What's the plan?"

The TV was already on, with a show about something historical humming in the background. Brooklyn pointed at the TV with the remote. "You're looking at it."

Kerri sat on the edge of the bed. Brooklyn tried to ignore her, but those laser-like blue eyes bore into the side of her head. "I have a feeling you want something," Brooklyn said. She was trying to be polite, but Kerri was infringing on her personal time.

"I wanted to pose a question." She sat there until Brooklyn finally looked at her.

"Yes?"

"Did you ever stop to think that part of the reason your travel is so boring might be because you never do anything?"

Brooklyn's eyebrows hiked up. "Do anything? I'm going to work on material tonight and I've got two shows tomorrow night. Since I get paid to do it, I consider it work."

"Of course you work." She put that soft, perfectly shaped hand on Brooklyn's leg. "But that's only about five hours of work out of forty-eight hours we'll be here. I need more activity than that, so I'm going out to explore. You don't have to come with me, but I'd think you'd like to air out a little."

"Air out. That's a funny way to put it."

"I always feel like I'm in a stuffy room when I'm in a hotel. Even a very nice one. For me a hotel is a place to sleep, not a place to be."

Brooklyn waved the remote. "But they have TV. It's just like home."

"Right. It is." Kerri showed that Mona Lisa smile that sometimes made Brooklyn want to bean her.

"What could we possibly do here? It's Dallas. I don't have a cowboy hat, or boots…"

Kerri stood up and gave her a quick wave. "I'm going to an art museum."

"Say hello to Frederick Remington for me."

She watched Kerri walk out, then focused on the TV. It was 10:15, and she wanted to go to sleep by four. That only left five and a half hours to watch…something about how submarines were made.

Rolling her eyes, she texted Kerri. "Stop by my room and pick me up. I'll buy a hat and boots at the museum store."

―∾―

Kerri had chosen the Kimbell Art Museum in Ft. Worth for their airing. The collection was quite small, but top notch in every way. They stood outside, braving the chill wind to admire the building.

"It's pretty cool," Brooklyn admitted. "I don't know much about Louis Kahn, but I know he's a big deal among architects."

"I'm not up on architecture, either, but I like to look at buildings."

"Let's go see the cowboy sculptures," Brooklyn said, "I'm freezing!"

Once inside, Kerri got a map of the collection. "Pick your poison. They have a very good European gallery, and smaller ones from Asia and Africa."

"You choose."

"Okay. Let's swing through Asia, then take our time looking at the European collection. They've got works by all of the biggies."

They stopped briefly at a sculpture of a bodhisattva that Kerri was taken by. She stared at it for a long time, then said, "Doesn't looking at his face give you a sense of peace?"

"Yeah, I guess it does. Who is he?"

Kerri continued to gaze at the peaceful figure. "It depends on what kind of Buddhism you're into. Some people think a bodhisattva was the Buddha before he became enlightened in this life, or in one of his previous lives. Others consider a person a bodhisattva if he's on the path to attaining enlightenment. I don't have a strong opinion. I just love how the artist captured that placid, content spirit. He really looks..." She stopped and shook her head, actually looking a little shy. "I don't have a good way to express how it makes me feel."

Kerri eventually moved away and Brooklyn walked alongside her. "Buddhism really means a lot to you, doesn't it."

"Yes, but so do Hinduism and Jainism. I have a real affinity for Eastern philosophies. They...reach me."

"Would you like to live in Asia?"

"Oh, sure. But I could live anywhere. The world is so interesting to me that I can't think of a place I'd rule out."

"Let's go look around Europe. I'm embarrassed to say I haven't been there. Or anywhere else, for that matter. But I've got enough Starwood points to stay somewhere nice if I ever leave the country."

They found a painting that Kerri was looking for. "I'm a big Caravaggio fan," she said. "The last time I was in Rome I spent a whole day tracking down every one of his paintings I could find."

"I've seen a couple of his at the Met," Brooklyn said. She looked around and whispered, "Where are the cowboys?"

"On their horses. Elsewhere."

—⁓—

After wandering around with no specific game plan, Brooklyn went to the information desk and spoke to the clerk for a long time. Kerri wasn't sure what she was trying to do, but Brooklyn eventually pulled out a charge card, then turned around and grinned happily at Kerri while the clerk processed it. After another minute or two, a scholarly looking fellow emerged from a door and shook Brooklyn's hand. Brooklyn signaled Kerri over. "This is Dr. Gutierrez, one of the curators of the museum. He's going to take us on a tour."

Now that was a unique way to see a museum, but it wouldn't hurt her body or her brain so Kerri was all for it.

—⁓—

Two hours later they braved the elements to head to their rental.

"Okay, I admit that I'm an idiot," Brooklyn said. "That was a kick-ass museum."

"Having Dr. Gutierrez with us made it a lot better. I'll admit I thought you were wasting your money to hire him, but you made a good call."

"I don't know enough about art to drill down and really learn something. I need help."

"Isn't it enough to just look at and enjoy?"

"Nope. Not for me. If I can't put things in context, I lose interest. I don't want to wander, I want to learn. Being able to ask a real expert questions gets my motor running."

Kerri chuckled. "I think you gave him a headache. He kept saying he'd never had anyone ask so many questions."

"Heh. After what I had to pay to get that tour, he should have carried me."

"Let's try to keep this up. Most cities have something to see. You just have to get out of your hotel room to see it."

"Make you a deal," Brooklyn said as she clicked open the car doors, "you find cool places to go, and I'll pay. I'll go to museums and historical sights and even movies. Getting out is a good idea." She was chuckling when she sat down and started to secure her seat belt. "Although I'll go broke if I have to join the Connoisseurs Circle at every place we go."

"I think I can make you happy at a fraction of the cost." Kerri watched Brooklyn start the car and carefully check the GPS navigation screen. Once again Brooklyn's remarkable desirability struck her. It was a crying shame. Brooklyn had every trait a woman could want, but a few that took her out of the game.

CHAPTER TWELVE

A WEEK LATER, BROOKLYN went to the dentist after *Reveille*. When she came home, she tossed a plastic container on the dining table and stood there, scowling at it.

Kerri came out of the kitchen when she heard the door close. "What's in the box? Snakes?"

"Almost." She stood stock still, glaring at the plastic. "My mouthguard."

Unable to stand the suspense, Kerri picked it up and opened it. Inside were two pieces of clear plastic, obviously molded to fit Brooklyn's bite; the pieces were held together by rigid pieces of plastic. "You won't be able to open your mouth with this on."

"I noticed." She walked over to the sectional and sat down. "I don't want to use that infernal C-pap machine, but this isn't a great second choice."

"Is it uncomfortable?"

"Yeah, but she swore I'd get used to it quickly."

"Doctors always say that." Kerri turned it around experimentally, trying to make sense of it.

"It's made so your lower jaw is forced forward. Having it stick out past your upper ostensibly makes your soft palate less able to vibrate."

"Well, it's better than climbing out of a fifteen-story window. Think of it that way." She shot Brooklyn a sunny grin and went to finish lunch, ignoring the lethal glare that followed her.

Brooklyn headed for bed at around four. She was just across the threshold to her room when Kerri called out, "Don't forget your mouthguard."

She stopped, then went back to pick it up. "Thanks a bunch," she said with false sincerity. "Are you hanging around?"

"Not for long. I'm going to finish this thing I'm working on, then I'll head home." She cocked her head the way she did when she was going to suggest something—usually something Brooklyn wouldn't like. "Why don't I come by at midnight and we can head to a comedy club?"

"Okay, but I'm not sure I can get on anywhere."

"So? Let's go hang out. Being around your people will get you in a good mood for your show."

"All right, but don't wake me up. I need to be rested more than I need to be around comics."

"It's a deal. I'll be as quiet as a mouse."

Brooklyn looked down at her and decided she sometimes looked like a cute little blonde mouse. She was tempted to reach out and ruffle that adorable hair, but thought better of it.

"Okay, Minnie. I'll see you later."

—⁓—

Kerri wasn't working on anything particularly time-sensitive. She could have gone home at any time. But she was truly worried about Brooklyn's sleep apnea and wanted to make sure she got used to her mouthguard.

It was very easy to hear over the relatively short walls of the bedrooms, so she moved to the kitchen, the spot closest to Brooklyn's room where she could work comfortably. She set her computer on the counter and perched on a stool, listening for signs that Brooklyn had settled down.

Pages turned for quite a while, then she heard a magazine hit the floor. After a few more minutes all was quiet. It usually took about fifteen minutes for Brooklyn to start snoring. But today—nothing. Stealthily, Kerri went to the bedroom door and slid it open. Brooklyn was indeed sound asleep. Her hair was pushed up onto the pillow beside her head, as she always placed it to avoid pulling on it when she moved around. Normally her mouth was open while she slept. But today it was closed, and her lower jaw did stick out a little, just as the device was made to do.

It was a little strange to be watching her sleep, but apnea was dangerous, perhaps fatally so if left untreated. Kerri didn't like to dramatize, and she had to admit that Brooklyn's sleep disorder was fairly minor. She merely cared about Brooklyn and wanted her to be happier and healthier. Okay, that wasn't entirely honest either. She cared about Brooklyn in a variety of ways and got pleasure from looking at her. Doing that while Brooklyn was asleep was ideal.

She was so pretty when she slept. When awake, her sharp, perceptive eyes never stopped roaming. The strangely attractive dichotomy of Brooklyn was that she was either hyper-aware or hyper-unaware. It was when she slept that she was serene, peaceful, and truly lovely. Surprisingly lush curves hidden by the sheet made Kerri twitch, wishing she could pull that sheet off to stare boldly. That, however, was something she'd never, ever do. Not even to Dakota. This was bad enough, even if she could vaguely justify her need to check on her.

Her conscience quickly asserted itself, and she left the room. Leering at a sleeping woman was beyond the pale, even if she had a valid reason. Things between them were unclear on many levels. It was possible Brooklyn would still be amenable to a physical overture, even though there wasn't the same kind of spark between them that had been present at first. Kerri could brave the risk of rejection, but she wasn't ready and wasn't sure she'd ever be. Until she was, she'd have to keep her lascivious thoughts to herself.

—⁓—

It was around one when they got out of a cab in front of Comicks on Lafayette. It was another seedy bar with a small stage surrounded by several dozen small tables and uncomfortable, unpadded chairs. Even though the place was less than luxe, Brooklyn looked and acted like she felt very much at home.

It always surprised Kerri how garrulous she was in the clubs. She turned into a back-slapping, high-octane chatterbox—something she almost never was at home. It was impossible to know which was the "real" Brooklyn, or which one was more attractive. They both had their advantages.

After talking to and tipping doormen, bartenders and waitresses, they sat down in the back of the club at a table on a low rise. Kerri had learned that many clubs had a special section where other comics sat and chatted or graded the talent, but tonight they were the only ones there.

Drumming her fingers against the table while the guy on stage tried to get through his set, Brooklyn seemed strangely antsy. The audience had clearly turned against the comic, not bothering to laugh even when he said something mildly funny.

"Like watching an execution," Brooklyn muttered.

"Does he have any talent?"

Blinking slowly, Brooklyn shook her head. "Not in comedy. I hope he can pick stocks or build things 'cause he's wasting his time."

She was about to ask how she could be so sure of her judgment when a woman came up behind Brooklyn and put her hands over her eyes. "Guess who?" she asked in a remarkably strong New York accent.

"Either Fran Dresher or Bridget McCleery," Brooklyn said, laughing. She grasped the woman's arm and pulled her around so forcefully that she landed right onto Brooklyn's lap. "That worked out well. I'm gonna have to try that more often." Then she kissed her on the cheek.

Bridget stayed right where she was, acting like she was settling into a comfy sofa. "You're nice and soft, York. I can see why the ladies love you." Then she made eye contact with Kerri and mouthed, "Sorry, honey."

"Oh, that's fine," Kerri said. "I'm just her manager. Feel free."

Bridget got up and took a chair from the next table. "No, I'm too old to try women. I missed my chance in college. It just looks desperate when you go gay because men don't notice you anymore."

Kerri decided most guys would probably be a little afraid of Bridget. She was shortish, stocky, sturdy, and loud—not the sort of woman a guy would find alluring at first sight. But she had a dazzling smile, and a ton of energy; traits you had to spend a moment to appreciate.

"So are you ready to date again?" Brooklyn asked. Then she looked at Kerri and said, "Bridget had a bad breakup last year. Hey! Did I introduce you?"

"Nope," Kerri said. She extended her hand. "I'm Kerri Klein."

"Hi, Kerri. Did you have Kat killed? I *know* York didn't fire her."

"I did too," Brooklyn said. "Well, she quit, but I didn't beg her to come back this time."

"Baby steps," Bridget said, pinching Brooklyn's cheeks. "Good girl. Are you working tonight?"

"I might, but I didn't ask yet. I just wanted to hang out. I'm trying to sleep in the afternoon and stay up all night, and I need to stay out of the house to avoid zoning out in front of the TV."

"Finally! That's the first sane thing I've ever heard you do. Kerri must be a good influence on you."

"She is," Brooklyn said so fondly that Kerri felt the flash of an ache in her heart.

A waitress checked on them and soon brought their drinks, a vodka martini for Brooklyn, a Manhattan for Bridget and a sparkling water for Kerri. It took all of her willpower not to chide Brooklyn, but she couldn't supervise her like a child. At least not every minute. She had to learn some things by her own mistakes.

They watched a few comics come and go, with either Brooklyn or Bridget saying something biting or complimentary. There seemed to be no middle ground. Jokes were either good or terrible. Bridget gave Brooklyn a droll look time and again and said just one word to characterize a bad set. "Abortion."

It took Kerri a little while to warm up to the brutal way they treated their peers, but Bridget started to grow on her. She was rough, but it was clear she was fond of Brooklyn, and that was a huge plus.

"You'll never guess who my sister tried to set me up with, Yorkie," Bridget said during a break. "A real estate agent."

She laughed hard and Brooklyn joined in. "Oh, that would be lovely. Make sure you invite me to go out with you two some night."

At the risk of sounding dumb, Kerri said, "What's funny about real estate agents?"

The look Bridget gave her was one you'd give to a young child who asked what quadratic equations were. "He's a straight guy who wants to live a normal life, honey. That can't work. It's impossible."

"Impossible?"

Both women nodded. "Impossible," Brooklyn intoned seriously.

"But why?"

Brooklyn shrugged. "It's a sad truth, but being an entertainer puts you in a different world. You can't go out with a straight couple and talk about little league and the PTA."

"But why? Lots of comics are married and have kids. Jerry Seinfeld, Chris Rock, all of those guys."

"Ding, ding, ding," Bridget said, acting like she was ringing a bell. "Guys. They have wives who do all of the normal stuff. Name five women comedians who have families."

"Roseanne..." Kerri trailed off, thinking she wasn't the best example. "Carrie Fisher?"

"She's funny, but she's not a comic," Bridget said. "She's never been on the road. Besides, she's had to have shock treatment to stay out of mental hospitals. That's what being a funny woman does to you. No, you can't do it."

"Sandra Bernhard!" Kerri declared. "I know she has a daughter."

"And a wife," Bridget added, looking superior. "Carol Leifer is another one. She had a child once, she turned gay and got a wife. No, Joan Rivers is the only woman I know who married a guy and had a kid while on the road. But her husband was her manager...and he killed himself."

"There have to be more examples," Kerri insisted.

"I'm waiting," Bridget said, smiling sweetly. "Ack! Time's up. Until I want to change teams, I'm stuck dating people in the biz." She reached over and ruffled Brooklyn's hair. "You're a lucky one, Bro-yo. A true dyke. All you need to live a normal life is a good-looking wife."

"A normal life is not in my future," she said dismissively. "Can you imagine having dinner with a couple who sell insurance or teach school?" She almost doubled over with laughter. "I'd hang myself."

———

At closing time, they went to a bar next to the club and Brooklyn had two more vodka martinis. Kerri was steamed, but she was determined not to say a word. Brooklyn knew better than to have four martinis before work. Did she have no memory of having to chew parsley and gum the last time? She could be so freaking infuriating!

Bridget pulled out her phone before they parted. "Where are you for the next few months? I'd love to hang out if we're ever in the same city."

With what looked like real pride, Brooklyn took her phone from her pocket and scrolled through her calendar. They chatted about possible overlapping dates, finding a good fit in New Orleans later in the year. Brooklyn put Bridget's name down and double-checked her cell phone number. Then they gathered their coats and said goodbye at the door. It was over a mile away, but Kerri successfully convinced Brooklyn to walk home even though it was barely fifteen degrees. There was a chance the walk would sober her up.

The cold, crisp air cut through their clothes like they were cheesecloth, but they trudged along the deserted streets. They'd gone about a block when Brooklyn leaned over and said, "Smell my breath."

Kerri wasn't enthusiastic, but knew she was the first line of defense for someone from *Reveille* calling Brooklyn out for drinking. She sniffed delicately. "You smell like olives." Cocking her head, she sniffed again. "Just olives."

Laughing, Brooklyn said, "I tipped both waitresses to bring me plain water with an olive. I paid fifteen bucks for each of those friggin' olives!"

Impulsively, Kerri hugged her, holding on for longer than she should have. "I'm so proud of you!"

Brooklyn looked equally proud, but also embarrassed when she pulled away. "I need to look like I'm drinking, but I can't afford to go to work soused any more. It's not worth it."

Kerri couldn't help it. She grabbed Brooklyn's arm and hugged it to her body. They continued to walk, and Brooklyn didn't try to shake her off, which was lovely.

Kerri's pique vanished now that she knew Brooklyn had learned such a valuable lesson. Being allowed to touch her even made her feel a little giddy. So much so that she wished they lived further away, despite the bitter cold. "Hey, why would it be so horrible to live what you call a normal life?"

Brooklyn didn't answer for a long time. It was hard to tell if she was thinking of an answer or polishing one she already had.

"It's tiring," she finally said. "When people learn you're a comedian they try to be funny. Especially guys. Actually, exclusively guys. They're the *worst*. They seem to think it's a competition, and they have to be in the game."

"And that bothers you?"

"Hell, yes!"

She said this with such fire that Kerri dropped her arm and stepped back.

"Wow. That was heartfelt."

"Sorry." She tossed her head so that her hair flung back over her shoulder, a chronic nervous tic. "It's just really, really annoying. When I meet a doctor, I don't try to act like I know how to remove a spleen."

"But you don't know how to remove a spleen. Lots of people are funny. I'd think you'd enjoy having someone trying to make you laugh."

Brooklyn stopped in her tracks and gave Kerri a withering look. "I'm a professional story-teller. This isn't a hobby. It irks the hell out of me when some guy thinks his story about his fishing trip where he fell in the lake is going to crack me up."

"But why? I hear what you're saying, but I can't see why it would bother you."

Brooklyn shrugged and shook her head. "I can't explain it any better. I enjoy talking to people and I enjoy hearing their stories. Just not when someone is clearly trying to impress me with how funny he is. It bugs the hell out of me."

They didn't speak about it the rest of the way home. Brooklyn's attitude seemed small-minded, even imperious. And neither trait was attractive.

―――

The next day, after Brooklyn got home from work, they went for a bike ride to soak up some much needed Vitamin D.

They'd been riding for a while when Brooklyn led them off the path and across Tenth Avenue. It was cold, but not quite as cold as it had been, and the sun was out. They locked up the bikes in front of a dry cleaner, where Brooklyn dashed inside to tip the owner to keep an eye on them. Then they climbed the staircase on Fourteenth Street to The Highline, the park created atop an abandoned elevated railway spur.

The park was fairly empty today, even though it was sunny. They went to a projection that allowed for a clear view across Manhattan where Brooklyn sat down on a wooden lounge chair and stared into the distance. "Nice, huh?" she said after a while.

"Very. And we're closer to the sun."

"Yep. Every few feet helps."

This was Brooklyn at home. Quiet, thoughtful, low-maintenance. Kerri was finding she liked this side equally as well as the hyper, glad-hander from the clubs. Actually, this side was nicer, seemed more elemental.

"Up for another question about comics?"

"Sure." Brooklyn grasped a knee with both hands and stretched her leg.

"Are women comics less neurotic than men?"

Brooklyn laughed immediately. "I know what you mean. A lot of us are. A lot of us are hard workers who found that we're funny and tried to make a living with it. Some of the guys are really tragic figures. They've got to find the humor in their desperation or end it all. Some of them are too dark even for me to be around and I can be positively sepulchuric."

"I'm guessing that means dark," Kerri said.

"I made it up when I couldn't think of a better word. I was gonna use funereal, but that wasn't quite right. I had to coin one."

"You could just say dark, but I know that's not your way." She chuckled. "I know what you're getting at, though. You don't hear of many women comics being found dead in a hotel room by the prostitute they picked up the night before. Thank goodness," she added.

Brooklyn sat quietly, her sharp eyes wandering all along the Manhattan skyline. "I'm really thankful you came along when you did. I was getting a little too guy-like when I was on the road."

"Guy-like?"

"Yeah. I was sitting in the back of a club most nights, leering at women with a bunch of guys while I drank enough to be able to sleep." She paused for a long minute. "That had to have had something to do with Ashley dumping me."

Kerri patted her leg. "It couldn't have helped."

"My schedule's just as whack as it was then, but at least I'm not drunk."

"You're barely drinking, much less to excess."

"I'm really trying to change. Not just to find a woman—for myself."

Kerri looked at her strong features, almost seeing the determination in her expression. She'd rarely been so happy to hear anything.

"Bridget was right when she was talking about dating. I've got to be content to find someone in the business. Dating a regular woman won't work. I need someone who can be on my schedule." She smiled. "Maybe a cop or a 911 operator who works the third shift."

"Why not? Don't limit yourself to other comics. There have to be plenty of night owls out there." *Just don't be in a rush to find one.*

"Oh. I keep forgetting to tell you how great it feels to keep my own calendar." Her grin was blinding in the strong, slanting light.

"I can imagine. It's important to know what's going on."

"No," she said slowly. "It's more than that. It lets me feel like I'm in control. My whole life has gotten better since I've been responsible for my own schedule, and that's all because of you. Thanks."

"You're welcome." She would have kissed her if Brooklyn had been the kind of person who could tolerate physical affection. So Kerri merely tried to show with a smile how much the compliment meant to her. It wasn't as good as a kiss, but she had to work with what she had.

———

Now that she was firmly committed and used to her new schedule, Brooklyn's entire personality seemed to change. She was drinking much less, and Kerri was certain she wasn't using any form of sleeping pill or tranquilizer. Her mouth guard let her sleep without constantly waking up, and that seemed to make the biggest difference. Just a week or two after starting to use it, she was the person Kerri had expected to meet just a few months before. Her mind seemed to work more quickly, and ideas almost flew from her lips. But the nicest change for Kerri was how Brooklyn now shared things with her on a routine basis. It was a little embarrassing to admit how little she contributed to their discussions, but Brooklyn didn't seem to mind a bit. She needed a sounding board, and Kerri couldn't have been happier to be one.

One afternoon, Kerri was sitting at the dining table working on some details for Brooklyn's next appearance. Unaware that Kerri was deeply engrossed in her work, Brooklyn walked up behind her and asked, "Do you think babies have the capacity for concrete thought?"

She might as well have asked how a zebra would look in a tuxedo. Kerri had never given a moment's thought to either proposition. "I don't know. What do you think?"

Brooklyn started to pace the six or seven strides between the dining table and the windows. "Thoughts seem to need language, right? I mean, feelings are one thing, but thoughts seem to be on a much higher level."

"Yes, I guess I can see that. So you think that babies just feel things?"

"Yeah." She nodded her head decisively. "I think I do. Once they have language, they can start to form thoughts. Until then, they're not much different than dogs."

All Kerri was able to add to the discussion was, "Did you have animals when you were growing up?"

"No. I wanted a dog, but my parents were pretty sure I wouldn't take care of it." She started to pace again and looked like she was going to say something profound, then she stopped and said politely, "How about you?"

"No, I didn't either. I'd love to have a dog, but I've never been in one place long enough to seriously consider having one."

Brooklyn stood there for a moment, then a slow smile lit up her face. "Maybe that's something we should investigate. If I got a small dog I could take it with me when I flew. That would be cool, wouldn't it?"

It seemed an utterly complex situation, but when Brooklyn smiled like that no one would be able to say no to her. It was all Kerri could do not to get on the internet, find the closest shelter and get a dog for her that very afternoon.

—※—

One afternoon when it was too cold and overcast to consider being outside, Brooklyn took on the task of putting all of the business cards she'd collected into a new app on her iPad. Kerri was in the second bedroom, and Brooklyn went to the door to ask her a question. When Kerri saw her, she quickly turned away. Brooklyn noticed she was on the phone and backed out, closing the door as she left.

A few minutes later, Kerri emerged. "Hey, I'm sorry. I was on the phone. What did you want?"

"You don't have to be sorry for talking on the phone. The room's got a door for privacy."

"I don't really need privacy... I just had to make a call." She had an odd expression on her face, one Brooklyn couldn't begin to read.

"Is everything okay?"

Laughing, Kerri nodded and sat down on the sectional. "Sometimes I get carried away with my secretiveness. The truth is, Dakota has started to see somebody, and I need to find a furnished apartment that will allow a month-to-month lease."

Brooklyn looked at Kerri for a moment, a burst of compassion welling in her chest. "Is that okay with you?"

A flash of feeling registered on her face, then was gone just as quickly as it had appeared. "You know, " she said, in a measured tone, "I'm pretty unhappy about it."

Brooklyn stood up and walked over to her. "Tell me about it."

"I hate to be cheap, but I truly hate to pay rent."

Brooklyn stared at her, waiting for her to get to her feelings, but Kerri merely stared back. "I think you might have gotten the wrong idea about Dakota and me."

She scratched her head, feeling shy and confused. "I assume you're more than occasional roommates, if that's what you mean."

"Well, we are, but we're not. I love Dakota, but I don't have any hold on her. I want her to do what makes her happiest."

Brooklyn nodded, thinking that was the right response, but she was thoroughly confused. "You're not sad?"

"No, not sad." She sat there for a minute, and when Brooklyn didn't speak, she added, "I'm a little disappointed, but mostly about her timing."

Brooklyn had no idea where to go with that tidbit, so she said nothing.

"Our relationship isn't traditional, so my reaction to this won't be either. I truly don't have a hold on her. I'm not kidding about that."

"Okay." *This is weird shit!*

"You look suspicious," Kerri said, smiling.

"I guess it seems odd to me that you have some form of relationship that's lasted for a long time, and you're not upset that she's moving on."

"Oh, I get it. You think I should be jealous."

"I would be. Or hurt."

"Right. Right." She sat quietly for a second, then said, "This is part of my quest. My Eastern practices." When Brooklyn looked at her blankly she added, "Meditation and that stuff."

"Okay…"

"One of the things I work hardest on is not being possessive. I had a tendency to be that way, and it wasn't healthy for me. So I work really diligently at letting things happen when they happen, and not being too clingy."

"Okay, I guess I understand." *Not a bit!* "So you're more like old friends who bunk together when you're in the same town."

Kerri shook her head. "No, that doesn't do our relationship justice. We love each other, but our relationship is…I guess it's just unusual."

It sure as hell is! "It's probably too unusual for my traditional mind to get around. So tell me about your housing issue. Do you always have to stay with someone when you're out of town? What do you usually do when you're on a job?"

"I almost always go away for a film, so I stay in the hotel or in the house the production company rents for my client. They always have a dozen spare rooms in the mansions they rent."

"I can't compete with that, but I definitely have a spare room, and I want you to take it."

"Oh, no, I couldn't. That wasn't part of our deal."

"Precisely. You wouldn't have taken this job if you'd known you would have had to pay for a decent apartment. Am I right?"

"You're kind of right," she said chuckling.

"I don't want to put pressure on you, but I'd like it if you moved in." She held her hands up, still looking directly into Kerri's eyes. "No ulterior motive."

"I'll move in on one condition. You have to cut my salary by at least ten percent."

"Okay. I've got one condition back at you. I'll cut your salary but I'll pay for your food."

"Fine, but I'll cook."

Brooklyn stuck her hand out and they shook. "It's a deal," they said simultaneously.

—⁓—

Brooklyn got home from the radio show the next day to find Kerri was completely moved in. She walked out of her new bedroom and waved. "Hi, roomie. How was work?"

"It was good. I was almost completely ignored, which is a cause for celebration. How in the world did you get your stuff over here so quickly?"

"I didn't have much. It just took one cab ride."

"You're a very efficient person. I guess that helps in your job, huh?"

"Pretty much. It's a lovely day, and it's supposed to break forty later. Do you want to go ride our bikes?"

"Absolutely. It's freezing and there's a brisk wind blowing across the river from Jersey. Perfect biking weather."

—⁓—

When Brooklyn got home the next morning, Kerri was busy making lunch. The kitchen was as big a mess as it had ever been, and four burners of the stove were in use.

"What in the heck is going on here?" Brooklyn stood with her hands on her hips, looking stern.

"I went to the organic farmer's market. I bought enough for lunch today and tomorrow and for dinner. Does it smell good?"

"I don't think I've ever smelled anything that smells quite like this. What is it?"

"That's probably the bulgur. That's for later. I'm going to make a ratatouille for lunch."

Brooklyn walked over and surveyed the bounty. "Cute little carrots." She popped one into her mouth and closed her eyes while she let out a sensual moan. "Oh my God. I haven't ever had a carrot that good."

"I don't want to keep harping on this, but I'd be surprised if it isn't because your sense of smell is working better. I bet all of your food tastes brighter."

"You know," she said thoughtfully, "it really does. I only miss cigarettes when I have a drink. And that's not even very often."

"Less is more, at least for me it is. When I have a drink it seems like a treat."

Brooklyn picked up another carrot and went to her room, saying, "You are one funny woman."

—⁓—

When Brooklyn came out of her room, she was very casually dressed. A clean but un-ironed, oversized, blue shirt covered some kind of knit, gray shorts which stuck out from the bottom of the shirt. Looking a little unsure of herself, she pulled up her shirt to show that she was wearing men's knit boxer shorts. "If we're going to live together, you're going to have to get used to my normal attire."

"That's totally cool." Kerri didn't bring up the obvious point that she'd seen her naked several dozen times, and that this was no big deal. She also didn't add that she hadn't paid much attention to Brooklyn's legs before, but she was glad to do so now. She had the legs of a tennis player, strong and muscular, and surprisingly lean. Kerri had always been a leg woman, and she decided that she was looking forward to getting used to Brooklyn's proclivities.

—⁓—

Since part of the deal was that Kerri would cook, Brooklyn sat down and started skimming through every headline that had come in on her iPad. Feeling remarkably happy, she realized after a minute that Kerri was singing to herself. She couldn't make out any words, and she wasn't familiar with the song, but having somebody so ridiculously cheerful making you lunch was a true mood elevator. Kerri had made it clear this couldn't be permanent, but for someone in a hurry to get back to LA she was dragging her feet awfully well. Whatever the reason for Kerri's sluggish pace, Brooklyn was going to do whatever she could to make this happy time last as long as humanly possible. Her life had never been better.

When lunch was almost ready Kerri brought over a fork with a piece of zucchini speared on it. "Test this and see if it's too spicy."

Brooklyn could see the steam coming off it so she put her hand atop Kerri's to steady the fork and her eyes wandered to her hand. Since the first day they'd met she'd been enthralled by Kerri's hands. They were perfect. Slender fingers, smooth skin, and beautiful nails. She knew Kerri didn't have a lot of free time, so they probably weren't the result of constant care. Perhaps she was just blessed with good genes. Whatever the reason, Brooklyn was blessed to be able to gaze at them. She just hoped Kerri didn't notice her interest.

Lunch was fantastic, and Brooklyn was effusive in her compliments. When they were finished eating she stood up and said, "We don't have a deal about cleaning, so I'll do it."

Kerri jumped up at the same time. "I'm on the clock. You've got plenty to do to get ready for work tomorrow."

"No, I'd like to." She walked over to the sink and stood there for a second, then asked, shyly, "Can you tell me how?"

—⁓—

Just a few words of instruction had Brooklyn working away efficiently. Kerri wasn't sure why she felt the need to clean the kitchen, but she wasn't going to dissuade her from doing anything for herself, nor from learning how to do the things most people had been taught at more tender years.

Brooklyn was washing up the last of the pans when her cell phone rang. Kerri got up and found it, calling out, "It's your agent. Want me to answer?"

"Sure."

Kerri held the phone to her ear. "Hi Melvin, it's Kerri Klein."

"Hey, how's it going?"

"It's going great."

"Let me talk to Brooklyn if she's around. I've got good news."

Brooklyn dried off her hands and came over to take the phone. "Hi, Melvin. What's up?"

"I got a call from the head of Oakleaf Publishing. He was listening to *Reveille* the other day, liked what he heard, and called to offer you a book deal."

She let out a yip of surprise. "Book deal?"

Kerri scampered over and put her arms around Brooklyn, and they jumped up and down in celebration at just the concept.

"I'm putting you on speaker phone, Melvin. This is important stuff, and I want Kerri to hear the whole deal."

After they hung up Brooklyn was grinning like a fox. "Tonight, you pick the restaurant, I'm buying. And make sure it's frivolously expensive. I can afford it."

Kerri chose a very high-end, vegetarian restaurant, where the chef was talented enough to make the dining experience so luxurious that only a rigorous carnivore would have missed the meat. It was a place that attracted a big after-theater crowd, so they served until one.

Brooklyn was at her most charming, riffing on ideas for a book that had no chance of being approved, but had Kerri laughing non-stop.

They had a fabulous time, sharing a split of champagne, a moderate choice that would have been beyond imagining just a few months before.

Kerri felt very close to Brooklyn, and hated to bring up a topic she knew wasn't going to go over well, but it was time. "My agent called with a job possibility for here in New York, but if I took it I wouldn't be able to travel with you."

Brooklyn looked nonplussed, but she quickly said, "Tell me about it."

Kerri laughed while making a face. "I don't know why I think it's funny. The job will probably be horrible, but it pays ridiculously well."

"Those two things often go hand-in-hand, don't they?"

"In this case, I think that's definitely true. There's a woman, who I can't name, who signed on with a French company that makes a diet pill that's supposed to be a miracle."

"Methamphetamine?"

Kerri shook her head while she took another quick bite of her dinner. "Right. That would *really* work. I'm sure this miracle pill is a load of bull.

Anyway, she's twenty-five pounds short of her goal, and she's only got twelve weeks left until the big reveal—on live television. She's getting a couple of million to do this, so the company is understandably concerned."

"What does she want you to do? Strap her to a treadmill?"

"She doesn't want me to do anything. It's the French company that wants to hire me. I anticipate a very contentious relationship, but it's in the contract that they can supervise her if she's not making her goals."

"My question remains. What are you supposed to do?"

"Supervise everything she eats, and make sure she's not sneaking anything. She's only eating a thousand calories a day…or so she says…so she's clearly cheating."

"That sounds like a pretty horrible job, but I can't wait to start seeing the commercials."

"You won't see them. The drug isn't approved in the US." She playfully rapped Brooklyn's hand. "Do you think I'd tell you as much as I did if you'd know who it was? She's a really big star, and very protective of her image."

"But people will see it in France and it'll get back here, right?"

"The company is French but the commercials are only going to be shown in parts of Asia, where the drug is legal. Big stars are always doing commercials in Asia and we never hear about them."

Brooklyn nodded, her expression contemplative. "Why do you want to take it? It sounds like it could be a really lousy way to spend your time."

"It might be, but it's what I'm used to."

"But…"

"Look." She put her hand on Brooklyn's and watched those brown eyes shift to gaze at them, one covering the other. "You're paying me too much to make you a latte in the morning and travel with you on the weekends. I know you don't mind, but it doesn't feel right to me."

"But I love having you." Her words sped up. She seemed to be throwing arguments out as fast as they came to her. "You make me lunch, you help me get ready, which is no mean feat. And you're doing so much for me on the road. Lots more than Kat ever considered doing. More than Melvin!"

"But it's easy for me. What I'm doing takes almost no time, Brooklyn. I can do almost everything I've been doing while taking this other job. I just won't be able to travel with you, and I probably won't be able to make your lunch."

"I don't care about lunch. That's the least of my problems." She sat there for a second, then looked at Kerri warily, intently. "Aren't we friends?"

Those words went right to her heart. Brooklyn had such a gentle, trusting soul, and her generosity had no bounds. That alone was reason to be particularly careful of taking advantage of her. "Of course we are. That's why I can't go on taking so much money for so little work."

"But you'll still manage me?"

"Sure. I really want to. I won't charge you much though. I just won't."

With a heavy sigh, Brooklyn said, "You're sure this is what you want?"

"I think so. I want to go to India soonish, so this would work out perfectly. The money is great, and having the extra cash will let me travel in business class, which will be a huge luxury for me. For a fifteen-hour flight I might just go nuts and spend big."

"What about going back to LA? I thought your mom needed help..."

"She says things are stable." She cut the topic off. "Now I have to decide if I can handle this client."

"Is she in New York?"

"Yeah. She's in one of those new condo buildings on the West Side Highway, and she has a big place in the Hamptons. Probably LA too, but my agent said the job would only be in New York."

"Are those the condos with the glass walls?"

"Yeah. The ones that face the river. They're filled with celebs."

"And you'd have to live there?"

She hated to admit that her decision hinged on this part of the conversation, but it did. There was no way she'd leave Brooklyn until she absolutely had to, but she wasn't about to reveal that...yet. "Technically, no. It would probably be easier if I did, but I think I'll need to get away from her as much as I can. My agent said she goes through personal assistants about five times a year, and he was trying to convince me to *take* the job."

Brooklyn laughed. "You don't have to tell me about agents. They're a necessary evil." She moved a bit of food around on her plate, then looked up said, "Why don't you stay with me? We can keep our same agreement. I'll pay for the food and you cook our meals. Would that be cool?"

"That'd be awesome! But only if you're sure you want me to stay."

"I do. I'm sure of that."

She looked so happy that Kerri almost teared up. Brooklyn was about as kind as people got, and that quality was as rare as hen's teeth in Hollywood—or anywhere else, for that matter.

—⁓—

They walked home from the restaurant, even though Brooklyn kept insisting that New York had a law against depriving cabs of their rightful business. "You know, I'm really excited about writing a book, but I'm worried that it'll screw up the schedule I've just gotten used to."

"Why would it do that?"

"I meant my exercise schedule. I didn't think it would happen, but I'm getting into it." She showed the wry smile that Kerri had seen on dozens of fan pages. It was very different from the full smile she flashed when she was relaxed and unguarded. This one was clearly intended to show she was making fun of herself. Maybe it was a self-defense, but Kerri had never known anyone who consistently pointed out how good her life was, and how little she'd done to deserve it. There was a working-class Jersey girl in there that would never feel she should be so richly rewarded for merely thinking and talking.

"Just do what we've been doing. Get your exercise as soon as you finish with work, and you can think about what you want to write while you ride your bike."

Brooklyn seemed to think about that for a few moments. "That could work, but I want to start playing tennis, and it's not the kind of game you can do while daydreaming."

"You'll want to get back into it slowly, so you probably shouldn't play tennis more than twice a week. That will leave you plenty of time to write. And once you get your competitive juices flowing, you'll easily be able to bang out a couple of thousand words a day."

"I guess I'll have to see how it goes."

"Well, you don't have to turn the manuscript in until June, and I think that's plenty of time. Just don't let it slide until April."

The look Brooklyn tried to hide was filled with hurt. She didn't say anything for a moment, then softly replied, "I've changed."

Kerri could have kicked herself. She reached out and took Brooklyn's arm, holding it tightly against her body. "I was kidding. One hundred percent kidding. You're a hard worker, and I really admire that about you. I bet you're going to start the book by the weekend."

She still looked a little hurt, but a gentle smile showed through. "I was plotting out the first chapter during dinner."

"Do you forgive me? I shouldn't tease you about something like that."

"Don't worry about it. When a comedian can't take teasing, it's time to hang it up. Did you hear how Arnie was on me today?"

"Yeah, I did. Does he think you're in charge of all government programs? How can you make FEMA respond to hurricane victims faster?"

"I'm the liberal, and I believe the government has a responsibility to act as a safety net during catastrophes, so I'm responsible for all of the screw ups. Idiots like him try to make everything black and white, when in reality, the whole world is various shades of gray."

They walked along the quiet riverfront, not saying anything for a while. Kerri broke the silence. "Do you think the show is good for your career?"

"Sometimes. Apparently this book deal came directly from the show. But you know how much I hate it."

"Have you given any thought to leaving when your contract is up?"

"And walk away from that kind of money? I'd have to be crazy."

"No you wouldn't. If you let it, money can become the most important thing in your life, but do you really need as much as you have?"

Brooklyn gave her a hangdog look. "I certainly don't live paycheck to paycheck, but to afford my lifestyle I've got to keep producing. I spent so much redoing my loft. Too much," she added glumly. "I like it, but the remodel took the majority of my savings. Ashley never would have let me get away with that." The self-deprecating smile showed again. "That was another issue between us. She didn't like it when I acted like a celebrity. She wanted to live in the suburbs and hang out at a local bar with the people we went to high school with. I can't imagine how much she would have hated TriBeCa."

"That would have saved you a lot of money."

"That she might have stolen." Brooklyn shook her head, still smiling. "Money creates problems—whether you have too much or not enough."

"It can," Kerri agreed. "But you don't have to let it. You just have to find a lifestyle that's worth what you have to do to keep it." She wasn't sure that Brooklyn really got the full meaning of her comment, but she hoped that she'd planted the germ of a thought that might one day allow her to reassess.

———

The next afternoon at bedtime, Kerri went into Brooklyn's room with her. They'd gotten into the habit of a short back rub to help Brooklyn relax. It was still hard for her to fall asleep at three or four in the afternoon, but a gentle massage helped immensely.

Brooklyn was lying on her stomach, and Kerri was sitting next to her, gently working on her stiff muscles. "Can I make a suggestion?"

"Sure."

"If you're ready to write a book, hire an agent and have him or her shop the idea around."

Brooklyn turned to look at her. "But Melvin's already got a deal."

"Melvin's not a literary agent. People in the book business can get you a lot more money than he can, and they know which publishers are best to work with."

"But won't that shut Melvin out?"

God, she was loyal to a fault! Why did she insist on sticking with people who weren't good at their jobs? Melvin might have been fine for a C-level local comic, but he was nowhere near what Brooklyn needed. "All he did was answer the phone. Is that worth ten percent of the whole deal?"

"That's what he gets. You can't pick and choose what you're willing to pay for."

"No, of course you can't. So if you ultimately decide to go with his deal, he'll get the commission. If not, your literary agent will."

"How do I find one? If I want one."

"I've got a few people I can call. Give me a couple of days and I'll make the preliminary calls for you."

"You'll make them?"

"Of course. I'm still the only manager you have."

"And the only one I want."

This poor woman could be robbed blind by her handlers and she'd just work harder to make up for it. Whoever instilled the loyalty gene had locked it tightly in place. Still, it was refreshing to know someone who wasn't always looking out for herself. Brooklyn's problem was just the opposite. Whatever she did, she did to the max, including ignoring her self-interests.

Chapter Thirteen

BROOKLYN ROLLED INTO THE loft at eleven the next morning. When the front door closed, Kerri called out, "Hi! Want to go to a big premiere tonight?"

Brooklyn poked her head into Kerri's room. "A premiere? Of what?"

"A big, noisy, superhero, comic-book movie. It'll probably be horrible, but the premiere is at midnight. Since that fits your schedule, I thought you might like to do it."

She was smiling so beautifully that Brooklyn would have agreed to anything. It struck her that Kerri was excited solely because she'd found something that might make *her* happy. She felt a burst of unexpected energy, and it had come directly from Kerri. "You know, I'd love to do that. But only if you'll go with me."

Kerri picked up her cell phone and started dialing. "I thought you'd never ask."

⁓

The premiere was held at the biggest theater in Manhattan, The Ziegfeld. Holding over a thousand people, it was the last of the big movie houses built in the country. The event planners for the studio that produced the movie were happy to have Brooklyn, since they wanted to attract people in her demographic. They offered to send a limo for her, but she refused. A taxi was just as fast and made her feel like a regular person.

When they arrived, they were herded along with all of the other celebs to wait in a queue to be photographed. Finally, it was her turn and she tugged on Kerri to accompany her. "No way," Kerri said, dancing away from her grasp. "I'm just your plus one."

It was a waste of time to argue when she had that look on her face, so Brooklyn handed her her jacket and stood on the proper spot. She posed for a few minutes, trying not to look as dumb as she felt. There was something truly stupid about standing on an X and having a bunch of people you didn't know take your photo so a bunch of other people you didn't know could look at it. But they wouldn't have been invited to the premiere if no one wanted to look at her, so it was part of the deal.

When they went inside, they were given action figures and lunch boxes and T-shirts and a large tote-bag to put everything in. Then Brooklyn spied the thing she liked best about premieres—free junk food. The main character in this particular movie turned a brilliant shade of orange so there were cupcakes and drinks and even popcorn tinted that color.

They grabbed bags of popcorn and found seats about halfway back. "This is fun," Brooklyn whispered. For some reason she felt about ten years old. It was like seeing a blockbuster movie with a buddy at the Paramus Mall—without their moms.

The theater filled up quickly, and the two and a half hours zoomed by. The audience applauded lustily, and Brooklyn found herself joining in. "That was excellent," she said, smiling happily. "I normally hate action movies, but this one had a heart."

"I thought it would," Kerri said. She stayed in her seat, avidly staring at the credits. "I know the second unit cameraman, and the best boy and…the key grip. Nice guys."

"Did you work with them?"

"No, no, not with them. But they were on film locations when I was working. You get to know a lot of people when you're hanging around a set for weeks at a time."

"Do you look at movies differently since you've seen them being made? I always thought that would ruin the magic."

She paused for a moment, her expression thoughtful. "No, it hasn't ruined it for me. Actually, I love movies more than I ever did. I know how hard it is to do certain things and make it look good, so it's more interesting."

"We should go more often. I tend to go for documentaries, but you could convince me to broaden my interests."

"It's a deal." She looked as excited as Brooklyn had seen her. "I'm a movie junkie, so say the word and I'm there."

"You pick one you want to see, and find one that plays around midnight and we can go tomorrow." *And any other time you promise to smile like that.*

"Super. Now let's hit the after party. I know someone who's going to be there, but he or she won't want to acknowledge me." She held up a hand before Brooklyn could say a word. "You know I won't say who it is, so don't bother asking."

"I'll just look around for the person who turns pale when he or she sees you."

They got up and headed for the exit. "They might not even recognize me. They were just out of rehab and I think they were seeing double."

"It's not easy to talk about people when you can't use proper pronouns, is it?" Brooklyn teased.

"That's why I could never be in the closet. The grammar alone is torture!"

———

A few days later, Kerri went to meet her new client. It was just supposed to be a quick introduction, but she didn't get back to the loft until Brooklyn was getting ready for bed. When she came in, she walked directly into the kitchen and put her head in the freezer. "Don't mind me," her muffled voice called out. "I've been trying to stop myself from committing homicide for the past three hours, and my brain is about to fry."

Brooklyn got up from the sofa and walked to the kitchen. Leaning against the counter, she sympathetically asked, "How bad was it?"

271

Kerri closed the freezer and stood there for a second. "I have to think about that." She poured herself a glass of water, drank a few sips, then said, "Most of my clients have been charming screw ups." She patted Brooklyn on the arm. "Except you, of course. My clients usually try to make me like them, thinking they can get away with more if I'm on their side. This creature, who I think I'll call Godzilla, has decided to treat me like a piece of gum she stepped in on the street."

Brooklyn gently stroked her shoulder. "Are you sure about this? We could split the difference between what I'm willing to pay and what you think I should pay, and tour together until you leave for India."

"You have no idea how tempting that offer is, but this will be good experience. I've spent a lot of time working to control my world by the way I view it. Working with Godzilla will really test my progress."

"I thought you were just going to meet her today."

"Yes, that was the plan, but she's decided to have a facelift so she'll look better for the commercials. She gave me a full indoctrination, and I'm to return after she recovers in one of those apartment/hospital things. I've gotten a reprieve of at least a week."

"So it was horrible, right?"

Kerri sat on the sofa and patted the cushion next to her. "Come sit next to me, and I'll tell you the whole story." As Brooklyn sat down, Kerri continued, "First we had to go over how I'm allowed to address her…"

After Kerri revealed the full extent of her meeting with Godzilla, Brooklyn suggested they go for a bike ride. It was time for bed, but Kerri looked far too wound up to sleep. Some exercise would definitely help her. It was a nice, warmish day, just made for being outdoors. To try something different, they went to Union Square for the Farmers' Market. Not surprisingly, Brooklyn had never been to a farmers' market, so Kerri took the opportunity to show her what to look for in vegetables.

Brooklyn had been thinking a lot about their relationship. Now that Kerri wasn't going to be her full-time employee any longer, things would probably change. They'd have much less time together, and, even though she'd never admit it, that might have been just the reason Kerri had taken another job.

While they were walking around, Brooklyn said, "Our schedules aren't going to sync once you start your new job. I…uhm…know we haven't talked about this, but you'll have a lot more time to yourself and…I want you to treat the apartment like it's your own."

"Okay. I don't know that I've been ignoring any deeply felt desires to claim it, but I'll keep that in mind."

"I meant…you know…maybe you want to have friends over. Or other people."

"People other than friends…" Her brow furrowed and she finally nodded. "You mean I can have a woman over."

"Yeah. Only if you want to, of course."

Kerri snickered softly. "I promise I won't bring a woman over unless I really want to."

That had been the most ineloquent few sentences Brooklyn had ever strung together. Why had she ever brought the topic up? Yes, she wanted to know what was going on with Kerri, but that had been one sucko way of finding out.

Thankfully, they moved on to less uncomfortable topics, like how to tell if lettuce is fresh. On their ride back home, Kerri said, "You know, I'm going to have to get out of the habit of treating you like a client. We're friends, so I shouldn't try to parse out information so begrudgingly."

"Were you parsing anything in particular?"

"Yeah, I was. I appreciated that you said I could have friends over, but I don't look for friends, especially intimate friends, when I travel, and I should have just said that."

Brooklyn grinned at her. That was fantastic news! "I've been interested in your love life, but when I've asked, you sure didn't tell me much."

"That's a bad habit. I'll gladly spill my guts, even though I don't have a lot to spill. The truth is, I don't like dating, so I don't do it."

"But you're a healthy, attractive woman. Don't you have any…needs?"

"Of course I do. But I don't get them satisfied very often."

"And that's okay with you?"

"Ideally, I'd have someone I saw more regularly, but Dakota's been my only outlet."

"I was wondering how that worked," Brooklyn said dryly. "I couldn't imagine sleeping with somebody as cute as Dakota on that sofa bed and having nothing happen."

"Things happen."

She grinned, looking a little naughty. That was something new. Something new and very attractive.

"We get along great sexually, and seeing her has given me something to look forward to."

"So, you've been exclusive?"

"We don't talk about that. She's been the only person I've slept with for the last five or six years, but I assume her appetite is broader than mine." She laughed. "Given that someone has replaced me on the sofa bed made that fairly clear."

Brooklyn said, "You look like you want to say more, but I can't tell what."

"Mmm, I do, but I'm used to being so discreet it's hard to know when I'm doing it because of habit, or if I have something to keep secret."

"I'm interested if you want to tell me more."

Kerri took a breath. "Okay. When Dakota left for New York, I was brokenhearted. Really brokenhearted."

"I hear you. Losing Ashley hit me like a truck, and I thought she was *stealing* from me."

Kerri stopped at the first set of benches and propped her bike up along side. "Sit by me," she said, looking at Brooklyn with an intense gaze.

It took a second to get her bike set, and when Brooklyn sat down Kerri was still staring at her. "I didn't realize how much my self esteem was locked into being with Dakota. It was like I'd lost myself in her. I was so disconsolate that I considered ending it all."

"Kerri!" Impulsively, Brooklyn threw her arms around her and hugged her tightly. "I can't stand to even hear you say that."

They hugged for a long while, then slowly pulled apart. "It's true. It was a really dark time for me. I decided I had to figure out a new way of being. Not long after that, I got into meditation and my various Eastern ways. All of them helped me a lot, and I slowly saw that I'd been trying to hold onto her when she didn't want to be held. That's when I doubled-down on doing my best to live in the moment and try not to force people to make promises they can't keep."

"But a lot of people want to make promises. And keep them."

"I'm glad to know you believe that." She patted Brooklyn's leg like she was an innocent child.

"You don't? Really?"

"I haven't seen it. At least where it concerns fidelity. I think people do their best, but most can't be satisfied with a single partner for long. That's why I've worked hard on letting go. The only people I've been able to trust without question are my grandparents."

"Only your grandparents?" Damn, that was awful! What kind of people did she surround herself with?

"Yes, pretty much. My dad's as hard to pin down as a gremlin, and even my mom comes and goes depending on what's going on in her life."

"That's not normal!" She wanted to take it back as soon as it was out. The look Kerri gave her was filled with hurt. "I didn't mean it that way. I just meant that it doesn't make sense to give up and assume everyone will betray you."

"But it's not a betrayal." The peaceful, zenlike smile that seemed so effortless showed itself. "People come in and out of your life depending on the things that are happening in their lives. You can't take it personally, or try to hold on tighter. You have to focus on yourself and know that they'll come back when and if it's right."

"If someone left me and wanted to come back, they'd better bring a locksmith. And an ax." Brooklyn tried to add a smile to take the sting out of her words, but she meant them with all of her heart. She gave people a lot of rope, but once they'd seriously wounded her—they were as good as dead.

—⁓—

As soon as they got home, Brooklyn got ready for bed. She knocked on Kerri's door just before turning in. "I wanted to say goodnight," she called through the closed door.

"Come on in."

Kerri was stretched out on her yoga mat doing something that looked like it should be impossible for anyone over three years old. She was flat on her back, her legs bent at the knee, feet at her waist, with her soles facing the ceiling. Her arms were resting on the floor, and she had a look of utter peace on her face. Brooklyn stood there for a moment, stunned by the beauty and flexibility of Kerri's body. She realized she was staring, so she forced her mouth closed and tried to look normal. "You're really good at that," she lamely commented.

"I've been at it for years." Kerri slowly released the posture and lay flat on her mat, breathing heavily. "It doesn't get any easier."

Brooklyn sat down so her knees didn't betray her. "Tell me more about…"—she gestured at Kerri's body—"that."

"The pose? That was the reclining hero."

"Huh. It looked super hard, so I guess that could make you a hero. But I was asking about your whole Eastern thing."

Smiling, Kerri pulled her T-shirt up to dry her face. She started to sit up, but Brooklyn said, "I interrupted you, didn't I. You weren't finished."

"I wasn't finished, but I don't mind talking. I'll just stay loose." She lay down again, and started to stretch her leg, quickly pulling it straight up until it touched her face.

"That's remarkable," Brooklyn said, trying not to sound like a heavy-breather. "You're so flexible."

"Practice." She switched to the other leg. "I was in India about fifteen or sixteen years ago, working with an actress who was in an English film about…well, that doesn't add to the story. There was a yogi on set who let me tag along with her lessons and I got into it. Meditation, focused breathing, everything. It felt right, so I adopted most of it."

"Is it...religious for you?"

"That's a little hard to answer. I'm not Buddhist or Hindu or any of the other spiritual practices that use yoga, but it's hard to do all of the elements and not have it affect me somehow. Does that make sense?"

"Not much," Brooklyn admitted, chuckling.

"Okay. I've worked with Buddhists, Hindus, Jains and Sikhs in India. If I hear of a good teacher, I'll seek him or her out. But I've never committed to any of the individual religions. There's always something about each of them that stops me from jumping in."

"Interesting. Isn't yoga a spiritual practice too?"

"Yes, it definitely can be. But I use it more for exercise and body shaping. It's made me so much more flexible and able to avoid injuries. It's been great for me overall."

Teasingly, Brooklyn said, "So you're like a cafeteria-style Eastern acolyte."

"Cafeteria-style?"

"You pick what you like, and leave the liver and onions on the steam table of religion."

"I guess you could say that. But I don't feel like I'm picking and choosing just to be difficult. I use the various techniques I've combined to focus on myself. Doing it all makes me calm. I sleep better, feel better, and my relationships are better. It's easier for me to stay on my side, if you know what I mean."

Having no idea what she meant, but deciding it was a lost cause, Brooklyn nodded her head. It was impossible to focus on Kerri's words when her body was moving so slowly and sexily. "You don't really have a lot of room in here. Why don't you exercise in the big room?"

"I'm used to making myself as invisible as possible," she said, laughing. "But since we're friends, I guess I don't have to be so rigid about that."

Brooklyn was still trying to get her own breathing under control. "Act like this is your house, just don't sell it when I'm not looking." She got up and turned to leave, adding, "See you around midnight—if you're up."

"I'll wake you up with your latte."

It was darned tempting, but she knew her fledgling independence was not built on bedrock. "I think I know how to do it myself. I've been watching you on the weekends, and I'm sure I won't be as good a barista as you are, but I can manage."

"Are you sure? I'm going to try to get back to an early morning schedule, but I'll still be up at midnight."

Brooklyn stood there, looking at her. Being independent was a very good goal but why rush? "Well, if you're up anyway I do love the way you make it."

She went into her room and tried to sort out the feelings and sensations that had just been racing through her body. Her goal had been to keep things at the friendship level, but Kerri was still getting to her. Watching her contort that smoking hot body was something few people would have been able to resist, but this was more than animal attraction. Kerri had made it clear she didn't want romance—not with Brooklyn or anyone else for that matter. Brooklyn had to focus on her oft-used technique of not wanting the person who didn't want to be wanted. But it was remarkably hard with Kerri. Maybe it was impossible, and that would suck...hard.

While Godzilla was recuperating, Kerri had nothing but free time. When Brooklyn announced she was going to join a tennis club, Kerri tagged along. The club wasn't too far away, just in Chelsea, and they rode their bikes, even though it was cold, slushy, and gloomy out. Brooklyn had gotten into the exercise habit, and jumped on her bike no matter the weather. She'd become a real trooper.

They met the coach she hired and got to work. Brooklyn didn't have a racket she liked anymore, so the coach, Chris, lent her one. They started to hit the ball back and forth, with Chris making a lot of encouraging comments. Kerri didn't know a lot about tennis, but she recognized that Brooklyn knew a lot. She was clearly not in good tennis shape, and was winded after just five minutes, but she moved to the ball gracefully, and seemed to be able to guess right where it would land.

Chris went over to Brooklyn's side and made a few adjustments in the angle of her elbow. Kerri couldn't hear them speak, but she found herself slightly resentful of how close Chris stood. She could have easily made those adjustments without physically touching Brooklyn.

After bringing over a basket of balls, Chris watched carefully as Brooklyn served them, one after another. After about twenty serves, Kerri thought Brooklyn had done quite enough. Chris didn't know how out of shape Brooklyn had been just weeks before, and it didn't make sense to overtax her. The last thing she needed was a shoulder injury that would set her back. Kerri had seen an awful lot of people give up on a new exercise regime because of an injury. She was just about to go over and interrupt when Brooklyn made a face and said, "I'm done."

She and Chris stood there talking for quite a while and when they finished Brooklyn joined Kerri.

"I feel like I'm seventy-five. That would have barely been a warm-up back in the good old days, but these aren't the good old days. I stopped as soon as my shoulder felt tight."

Kerri could feel how widely she was grinning. Brooklyn was starting to develop some good instincts. She just had to keep them up.

—⁓—

That night, they went to a comedy club together. Kerri had just a few more days of freedom before she'd have to go back onto a morning schedule, and she wanted to spend as much time with Brooklyn as possible.

It was a club in SoHo, so they walked, even though it was freezing and the streets were slick with slush.

"Hey, remember a while ago when you told me I was a Luddite?" Brooklyn asked.

Kerri had no idea what she was talking about. "Not really."

"Well, you did. And you said I should do a bit about it."

"Right! Now I remember." She grinned, amazed that Brooklyn had taken her seriously. "Did you use it?"

"Yeah. I've been working on it. I'll try it out tonight if I can get a few minutes."

"Excellent! Did I really help?"

"Of course. I told you, the idea is the hard part." Brooklyn grinned, but it wasn't clear if she was teasing or genuinely thanking Kerri for the idea. Time would tell.

—◆—

Brooklyn did, in fact, get a few minutes, and Kerri sat there in the audience listening to the idea she'd given Brooklyn.

"Not long ago, a friend told me I was a Luddite. I've got no Twitter, no Facebook, no web page, no blog. I know what they are, and I know what they do. I'm not one of those people who thinks it's called the Interwebs."

The crowd laughed softly.

"I get it—from afar. I'd love to have a web presence, because I'm very full of myself. Hell, the entire web could be devoted to me and I'd be fine with that. Get rid of all the porn and there'd be a gaping," she held her hands up and made a circle, then dipped her head and peered into it. "Bad choice of words—hole. Ohh, another bad choice."

That little bit of naughtiness made the audience follow right along. You could feel the excitement start to build. They wanted her to be funny. It was palpable.

"I digress. I'm a narcissist, but I'm a little ashamed of it. Just a little. Not enough not to *be* a narcissist, but enough to be tolerable to real people in real life.

"As soon as I see something worthwhile being tweeted I'll reassess. But I've seen one too many instances of thousands of people retweeting the one guy who says something vaguely…and I do mean vaguely… interesting."

The crowd had all felt this, and they nodded and elbowed their friends who re-tweeted too much crap.

"It's like in grade school when the teacher was droning on about reciprocal pronouns dangling a modified adjectival phrase and the freakiest kid snarked the dumbest, most hackneyed joke. The class exploded in laughter! Metaphorically exploded!"

The crowd laughed hard, thinking, en mass, of the dumb kid in their class who everyone laughed at just to have a break in the tedium.

"Listen. He wasn't funny, people! The dork huffed glue during recess, and could barely sit upright. But you were all so bored that you guffawed.

"That's what Twitter seems like—a bunch of terminally bored people trying so very hard to be engaged. To be ripped from their torpor. Go for a friggin walk!"

She used her thickest Jersey accent when she said that last phrase, and the accent alone made people laugh. But the truth of the sentiment was the funny part. Everyone who used Twitter had to acknowledge it wasn't much more than a techno time-waster…and that that was part of the fun.

Brooklyn's voice grew quiet and she acted as though she were telling a secret to a group of close friends. "Here's the sad truth. Most people who tweet should stick to a very, very private diary." She was truly whispering now; the crowd leaned forward to hear. "One that ignites spontaneously upon their deaths so that no one ever, ever has to read it. One out of a thousand of us is clever." Now, at full voice, "Do…the… math!"

They roared. They truly roared. It wasn't the funniest joke in the world, and retelling it to another person would never work. It was Brooklyn who made it work. Only her timing and her experience and her personality gave it life.

Kerri had chills listening to the crowd still murmuring about their own experiences after Brooklyn departed. Yes, Kerri had given her the idea. Just like Einstein got the idea of relativity from a clock. That's what Brooklyn had meant when she said hanging out with amateur joke tellers drove her nuts. Now it made sense. It must have been like being a pro quarterback and having guys tell you their glory days in the Pop Warner league when they were eleven. Or being a professional boxer and having dopes try to take a punch at you.

Brooklyn was a pro, and having amateurs try to best her was never going to be fun. It might be fun for the amateur, but never for her. Kerri got it. She truly got it.

———

That weekend Brooklyn was playing Toronto, their last planned gig together. Since the flight was short, they stayed in New York until Saturday morning. It was so rare that Brooklyn had a weekend night off that she was itching to do something fun. They were sitting on the sectional, going through ideas when Kerri said, "Maybe we should go out to a club."

"Eh." Her expression couldn't have shown less interest.

"I'm beginning to doubt how serious you are about finding a woman."

Brooklyn's eyebrows waggled, and she adopted a lecherous look along with her Russian accent. "Finding a woman for what?"

Slapping at her, Kerri said, "You know exactly what I mean. You're tremendously attractive, whip smart, you make a great living, and women throw themselves at you. Are you ready to start dating?"

"Yeah, I am. I know I'm picky, but I'd rather be alone than waste even a single evening with someone I wasn't into. But believe me, when I meet someone I think is right, I go for it."

"I'm not convinced. It's been months and you haven't…"

Brooklyn leaned over until their faces were just a few inches apart. "I was motivated towards you," she said softly, "but you shot me down." Her dark eyes looked so beautiful in the fading sun, and her skin had a peach tint that made it look like it was actually edible.

"You were a client." She felt herself leaning closer. "But I guess that's in the past, isn't it?"

Brooklyn closed the distance, tilted her head, and spoke while her lips were mere millimeters away. "It is." She pressed her lips against Kerri's, pulled away briefly, then kissed her again, very, very gently. While moving away, she trailed her hand down Kerri's cheek. "What do you think?"

Kerri grasped both of Brooklyn's hands and held them against her chest. "Ooo, I want to. I really, really want to." More than she could put into words. But this was so unexpected, and she still had so many doubts. About Brooklyn herself, about being intimate with a client, about getting into another situation with someone who lived so far from LA. Knowing Brooklyn, she'd be hurt, maybe badly, if Kerri expressed many of those fears. Still, she was so remarkably appealing. If they kept things very, very casual there was a chance it could work. But Brooklyn wasn't a very casual person. "My situation isn't great for getting involved. Especially not seriously involved. How do you feel about that?"

Solemnly, Brooklyn nodded. "I think I know your boundaries. You don't want to be in an exclusive relationship, and you can't live in New York."

Still holding on tightly, Kerri said, "That's true, and I don't see either of those points changing in the near future. I'm only able to be… I don't have a word for what I'm able to be, but I'm not able to be anyone's wife."

Brooklyn moved so she was right in front of her again, their noses almost touching. "I'm not sure what I want. Maybe I want a…whatever it is you can be." She smiled, her tender emotions clearly visible. "It just seems like a waste not to see if we have something here…if you're into me as much as I'm into you."

Kerri tilted her head and pressed several soft kisses onto Brooklyn's lips. "I'm very into you. Very, very into you." That was the absolute truth. Her desire for Brooklyn made all of her qualms seem unimportant. This chance made the reward seem worth the risks. But Kerri Klein was possibly the most risk-averse person in the entire state of California.

Brooklyn gave her the sexy grin that lesbians all over America loved. But tonight, Brooklyn was giving it only to her.

They kissed for a few minutes, keeping things light and casual. Kerri leaned back against the sofa and let out a sigh. "You kiss like an angel."

All of a sudden Brooklyn lost the self-confidence that had filled her mere moments before. "I'm not sure how we…do this," she said, cringing at how inelegant that sounded.

They were clearly no longer employee and client, because the look Kerri gave her was close to salacious.

"You've been concentrating too much on current events if you don't know how to do this." She reached out and grabbed Brooklyn by the shirt and pulled on her until they were prone, one atop the other.

That was such an unexpected response that Brooklyn laughed at the whole situation. "I know how to do that," she said gesturing with her head towards the bedroom. "But I've never had sex with somebody I care about, while hoping it doesn't turn into a relationship. How do you do it?"

"Oh." Kerri frowned, clearly thinking.

Brooklyn slid off her body and sat on the floor in front of her. Their heads were very close, and she could hear Kerri's breath when she exhaled slowly. Kerri would have thought it was crazy, but she could have been very happy sitting right there feeling that warm breath. Just being near her was intoxicating.

"I'm not sure this works for other people, but for me I try to keep it more fun than passionate." She frowned, shaking her head. "No, that's not right, it can be passionate, but it's less about love, and more about sex."

"More about sex, huh?"

"Yeah, but not in a cold or unfeeling way. Does this make any sense?" She looked adorably confused.

"Not entirely. I want to have sex, of course, but not like I've had with strangers." Just thinking about those encounters turned her stomach. She needed more, a lot more, from Kerri.

"Oh, Brooklyn, I could never treat you like a stranger." She leaned over and placed a very tender kiss on her lips. "You know I care about you. But at this point in my life, I can only safely offer sex. Just playful sex."

Hmm…that was…different. But if that's all she could do… "When I was really young I just wanted to have sex. I had no intention of being in a relationship. But that's a lot like a one night stand."

Kerri reached out and started to play with Brooklyn's hair, tucking it neatly behind her ears. "What I want is definitely more than a one night stand. I'm sure of that. I'd like something similar to what I had with Dakota. A loving 'friends with benefits' situation."

"I've never ever had that."

"It takes a long time to get there. There are land mines everywhere."

"How should we start?" She tried for a sexy smile but knew it probably looked overly anxious.

"I could spend a few days playing with your hair."

The sexy timbre of Kerri's voice made Brooklyn's skin pebble. "Do you like it?"

Filling both of her hands with the long tresses, she threaded her fingers through it and let it fall against Brooklyn's back. "It's the most beautiful hair I've ever seen. The first day we met I wanted to touch it."

Chuckling, Brooklyn said, "I thought you were getting fresh when you touched my hand. I would have run if you'd touched my hair."

Kerri leaned over and kissed Brooklyn's silky soft cheek. "Do you not like to be touched?"

"No, I love it. But only by people I'm intimate with. I'm not into that 'kiss the guy who cuts your hair' thing. Touching breaches my barriers."

"Maybe I touch too much."

"You can touch me now. Anywhere you want."

Kerri placed her hand on Brooklyn's cheek and turned her enough for a kiss. "Let's keep it really casual at first. Ultra-casual. Let's act like we're relative strangers who're hot for each other."

"We're not strangers, but I'm so hot for you it makes my knees weak when I see you doing yoga. You should stay in your room if you don't want me to leer at you."

Kerri laughed softly, reminding Brooklyn once again of the angels telling jokes. "I don't mind being watched. As a matter of fact, I kinda like it. I work hard on my body, and it's nice to know someone digs it."

Brooklyn knew she was looking at her lustfully, but she'd been given permission. "I dig it a whole lot." She turned and got on her knees, then grasped Kerri and pulled her up enough to kiss her with a flood of emotion. It felt like her whole body was alive with a thrumming sensation she hadn't felt in years. "I want to make love to you," she whispered.

"Ooo, that sounds dangerous. We'd better take it a lot slower than that."

"Slower?" She dropped back onto the floor. This wasn't going well. Sex shouldn't be about following rules! "Uhm, how?"

"I was thinking we'd act like I've told you I have a really bad itch and I can't reach it."

Oh my God! An itch? "That's a long, long way from making love. I don't think you can even see love from there."

"We only start off being super casual. We'll slowly get closer once we build trust and know we want the same things." She sat up a little bit, gazing deeply into Brooklyn's eyes. "But we have to be honest. Painfully honest. Can you tell me what you're feeling when you're feeling it?"

"I can try." Taking a deep breath, she said, "I really care for you. If you were into it, I'd want...something that could lead to marriage. But since you're not, it seems kinda silly to walk away from something that might be really good."

"That's only true if you get something out of this, Brooklyn."

She once again ran her fingers down Brooklyn's hairline, tickling just behind her ear.

That simple touch made Brooklyn's skin pebble at the same time her heart started to race. She desperately wanted to pick Kerri up and take her into the bedroom, but that didn't seem right when you were just scratching each others' itch. *This is nuts!*

"Having this kind of relationship worked with Dakota because we both wanted to be intimate while having complete freedom. But if that's not what you want…"

"How do I know if I don't try? Maybe a casual connection with someone fantastic is better than a deep connection with someone less great."

"Only you can know that."

"I'll tell you one thing for sure." She shifted on the floor until they were nose to nose. "It's going to be hard not to fall in love with you."

"There's nothing wrong with loving each other." As Kerri stroked those beautiful fingers all across her features, Brooklyn's body shivered from the touch and she found herself leaning in for more.

"I love Dakota, but I'm not unhappy that she's with someone else."

"Maybe that's what I meant," Brooklyn admitted. "I might have trouble feeling possessive."

"Possessiveness doesn't work. At all. So if you're not sure, we shouldn't do this."

"No, I'm sure I want to try." It felt almost mandatory to take on a new challenge. This was a big one, but she was ready. She shifted her eyes, looking at the bedroom again. "Do we go in there?"

"No need. I'll show you just how casual this can be."

Kerri slid to the floor, grabbed her and gave her a sizzling kiss before tumbling both of them prone. Without warning, her hand slipped between Brooklyn's legs and she started to massage her through her jeans.

Brooklyn couldn't have spoken if she'd had a gun to her head. She'd dreamed of making love a thousand times, but this scenario was never, ever in play.

She tried to move her head to kiss Kerri, but Kerri pulled back, grinning lasciviously while she unzipped her and slid her hand inside.

No fucking way! She could have had this with hundreds of women, but she didn't want it with them. Why settle for humping with Kerri? Brooklyn grasped her hand and pulled it out, then tried to kiss her very, very tenderly. But Kerri broke the kiss and shook her head. Her expression was wary. "I don't think that's wise."

"I don't think so either." Brooklyn rolled away and stood, wanting to tug on her jeans so her pussy would stop tingling. She reached down and extended a hand to Kerri, who stood gracefully, with almost no assistance. "I guess I'm not the casual sort."

Kerri put her arms around her and they hugged for long minutes. "I wish I could offer more. I really do. I think we could have something good if we wanted the same things."

"I do too. But I don't think we're close to having the same needs." Brooklyn was hurt. So hurt she almost said what she felt, that Kerri just wanted a warm body to fuck. But she forced herself to put it more delicately. "Is it really too intimate to kiss?"

"No, of course not. But the look in your eyes said you wanted more than a kiss. It scared me. A lot."

"I do want more than a kiss." Her shoulders rose and fell dramatically. "I want to love you. Sex isn't gonna be enough." Brooklyn's heart felt like it would break. The look in Kerri's eyes said she wanted more too. Why was she being so inflexible? "I guess it's better to know now than…later."

"It's hard to make something like this work. Actually, it's very hard. It took a long time for Dakota and me, and we'd been lovers for years."

"Maybe it's easier to go from being intense lovers to being casual lovers. I need tenderness and intimacy. Lots of it."

Kerri put her hands on Brooklyn's waist. "If you want to work through it, we'd get to tenderness and intimacy. I'm simply not willing or able to start there."

Sadly, Brooklyn looked into her eyes. "And I'm not able to start anywhere else. I can have sex at the drop of a hat. I want a lot more from you."

Kerri hugged her briefly, then pulled away. "I'm feeling pretty raw. I think I'll go do my yoga for a while. Is that okay?"

"Sure. I'll go take a walk. I might go to the Comedy Cabin if I'm in the neighborhood."

"Okay. See you tomorrow." She walked away, with Brooklyn unable to take her eyes off her until she closed the door to her room.

—◊◊◊—

Instead of yoga, Kerri tried to meditate. But she couldn't get her mind off Brooklyn. The way she'd handled it had been ham-handed, crass. But Brooklyn had been racing along far too fast for comfort. Kerri'd tried to slow her down and make it playful, but it had probably seemed like she was proposing what amounted to an anonymous hook-up. Sadly, what made Brooklyn so appealing was that she'd refuse something she badly wanted for fear of getting hurt. That sweet heart was undoubtedly easy to bruise, and Kerri was proud of her for standing her ground.

It had been so tempting. So very, very tempting to let her really get in. The thought of opening herself to Brooklyn fully was so remarkably compelling, but she knew Brooklyn didn't look at relationships like she did. One of them would get hurt, and hurt badly.

If only Brooklyn could see how much fun it could be to let their bodies merge with no expectations. But she clearly wanted a spouse. Someone she could call her own. And Kerri had been working for fifteen years to remove that kind of possessiveness from her life. She had no desire to throw that hard work away. Even for Brooklyn.

—◊◊◊—

Kerri walked into Brooklyn's room not long after midnight and set her latte on the bedside table. Her instinct was to gently wake her, then run and hide. But that was being a coward. If Brooklyn was hurt or angry about what had happened, they'd have to work through it. She reached down and patted her on the shoulder. Brooklyn grabbed her pillow, held it over her head and turned, belly down.

"Come on now," Kerri cooed. "I've got a delicious latte for you."

The pillow lifted slightly. "Right here?"

"Right here." She sat on the edge of the bed. "Turn over and I'll hold the mug."

Opening her mouth, but not her eyes, Brooklyn flipped over and sat halfway up. Kerri smiled while holding up the mug.

She slurped noisily, smacked her lips and flopped against her pillow. "Delightful."

Her eyes were still closed, and Kerri spent a few moments carefully looking at her. She looked the same as always. Sleepy, reluctant to get up, but otherwise happy. After a few more sips, Brooklyn stumbled out of bed and went into the shower, holding onto her precious coffee cup while leaning against the shower door, waiting for the water to warm up.

—∿—

Brooklyn stood in the shower, letting the hot water take away some of the...what was it? Sadness, anger, disappointment? Whatever it was, her body ached with it. She wanted Kerri Klein, goddamn it! But she didn't want a piece of her while Kerri held onto the good parts.

There was no way she'd be able to be casual about this. How could Kerri not see that? Hell, she didn't act very casual herself. But if that was her game—to be close emotionally but distant physically or close physically but distant emotionally—she could keep it. Brooklyn wanted, needed, and deserved the whole package. And she was going to get it. She'd have a girlfriend who was emotionally connected, physically connected, and honest. If she couldn't have all three, she'd much, much rather be alone. Fuck it all.

—∿—

Going to work for Godzilla now seemed like a very, very bad idea. Brooklyn acted like things were fine between them, but Kerri would have been much happier if she could have spent the day with her, making sure her upbeat facade was genuine. But she spent her first official day sitting around the loft, waiting. The arrangement she and Michelle, Godzilla's current personal assistant, had worked out was that Michelle would call her the minute Godzilla awoke, and Kerri would dash over there.

Kerri was to be at Godzilla's side whenever she was awake. Another, less expensive minion would stay outside her bedroom at night to make sure she didn't run to the kitchen and jam calories down her throat.

Poor Michelle had only been on the job a few weeks, and since assistants were fired constantly, Kerri hoped the woman wasn't planning on a long relationship with the notoriously difficult star.

She cooled her heels until two o'clock in the afternoon, but that at least allowed her to have lunch with Brooklyn. They stayed on safe, pleasant topics, and when she finally left, Brooklyn seemed happy.

"God knows when I'll be home, but I have your dinner ready for you in the refrigerator."

"Have fun. Or should I say, 'Don't kill her'?"

―⁓―

Kerri returned home the next morning after Brooklyn had left for work. She'd had such a long, tough day and night being insulted, treated rudely and screamed at several times that she craved a friendly face. Sometimes working for idiots wasn't worth even really good money, but she'd made her bed, and now she had to lie in it.

She was still home later that morning when Brooklyn returned from work. Brooklyn dropped her things on the dining room table and went to sit next to her on the sofa. "Tell me how it went. I've been thinking about you since you left yesterday."

"It wasn't great." She slapped Brooklyn on the thigh and got up to go to the refrigerator. "But I made a great lunch for both of us." She started taking out plates and silverware. When Brooklyn came up behind her and put her hands on her shoulders, she visibly started.

"You don't seem like your usual cheery self. Do you want to talk about it?"

Kerri didn't turn around, but she leaned back and rested her head against Brooklyn's shoulder for a moment. That was such a nice sensation. Being able to touch her might actually make up for not being sexual. It certainly wasn't optimal...but much better than nothing. "I don't think

I've ever felt as unwelcome as I did yesterday, so it's nicer than usual to have you come home."

Brooklyn let her go, then moved over to the sink and washed her hands. "I'm glad to be home. I hope she sleeps all day."

"She's still on pain pills from her plastic surgery, so she's sleeping a lot. It's a good thing I wasn't in charge of giving them to her, or I might have overdosed her."

Her phone rang, and she made a face when she saw who it was. "It's alive," she said, with an overly dramatic flair. "I've got to go." As she walked by, she kissed Brooklyn on the cheek. "I'll try to remember that there's someone who cares for me at home when Godzilla is cursing the day I was born."

"Don't let her get to you," Brooklyn said, giving Kerri a heartfelt look. "There's someone at home who's very glad you were born."

—⁂—

That weekend, Brooklyn arrived at Lambert Airport in St. Louis. A man in a black suit stood by the luggage pickup area, holding a printed card that said, "YORK." She didn't have any checked luggage, and she ambled over to him. "Brooklyn York," she said. "Are you my driver?"

"Yes, I am." He held out his hand. "I'm also your tour guide for the day."

Her face lit up. Kerri had been working her magic. "My tour guide, huh?"

"Yes. I'm Stephen Halsey. I'm an astrophysicist at Washington University. Your manager hired me to take you to the planetarium and answer every question you might ever have about the solar system." He chuckled. "She said you're the most inquisitive person on earth."

They started to walk to the parking lot. "How did she find you?"

"I'm not sure. I've never been asked to do anything like this, but it sounded like fun. Ms Klein said to keep you busy until three p.m.—no later."

"Oh, I'm sure Ms Klein gave you a whole raft of instructions." She was so happy to have been so well taken care of that she was tempted to call Kerri right that moment. But she didn't want to disturb her at work. Sending her a big bunch of flowers would be nice. She'd do it as soon as they got into the car. It had to be easy, right? Maybe the astrophysicist knew who to call.

—⁓—

Early in the morning a week later, Kerri was just waking up to her radio. She was still groggy; her irregular hours made her feel sluggish and slow through most of her day. Luckily, she barely needed to use her brain to work with Godzilla. Actually, a bright German shepherd could have done the job, and the dog might have done it better since it probably wouldn't get its feelings hurt by being treated like what it was.

The job was making Kerri unnaturally grumpy, but she had to hide her bad mood at work. As a result, at home, she avoided negativity as much as possible. Arnie was grumbling about something or other and she was just about to turn it off when she heard Brooklyn clearly say, "You should be ashamed of yourself for saying something so insensitive."

That was different. There were some days that you wouldn't have known Brooklyn was even in the studio. Arnie was in charge, and Brooklyn said they were cued by him making eye contact. If he didn't look at you, you were supposed to keep your mouth shut. But it was highly doubtful Arnie had asked for Brooklyn to chide him. Kerri braced herself, waiting for Arnie's response.

"It looks like Madam Resident has woken up," Arnie said, the derision dripping from his voice. "Are you interested in earning your salary today?"

"I've been getting a check regularly, so someone must think I've earned it."

"That makes one of us,"

"It's not too late to step back from the ledge. If you could think about what you just said and apologize to the people you've offended, you might avoid taking another quote vacation unquote while the company decides what to do with you."

Kerri was sitting on the edge of her bed, so amazed that her mouth dropped open as she stared at the radio.

"You're the last idiot I'd take advice from."

"Since I'm here every day to remind you what happened the last time you insulted an entire group of people, I think I'm the best person to give you advice on how not to screw up again. All Muslims are not terrorists, and saying that they are just shows the world how insular and childish you are. You're a very well-known personality, and I think you have a responsibility to the country not to be so xenaphobic."

Sputtering, Arnie got out, "What do you call a bunch of people who blow up buildings and try to take down airplanes and cargo ships?"

"I call them terrorists," Brooklyn said calmly. "And there are Christian terrorists and Jewish terrorists and agnostic terrorists and atheistic terrorists. One is a subset of the other. They're not equivalent."

"I've got nothing to apologize for. It was a bunch of towel-headed, Allah-worshiping, virgin-humping Muslims who attacked us, and I will never stop telling the truth about that fact. You and your politically correct, lefty friends might think they're the same as we are, but they're not. And if you don't watch out, they'll be running this country openly, instead of behind the scenes like they are now."

"Do you wear that baseball hat to hide the tinfoil on your head?"

"Out! Get out of here right now, you stupid cunt!" While Kerri gawped, there was a momentary silence, then they went to commercial. She jumped to her feet and started dancing around the loft, punching her hands in the air, rejoicing that Brooklyn had finally reclaimed her integrity for all to hear.

CHAPTER FOURTEEN

BY THE TIME BROOKLYN'S limo hit her street, a gaggle of photographers was there waiting to meet her. Brooklyn wasn't sure how they'd done the research to find her home address, disseminate it, and find her *en masse* in less than an hour, but she had to applaud their industriousness.

She had been given explicit instructions from the suits at Spectrum, so when Terry opened her door, she stepped out and stood there for a moment amidst the glaring blur of flashes and shouted questions. Having no intention of scurrying away like a guilty animal, she tossed her hair back, straightened her shoulders, and smiled. After generously allowing every photographer to shoot her at any angle they wished, she pushed through them to her front door. She said not a word until she'd ridden the elevator up to her apartment. Kerri was standing in the open doorway, a happy smirk on her face.

"Your lawyer will be by in about an hour. Who wants lunch?"

"That's all you have to say?"

"This is the only time I've ever been proud of a client for being thrown out of her place of business." She stepped into the hallway and gave Brooklyn a hearty hug. "I'm really happy you stood for something you believe in."

"I am too. Being cussed out works up an appetite. Let's have lunch."

The lawyers got together and agreed that Brooklyn would take the rest of the week off, with full pay. She agreed she would not discuss the incident while under contract, and Arnie agreed to issue a press release apologizing to her and to the millions of people he'd insulted. After a day, the reporters found something more interesting and she was once again left alone.

———

At about two a.m. one night after she returned to work, Brooklyn was in her room, lying on her belly in bed when Kerri came home. Kerri poked her head into Brooklyn's room and waved. "Who's that well-rested woman playing with her iPad?"

"It's me."

Kerri went in and sat on the edge of the bed. "Did you just wake up?"

"No, I've been up for about an hour and a half. I have to read all my mail and get caught up on the news before I can put my butt into gear."

"You haven't had your latte?"

"I haven't even turned the machine on. But I will."

Jumping up, Kerri headed for the kitchen. "I'll do it for you. I know you like my barista skills."

"You don't have to," Brooklyn called out. "Just because I haven't done it yet doesn't mean I'm not going to. I'm just slow."

Kerri's shoes squeaked as she walked back across the floor. She leaned on the doorframe and looked at Brooklyn for a second. "That is exactly how I would describe you. You're not lazy, and you're more than capable of doing whatever you need to do. You just like to do it at your own pace, which is slooooow."

"Slow and steady wins the race."

"I'm not antagonistic to slow, but it's certainly not my style. Maybe that's why we get along so well."

"Maybe," Brooklyn said, thinking there were many other reasons, but none of them seemed able to close the gap that kept them apart.

"I think the machine's warm enough for me to make you coffee. I'll be back in a minute."

Brooklyn got up and wandered into the living area. She turned on the television and flipped through channels until she found some news worth watching. When Kerri brought her the latte, Brooklyn took a big, first sip and gurgled with pleasure. "This is the nicest thing anyone's done for me today." She sat down and Kerri joined her.

"You look a little troubled. Something happen at work?"

"No, it's not the radio show for a change. You remember that I was going to the Caribbean with Kat and a couple of other friends for Christmas, right?"

"Of course."

"Well, I went through all of the bits I have for a new act and it's just not enough. I'm going to have to spend my Christmas vacation working the clubs."

"Oh no! That's horrible news."

"I certainly wasn't happy about it, but the thing that really hurt was Kat's reaction."

"Did she say something that hurt your feelings?"

Brooklyn nodded. "Yeah, a little bit, but what has me more upset is the realization that she's no longer a true friend."

Kerri reached out and grasped her arm. "Why would you think that?"

"I have a bunch of reasons, but two of them bit me on the butt today. One, she didn't have a bit of empathy for me even though I desperately need a vacation, and a real friend would've wanted me to have one. And two, she thinks that she and our other two friends should get to go without me."

Looking confused, Kerri said, "Why would it bother you if they go without you?"

"Because I'm paying!"

"Oh my God! That's horrible. Actually, it's unconscionable. Shameless."

Brooklyn started laughing. "I wish you would've come home much earlier. You could've saved me a few hours of sulking. Just knowing that you agree I wasn't being childish for feeling used makes me happy." She desperately wanted to reach over and take Kerri's hand. But she knew that was something she shouldn't start.

"You're not being childish in the least. I don't want to talk bad about Kat, but that was a ridiculously insensitive thing to do."

"Knowing you has let me see what a real friendship is. I think Kat and I were fairly good friends when we were younger, but that's changed. Now part of the reason she likes me is because I pay for things and that feels awful. I've been really generous, but I can't stand it when people expect me to give them money."

"That's one of the worst things about celebrity. It's hard to know who to trust."

Brooklyn couldn't keep from smiling as she looked into Kerri's guileless eyes. "That's why you have to choose the people who get close to you very carefully."

―〰―

Since she had no idea when she'd have to get up the next day, Kerri headed off to bed. She tried to clear her mind by meditating, but thoughts kept bombarding her. She knew Brooklyn needed a vacation to get away, and it was ridiculously unkind for her to be secretly happy she'd have to stay in town. It was selfish and selfishness was something that she'd tried hard to overcome. But the thought of Brooklyn being away for two weeks had been on her mind for a month, and she'd been dreading it. Having her there when she got home was the only thing that helped her keep her rotten job. As penance for her selfish thoughts, she vowed to take excellent care of her roommate while she was stuck in New York.

―〰―

Two weeks later, Brooklyn woke and walked out of her room to find Kerri sitting on the sectional. With her knees tucked up to her nose and her arms wrapped tightly around her shins, she rested her chin on her knees and stared into the distance. Tentatively, Brooklyn quietly asked, "Are you okay?"

Kerri's automatic smile was weak. "I just got some bad news." She got to her feet. "I turned the coffee maker on. Let me make your latte."

Brooklyn put a hand on her shoulder, holding her in place. Then she sat down and tugged on Kerri's hand until she sat next to her. "Tell me what's wrong."

"My dad called a while ago to tell me that my grandfather had a stroke today."

"Oh Kerri, I'm so sorry to hear that. How serious is it?"

"It might be serious enough to kill him, but they won't know that for a little while. My dad has decided not to use any medical intervention to keep him alive."

"How do you feel about that?" Brooklyn asked gently.

She lifted her head and met Brooklyn's eyes. "I don't know. I'm still processing that."

"Why don't you process it with me?"

"I'm not sure I have words for it yet. I'm still in shock thinking about not having my grandfather in the world."

Brooklyn leaned back against the cushions and spread her arms out against their backs. Surprisingly, Kerri took that as an invitation to cuddle up next to her. It wasn't an unwelcome contact, but it still caught Brooklyn by surprise. She tried to keep that out of her voice when she said, "Tell me about why your grandfather means so much to you."

"That's easy." Her smile seemed reluctant, but it showed through her sadness. "Things weren't always calm at my house, but I could always count on absolute normalcy from my grandparents. All I had to do was call them and they'd come pick me up. Luckily, my mom didn't care if I just left her a note and went to stay with them for a couple days."

That was different. "How old were you when your parents broke up?"

Kerri let out a short laugh. "They were never together. Well, they were together physically, but not emotionally. My mom got pregnant after being with my dad for a pretty short time. She was in her thirties and assumed she wouldn't get a chance to be a mother, so she was happy about it. But my dad wasn't really down with it."

"How not down was he?"

"I saw him, but not on a regular schedule. Apparently, he was around a lot when I was a baby, then he got interested again when I was in high school."

That was very different. That wouldn't play in Paramus. "Did he help your mom financially?"

"I don't really know. My mom never complained about that, so maybe he did. But it's more likely that she felt it was her choice to have a baby and that he didn't owe her anything. She's a bit of a libertarian."

"I bet she was glad that her parents helped out so much."

"Her parents didn't help out at all. They divorced when my mom was little and she has no idea where her father is. Her mom is still alive, but she's not crazy about kids. We had more of a greeting-cards-on-holidays kind of relationship."

"So who is your grandfather?" These Los Angeles-style relationships were even more complex than they seemed.

"Didn't I say he was my dad's father?"

"If you did, I missed it. That's an interesting set-up. Why's he living with your mom?"

"Because she stepped in when my dad was going to put him in a home. She's goodhearted about most things. My dad can be…less so."

"That's not surprising your mom is kind. So are you." It was hard to know what else to say, especially since it wasn't clear what Kerri thought about her father, but he sure sounded like a prick. "Did your dad ever get married?"

"No, but he had two more daughters. He's never encouraged us to know each other, so we didn't. I'm actually glad, because it would've been hard to hear that one of them got more time with him than I did."

"I can imagine that would have been hard. Did your half-sisters spend time with your grandparents?"

"No, they didn't. I don't know if their mothers didn't encourage it or my dad didn't encourage it, but to my knowledge they've never met."

Chuckling softly, Brooklyn said, "I'm kind of glad for that. You got to get all of their attention."

They sat there quietly for a few minutes.

"I think one of the reasons I was so ready to jump into Eastern practices was that many of them stress being self-sufficient. I had some real problems when I was a kid, and meditation and yoga have helped me get rid of the competition I felt over my dad." She turned to Brooklyn, revealing the tears in her eyes. "I never, ever had enough time with him."

"I'm so sorry he wasn't more available. That must have been hard for a little girl to understand."

"It would be hard for a big girl if I didn't have a better grasp on how limited most of us are. I've learned not to expect much from other people. I'm the only person I can control."

Brooklyn thought that expecting good things from those you loved was one of the main joys of life. But Kerri clearly had her mind made up. "I'm glad your grandparents were reliable."

"They were," she agreed, sniffing. "I think that's why my mom so willingly agreed to take care of my grandfather when he needed it. They were substitute parents and their help allowed her to date and not have to worry about coming home to cook a meal for me."

It was hard to keep up with who was connected to whom, but Brooklyn wanted to make sure of one last connection. "Did your mother ever marry?"

"No. She had"—she narrowed her eyes and ticked off numbers on her fingers—"four long-term boyfriends."

"Were you close with any of them?"

She looked heartbreakingly sad. "Just the first. He was there from the time I was about three until I was in third grade. But they broke up and I never got to see him again."

"Never?" *That was child abuse!*

"Never. I didn't even get to say goodbye. He must've done something bad, but I never asked what. My mom doesn't like to talk about her personal life much."

Her personal life? Christ!

"She told me in recent years that she didn't get married because she knew she couldn't commit to one man." She looked heartbreakingly sad when she added, "I guess I'm a lot like her."

"There's nothing wrong with doing what makes you happy. You seem happy with the way you've set things up."

"I usually am. But when things like this happen, it would be awfully nice to have a partner who I'd know would be there for me."

"How about Dakota? She probably knows your grandfather, right?"

"Yes, she does. I called her, and she was very sympathetic, but there's still a difference. Dakota would do anything I ask of her. But a partner would be making plane reservations right now." She got up again and started to walk over to the espresso maker. "There are tradeoffs in everything. You can't give a little piece of yourself to people and expect them to give all of themselves back. But it's okay. Now I just have to decide if I should go home to see him right away. I've never walked out on a job, but I should be there, both for my parents and to show my respect for my grandfather."

"You don't think you could get just a few days off?"

"This is my last week. But that's not what's really bothering me. I really hate to admit this, but I'm going to." She came back to the sectional, stood in front of Brooklyn and looked her in the eye. "I don't want to go home until he dies." Tears started to roll down her face, and she nearly collapsed against Brooklyn. Burying her face in her shoulder, she sobbed quietly.

"It's really hard to see someone you love when they're in bad shape."

"I've never admitted this to anybody, but I took this job to stay away from home for as long as possible. The thought of having to help my mom feed him and do every other thing for him weighs on me like a ton of bricks."

"Don't feel bad about that. Nobody likes caring for a sick relative."

"You don't understand. I've been working for years and years on how to be more selfless, but when my prime opportunity came up, I ran. I'm so disappointed in myself."

"Did your mom want you to help sooner?"

"No. I guess not." After a moment she shook her head decisively. "I'm sure she would've told me. She's not the kind of woman who suffers in silence."

"You did everything you needed to do, Kerri. You offered to help, and you would have. Being selfless doesn't mean liking to do difficult things. Just doing them makes you selfless."

"Do you really think so?" she asked, her voice quaking with emotion.

"I know it. If your grandfather recovers and your mom needs help, I know you'll be there."

"I would be," she agreed.

"That's what matters. You're a very good granddaughter."

Sniffling, Kerri managed to say, "Thank you."

They each sat on the sectional and had a latte. Kerri was still much closer than normal, but somehow it didn't feel very different from their norm. They'd been talking for about an hour when Kerri's phone rang. She stared at it with fear. "My dad." That's all she had to say for Brooklyn to feel her stomach fly to her throat.

Kerri's hand was shaking noticeably when she hit a button and said, "Hi, dad." After just a couple of seconds it was clear this was not worse news. "All right. If they're that uncertain, I'm coming home in the morning. I really need to talk to him." She smiled while she listened, then said, "I'll fly into Burbank and take a shuttle to the house. I'll see you when I get there. I love you dad." She pressed a button and let the phone drop in her lap. Then, as though this was what they always did, she scooted over until she was right next to Brooklyn. She tilted her head up and said, "You don't mind, do you?"

Silently answering, Brooklyn wrapped an arm around her and pulled her even closer. "What did your dad say?"

"He said that my grandfather had regained consciousness, which is obviously good, but the doctor can't assure him that it will last long. If he's awake and can understand me, I've got to get there."

303

"Of course you do. How can I help?"

Kerri snuggled in a little deeper. "You're doing a lot. Touch soothes my soul more than words ever do."

"Words come first for me," Brooklyn said, "but I'll bet you knew that."

"I do. Other than a long hug, I don't think I need anything. I'll make a reservation to fly home, then I'll call my agent and tell him he's got to have somebody at Godzilla's house as soon as the villagers ring the bell to alert the town that the beast has risen."

They spent the next couple of hours talking, mostly about Kerri's grandfather. She shared dozens of stories about him and her grandmother and the fun they had doing the simplest of things. Just watching her eyes light up when recounting a trip to Griffith Park or some time spent cooking in her grandmother's kitchen would have made Brooklyn fall in love with her if she hadn't been already.

It was very late when Kerri got up to go to her room to get ready for bed. She came back a while later and sprawled out on the chaise longue part of the sectional. Brooklyn wasn't sure if she should put an arm around her again, but Kerri answered that question when she leaned against her and let out a satisfied sigh. "I don't know if I was cuddled too much or not enough when I was a baby, because when I'm upset there's no limit to how much I need."

"I bet you were cuddled a lot, felt how great it was, and realized, even at that young age, that this was a habit you had to keep up."

Kerri tossed her long bangs out of her eyes, smiling placidly. "I like that." They sat there for a while, neither one speaking. The windows and doors were all closed, but you could still hear the occasional cab horn bleating. "I appreciate your being here for me tonight. It's helped a lot."

"You don't need to thank me. In my opinion, friends are obligated to help each other. If you can't count on a friend, she's an acquaintance."

"You're very deep tonight." She turned and smiled, her loveliness never more vidid. There was a moment, just a moment, fraught with anticipation. Then she moved closer and put her hand on Brooklyn's cheek. She held it there for a few seconds, as though she was making up her mind. Brooklyn was frozen. She desperately wanted Kerri to kiss her and was just as desperately afraid that she would.

Closing the remaining distance, Kerri gently pressed her lips against Brooklyn's. She held the touch longer than a friend would, and when she pulled back her blue eyes were hazy with desire.

Brooklyn had no idea how to respond. She wasn't interested in joining Dakota as a member of Kerri's rotation, but she'd made that crystal clear. And Kerri wasn't the kind of person who'd push her to do something, no matter how much she needed touch.

Getting to the answer felt like hacking through a jungle, but mere seconds had passed. What made sense was that Kerri needed a lot more touch than most friends did. Given that she was hovering an inch from Brooklyn's lips, she clearly wanted some response. So Brooklyn tilted her head and placed an equally gentle kiss on Kerri's lovely lips, then held her tightly while Kerri let out some more of her pain while sobbing against Brooklyn's shoulder.

They sat just that way, cuddling on the sectional. Kerri's tears had lasted only a minute or two, then she collected herself and said very little. It seemed like the physical contact Brooklyn offered gave her some comfort, which made Brooklyn feel great—on a friendship level. But sitting this close to the woman she needed for much more than comfort was sweet torture. She'd never been this close to Kerri for this long, and it was almost impossible to merely hug. All she could think of was the kiss, and how blissful it had felt to touch those delightful lips.

Suddenly, Brooklyn's certainty turned shaky. Kerri had to have wanted more than comfort. You didn't kiss someone on the lips because you were sad. You kissed her because you wanted to feel a greater physical connection.

Letting her guard down, Brooklyn took a huge risk. Kerri's golden hair was right next to her lips, so she kissed the crown of her head several times. Each time Kerri cuddled closer, asking for more. So Brooklyn tried to calm the butterflies in her stomach and kiss her forehead. Kerri tilted her head back, presenting her cheek and throat to Brooklyn's lips. She froze once again, but it was one hundred percent clear that Kerri wanted her to continue. Down the baby-soft skin of Kerri's cheek, then let her lips trailed along her throat until she could feel her pulse. Now Kerri shifted and placed another soft kiss on Brooklyn's lips. Frozen, Brooklyn gazed at Kerri's lips as they drew her towards them. It had just been seconds, but it felt like minutes had passed. Finally, Brooklyn broke through her indecision and slipped her hand across the short, bristly hairs on the back of Kerri's neck, and she kissed her, exactly mirroring Kerri's kiss. She settled back against the cushions, making her body language show that she was open to anything Kerri needed. It was putting her heart at great risk, but she trusted Kerri explicitly.

It felt like she'd sat there, vulnerable and exposed forever. But Kerri didn't move closer. They were at a total standstill, and Brooklyn had no idea what to do to break it. Kerri looked like she desperately wanted to fall into her arms, but she didn't. She just sat there, gazing into Brooklyn's eyes, her sorrow and pain-filled expression completely confusing Brooklyn's already flummoxed brain. Finally, Kerri scooted back to sit alongside Brooklyn and let her head rest on her shoulder. The sigh she let out could have been one of frustration, sadness, desire, desperation, or any one of a hundred different emotions. All of them totally hidden from Brooklyn's understanding.

Kerri's phone alarm rang at four a.m., waking her from a sound sleep. It took a few seconds for her to remember why she was lying on the sofa with Brooklyn, who hadn't flinched. She had to get moving to make her flight, but first she had to think about what had happened just hours before.

It had all seemed so possible last night. Brooklyn was open to her, supremely available. But after just a kiss or two, a wall seemed to come between them. Had she merely caught her in a moment she now regretted? Or was Brooklyn unable to be more decisive? It seemed like she'd been waiting for Kerri to make a move, but she would never do that. Brooklyn had made it clear she wanted more, much more than Kerri could offer.

It had been a mistake to even kiss her, but she was so tantalizing. Brooklyn was the real deal, and having a second chance at even a tentative kiss had been awesome. Kerri had never gotten so turned on so quickly by such fleeting contact. But Brooklyn was wedded to the idea of being in an exclusive, monogamous relationship. She'd made that clear. Then why had she returned that first kiss? They'd have to talk about this, but not right now. Right now she had to gently wake Brooklyn up and get to the airport.

———

Kerri called the next afternoon, reaching Brooklyn just after she got home from work. Brooklyn's greeting warmed her all over.

"Hi," Brooklyn said. "I've been thinking about you constantly. Have you been able to talk to your grandfather?"

"I have. I'm sorry I didn't get to call you yesterday, but it really takes two of us to take care of grandpa now."

"Is he at home?"

"Yeah. After they decided he'd had a stroke, my dad insisted on bringing him back home. I think it makes sense to have him in an environment that he's used to, but my mom and I are trying to figure out how to be nurses with no training."

"Are you going to call hospice?"

Kerri let out a short laugh. "That's my dad's contribution. He's going to go through the paperwork to get them to come as soon as they can. I think they'll be able to give us some tips on how to keep grandpa comfortable."

"How's his mental state?"

"I'm not sure yet. He doesn't seem to understand what's happened and he definitely doesn't recognize any of us. But that could be from Alzheimer's."

"How do you feel about...caring for him?"

She thought about the question for a full minute. A thousand thoughts zoomed through her brain, but the one that stood out was clear. "It was crazy of me to dread this so much. There's nothing I could have done to show him how much I love him more than to take care of him when he's most vulnerable. I'm looking at this as a gift."

It sounded as though Brooklyn were sniffling. "I really admire you, both for going and for seeing it in such a positive light."

"Well, I am an optimist." She found herself laughing a little, something she hadn't done for quite a few hours. "It's awfully nice to talk to you. How are you doing?"

"I'm doing fine. I want you to promise you'll call me any time things get too intense or you need someone to share things with. Promise?"

"I promise. My mom's calling, so I have to go. I'll call you tomorrow."

"Okay. Just remember to take care of yourself too."

Kerri, hung up, not realizing until after she did that she hadn't brought up what had happened between them. It was too confusing to even think about right then, and if Brooklyn needed to talk, she was forthright enough to say so.

CHAPTER FIFTEEN

WHEN KERRI CALLED A week later, Brooklyn almost jumped for the phone. She was amazed at how much she missed her face, her voice, the way she sang quietly when she was working around the house. There were so many parts of Kerri that she loved, and having her gone had highlighted all of them. Talking for a few minutes every day had only taken some of the sting out of her loss.

"Hi."

"Hi. I wanted to let you know that my grandpa died this afternoon."

"Oh, Kerri, I'm so sorry to hear that."

"I know you are. That helps a lot." She sniffled a little. "But the best thing happened this morning. Actually, when I think about it, it seems like a miracle."

"Tell me."

"I went into his room first thing to see how he was. It was probably five-thirty or six, and he was wide awake. Awake and alert in a way I haven't seen him for a year."

"That's amazing."

"It was more than that. It was like he was able to fight through the fog and be the man I've known. It didn't last long, and he didn't say much, but it meant the world to me, Brooklyn. I can let him go now that I had just a few seconds with him."

"That makes me cry."

And cry she did, until Kerri made gentle "shooshing" noises into the phone. "Don't be sad. He lived a long life, and he was happy for much of it. That's a lot to be thankful for."

"I know. I guess I'm happy more than sad. Hearing that you connected with him, even though it wasn't for long, really got to me."

"Thanks." Kerri was quiet for a few moments, then she said, "I have to go now. There's a lot to do for the funeral."

"When is it?"

"Tomorrow morning."

"Really? That seems so soon."

"It is, but that's how we do it. Where are you going to be this weekend?"

"Florida. I wish you were going with me."

"I miss you too. But I'll come back to New York soon."

"That would really make me happy." *Especially if it means you're ready to give us a chance.*

The next day, a cab dropped Kerri off at her apartment at around three p.m. She was absently searching her purse for her keys when she started in alarm. Brooklyn was sitting on the stairs, smiling shyly. "I… couldn't decide whether to call you or not. I didn't want to…"

Kerri launched herself at her, holding onto her so tightly that her arms ached after a few seconds. "You are such a dear woman. I can't believe you went to so much trouble for me."

"I thought of you coming home tonight, and I knew you'd be sad. I wanted to make sure you had someone to talk to."

"Damn, Brooklyn, this is the most thoughtful thing anyone has ever done for me." She kissed her cheek, then hugged her tightly, not able to let her go. She'd been talking all day, and being held was much, much nicer.

"Let's go inside."

They went up the stairs and entered the stuffy apartment. "I haven't been here since I got back."

"I knew you were at your mom's up until now, but I had a feeling you'd come back here. If you didn't get home by four, I was going to call you."

"I wish you would have called the minute you got in. You could have come and met my family."

"I didn't want to interfere. And I didn't want to get dressed up either."

"Still…I stayed and helped my mom clean up, but she had enough people to do that. When did you get in?"

"Around ten."

Kerri stopped opening doors and windows to gawp at her. "And you've been sitting here for four or five hours?"

"No." Brooklyn shook her head. "I dawdled. I had lunch, then went to the beach and watched the waves for a while. I've only been here for a couple of hours. I slept in my rental car for a while, then sat on the steps to get some fresh air."

Kerri felt herself drawn to be as close to Brooklyn as was polite. "How can you afford to be here at all?" They were just a foot from each other now, and Kerri could get a mere hint of Brooklyn's scent. Her mouth watered and she had to force herself to back away or do something rash.

"I can only stay until nine. I'm taking the red eye to Florida. It'll be fine. You know how well I can sleep if I'm in business class."

"You came just to see me for a few hours?"

"Yes."

Her brown eyes were so full of empathy that Kerri's breath caught in her throat.

"I wanted to let you know how much you mean to me. I'm here to help you get through this in any way I can."

Feeling abnormally shy, Kerri forced herself to ask for what she needed the most. "Could we sit and hug for a while? I feel awfully raw."

"Absolutely."

Brooklyn took her hand and led her to the sofa. They sat and Kerri immediately snuggled closely against Brooklyn's body. "This is the best gift I've ever gotten. Having someone know what I need without having to ask for it is fantastic."

"I'd give anything to be able to do that for you all of the time."

All of the time. Was that a subtle way of restating her need for commitment? Or was she only saying something unbelievably sweet? Thoughts rushed around Kerri's head, banging into each other until she wanted to slap herself. It was so fantastic to smell, feel, and touch Brooklyn's body, but she wanted so much more. If only they could kiss—just once, she felt like her raging thoughts could calm and she'd get a moment of peace.

She snuggled closer and tentatively lifted her chin. Brooklyn looked into her eyes and everything seemed to stop for a second. It didn't matter what they'd said before. It didn't matter that Brooklyn wanted a serious commitment. When their eyes met, all that ceased to exist. There was only the two of them, their warm bodies pressing against each other, and the thrum of excitement that was completely undeniable. Seconds ticked by slowly, and Brooklyn haltingly inched forward. Now they almost touched. Almost. Kerri couldn't stand it. She closed the scant distance and let her lips finally find the succor that only Brooklyn could provide. When they touched, a flash of electricity surged through her, and she was certain she'd been struck by some force of nature. The energy that bubbled up in her couldn't be from a simple kiss. But as her heart slowed to its normal rhythm, she realized the phenomena came only from Brooklyn. Her concern, her caring, her gentleness—all combined to create a wellspring of feeling in Kerri's body that she was sure she'd never felt before.

Now she sat, transfixed, waiting for Brooklyn to return the kiss. To show she was as enthralled by their connection as Kerri. But the moments produced only anticipation. Kerri was ready to burst into tears when Brooklyn finally moved towards her and mirrored her kiss. The energy surged between them again, and she heard a throaty purr. Good god, that was the sexiest sound in the universe. But as she felt herself surrender to the moment, Brooklyn pulled back and gazed at her with an inscrutable expression on her lovely face. Did she want more? It didn't matter any longer. Kerri needed more. Restraint wasn't an option. She shifted her weight to lean heavily into Brooklyn's body, then threaded her hands through her glorious hair. Holding her lovely face still, she peppered her with kisses, touching her forehead, her eyelids, then her flushed cheeks. Finally, Kerri captured the pink lips that seemed to quiver as she pressed into them. Immediately, strong hands settled on her shoulders, holding her tight. Brooklyn gripped her firmly, and their lips met again and again.

Kerri's whole body hummed with feeling, settling in her breasts, then between her legs. Her skin was alive in a way it had never been, not even in the most heated passion. Brooklyn was all she wanted. All she needed. Her head throbbed with an interplay of thoughts, feelings and sensations too fantastic to name. Their kisses were nearly frantic, as though they were trying to make up for all of the opportunities they'd both let slip by. They continued to kiss and nip at each other's lips for so long Kerri was weak with need. But Brooklyn didn't move one millimeter past her kisses. She hadn't even allowed her tongue to slide inside Kerri's very willing mouth. Was she shy? No, there was no way Brooklyn was too shy to press forward. Either she was waiting for Kerri to take the lead or... Or she didn't want to go further. But the passion that rose from her body showed she was dying to go further. Her skin was hot, her body flushed with perspiration. Her breathing was labored and sexy sighs continued to spring from her. That meant only one thing. She wanted Kerri to assure her that she'd changed her mind. That Kerri was ready to take their relationship to the next level. What had she said? That she wanted something that would lead to marriage. Marriage. That was so far from Kerri's life plan that it hadn't even made it onto the paper. And if she couldn't go there, she had to stop. For Brooklyn.

It took all of her strength, but Kerri managed to slow down. She made each tender kiss a little softer, a little shorter. Finally, she kissed her way back up; past flushed cheeks, salty eyelids and damp forehead. Then she slowly let Brooklyn's hair slip from her fingers, feeling the loss in her gut. She couldn't let Brooklyn see how close she was to crying, so she put her head back onto her shoulder and tried to keep herself together.

They sat just that way for well over an hour. Neither one said a word, but Kerri intermittently let out a few tears, wetting Brooklyn's sky blue shirt. Once she felt in control again, Kerri said, "You mean so much to me. I can't thank you enough for—everything."

Brooklyn's voice was rough from lack of use. "I'm very glad I came."

"I think I'll go with you to Florida. There's nothing vital for me to do here."

Brooklyn sat up, dislodging Kerri from her body. "I don't think that's a good idea. I'd love to have you, but you need to take some time to mourn. Don't come back until you feel like you're completely ready."

What did that mean? Did she want to be alone? Or was she being thoughtful? "I feel like I might be ready."

Brooklyn touched her chin tenderly, and held it until Kerri met her eyes. "You seem very shaky to me. Take some time for yourself. You've been taking care of me or your grandfather for an awfully long time. Try to relax for a while."

"Okay. You're probably right. But I owe you an awful lot for being here for me."

"No, you don't. It's not a gift if it has to be reciprocated."

Kerri leaned back and looked at her for a long minute. "You're really very zen every once in a while."

"Maybe you've rubbed off on me. I hope."

——

A few weeks later, Kerri finally felt able to return to New York. Brooklyn had been right, of course. She had needed quite a while to feel like herself again.

It took a little nerve, but when they were on one of their daily phone call, she asked, "Do you still want me to be your road manager? Please be honest if you think you can handle things on your own."

"Of course I want you here! There's nothing I'd like better."

"I can't guarantee how long I'll be able to do it, but I like it and I'd like to avoid stress for a little while. Don't even think of offering me some ridiculously high salary. I'll only take a normal manager's cut."

Chuckling, Brooklyn said, "As Kat would tell you, real managers get fifteen percent and I'm more than happy to pay it."

"Then we're set. I'll be home...I mean back in New York for your weekend gig."

"There's just one thing you should know," Brooklyn said. Kerri could almost see the teasing expression that always accompanied that particular tone of voice. "I'll never, ever look for another manager."

———

Brooklyn's gig that Saturday was in Chicago, so rather than go to New York and fly back out, Kerri met her there. Kerri reached the hotel not long after Brooklyn and as soon as she dropped her bags, she knocked on the adjoining door.

Brooklyn threw it open and smiled while extending her arms. Kerri fell into them and when they closed around her body, she felt something click in her heart. She loved Brooklyn, and was willing to give whatever it took to get her. What that meant was another story.

———

It took Kerri a few days to readjust to Brooklyn's schedule, but by the end of the week they were both going to bed mid-afternoon and getting up around midnight. Kerri seemed generally fine. She'd had a long time to prepare for her grandfather's death and, apparently, once the shock of it was over, she was able to get her feet back under herself quickly. But she didn't bring up what had happened between them. It was on Brooklyn's mind so many times that it could have driven her to drink. But she felt much better drinking less, and she wasn't going to change that just to relieve some tension.

There was one big change in the way they related. Since the day Kerri returned, they hugged each other before bed and after Brooklyn got home from work. Kerri also put her hand on Brooklyn's shoulder or arm for no particular reason, or brushed her hair across her shoulders, and a dozen other small, but intimate gestures. It was different, but pleasant, and Brooklyn was a long way from complaining. But what did it mean? Was it a tiny step towards commitment? If so, it might take a year until they got there. Brooklyn wouldn't have minded even that, if she knew for sure that her patience would be rewarded. But as things stood, nothing was guaranteed.

—◁◇▷—

Kerri was certain that Brooklyn was the kind of person who would speak up if she had something to say. But a week passed with them both in New York, and she still hadn't mentioned what had happened between them. It was driving her crazy, so she was resolved to bring it up that day. Now all she had to do was stop her stomach from flipping and keep her hands from shaking.

When Brooklyn got home at her usual time, Kerri got up to hug her at the door. She held on for a long time, longer than she knew she should have, but the longer they hugged the more time she had to change her mind about talking. She could tell Brooklyn was getting uncomfortable, so she finally backed away. The only way to get through this was to gut it up and do it.

"Do you remember the night my grandfather had his stroke?"

Brooklyn was standing by the table, and when Kerri brought up the topic, she leaned against it and said somberly, "Of course I do."

"I think we need to talk about what happened between us that night. And after his funeral."

If it was possible for someone's knees to turn to jelly, Brooklyn shouldn't have been able to hold herself up. All of the color drained out of her face, and Kerri felt a small guilty pleasure that Brooklyn clearly was as nervous about the topic as she was. It was so nice not to be alone.

"Sure," Brooklyn said, her voice quivering. "I'm open to talk about anything."

"I hope I didn't come across as some lunatic who does crazy things when the people closest to her are in danger." She'd meant that as a joke, but Brooklyn's expression was dead serious.

"I never thought that."

Given her expression that's exactly what she'd thought. "I needed to be close, and I felt so understood that I needed as much intimacy as you were comfortable giving me."

Brooklyn stood and put her arms around Kerri, hugging her close. "I'm glad you did. I really care for you, and I'm glad you know that." She released her hold and stood back, smiling uncertainly.

What did she mean by that? Where did they go from here? Brooklyn looked like she didn't have another word to say, so Kerri put her arms around her waist and hugged her until she could feel Brooklyn stiffen up. Having no idea what to do next, she let her go. Brooklyn was still smiling, but she looked confused. Unable to stand there for another moment, Kerri went into the kitchen and worked on finishing lunch—one thing she felt completely confident doing. *Now what?*

As springtime was hinting that it was ready to come out and play, they enjoyed each warm moment to the hilt. They were able to ride their bikes without mittens and two pairs of socks, and the jonquils and daffodils popping up along the bike path were a healthy tonic to a long winter. They had synced their schedules, and most days the only times they were apart were during *Reveille* and when they slept. Now even yoga wasn't enough to relax Kerri before bed. Spending so much time with Brooklyn and wanting her so badly could only be vanquished by fantasizing about her. She wasn't sure if that was an Eastern discipline, but it worked like a charm.

She'd had time to find Brooklyn a top-notch literary agent, and after kicking around ideas for several weeks, they finally came up with a good pitch which her agent, Michelle, shopped around. A few weeks later Brooklyn came home from work with a decided spring in her step. This time when she hugged Kerri, she picked her up from the floor and twirled her in a circle. "I'm getting an awesome book deal!"

"Fantastic! Tell me all about it."

"I get to write the book I really want to write, and they're going to give me a massive advance—three times more than the other place offered. And I'm going to get to work with an editor who's done both political books and more lighthearted things. He's just about my age, which should help since we want to appeal to the eighteen to thirty-five demo."

"Listen to you, all hooked up with the demographics." She gave Brooklyn another hug and started to lead her into the kitchen for lunch. But she stopped and said, "You'll probably want to charter a jet and go to Vegas for lunch. You could pick up a couple of girls, a few bottles of champagne, and really celebrate."

It only lasted a second, but no one would've missed the hurt expression that flashed across Brooklyn's face. "I'm a simple girl. I'm happy to have lunch with you. I can go pick up a couple of girls later." Now her smile was back, but she still looked a little wary.

Kerri went into the kitchen to plate their lunch, then Brooklyn carried everything into the dining room with Kerri following behind with their drinks. After sitting down they toasted with their glasses of sparkling water. It was clear Brooklyn was still troubled by what Kerri had said. "You know, I couldn't have sex with a prostitute even if she paid *me*."

Okay. She *was* hurt by the comment. But was she hurt because having sex for money was something she didn't do, or did it offend her in some other way? It was so hard to tell with her!

"I know what you mean. Given that I wouldn't go outside of my comfort zone with Dakota all of these years either shows that I'm lazy or I need a deep connection before I'm ready."

Brooklyn's smirk returned. "Or your sex drive has become a sex walk."

"That's definitely not the case." She was going to elaborate, to tell Brooklyn that she was touching herself so frequently while thinking of her that her wrist ached. But there was nowhere to go with that line of thought. "How well do you have to know somebody before you're comfortable having sex?" Maybe she just needed a year or two to really get into it.

Brooklyn chewed on her cheek for a few seconds. "If I'm interested in a relationship?"

"Yes. I assume you can have sex with a stranger fairly quickly."

Brooklyn chuckled at that. "I only need about five minutes for a stranger. But for a relationship it's got to be at least five dates. It can be longer, but never shorter."

"You sound like that's a rule."

"It is. I take sex very seriously when there's some permanence involved. I won't open up to a woman unless I'm sure I could love her. I can't fall in love in only five dates, of course, but I can always tell by then if there's real potential."

"Is that how it was with Ashley?"

"Yeah. That was a sticking point, because she was ready right away. But I knew she had potential to stick around and I didn't want to get started unless I was sure."

"I don't have a number, but I approach it the same way."

"Better safe than sorry. I've had sex with more women than I should have, but I've been very careful about relationships. They're too important to rush."

That was fine and dandy, but how safe did they have to be? Were they dating? If so, they'd had many, many more dates than five. It struck Kerri that she might have been fantasizing about the entire relationship. She'd almost forced Brooklyn to kiss her in Santa Monica, and she'd been the one to try to discuss it afterwards. Brooklyn obviously hadn't wanted to. Maybe her interest had flagged or even evaporated. That was a disgusting thought, but it wasn't something to ignore.

— ··· —

April and May were both rainy and cool. Most of the rain came in the afternoon, spoiling their afternoon exercise routine. They were still able to go for bike rides, but now they went at midnight or one a.m. Kerri found it strangely exhilarating, being from a place where exercising outdoors at midnight would've been considered very, very strange. But they were never alone on the bike paths. It was hard to figure out who the

319

other people were, and what kind of jobs they had, but she guessed many of them were writers or artists. Or vampires.

Brooklyn had been working hard on the first chapter of her book. She and her editor had sent it back and forth three times, and she was very close to finishing it. *Reveille* was dark the last two weeks of June, and now that she was in good shape with the beginning of her book, Brooklyn announced she was taking a real vacation.

Kerri was a little surprised when Brooklyn decided she wanted to rent a house on the Jersey shore. She'd heard of it, of course, but she didn't have any real idea of what one did there. She got her chance to see for herself when she and Brooklyn set off just before midnight on a Sunday for Toms River, a community on the Atlantic shore of New Jersey. Traffic was horrible going towards New York, but not bad at all heading down the shore. "Most rentals start Sunday at noon," Brooklyn said. "So it's hellish coming down here on Sunday morning. People should really wait, but no one can stand to." It took about two hours to get to their destination, and when they pulled up to a gate blocking a drive to a residence, it looked like they were in another country.

The house was ridiculously large and resembled a Tuscan manor with a long curved road to the front door. Kerri expected a dozen servants to emerge and take their bags, but it was just the two of them, she and a grinning Brooklyn.

"I think I can be happy here for a couple of weeks. What about you?"

"Everybody I know could be happy here. Did you really want someplace this big?"

"I want my family to come down, so I needed four bedrooms. But most places had six or seven. It hardly matters. The big houses all rent for about the same amount." They each took their bag and went into the house which was even more spectacular inside, if not a little too ostentatious. The best part of the place was outside where there was a pool, a spa, a huge outdoor kitchen, and a dock. The small body of water that was just off the back of the house look barely wider than the pool, but there were large power boats lined up along it. "That sure doesn't look like the ocean," Kerri said.

"It's a little inlet off Barnegat Bay. You go down this to get to the bay and then you go across the bay to get to the ocean. Or, you can go out the front door, cross the street, and you're there. It depends on if you want to be on a boat or on the beach."

"I like both."

"That makes two of us."

They had decided to try to keep to their schedule, so they stayed up all night. They spent much of the gorgeous evening walking up and down the sand-covered beach, admiring the few homes that had enough light to be seen clearly.

It seemed so far away from home, like they were hours and hours from Manhattan. Nothing about it was like New York, and that gave it an exotic flair that was remarkably attractive. Equally attractive was Brooklyn, with the wind tossing her hair and the pale moonlight revealing, then shadowing her features. Kerri couldn't help herself. She had to touch her in some way. But all she could get up the nerve to do was hold her hand. Brooklyn flinched a little when she took and held it, but they walked that way for another hour.

Somehow it seemed they'd reached another milestone. Now Brooklyn acted as though it were perfectly normal to hold hands, and she even pulled Kerri closer when she strayed a little too far away. But she didn't go one step further—making Kerri wonder if they were really making progress or just slightly lowering their guards.

It was late when they got home, and very, very quiet. There wasn't a light on at any of the nearby houses, and the canal was pitch black and silent. Not even a bird was chirping, and the sounds of the ocean were very muted.

Before they entered the back of the house, Brooklyn stopped. "Let's go swimming. It's too nice a night to be inside."

"Okay. I'll go get our suits."

"Who needs suits? You've seen more of me than my gynecologist has."

She had the playful smile she wore when she was feeling particularly youthful. Kerri was one hundred percent powerless over that smile, and found herself nodding. But Brooklyn had never seen her naked, and she was slightly skittish about stripping. *Don't be an idiot! You've seen her naked, and that was no big deal. Get over yourself.*

That tiny pep talk did the trick, and they both dropped their clothes onto nearby chairs. It was really too dark to see a heck of a lot, but Kerri found herself trying to make a good impression—thrusting her shoulders back, and making sure the curve in her back showed off the thousands of hours she'd spent developing the best ass she was capable of.

But Brooklyn didn't see a thing. She jumped into the pool as soon as she was naked, avoiding looking in Kerri's direction until she'd joined her. "If there's anything that feels better than skinny dipping, I don't know what it is." Brooklyn lay on her back, her hair billowing around her like a sea nymph's.

"I love skinny dipping, but there are things that feel better. A lot better." There. It was time to stop acting like they were ninety-year-old sisters. At least they could talk about sex—even if they didn't have it.

Laughing, Brooklyn said, "Yeah. I suppose that's true. I guess I've almost forgotten."

Then…nothing. She wouldn't run with the ball when it was thrown right to her.

Kerri was so frustrated, she wanted to grab her by the shoulders and shake some sexual desire into her. But she was pretty sure it didn't work that way. Brooklyn kept floating around the big pool, her lovely hair floating around her, looking like some kind of chaste, lovely angel. Emphasis on the chaste.

—⁂—

Much later, Brooklyn wrapped herself in a bath sheet and led the way back into the house. She stood in the doorway holding it open for Kerri who had to pass right in front of her. Kerri paused for just a second and their eyes met. She could have sworn that Brooklyn was going to kiss her. It looked like she'd leaned toward her just a little bit. But then she straightened up and squared her shoulders against the door, making it clear...or as clear as anything was with her...that Kerri should keep going.

———

After breakfast they went to the beach. Early morning at the shore was transcendently beautiful. Kerri decided that this part of the Atlantic was just as pretty, if not prettier, than the Pacific. She braved what she knew would be bracing cold water, but stopped and exclaimed, "It's not bad at all!"

Brooklyn let the waves crash up to her shins. "I'd say it's about seventy. I can go in as long as it's above sixty."

"It's delightful!" Kerri timed the next wave and dove in, letting the chilly water wash over her body. She always felt a little like she was in a huge effervescent drink when she dove into a wave. There was something about the water burbling around that felt like bubbles. She tossed her head, flipping her hair from her eyes. Brooklyn was still on the shore, looking tentative. "Come on!" Kerri called out.

"I like to wait until I'm hot. It's not hot at six a.m!"

"Chick...chick...chick...chicken!"

That did it. Brooklyn ran through the breaking wave, looking like she wanted to scream but was fighting the urge mightily. "Shit, shit, shit!" She obviously couldn't hold back for long. "It's freezing!"

When they got out to where the waves were breaking, Kerri lay on her back and stared up into the clear, blue sky. "I love this more than I can say. The ocean is my favorite place on earth."

The water was up to Brooklyn's neck, letting her stay upright without having to tread water. "I'm with you. No place on earth makes me feel better. Of course, I haven't been to as many places as you have."

"I've been just about everywhere that has water, and this is pretty perfect. Why don't we live here?"

"I've considered getting a place down here. A nice two or three bedroom that my family could use all summer. Maybe we should shop while we're here."

"Wouldn't it drive you crazy to have a place you couldn't visit very often? You're gone every weekend." Kerri wasn't possessive about much, but having a nice place on the beach that she couldn't use would not be pleasant.

"Right. I forget I don't have a normal life." She smiled devilishly. "My family can buy their own damned house."

—⁓—

Kerri went exploring while Brooklyn spent some time on the phone with her agent. When she returned, she called Brooklyn out to the back yard. They went to the lagoon that led to the bay and Kerri pointed at a big thing that looked like a large surfboard. "A guy down the street let me borrow his paddleboard. Wanna try it?"

"Looks hard."

Kerri elbowed her playfully. "Come on, it's fun. He showed me how."

Brooklyn shook her head, but Kerri could tell she was interested. They sat on the edge of the dock and eventually Brooklyn was able to stand and balance.

"Now you've got to use the paddle to move." Kerri handed it to her and she almost fell over just from that slight movement.

"Shit!" She wobbled dramatically, but her balance was good and she stayed up.

"You've got it," Kerri said encouragingly. "Just flex your legs and stay centered. Let the paddle do the work."

Brooklyn took instruction well, and she flexed those long, muscled thighs, managing to stay upright and move the board a few feet through the water. Kerri jumped in and swam right next to her, encouraging and offering tips. By the time they got to the entrance to the bay, Brooklyn looked fairly competent. They turned and went back down the lagoon, where Kerri took over. They traded back and forth for a long time, then

Brooklyn sat up on the dock and called out, "Even though my back muscles are on fire, as soon as the stores open we're buying two!"

—⁓—

They went to bed as usual—at around four o'clock. It was odd to go to sleep at that hour in Manhattan, but even odder to do so when they were right on the beach. But it was crazy to try to move the schedule around—only to have to get acclimated again once vacation was over.

When Kerri woke at midnight, the sound of thunder was rolling in the distance. Brooklyn knocked and entered a few minutes later. "It doesn't look like a good day to walk on the beach. I have a very healthy respect for lightening."

Kerri sat up and thought for a second. "Do you know how to play poker?"

Brooklyn's eyes lit up. "Did you say poker? There are few things I like more than a good poker game."

"Isn't Atlantic City somewhere around here?"

"It will be in an hour. Get dressed and we're on the way!"

—⁓—

They walked into the biggest of the Atlantic City casinos just as the heavens opened up and dropped a massive amount of rain, accompanied by thunder, lightening and everything else the sky could deposit. "Nice day for a casino," Brooklyn said. "People here think 1:30 in the morning is a perfectly normal time of day to play cards."

"Most of them have been up for hours. We're fresh."

Brooklyn rubbed her hands together. "Patsies."

They found the poker area and strolled around looking for a good game. "I like no-limit hold 'em," Kerri said after surveying all of the possibilities.

"No limit? Really? You can go broke in one hand."

"Or do really well after making the other guys go broke."

Brooklyn moved back a couple of inches, her eyes scanning Kerri's face several times. "No limit, huh? I think I'll just hang around and watch you play a few hands. I hope you brought your checkbook."

Kerri flicked her fingers under Brooklyn's chin. "Checkbooks are so twentieth century." She reached into her wallet and pulled out a rewards card for the casino. "There's a Vegas branch too." Then she marched over to the table, handed the dealer her card, took a seat and grinned at Brooklyn who merely waved.

—————

Kerri didn't win much at all when all was said and done. But she sat right there for over four hours before coming out about fifty dollars up. Brooklyn had moved from table to table, trying to find a lucky one before giving up. She'd lost a few hundred—nothing to cry about—but she was mesmerized by Kerri's nerve. She couldn't have looked more out of place. Her angelic features, pale hair and intelligent blue eyes made her look like she should have been running the casino child-care center. But she didn't bat an eye when a pot went far higher than Brooklyn ever felt comfortable playing.

Watching her gave Brooklyn new respect for Kerri's demeanor. She was clearly a determined, calm, and placid woman. But she also had the ability to stare down a big table full of older, richer men when she was holding cards she liked. Brooklyn hated to admit it, but she'd never been more attracted to her. There was something inherently sexy about a woman risking a good chunk of money just because of her self-confidence. That was it. That's what Kerri had in spades. She didn't do risky things. She did things she was good at that would have been risky if she'd been inept. But looking at her sitting at that table, it was clear that Kerri Klein was very, very 'ept.'

—————

By eight a.m. they were both toast. Kerri finally stood up and stretched, with every man around watching her blouse rise up to almost…almost reveal her flat belly. Brooklyn could see the regret in their eyes when she picked up her few chips and walked away. "I didn't do very well," she admitted, "but I still have my shirt."

"The guys sitting by you wished you'd lost it."

"Huh?" Kerri turned around and looked back at the table. "Oh. Guys always stare at me when I play. They're not used to women who know cards."

"Yeah. That's probably it." Kerri couldn't be that oblivious. Those guys had been treating her like she was minor royalty. They went to the cashier's window for Kerri to collect her winnings.

"How'd you do?"

"Not good. You get to buy lunch."

"You didn't bet the title to your car, did you? I'd hate to have to hitchhike home."

"No, I've still got my car." They went outside to wait for the valet to bring the car around. "How long have you been playing? You look like it's been years."

"Yeah, definitely. Remember me telling you about the rock band I traveled with?"

"Yeah."

"They got me started. They played a lot, and after I got the kids settled for the night, I'd play too. It was something to do on the tour bus that didn't involve hookers or blow."

Laughing, Brooklyn said, "It sounds so funny to hear you talk like that. You look so innocent that to hear you talk about hookers just cracks me up."

"I don't think I look innocent now, but I did when I was just starting out. I got carded at every casino I went to, and I went to a lot of them."

"What's the best?"

"Mmm, that's hard to say. But I had the most fun on Macau. The Chinese really know how to do things up big."

"I don't think I could find Macau on a map if you gave me a dozen hints."

"It's not far from Hong Kong. That's where I was working. You can take a high-speed ferry that's fun in itself. I played fan-tan while I was there and didn't do too badly." She looked very pleased with herself.

The car arrived and Brooklyn got in, after handing the valet a tip. "Where shall we go? Since you're buying, you get to choose."

"We're near the shore, so let's find a place to have chowder. Know of anywhere?"

"My car does." She played with the GPS, asking it for the closest seafood restaurant. Kerri took what the car suggested and used her phone to double check on other people's reviews.

"I've become so inundated by technology that I don't think I could find my own butt without an app," Brooklyn said.

"Welcome to the twenty-first century. You're a few years behind, but you're catching up nicely."

Friday night a big SUV pulled onto the grounds of the rental house and deposited Brooklyn's brother Austin, his wife Emily, their son Cody, and Brooklyn's parents. After hearing, in great detail, how horrible traffic was, they all went into the house. Brooklyn had obviously not spent a lot of time developing hostess skills, so Kerri took Donna and Emily on a tour of the house, while Brooklyn walked to the pool with the men following.

Kerri was a little uncomfortable acting as though she'd rented the place. She'd met Emily and Donna only once, and she wasn't sure what role they thought she held in Brooklyn's life. But both women were friendly and treated her as if it were perfectly normal that she was showing them around. Maybe they thought that's what a manager did.

The next afternoon people were spread all over the property. It was a warm day and Kerri found herself sitting under a large awning with Donna. Brooklyn and Austin were playing tennis at the public court just down the street, Richie and Cody were surf casting at the beach and Emily had gone out to buy something to barbecue for dinner. Kerri was still a little anxious at being alone with Donna, even though she couldn't have said why. The only thing that made sense was that she was afraid she was going to ask about her relationship with Brooklyn and she had no idea how she would respond.

"I was so pleased when Brookie told me she'd started to play tennis again," Donna said.

"Yeah, she seems to love it. Does Zack play too?"

"All of the kids played when they were young, but Brookie was the best. She probably could have gotten a tennis scholarship, but she didn't need it."

Donna had that "ask me to tell you why" look that she got when she was parsing out information. Kerri didn't find it too irritating, so she played along. "Why didn't she need a scholarship?"

"Because she had one based on her grades." The look on her face was almost bursting with pride. "You knew about that, didn't you?"

"No, I don't think she mentioned getting a scholarship."

"To Yale," Donna said, enunciating crisply. "Do you know how hard it is to get a scholarship to Yale?"

"That's the school she dropped out of?" Kerri's head ached at the mere thought.

"That's my girl. She got up there and went to a comedy club before she'd ever been to a class! Once she saw that she had the guts to do it, she was ready to get started." She put her hand over her mouth, trying to hold back a laugh. "Oh, my God, you should have seen the look on Richie's face when she called home and told us."

"That's…amazing. Really amazing."

"She practically got a perfect score on the SAT, and I don't think she ever got less than an "A" minus in school. She's actually a genius, Kerri. Where she gets it from, I don't know…" She laughed hard, and shook her head.

"I'm not surprised she doesn't talk about it," Kerri said. "She never boasts about anything."

"She never has. You just never know with Brookie." She lowered her voice, even though no one else was around. "Do you think it would bother her if I told her I ran into Ashley?"

Kerri noted that Donna didn't explain who Ashley was. That alone implied something, but she wasn't sure what. "She doesn't talk about her very often, but when she does she certainly doesn't seem upset."

"It's so hard to tell with her."

Kerri could have gone on all day about how hard it was to figure a lot of things out about Brooklyn, but she was too discreet to do that. "Yes, she plays her cards pretty close to the vest."

"I could never tell how much she loved Ashley. With Austin and Emily, I knew they'd be together after just a couple months. But Brooklyn wasn't like that. I used to tell Richie that Brooklyn wasn't satisfied, so I was shocked when Ashley broke up with her. I would have bet money it would've gone the other way."

It wasn't wise to get into discussions like this, but Kerri couldn't help herself. "Why do you say that?"

"It wasn't anything she said. Brookie isn't the type to tell tales out of school. But I never thought Ashley was bright enough for her."

"Not bright enough? Really? I never got that impression from Brooklyn."

"Ashley was smart in her own way, but she didn't read much, and she's not interested in the world. And if you've spent any time around Brooklyn, you know she barely cares about anything practical." She laughed, long and hard. "It drives Richie crazy, but the rest of us have gotten used to her. I'll never know where she got it from, because nobody in either of our families is like that, but she's always been interested in knowing everything there was to know."

"And you'd really think she couldn't love someone who didn't share that?" It felt like someone had just turned the heat up, and Kerri could feel her pulse quickening.

"Sure, she could fall in love with someone who didn't like the same things, but how long could it last? I think Brookie finally figured out that she has to be with somebody who's more than just pretty or fun. I think she's grown up a lot and now knows that having things in common is the only way to make sure you can stay together permanently."

Kerri found herself laughing nervously. "But they say that opposites attract."

"They also say that half of all marriages end in divorce. I don't think Brooklyn wants to be in that half. Having Ashley leave her broke her heart. She won't make that mistake twice."

—⁓—

Brooklyn graciously gave her parents the room she'd been using since it was the biggest one in the house and had a bathroom in the suite. She moved to one of the smaller rooms that shared a bathroom with Kerri. Everyone else went to bed not long after they got up, and they sat together in Kerri's room, making plans for the day.

"How do you think the weekend is going?" Brooklyn asked. "It's kinda weird sleeping all afternoon while everyone else is at the beach, but they don't seem to mind."

"I think it's going great. Cody seems happy to be here and all of the adults seem like they're able to relax. Our being on another schedule lets everyone have some alone time."

"What were you and my mom talking about this afternoon when I got home? I like to keep an eye on her, because she has a tendency to try to use other people to find out things I don't tell her." She laughed mischievously.

Kerri was close to tongue-tied. "She wasn't trying to get information out of me. I don't remember what made her say this, but she paid you a compliment. She said she thought you'd grown up a lot in the last few years and you were ready to settle down."

Brooklyn rolled onto her side and supported her head with her hand. She looked right into Kerri's eyes for a few long seconds, then said, "She's right. My next relationship will be my last."

The laugh that bubbled out of Kerri sounded like she'd taken a hit of laughing gas. She wished she could pull it back in, so as to not sound so crazy. "That's a pretty bold claim."

It seemed that Brooklyn drew closer, or that her eyes had grown bigger and more soulful. "I mean that sincerely. I'm ready for the love of

331

my life." Her eyes blinked slowly, then she let them remain closed for another second or two. Kerri desperately wanted to, at the very least, touch her lovely cheek or kiss her lips, but she did neither. They were just a few inches from each other and that tension was palpable, but it somehow felt like most of the tension came from her and not Brooklyn. She was so confused, she felt like screaming, but she sat there quietly and waited, pleading for Brooklyn to say another word. But when those lovely eyes blinked open, the look Brooklyn gave her didn't make things clear. It wasn't devoid of emotion, but it didn't give Kerri a clue as to what the unreadable feeling was.

Kerri was putting things out for breakfast when Richie walked into the kitchen the next morning. "Are you still awake?" he asked.

"Yes. We normally go to bed at three or four and sleep until eleven or midnight. That lets Brooklyn go to a club and work out new material, while still being able to be alert at six. She's doing a lot better with this schedule."

Richie poured himself a cup of coffee and sat at the breakfast bar, silently watching Kerri work. It was disconcerting at the least, and the strong physical resemblance he and Brooklyn shared was equally odd. Kerri wanted to escape and find out where Brooklyn had hidden herself, but Richie stopped her. "If Brookie's doing so well, why are you still in town? I thought you promised me that you were going to leave as soon as she got on a good schedule."

Even though the words were blunt, it didn't feel like he was making an accusation. Instead, he truly seemed interested.

"I was planning on going back to LA to deal with some personal business, but those plans changed. Brooklyn's happy with the way I've managed her schedule, so I'm staying on for a while."

"How long a while?" he asked, gazing at her with eerily similar eyes.

"I'm not sure. I've never managed a performer, and I'm finding I like it. Plus, Brooklyn's so easy to work for that it barely seems like a job."

"But you're taking a salary. I think Donna said it was fifteen percent, right?"

"Uhm…yeah. That's standard."

"That's off the top, right? Before Uncle Sam takes his cut? Fifteen percent of gross?"

"That's the way it works."

"You make it sound like that's the law. You could take less if you wanted to, right?" Again, it didn't sound like he was casting doubt on her motives. He just seemed like he was trying to understand.

"Sure. I could do it for room and board. But you could live with the person whose house you're papering and just get paid for materials, right?"

He showed such a broad, handsome smile that Kerri briefly thought Brooklyn wouldn't look bad at all as a man.

Richie laughed, "I can see why she likes you. You're scrappy."

"I'm not really very scrappy, to be honest. But I'm glad you think she likes me. We've become close."

"How close?" Now his eyes bore into her and she felt like she was far too exposed.

"Closer than any client I've ever worked for. We're friends as well as colleagues."

"Hmm. I never charge a good friend for a job."

"How many jobs do you do for friends?"

"Not a hell of a lot. I couldn't afford to."

She merely smiled at him, waiting until he nodded, then took another sip of his coffee. "Okay. I get it. You've gotta make a living too."

"I do. And Brooklyn's the one who insisted on my taking fifteen percent. I would have happily done the job for less. Actually, I would have done it for room and board."

"That's what Brooklyn tells Donna." He smiled like a fox. Luckily, Kerri had never felt like Brooklyn had quizzed her about something she already had the answer to. That was one trait she wouldn't have wanted Brooklyn to share with her dad. But Kerri had to admire the fact that he obviously cared about his daughter and wanted to make sure she wasn't being taken advantage of.

—⁓—

Brooklyn and Kerri packed up their chairs at one to head back from the beach. They liked to have a light meal a couple of hours before bed, and, having arrived on the beach not long after dawn, they were tired of the sun.

Donna got up with them and said, "Let me walk back with you. I need to get some more snacks for Cody."

When they arrived at the house, Brooklyn went to shower while Kerri started their lunch. Donna was poking around, looking like she was wasting time. As soon as Kerri had laid out the ingredients for their dinner, Donna started asking questions. "What's that?" she said, pointing.

"Jicama. I'm going to make a jicama and watermelon salad with a lime vinaigrette."

"For you or for Brooklyn?"

"For both of us. That'll go along with the veggie burgers I made this morning." She took the burgers from the freezer. "They hold together a lot better if you cook them while they've been in the freezer for a while."

Donna stood there, open-mouthed, for a full minute. "Brooklyn won't eat that."

"Sure she will. She likes anything that's spicy, and the vinaigrette I make really packs a punch."

"She doesn't like vegetables. Except for potatoes."

"She does now." Kerri tried to keep from sounding proud of her accomplishment, but getting a vegetable hater to be almost vegetarian was one of her signal accomplishments as a talent wrangler.

"I know what my girl likes, Kerri, and it's not some weird-looking..." She held up the unprocessed root. "Thing. What is it, anyway? It looks like a turnip."

"It's a root, like a turnip. It's really good cubed or sliced in a salad. I like to use it with dip. It's much better for you than chips."

334

"Brookie likes chips." Donna was almost glaring at her, and Kerri flashed on the time Brooklyn told her that Donna and Ashley clashed on what food Brooklyn liked. Now it didn't seem so preposterous. But she and Donna were not going to clash. No way.

Kerri stood at the counter for a moment, collecting herself. "I have chips right here." As per Brooklyn's instructions, she'd bought an unhealthy supply of junk food for the Yorks, and there was still a bag of potato chips left unsullied. "And I have regular hamburger if she'd prefer that."

"She would," Donna said firmly.

A few minutes later, Brooklyn walked into the kitchen. Her nose started twitching and she went over to the grill where Kerri was cooking a vegetable burger and a hamburger. "What's this?"

"I told Kerri you wouldn't want a vegetable burger," Donna said, looking proud of herself.

"Since when?" She put her hands on her hips and stared at Kerri. "I love those veggie burgers. They've got more taste and texture than a regular burger."

Donna broke in. "Brookie! You don't like vegetables."

Without a moment's hesitation, Brooklyn said to Kerri, "Did you make two veggie burgers?"

"Yes. There's another in the freezer."

"Would you mind?" Brooklyn pulled it out and placed it on the grill. Then she leaned in and placed a gentle kiss on Kerri's cheek. "Thanks," she said quietly. Then she turned to her mother. "See this?" She lifted her shirt and slapped her relatively flat belly. "Having Kerri cook for me has let me take off fifteen pounds. I've got another ten to go to be the same weight I was in high school. Vegetables will get me there. Hamburgers and pizza and kung pow chicken and potato chips and Coke will pull me right back to where I was."

"I didn't know you were trying to lose weight." Donna paused for a moment. "You looked fine before!"

Brooklyn put her hands on her mother's shoulders and gazed at her, the affection she held for her obvious. "You don't see me like other people do, Mom. You're very biased, and I love that about you. But I'm on television every day, and I've got to look good." She turned and caught Kerri's eye, giving her a smile. "And I feel better eating less fat and grease. So I'm not going to change something that's working for me. Kerri might be the only manager in America who cooks for her client, and I'm really, really lucky to have found her."

"So that's why your freezer still has the food I left for you a month ago in it." Donna's voice was filled with hurt.

"Yes. That's why. I know you bring me food because you love me, but you don't have to do it any more. Use that time to do something for yourself."

"Taking care of you is what I love to do."

"I know." Brooklyn didn't add another word. She put her arms around her mother and hugged her for a long time, then walked her back to the beach. Kerri sat at the breakfast bar and marveled at the change she'd witnessed. Brooklyn had not only acted like a competent adult, she'd stood up for Kerri, something she admitted she never did for Ashley. Remarkable.

───※───

The sun was blazing, there were hundreds of people crowding the beach just outside their windows, and music from various sources could be heard in the house, yet Brooklyn and Kerri were getting ready for bed. The curtains were drawn and the air conditioning blew cold air around the dim room as Kerri finished a short meditation period and got into bed. There was a knock on the door that led to the bath. Brooklyn popped her head in, then entered Kerri's room and sat on the edge of the bed. "I wanted to thank you for putting up with that little tantrum over lunch."

"That wasn't a tantrum. Your mom loves you. She'd do anything for you, and I know she thinks those hearty meals she makes are good for you."

"She and I might be the only two people in America who still think that," Brooklyn said, chuckling. "But I've left the fold and I think she feels a little...I don't know...left out?"

"Maybe. I know she likes doing things for you, but maybe you can work on doing things together. Make it less one-sided."

Brooklyn blinked. "What's in that for me?"

She looked so serious that Kerri was caught flat-footed when she began to laugh.

"That look was priceless!"

Slapping Brooklyn on the shoulder was scant recompense for the trick. "You devil!"

Brooklyn lay crosswise on the bed, looking like it was perfectly natural to drape herself across Kerri's bed. "You're right. I've got to act like an adult, rather than her baby."

"You're not a baby." Kerri couldn't help it. She had to run her fingers through the prettiest head of hair she'd ever seen. Brooklyn purred like a kitten and turned to present her whole head. "Why don't you make it a point to spend some real time with your mom every week? I know she'd love it."

The head rub had only lasted seconds, but Brooklyn's voice was already soft and slow. "You're right. I'll figure out some time we're both awake and make a standing date with her. She's off on Wednesdays. Maybe I could..."

Kerri waited for the sentence to end. But Brooklyn's soft snore was her only answer. She knew she should have wakened her, but there was room for both of them in the bed if she moved around to sleep on the diagonal. She let her hand continue to glide through Brooklyn's hair, hoping against hope that one day a long head rub would precede or follow a very satisfying bout of lovemaking.

They were back in the city on the Fourth of July weekend and Brooklyn had a ton of personal mail to go through. "Here's a cool one," she said, holding up what looked like a formal invitation. "Do you want to be my plus one for a party at Winston White's house?"

"Should I know who Winston White is?"

"You'd know if you were in the New York social scene or if you followed the publishing industry. He's a very big wig in both."

"What's the party for?"

"It's a book party for Jeffrey Wolfson's new book about the first Iraqi war."

Kerri smiled. "Well, since I'm never going to read that book, this will be my only chance to learn anything about Jeffrey Wolfson. I'd love to go." It took a second to realize, as she tossed off that comment, that this was exactly the type of thing that Donna had mentioned. Could Brooklyn be happy with a woman who didn't know the first thing about her world? Maybe Brooklyn was trying to figure that very thing out.

The night of the party, Brooklyn came out of her room looking beyond fantastic. Surprisingly, she had agreed with Kerri's edict that her basketball shoes and jeans were not appropriate for an evening event. "If I were a lot more famous I could get away with that. But I'd just look like an idiot if I tried to do something goofy at my level of fame."

She wore a black linen jacket, a snug white tank and a pair of white jeans. It was a hot night, and her mostly white outfit made her look summery, tan, and fit. Her sandals weren't the most fashionable, and they didn't have high heels, but they were unobtrusive and didn't detract from the rest of her look, that of a stylish lesbian who was dressing for other lesbians, not fashion mavens or taste-makers. That gave her an élan that most women, even some serious fashionistas, lacked.

They took a cab up to the East Seventies and stood on the sidewalk for a moment watching people climb up the stairs to the townhouse. Most of the women were dressed much more formally than they were, with a lot of tight cocktail dresses and high black heels, but some of the younger people looked more casual than they did. Brooklyn didn't seem to notice, and she didn't seem nervous in the least, even though Kerri knew this was not her usual crowd.

When they got up to the doorway, Brooklyn told the tuxedoed fellow her name and he graciously welcomed them. They went inside and Brooklyn made a soft whistle through her teeth. "Have you ever been in one of these places?"

"Yeah. A time or two. Owning an entire townhouse would be pretty cool."

"It's ridiculous. Let's sneak around and see the whole place." She appeared perfectly comfortable wandering around the huge home, casually looking in each room that had an open door. When they got back to the living room where most of the other guests were, she went to get Kerri a flute of champagne. They toasted and she stood there looking rather smug, a look that Kerri found intensely appealing. It was rare when she projected that "I'm-pretty-cool-and-I-know-it" look, but when she did Kerri was lost. Most people got slightly irritated when someone showed off. She got hot. Michelle, Brooklyn's literary agent, saved Kerri from drooling when she came up and said hello.

"Are you two enjoying yourselves?"

"Great party," Brooklyn said. "It's especially nice to come to a party with this many famous people and not have any paparazzi outside."

Michelle laughed. "The paparazzi don't care about people who write. If you're into publishing, there's some huge names here, but most people wouldn't know them from a famous mathematician."

"I shouldn't laugh. I don't know any famous mathematicians," Brooklyn said.

"How about philosophers?"

"I read some philosophy, but it's not in my wheelhouse."

"This is a funny time to be asking this, but since I know Kerri is your manager and probably isn't your date, can I assume you're single?"

Brooklyn stood there for a second, looking like she had no idea how to answer that question. "Ahh, yeah, I'm single. Why?"

"Do you see that woman over there?" Michelle asked, pointing to a brainy-looking woman with big black glasses, dark blonde hair that curled around her shoulders and cheek bones to die for. She was also very thin and dressed like she had enough fashion sense for three *Vogue* editors.

Brooklyn nodded. "I think everybody sees her. Why?"

"She asked me if I would introduce her to you, but I didn't want to if you were involved with somebody."

Unable to help herself, Kerri said, "She could make you break up with a lot of people."

Laughing, Michelle said, "I wasn't going to be that blunt, but that's exactly what I was thinking."

"Why does she want to meet me?"

"She said she's a fan, but I assume she's also interested in you. She asked if you were single…"

"Who is she?" Brooklyn could not have looked less interested. It was as though she were asking about someone's particularly homely cousin, and was merely being polite.

"That's Appoline Duprey."

Brooklyn's eyes got big. "I'd love to meet her! I've been reading little tidbits about her philosophy for a couple of years now, but none of her books have been translated into English."

"That's about to change. Her latest will be out in English within the month."

"That's very cool. I'd love to meet her." She started heading her way, leaving Michelle and Kerri behind. Kerri couldn't help but laugh, thinking Brooklyn was one of the few people who would be more interested in her philosophical ramblings than her gorgeous face. It was also a laugh of relief.

When Brooklyn was in her bedroom getting ready for work on Wednesday, she called out, "Hey, don't make lunch for me today. I'm going to have Terry take me to my mom's house and she'll give me a ride home after we have lunch."

Kerri strolled into Brooklyn's bedroom to find her carefully adjusting her shirt to hang properly over her jeans. "That's nice. I know she'll love that."

"Actually, I've got my Wednesday afternoons blocked off for her. We can go shopping or have lunch or go to a movie. She gets to choose."

Kerri moved over and tugged on the back of Brooklyn's shirt. "You need some new jeans. These are bagging in the back and making your shirt stick out."

"Will you buy me some?" She made eye contact in the big mirror.

"Sure. But you could get your own. That'd give you something to do with your mom."

Brooklyn smiled slyly. "I don't want "mom" jeans. I want to look as good in mine as you do in yours." She turned and tickled Kerri under her chin. "That might take magic, but you can probably do that too."

Kerri watched her walk into the main room, letting her eyes linger on Brooklyn's butt. Buying her new jeans wasn't exciting, but watching her try them on might be.

A few weeks after the party at Winston White's house, Kerri brought in the mail and found another invitation for Brooklyn, this one addressed in an elegantly flowing European hand. Brooklyn picked it up when she got home, nodded, then tossed it back on the table. Kerri's curiosity was killing her. She hated to be so childish, not to mention so nosey about Brooklyn's business, but later, when Brooklyn was heading to bed, she had to ask. "Did you see that letter you got?"

"Hmm?" She stopped on her way to her bedroom. "Oh, yeah." She took a detour to the table, picked it up, and took it into her room. Now Kerri had to stew in silence and hope Brooklyn mentioned it.

For three days, Brooklyn didn't say a peep about the invitation, but on Friday, when they were getting ready to leave for St. Louis, she asked,

"How do you feel about being my social secretary? Not that I have much of a social life."

"Fine. I'm happy to do it." *Especially if I can spy in the process.*

"I got invited to a dinner party by that French woman we met a few weeks ago. Remember her?"

"Yeah, I think I recall a gorgeous blonde woman who Hollywood imagines sexy, but evil scientists look like."

Brooklyn threw her head back and laughed heartily. "That's exactly what she looks like! You hit it right on the head. Like she'd whip off those glasses, take her hair out of a bun and make men die from lust."

"Do you want me to find out the details?"

"Nah. Send my regrets." She chuckled. "I like how that sounds. Like a rich person back in the thirties when the butler brings an invitation in on a silver tray."

"Is it on a weekend?"

"No. It's a Tuesday."

"Oh. You can't go because it's too early."

"No." Brooklyn looked like she was having fun with this. "It's for nine o'clock at night. I could easily get up for it."

"So why aren't you going?"

"I'm not part of that literary crowd. It'd probably be boring."

"But you really liked talking to her. You brought it up several times the next day."

"Yeah, she's cool. But I don't know how big it's going to be or anything."

"Show me the invitation. I can tell you based on how it's worded. I have a lot of experience with turning down invitations because my charge was too strung out to feed himself."

Brooklyn was laughing to herself on the way to her bedroom, and she returned a minute later with the invitation. Kerri looked at it for just a second, then said, "She's inviting you to have dinner with her. Just her."

"Really?" Brooklyn looked over her shoulder. "How do you know that?"

"Well, it's handwritten, which makes it pretty intimate, and she only mentions you. She doesn't say 'dinner party,' she says 'join me for dinner.' I'd be amazed if anyone other than the two of you were there."

The small wrinkle between Brooklyn's eyes appeared. "Huh. I guess I have to call her myself to refuse. I'm not famous enough to have you do it." She reached over and pulled the invitation from Kerri's hands.

"But you said you think she's cool."

"Yeah, I do, but this sounds like a date."

A beautiful woman wants her to come to her hotel room for dinner, but Brooklyn dismisses it out of hand. What in the world does that mean? She couldn't let it go. She just couldn't. "What's wrong with going on a date?"

Brooklyn stood there, looking like she didn't know where to let her eyes land. "Nothing."

The devil himself must have taken over her mouth. There was no other reason to have said what she did. "Then go. You might have fun."

It took just a few seconds for those brown eyes to land right on Kerri. Brooklyn's voice had a definite edge to it when she said, "Fine, I will. Thanks for the push. I obviously need one."

That night, all through the flight to St. Louis, Kerri went over what had happened. Why had she pushed her? Brooklyn didn't want to go, but she'd practically forced her. How crazy was that? She took a long look at her...so lovely when she slept. Kerri hadn't known it before that moment, but she'd intentionally pushed her. Given how little had transpired between them in the past months, Brooklyn was certainly not going to make a move. Maybe Appoline would stir something in her that Kerri hadn't. If that was true, that's where she should be. No one said selflessness was going to be fun.

On the night of her date, Brooklyn emerged from her room looking very spiffy. She'd somehow found a block of time when Kerri wasn't with her to buy some very attractive black boots. She wore her new sexy-looking jeans, and one of her tailored shirts, this one a purple and white check. Her newish black blazer made her look perfectly stylish, but not overdone.

"You look great," Kerri said, trying hard to sound lighthearted.

"Thanks. I probably won't be home too late. Wait up for me." She smiled and held Kerri's gaze for a little longer than was comfortable. "That's a little joke. Normally you say 'Don't wait'—"

"I get it. Have a good time."

"I will." She stood there for a second, as if she was waiting for Kerri to do something. Then she shook her head and left quickly. It took a moment for Kerri to realize that they hadn't hugged goodbye, and that Brooklyn was waiting for her to take the initiative. It was like they always eventually got on the same page, but each time one of them was a beat or two late.

Brooklyn hailed a cab, and instructed the driver to go to a bar in a tiny hotel in Chelsea rather than to Appoline's hotel. She went in and found her sitting at one of a pair of club chairs in a quiet corner of the room. "Hi," Brooklyn said. "Thanks for agreeing to meet me here."

Appoline extended her hand and Brooklyn shook it. "It's my pleasure. You were very kind in your refusal of my invitation."

"I wasn't refusing."

"Yes, you were. But I like your honesty. I'd love to have another friend I could trust. What do you think?"

"I think that would be fantastic." She sat down and signaled the waiter. "I'd like a vodka on the rocks. Appoline? Would you like another?"

"Yes, thank you." The waiter left and she leaned close and said, "I want to know more about this woman. You say her name is Kerri?"

After talking and drinking for several hours, Brooklyn realized she'd had one too many. Appoline was a hell of a drinker, and Brooklyn had lost track of how many they'd had. But it was only two a.m.; she still had four hours to sober up. She'd been in worse shape.

"I disagree with your presumptions," Appoline said. "I think she cares for you very much. You merely must make her tell you this."

"I have no idea how to do that." Brooklyn was slumped down in the big chair, her chin resting on her hand.

"You give up so easily! She doesn't know you want to be with her. Tell her!"

"I have told her. But she knows I only want a monogamous partner. I think that's the sticking point."

"And yet, she dates no one. No one!"

Brooklyn showed a half smile. "True."

"And she's been with you—alone—for how long?"

"Uhm, she's been single and living at my place for...gosh...I guess it's been seven months."

"Brooklyn," she said, the name sounding extremely cool with her soft accent. "I think she's either afraid of commitment, or she thinks you'll change your mind and give in to what she wants if she stays with you long enough."

"I won't do that. Compromising on something I know I need isn't wise."

"Maybe she's afraid then. You must do something to blast her out of her torpor."

"You look like you have an idea."

"Meet me at Bergdorf's on Thursday at two. You'll know soon enough if she can be had."

———

Brooklyn had almost nothing to say when she returned from her date. She seemed in a good mood, but that was little to go on. Kerri watched her sit and start to watch a news show on television. She looked completely oblivious to the eyes staring at the side of her head.

Talk to me! What did you do? Where did you go? Did she kiss you? If I sniff all over you will I smell her undoubtedly fabulous French perfume? Could I make myself any crazier about this whole episode? No, I could not!

———

Over the next few weeks, Brooklyn saw Appoline occasionally. Not enough for a predictable schedule. Just enough to drive Kerri mad. But worse than that was the way Brooklyn spoke of her. They were watching TV very late one night and Brooklyn said, "Appoline is so good at taking a political commentator and cutting his legs off almost bloodlessly. She's showed me a couple of clips of shows she's been on in France. She had to translate, of course, but they were totally cool. I wish we had more programs like that here."

"I thought she was a philosopher."

"She is. The clips I saw were on talking heads shows like we have here, but the people were actually intelligent. And the best one had a moderator who cut people off when they were too strident or went on too long."

"Were they talking about philosophy?"

"Yes and no. Most of them were about morality. Philosophers are the go-to guys for that. She's ridiculously intelligent, Kerri. Some of the stuff she says is so over my head that I feel like a dunce."

Kerri stewed about that for a few minutes. If Brooklyn felt like a dunce, she'd feel like a bag of hammers.

Brooklyn carried a small shopping bag when she walked into the house one morning. Whistling to herself, she went into her bedroom and moved things around for a while, making just enough noise to compel Kerri to walk to the doorway.

"Hi. Did you just get home?"

"Yeah. I'm getting some things organized. Want to go out to lunch?"

"Uhm…sure. I made salads but they'll keep."

"Let's go to the Boathouse in Central Park. It'll be fall before we know it, so we have to squeeze the life out of summer."

"It's a deal."

The next day, Kerri picked up Brooklyn's laundry. It was always organized in neat piles that were then jammed into a big nylon bag. Socks and underwear on top, then t-shirts, then jeans, then towels, then sheets. They did a decent job, but not nearly as good a job as she could have done if Brooklyn had let her use the machine in the building.

Kerri picked up the underwear and started to put it away when she dropped everything and clapped her hand over her mouth. There were three beautiful sets of matching bra and panties lying in the drawer. They were absolutely gorgeous. The kinds of things you wore the first time you...

She crossed her legs and slid to the floor, winding up in the lotus position. Damn it all! This was all her own fault. She could see that clearly. But what could she do now? In a complete funk, she finished putting the laundry away, then got on her bike and rode until she hit the northern tip of Manhattan. On the way home, she slowed down and tried to think of how to get what she so desperately wanted while letting Brooklyn fulfill her own needs. Nothing came to her. Brooklyn was taking what she wanted, and Kerri was going to be left holding the bag.

The "Praise Appoline" train continued to roll through New York. Brooklyn certainly didn't do it all of the time, but she did it often enough to drive Kerri slightly mad. While having coffee with Dakota one morning, Kerri found herself grousing nonstop.

"What's up with you?" Dakota asked. "I've never heard you sound jealous about anyone."

She dropped her head onto the table and thumped it against the surface a few times. "I know. But I'm crazy about her. You know that."

"Then tell her for god's sake! This has gone on way too long, sweetie."

"I can't tell her now. Besides, I don't think I'm what she wants. She needs someone like Appoline. Someone who makes her living with her big brain. Someone who can afford to hire someone like me to take care of them. They can talk about stupid politics and morals and hire someone to baby both of them!"

Dakota sat there for a moment or two, staring at Kerri like she barely recognized her. "Have you been meditating?"

Vaguely ashamed, Kerri shook her head. "I try. God knows I try, but I haven't been this blocked in years. I sit for twenty minutes in the morning, and twenty minutes before bed, but I can't stop myself from sulking about Brooklyn."

"Listen to me," Dakota said slowly. Kerri looked into her eyes and waited for her to speak. When Dakota sounded like this, it was time to listen. "I think you should tell Brooklyn how you feel. But no matter what, you've got to get back into your meditation practice. You'll drive yourself crazy if you don't, KK."

Kerri found herself nodding obediently. Dakota was right. Meditation would get her through this. She just had to find the way back to it.

———

Luckily, Manhattan had more meditation practitioners than most towns had people. Kerri was able to find a well-recommended place that had day-long silent retreats for advanced students who were struggling. She was able to secure a place the next week, and slipped away right after Brooklyn left for work that morning.

The retreat was in a dingy building in Chelsea, and a dozen or so people filtered in and out of the space, getting in some group meditation before they headed off to work. Because her class did not begin until seven, she lingered by the entryway, reading her e-mail and catching up on some to-do lists until her instructor showed up.

A few minutes before seven, a youngish, gentle-looking man appeared and gathered up the members of his class. They laid out their meditation cushions while he instructed them as to the flow of the day.

"I'm Andrew," he said, taking a slight bow. "We're going to be silent for the majority of the day, so get all of your verbal interactions out of the way now. Our first period will be guided meditation for about two hours, then we'll do a period of walking meditation, and then another several hours I'll guide you through. Throughout the day, I'll call each of you into the next room and we'll chat about whatever comes up. We'll finish at seven o'clock this evening. Any questions?"

"Were we supposed to bring something to eat?" a nervous-looking woman asked.

"No. We'll have fruit and some veggies and juice set out when the office staff gets here. You'll be taken care of."

Since there were no other questions, they all seated themselves in whatever position worked and started their day. Kerri found herself fighting from the first minute, feeling every bone in her body protest, and every muscle and nerve join in the complaint. Seven p.m. was about eleven and a half hours away, and it felt like it would take two lifetimes to get there.

Kerri's turn for her individual conversation didn't come until two. She'd sat, she'd walked, she'd gotten into every yoga posture she could think of—still nothing. She was completely unable to clear her mind. When Andrew gently touched her shoulder, she almost shrieked. But she got up and followed him next door. Her mouth was dry, and her emotions were bubbling near the surface when he looked deeply into her eyes and asked, "What brings you here?"

He didn't flinch as she burst into tears, but Kerri was shocked by her reaction.

"This never happens," she managed through the tears. "But I'm so out of touch with myself."

"Oh." His face and calm, empathic voice were the essence of compassion.

"I've been meditating for fifteen years, and I practice yoga on a daily basis. I've made so much progress over my biggest vices...or stumbling blocks."

"What are those?"

She sat there for a moment, trying to make sure she explained herself properly. "I can be covetous, and too attached. I've been able to let go of so many hurtful feelings and situations through meditation over the years, but now I'm obsessed with a woman who's on my mind all of the time!" She cried more tears of frustration. "It's driving me crazy!"

"Has this happened before?"

She thought about the question thoroughly. "No, not really. I've had my heart broken before, but meditation helped me let go of the hurt. It's not working this time, though, and I feel absolutely aimless."

"Tell me about the obsession. Do you know the woman?"

She blinked. "Of course. Oh! You think I'm obsessing in a delusional way. No, no, I know her very well. Actually," she started to cry again. "I obsess about her because I love her. But I can't commit to her, and she won't be with me unless I can."

A tiny smile formed on his sweet face. "Why can't you commit to her?"

"That's not wise." She felt like she was instructing him! He should know about not letting your desires rule your world.

"Why not?" Again, he fixed her with his dark eyes, making her feel like she couldn't move without his permission.

"Because...I want it too badly. I have to maintain some sense of detachment or she could consume me!"

"We can't detach from our feelings," he said so quietly she had to lean forward to hear. "Our feelings guide us to our higher selves."

"But detachment is my path."

His tiny smile grew bigger. Then he lifted his hand, reared back and slapped her hard across the cheek.

"Shit!" she cried, grabbing her scalded cheek with her hand. "Why did you do that?"

"Do you feel detached?"

"No! I feel like I'm going to hit you back!"

"That's very good," he said, his peaceful affect seemingly intact. "When I slapped you, your skin tingled. You felt an authentic sensation. You need to feel what you feel, Kerri. If you love, let the love in. Don't try to starve your heart and your soul from experiencing all that life has to offer."

"But how to I let myself...go?" Her heart started to race merely thinking of surrendering to her overwhelming desire to possess Brooklyn and every one of her adorable idiosyncrasies.

"You do just that. You express your love with your whole soul. You give of yourself selflessly, completely, effortlessly. If she loves you as well, she'll do the same."

"But…what if she doesn't?"

"Life itself is impermanence. You embrace the possibility of loss when you embrace the love. They're entwined. But loving a person is one of the greatest gifts of life. Allow yourself to take risks." Then he got up, gently touched her head, and left her alone. She sat there, stunned, for just a few moments, then she got up, went back to her cushion, seated herself in the half-lotus position and tried, once again, to meditate. This time, she was struck by the image of Brooklyn, as big and vibrant and colorful as the images of the gods she'd seen everywhere in India. A golden, throbbing aura floated across Brooklyn's chest, right where her heart should be. Kerri felt herself entering that golden orb and being accepted into Brooklyn's very essence, where she stayed, in total peace, until the sun set across Chelsea. Andrew rang a bell, wordlessly letting them know their day was done.

CHAPTER SIXTEEN

BROOKLYN WAS ALREADY IN bed when Kerri returned home. Because she was energized from her retreat, it took her a long time to relax enough to sleep. She finally woke at around two to find a note.

> Hi,
> I'm going out with Appoline. I don't know how late I'll be, but if it's really late I'll just go to work. Have a good evening.
> Love,
> Brooklyn

She had to look. Kerri marched into Brooklyn's room and found that one set of the new underwear was gone. That did it. Somehow, that simple discovery lit a fire that nothing else had been able to. She went to the computer and brought up Brooklyn's calendar. Tonight was their sixth date. One more than the minimum Brooklyn required before sleeping with someone. She'd mentioned earlier that Appoline was going to France for a few weeks, so this would be a perfect night to send her off with a bang. Poor choice of words.

It felt like steam was coming out of her ears, just like in cartoons. Images of the two of them lying in bed together made her want to break everything she could get her hands on. Then a wave of sadness hit her so hard she had to grab onto a chair to steady herself. She sat down heavily and thought of her last conversation with her grandfather. He'd only said a few words, but he was undoubtedly in his right mind. His eyes were clear and he knew just who Kerri was when he said, "I'll finally see my Elsie today."

Just thinking about it made her cry. Thinking of being reunited with his wife of sixty years had allowed him to fight past the stroke and the dementia to feel the joy of that promise. She wanted that! She desperately wanted Brooklyn to lie on her deathbed and be filled with joy at the thought that they'd be reunited. She wanted to be missed! And the only way to be missed was to commit. Brooklyn was the one. There was no question of that. She just had to make her case and hope she won.

Brooklyn and Appoline were in a crowded, noisy bar in SoHo, trying to have a conversation. Brooklyn's phone was in her back pocket, and when it vibrated she held it up to show Appoline she was going outside to answer. Seeing Kerri's name made her heart start to race. It was three a.m. and Kerri knew, or thought she knew, that she was on a date. "What's wrong?" she asked, short of breath.

"I have to see you."

Shit! It sounded like she was crying. "Kerri, tell me what's wrong. You sound really upset."

"I am, but I can't tell you on the phone. I have to see you."

"I'll come home."

"No. I'm already hailing a cab. Where are you?"

Brooklyn looked up and saw one of the conversions that had turned a factory into a high-end hotel. "I'm at the Mercer." That wasn't true, but that address would be much easier for a cab to find than the rat-hole, after-hours club that Appoline had taken her to.

"The hotel or the restaurant?"

"The hotel."

"Great," Kerri growled, before hanging up.

What the fuck? She sounds pissed!

Brooklyn went back inside and tried to tell Appoline what was up. But it was far too noisy to be heard, so they went outside. "Kerri says she needs to see me right now. She actually sounded angry."

"Oh, that's excellent!"

"Excellent? I want her to be mad?"

"Yes! Mad, sad, excited, anything but the flatlining you two have been doing. I think she's finally feeling jealous."

"I'm not sure I want her to be jealous. Wouldn't it be better if we just told each other exactly how we feel?"

"Yes. When is the last time you've done that?" Appoline crossed her arms and gave Brooklyn a playfully haughty look. "I've made my case."

"She'll be here soon, so I suppose we'll find out if you're right."

"She's coming here? Right here?"

"Across the street. I told her to meet me at the Mercer Hotel."

"Fantastic! Let's go!"

—⁂—

Kerri stormed into the hotel and barreled up to Brooklyn. "I'm the one you should be here with!" Her face was pink with outrage, and her eyes blazed with blue fire. "Me!" She poked Brooklyn in the chest with a finger, and immediately two men with bespoke suits were on either side of them. They each wore an earpiece and one was quietly speaking into a microphone on his lapel.

"We're fine," Brooklyn said. "Nothing to worry about."

"You'll understand, Ms. York, that our guests like a peaceful atmosphere."

"I certainly do, and I promise we'll be peaceful." She took Kerri by the arm and led her to the elevator. "You don't have to shout," she said quietly. "I can hear you perfectly fine."

"Where are we going?"

"Up to a room. We can talk there."

"With Appoline?" she asked, once again far too loudly.

One of the gentlemen appeared right before them and shook his head at Brooklyn. "She's the loud one," she said, but he continued to look only at her. "Sometimes it sucks to be famous," she grumbled. They got onto the elevator and zipped up to the fifth floor where Brooklyn took a key card from her pocket and slipped it into the lock.

"I want to talk to you alone. This isn't Appoline's business."

"She's not here, Kerri." Brooklyn gently pushed Kerri back a step into the room, then another. The stunned look on her face was priceless, so Brooklyn pushed one last time and the door closed behind them. "Now, what did you want to say?" She put her hands behind her back and rocked to and fro, like she was waiting to hear some very good news.

Kerri threw her arms around Brooklyn and buried her face in her neck. "I love you, and I'm so stupid for not telling you before now." She pulled back a little and looked into Brooklyn's eyes. "Please, please don't sleep with Appoline yet. Give me a chance. Just one chance." She buried her head again, hot tears falling onto Brooklyn's neck. "I can make you love me. I'll start reading more and being interested in the world. I'm smart enough to learn to keep up. I really am."

Brooklyn soothed her, rubbing her back gently while rocking her. "You can't make me love you," she whispered.

Kerri's head jerked up and she looked at her with shock. "I can!"

"You can't. I already love you." She placed her hands on Kerri's damp cheeks and held her for just a second before placing a long, loving kiss on her trembling lips.

"You love me?" Kerri finally asked when the kiss was broken. "But why haven't you told me?"

"I was waiting for you to tell me." She rocked her in her arms, unable to let go for even a second. "I didn't think you ever would."

"But why did I have to be first?"

Brooklyn pulled back a little, and looked into Kerri's eyes. "Because I'd already told you what I needed in a partner. It was up to you to decide if you could commit to me." A flush of panic hit her and she grabbed Kerri by the shoulders. "You can commit to me, can't you?"

"Yes." Kerri's eyes closed for a few long seconds. She looked entirely at peace, and a burst of emotion welled up in Brooklyn's chest.

"I'm so happy." She grasped Kerri and held her so securely no one could have broken them apart. "You make me happy. Only you." She kissed her cheek, the only thing she could reach when they were so

355

closely entwined. "I swear you're the only woman I've ever wanted like this."

"What about Appoline?" Kerri asked sourly. "You were in this very hotel with her not ten minutes ago."

Brooklyn relaxed her hold and laughed. "Yes, but she was just helping me get a room. She was sure we'd need one."

"What?"

"She's been tutoring me on how to capture you. To be honest, she's a natural."

"What?" This time she was almost loud enough to make one of the black-suited men come back.

"Shh." Brooklyn led her to the sofa, where they sat close enough to take up only one cushion. "I told her I wasn't interested in going out with her because I was completely stuck on you." She poked Kerri's chest with a finger.

"You did?" Now that lovely face exploded in a warm, beautiful smile. It was like the sun shining after weeks of rain.

"I did. And she and I have gotten together to talk about you while we've gotten to know each other. She's a great person. You'll like her."

"She could be a combo of the Buddha and Vishnu and I'd still be more interested in you, but she's...she's everything a woman could want. Have you looked at her?"

"I have," Brooklyn said somberly. "She's attractive, but she's no match for you."

Kerri blinked. "You're clearly not able to see very well, but"—she stopped to take in a breath—"you deserve someone who can talk to you. Someone who's as bright as you are."

"Kerri, what in the heck are you rambling on about? You're as smart as anyone I know." She stopped for a minute and found herself unable to resist teasing. "Well, Appoline is smarter than both of us put together, but what does that matter?"

"I..." She sat there for a second, looking like she'd burst. Then she buried her face in Brooklyn's neck and nuzzled into it. "I was being insecure. Forget it."

Brooklyn grasped her by the shoulders and looked at her carefully. "Are you insecure about your intelligence?"

"Not normally. But you're a genius of some sort and Appoline..."

"Is too much like me. Why would I want a girlfriend who likes to sit and read all day? I want a woman who likes to move, to be outside, to do all of those things I'd never do without prompting." She kissed her quickly. "A woman like you. Someone who's very, very bright but isn't all up in her head every minute."

"Are you sure I'm bright enough for you?"

"Damn, Kerri, where does that come from? You're very, very bright. You don't have to read the crap I'm interested in to be bright."

"Sorry. I'm sorry. I'm obviously a little nervous." She dropped her hands and shook them roughly. "Okay. All better now."

"Not so fast. I need to hear a few more things from you. Like how you know you can commit. This isn't something I can be flexible about."

Kerri's expression turned sober. "I don't want you to be flexible. I want to be your lover. For the rest of my life." She shivered roughly, and Brooklyn held her tighter. "My grandmother told me something years ago that took until today and a guy named Andrew to reach me."

"Who's Andrew?"

"A guy who packs a mean punch. But he's not the important one. My grandmother is."

"Okay. I think."

"My grandmother wasn't crazy about my Eastern practices, so I didn't take most of her comments very seriously. But she said one thing many times. She said it was harder to love one person than to love the world." Her eyes softened and she shed a few tears while Brooklyn lovingly held her.

"I'm not sure I understand."

"I've tried to be a loving soul. To love everyone on earth. To not make a claim on anyone. But my grandma was right. That's easy compared to giving yourself to someone. I've been fighting it for months and months, but I give in"—she kissed Brooklyn gently—"to you."

Brooklyn stood and pulled Kerri up with her. "I think I'm in love with you...and your grandmother."

"I don't know your grandmother, so I'm only in love with you." They held each other closely, and Brooklyn soon noticed that Kerri was trembling.

"Are you all right?"

She pulled away and smiled brightly. "I'm fantastic. I'm frightened, and giddy and confused and I feel like I'm going to burst. But everything will be fine now that I have you." She shook her head roughly. "Have. That's hard to even say, but it feels so right. I have you."

"Do you want to tell me about whoever punched you? That sounds kinda important."

"I will. But we've talked an awful lot in the last few months. Maybe we should let our bodies say a few words."

Her smile had just enough of a racy edge to make Brooklyn's body heat up. "Great idea. Fantas—"

Before she could finish her thought, Kerri's mouth covered hers. The first kiss was almost like the kiss they'd shared in Santa Monica, but there wasn't a shred of hesitation this time. Kerri poured herself into the kiss, and Brooklyn was the happy receptacle of every bit of emotion she let flow.

In seconds Brooklyn felt her temperature rise, her body starting to tingle with need. Kerri was everything she'd ever desired, and finally having her in her arms was a highlight of her entire life. Kerri was hers. The mere thought made her pulse race, and when Kerri's fantastic body pressed against her it was tough to keep her wits about her. But then she realized she didn't need to. It was time to throw the off switch to her brain and let her body take over.

She wasn't sure who led, but they moved, locked together, to the edge of the bed. There she slowly started to undress Kerri. All of her summer clothes were light, thin and unstructured. One tug on a string had Kerri's white linen slacks on the floor, and a few buttons later her sky-blue shirt joined them. A rush of sensation weakened Brooklyn's knees as she let her hands glide up and down Kerri's bare shoulders, waist and thighs.

Kerri had the most sensational body she'd ever touched. Strength, suppleness, firmness and luxuriant softness all rolled into one delightful woman. Her hands shook as she let them explore the dips and swells of muscle, tendon and silky smooth flesh. Kerri rubbed against her, making Brooklyn's sex pulse with longing and unquenched desire. But she'd wanted Kerri for so long, she couldn't bear to rush at this point. This was the only first time they'd ever have, and it was going to be very, very special.

When she felt as though her legs would give out Brooklyn finally reached back to unfasten Kerri's bra. It fell from her shoulders and, for the first time, Brooklyn was able to fill her hands with the breasts she'd fantasized about more times than she could count. Her imagination had been a poor predictor of how glorious it felt to actually palm, squeeze and fondle the supple flesh, especially when accompanied by Kerri's pleasured moans.

They fell onto the bed, and Brooklyn made quick work of the panties that kept her from devouring Kerri. Now the dim illumination from the bedside lamps cast a golden glow all along Kerri's lovely body. Brooklyn was speechless for once in her life. Words could not ever do justice to the work of art that was Kerri. Her body was flawless, absolute perfection. The scent she'd grown to love was no longer obscured by fabric and she let herself breathe in, her head reeling from the sensation. Her sex throbbed from being enveloped in Kerri's scent, yet they'd barely begun.

Hands fussed at her, and she realized Kerri was trying to undress her. She almost balked, but even though she didn't have the glorious body to offer as Kerri did, she wouldn't refuse her anything. Patiently, she rolled onto her back and let Kerri slowly remove her clothing. Soon, they were rubbing against one another, their naked bodies sliding sensuously along their lengths.

"I love you," Brooklyn whispered, not even realizing she had spoken. This was the absolute truth. Kerri's body was a wonder, but it was her soul that Brooklyn loved. Her kindness, her gentleness, her concern for other people. Especially her moral code. There was nothing haphazard about Kerri Klein, and Brooklyn loved her perseverance easily as much as her flat belly and shapely ass. But those were great perquisites, and she set about to explore her physical attributes in depth.

Kerri lay beneath her and let out a series of sexy moans that made the hairs on the back of Brooklyn's neck stand on end. She switched her hips to and fro while Brooklyn licked and suckled her breasts, then wriggled around so her thighs clamped against Brooklyn's leg while she thrust against her.

It seemed like they'd only been touching each other for moments, but Kerri's voice finally broke through Brooklyn's frazzled brain, saying, "Please, baby, please touch me."

Pulling back, Brooklyn saw the raw need in those beautiful blue eyes. Her chest filled with emotion when she realized that she'd created that need. Slowly, she inched down Kerri's belly, finally settling between her legs, which parted to meet her. "Yesssss," Kerri groaned when Brooklyn dipped her head and tasted her for the first time. It was revelatory. Like finding the Rosetta Stone in the recesses of a great monument. Kerri's legs slid along Brooklyn's back as she feasted on her. She shivered roughly, calling out Brooklyn's name, sighing heavily, then letting her voice rise as her breathing grew more labored, finally crying out her release after all too short a time.

Unable to stop exploring, Brooklyn was still for a few moments, watching Kerri's body react to her orgasm. As soon as her flesh stopped quivering, she dove back in, nuzzling her face into her slick skin until Kerri climaxed again and again. She'd lost track of how many shuddering orgasms she'd wrung from her when Kerri placed her hands firmly on Brooklyn's shoulders and croaked out, "You're going to kill me."

Grinning, Brooklyn climbed up and wrapped her in a fervid embrace. "You can't die from love. I promise you."

"Hold me," Kerri murmured. "Hold me just like that. I've been dreaming about how it would feel to hold you after we make love."

"I'm holding *you*," Brooklyn teased.

"It was pretty close to this. Almost the same." She kissed Brooklyn gently. "I love you. I love you so very, very much."

"I'm happy. I've never been so happy."

"You speak too soon." With a rush of energy, Kerri swept into action. Brooklyn found herself flat on her back, vivid blue eyes gazing avidly into her soul. "I'm going to make love to you," she whispered. "Be in the moment with me."

It struck Brooklyn at that moment how distant she'd been with her former lovers. Even with Ashley. But she wasn't going to make that mistake with Kerri. She forced herself to overcome all of her insecurities and allow Kerri to know her to her depths.

It was harder than she'd imagined. Kerri's eyes were like lasers, searching her for every thought, every feeling. Brooklyn felt splayed open, unable to hide even a single emotion. But this was Kerri...her Kerri. There was no need to hide anything, and she braved the wilderness of fully opening her heart to the woman she loved.

They gazed into each other's eyes while Kerri delicately touched her breasts. Her touch was so achingly tender that Brooklyn had to bite her lip to stop tears from flowing. Like a slap, it hit her again. Don't hold back. As soon as the thought lodged in her brain her eyes welled with tears and for the first time in her life she didn't try to stop them, or laugh them off. She lay there and shared the intensity of her feelings with Kerri, and was rewarded by a soul-stirring kiss.

Their lips merged again and again, then they grasped at each other, holding on hard as they cried together for a few moments.

"I don't know why I'm crying," Brooklyn whispered. "I just feel so much it's…"

"I know." Kerri pulled away and hovered over her. "It's hard to let someone inside. But it's wonderful too, isn't it?"

All she could do was smile and nod. That lovely face was mere inches away, and it was hers. The bright eyes, the cute nose, that ridiculously adorable dimple; all were Brooklyn's now. It was almost too much. But it was really just right. Exactly right.

She forced her body to relax and stay open to whatever happened. Her cheeks ached from grinning, but Kerri must have sensed that, because she kissed her again, taking one ache away and replacing it with another—centered much further down her body.

Whatever thoughts had been racing around her brain were almost completely erased when Kerri's kisses grew more sultry. For such an angelic looking woman, she kissed like the devil herself!

Kerri's beautiful hands roamed all over her body and Brooklyn couldn't stop her mind from recalling that first day in the loft, when she'd been struck by how lovely they were. Now they glowed in the soft light as they caressed her, growing more gorgeous by the moment.

Her skin tingled everywhere those remarkable hands touched, waiting for the powers within them to soothe both body and spirit.

Brooklyn had always closed her eyes while a woman made love to her, letting her fantasies take her wherever they wished. But now her fantasy had come to life and was making love to her. Avidly watching her was a huge part of the fun. And this was as fun as fun could be. She found herself giggling when Kerri enveloped her breast in her warm mouth.

"Ticklish?"

"No," she said, trying not to sound like an idiot. "This is just so much fun!"

That earned her another long, luxuriant kiss. "I cherish you," Kerri whispered. "You're the top nine or ten kinds of women I'm most attracted to."

"Nine or ten?"

"You've got so many different personalities wrapped up in there," she said, tapping various places on Brooklyn's body. "At least nine or ten."

"Well, you've only got one personality and it's a winner."

"I'm glad you like it." She kissed down Brooklyn's body, slowly making her way to her sex. "I'm going to do something else I bet you'll like." Then she looked up, showing a sexy grin.

Brooklyn started to answer, then reminded herself she had to shut up at some point, or she'd die of anticipation.

It was scary. She hadn't let anyone touch her intimately since Ashley. But a few deep breaths eased her trepidation, and when Kerri's soft tongue first touched her skin, she almost melted into the bed. It had truly been worth the wait. Having the woman she loved touch her so intimately was orders of magnitude better than being touched by some anonymous hookup. There was no comparison.

Brooklyn felt herself open even more fully to Kerri, willing her gentle spirit into her body in every way. Her head swam with feelings, images, inchoate thoughts and sensations as Kerri's tongue swirled against her.

Then fingers joined the fray, filling a need she'd not known she'd had. Her heart was filled to bursting, and her body spoke for her, climaxing roughly, as if it would pull Kerri right inside and keep her there.

Then Kerri's warm body was cradling her, cooing into her ear, caressing her fevered cheek. She'd never been more fulfilled in any way. She was home.

They slept at some point, enjoying the luxurious bed and fine Italian linens. But they were off schedule, and woke before dawn, ready to spend the day in each other's arms. Kerri got up and, after opening the French doors that exposed the big Roman tub, ran water for a bath. When the bath was ready they got in together, giggling while they tried to find a way to avoid putting out an eye.

From behind, Kerri patiently braided Brooklyn's hair and placed it over her shoulder to avoid getting it wet. "I'm never going to stop playing with your hair, and if you cut if off I might renege on my promise to love you forever."

Brooklyn's voice was a little rough, adding to its sexiness. "Think of how silly you'll look standing before a judge and asking for a divorce on the grounds of tonsorial cruelty."

"Definition?"

Brooklyn laughed. "Relating to the cutting of hair."

"Still…you promised, and I know you never break a promise."

"You promised to love me forever. I promised nothing. You have no grounds for a divorce. Sorry."

Kerri leaned over Brooklyn's shoulder so she could look into her eyes. "Are you asking me to marry you?"

"I am." She took Kerri's left hand and kissed her ring finger. "I'd like to place a big, brilliant diamond on this lovely hand to show the world to keep its paws off my wife."

Leaning forward again, Kerri took a playful bite from Brooklyn's ear. "Not the most romantic proposal in the world, but I—"

With a swoosh of water splashing onto the floor, Brooklyn turned and wound up kneeling in front of a stunned Kerri. Grasping her hand, Brooklyn once again gently kissed it. "I will never in my life ask a more important question, and I'm sorry for teasing about it." She took in a visible breath as her eyes glowed with feeling. "You'd make my life complete if you'd agree to marry me."

Tears rolled down Kerri's cheeks as she answered in a shaking voice. "I will. I'd be honored."

"Can I buy you a ring?" Brooklyn was gazing at Kerri's hand with a strange intensity. "On the day we met I couldn't stop staring at your hands. They're extraordinarily beautiful, and I'd love to see a ring I gave you every time I looked at your hand."

"Yes, of course. We'll both wear a ring." They'd talk details later. Maybe they could incorporate something Buddhist or Tibetan… But that might be too strange for Brooklyn. She snapped out of her daydreaming—"What?"

"I said, maybe we could think about what kind of rings we'll wear while we're in India. We could get something kinda Eastern."

"India?" She felt like she was a step behind. "We're going to India? For a gig?"

Laughing, Brooklyn grasped her by the waist and manipulated her until they were face to face, half submerged. "We're going to India at the end of next month."

"We are?" Her brain was fuzzy, filled with so many thoughts and feelings. What was she missing?

"I decided not to renew my contract. We can take off and stay as long as we like."

"What about your tour dates? You've got something every weekend."

"No I don't. I had Melvin re-schedule those dates two months ago. I was going to surprise you with the trip." She kissed her, letting the kiss build slowly. "Surprised?"

"Oh, Brooklyn. You are such a wonderful woman." Kerri started, sending another small spray of water onto the floor. "Are you sure you're comfortable quitting *Reveille*?"

"Yep. I'm never going to take another job I hate. Life's too short."

That simple sentence was the second nicest one Brooklyn had ever said. Right after "Will you marry me."

A COLD, BRISK WIND blew into the apartment, fluffing some strands of hair from Brooklyn's wet neck. Her t-shirt clung to her back, and she moved to sit on the sill of the open bedroom window. Kerri poked her head in, saying, "You don't have to put the books away yourself, honey. The movers will do anything you ask them to."

"I know, but I'm fussy about how I like my books shelved."

Kerri walked over to her and perched on her lap. "You're strangely fussy about a lot of things. When I met you, you hardly seemed to notice if your clothes were on the floor. You've gotten very neat and orderly."

Brooklyn patted her ass, then let her hand rest there. "I've had a good example. Besides, I've got to be orderly to go from a loft down to a simple apartment."

It was a remarkable thing, but Brooklyn honestly thought she was downsizing significantly. But the new apartment on the Upper West Side near Riverside Drive was a three bedroom, three and a half bath with a big terrace. Granted, it cost less than half what she'd sold the loft for, but only Brooklyn would think she was being virtuous by buying an 1800-square-foot Manhattan apartment.

"It's a lovely apartment. And as soon as we're finished unpacking we're going to go buy a big Christmas tree."

"You celebrate Christmas?"

"Of course. But I've never been in a cold climate over the holidays. I'm hoping for snow."

"I guess I wouldn't mind a little snow, since I won't have any in Santa Monica."

Kerri turned and nibbled on her ear. "You were the one who wanted to be in a warm climate during the winter. Don't act like you're going to miss snow." She stood and signaled Brooklyn to get out of the window, which she closed.

"I won't miss it, but I'm not sure how I'm going to fare in your apartment. I'm used to a lot of room to move around."

"True." She linked her hands behind Brooklyn's neck and gazed at her contemplatively. "I think you'll be fine. We'll be outside most of the time, anyway."

"I've gotta buy a new sofa. I can't sit on that futon of yours for long."

Giggling, Kerri nodded. "Okay, but you have to remember there's no TV to watch while you're sitting there."

"Arggh! You've gotta let me at least put cable in."

"No deal. You can watch everything you need to see on the internet. I don't want my apartment defiled by a big TV set."

"Your apartment? Why is that your apartment and this is our apartment?"

"Because we're engaged, silly. This is our home. Santa Monica is my crash pad. And where I crash, my lovely fiancé crashes."

"We could easily afford a nice condo by the beach. Are you sure I can't persuade you?"

"Hey, what happened to the woman who stood in the cave temples in Ellora and proclaimed she was going to divest herself of her attachment to material goods?"

Brooklyn grinned, dipped her head and kissed Kerri, holding the kiss until one of the movers dropped a box in the hallway. "I sold my loft," she said, her eyes taking on a dreamy quality they often did when she wanted to make love. "And my car."

"I was proud of you for doing that. Not having a car payment or a mortgage is nice, isn't it?"

"Yeah, it's nice to know I don't have to worry about being foreclosed on if my career dries up."

That was a long, long way from happening. Since she left *Reveille* she'd gotten to play bigger houses, making appreciably more money. She'd released a very successful DVD of a live show, and they were deep in negotiations for her second book. Kerri just hoped that Brooklyn would continue to evolve and see that material goods owned you more than you owned them. But even if she didn't—she was nearly perfect. Those perfectly beautiful brown eyes gazed down at her, and Kerri wanted to shoo the movers out and break in the new bed in the guest room.

"Whatcha thinking?" Brooklyn asked. "You look like something important is on your mind."

Kerri tightened her hug and nodded enthusiastically. "The most important thing in the world is on my mind. And that's you."

Brooklyn placed another quick kiss on her lips and whispered, "Don't go anywhere."

Kerri watched her leave, and a few minutes later she returned, smiling victoriously. "We have an hour. Got any ideas on how to spend it?" Her arms wrapped around Kerri tightly, and the kiss that followed almost made her forget the question.

"Where are the movers?" she finally got out.

"At lunch. I suggested they take an hour—paid—and they agreed it was a good idea."

Her smile was so playful and childlike that Kerri couldn't resist it for another moment. She kissed every part of her pretty mouth, then added a few tiny kisses to the laugh lines at the corners of her eyes. "Normally, I'd think you were being frivolous. But I'm itching to baptize this new apartment. Where should we go?"

"We start in the shower," Brooklyn decreed. "Where we end up is your choice."

They dashed for the big bath near the master bedroom. It was old and tiled in white subway tile, making it look even bigger than it was. It was the perfect size for two adult women to quickly strip each other from their dusty clothes and jump into the rainfall shower.

It looked like the fixtures were from the 1920s, but Kerri was quite sure they were of a recent vintage made to look old. The chrome gleamed, and the water pressure was good—something truly old fixtures probably couldn't match.

The warm water hit Brooklyn's fit body. Gone was the layer of fat around her midsection, replaced by a feminine curve that Kerri was addicted to. She ran her hands over that curve now, feeling the essence of womanhood flow from Brooklyn's body into her hands.

When she let her hands drop to the curvy ass that biking and tennis had created, she felt her heart-rate quicken. Not just because of the animal attraction she had for curves, but for the pride she shared with Brooklyn because of her determination. This altered body was the result of work and stamina, and those were traits that Kerri was dearly attracted to.

"I need to feel more of that ass," she murmured, turning Brooklyn around. She ground herself against her lover, feeling her temperature spike when those smooth mounds rubbed against her belly. This was pure pleasure. Grinding against Brooklyn's ass while she grasped and played with her breasts was every good sensation all at once. And hearing Brooklyn's sexy sighs while she touched her made the whole world spin just a little faster.

Brooklyn's hips twitched rhythmically, making Kerri's match the beat, and soon they were groping each other blindly, warm water, soap suds and lust ratcheting up the frenzy. Suddenly, they were facing each other, fingers sliding in and out of the most sensitive spots, kisses blessed with the wet spray. "There's not one thing on earth better than fucking you," Kerri growled, her breath hot in Brooklyn's ear.

"Uhnnn." Try though she might, Brooklyn never seemed able to speak when they were in the midst of sex. The best she ever managed was a series of grunts, and Kerri took that as high praise. She increased the pace and the pressure, then covered Brooklyn's mouth with her own and pumped into her until she moaned her release. Hearing that guttural sound and feeling that wet flesh spasm around her fingers sent Kerri right over the edge as well. They grasped each other hard, then their more tender emotions took over and they became very gentle with each other, as they almost always did.

"I love you," Brooklyn whispered. "I'm going to love you many, many times in this fantastic shower." She started to giggle, the girlish sound music to Kerri's ears. Her beautiful, tender, stoic, funny, quiet, gabby, brainy, absent-minded lover was as close to perfection as a woman could be.

Kerri kissed her again and again. The thoughts in her heart were too precious to speak at that moment. But she'd have another chance to tell her how she felt. Many, many more chances. And, besides, Brooklyn already knew.

———

THE END

By Susan X Meagher

Novels

Arbor Vitae
All That Matters
Cherry Grove
Girl Meets Girl
The Lies That Bind
The Legacy
Doublecrossed
Smooth Sailing
How To Wrangle a Woman

Serial Novel

I Found My Heart In San Francisco
Awakenings: Book One
Beginnings: Book Two
Coalescence: Book Three
Disclosures: Book Four
Entwined: Book Five
Fidelity: Book Six
Getaway: Book Seven
Honesty: Book Eight
Intentions: Book Nine
Journeys: Book Ten
Karma: Book Eleven
Lifeline: Book Twelve

Anthologies

Undercover Tales
Outsiders

To purchase these books go to *www.briskpress.com*
Author website *www.susanxmeagher.com*